The
Starchild
of Atarashara

The Field of Unlimited Possibilities

M. Louise Cadrin

www.InfluencePublishing.com

Published by The Starchild of Atarashara Publications,
November 2018
ISBN: 9781999499808

Editor: M. Louise Cadrin
Typeset: Greg Salisbury
Book Cover Design: Judith Mazari
Proofreader: Lee Robinson
Portrait Photographer: Paige Fraser

DEDICATION

This book is in memory of Fay Cadrin, who passed into Spirit
before its completion. Mom delighted in the characters of this
story and took great pride in sketching them. She is present
in the book, through her sketch of the character,
Dineah Firefly.

Thanks, Mom – love you!

"To believe in magic is our birthright.
In opening our senses to its existence,
we open ourselves to a world of
unlimited possibilities."

M. Louise Cadrin

TESTIMONIALS

"It's an imaginative story about a young girl's journey discovering herself and who she can be against all odds with the help of her family, friends, and magical creatures. I could definitely relate to the main character and the idea of being different and not like everyone else. This story reminded me that each of us is special in our own right and that we all have somewhere to belong."
Jenny Story, Bestselling fantasy author of *Dysnomia*

"I spent a week with Louise in Mexico when she attended my writers retreat to work on her novel. I don't usually publish fantasy books, but this book came to life with magic, and I experienced the characters even before they appeared on the written page I had not yet read. I took that as a sign that I was destined to help Louise bring this magic to the world, and so I took on real magic again for only the second time out of 150 non-fiction books."
Julie Salisbury, TEDx speaker, author, and publisher

ACKNOWLEDGEMENTS

A number of years ago, I travelled to Europe, the last seven days of which I spent in rural Tuscany, Italy. Every night, as darkness fell, I would walk down to the river and be filled with wonder as the woods came alive with the presence of fireflies, their lights reflecting on the water. That mystical view, coupled with the song of the bullfrogs, pulled me into a world of magic and awe. Upon returning from that trip, I felt a pressing need to write but did not know where to start. I will always be in debt to my friend, Joan, who during one of our many coffee dates, remarked, "Why don't you write out of your head, Louise. You have such an active imagination." *And so it began …*

Less than two weeks after my return from Italy, I wrote the Prologue of this book. I still clearly recall the first time I announced to my family that I was writing a book. We had gathered in the living room of my parents' home. No one pointed out that I had never written a book before. Rather, my nephew, Jared's, immediate response was, "Who is going to be your illustrator?" as he proudly pointed at my mother, the artist. I would like to thank my incredible family for their support through this creative project. I would also like to thank my nephews, Tal, Evan, and Jesse, for lending their youthful, creative minds as we playfully brainstormed character names.

Thank you to the test readers of the book, both in its very early stages of inception and final stages of completion. Dan Cooper, Philip Cameron, Sharon Odnokon, Debbie James, Fay Cadrin, Mahalia Nagel, Michelle Hankes, Joann Noll, Jesse Zdunich, and Jenny Story, your support and feedback were deeply appreciated and invaluable.

Thank you to my incredible publisher, Julie Salisbury, the most free-spirited, intuitive, wonder-woman I have ever met.

You so fiercely protected the integrity of the book's voice, and continually guided me to do the same. Thank you, Greg Salisbury, for the beautiful layout and presentation of the book, and Lee Robinson, for your incredible attention to detail.

Thank you to Spirit, for continually teaching me to trust, and for bringing into my life the circumstances and people that allowed the book to grow into its completion. And thank you to the characters of the book, who so kindly told the story through me, often bringing the storyline into my awareness while I walked in nature. It has been an honour to tell your story.

M. Louise Cadrin

TABLE OF CONTENTS

PRINCIPAL CHARACTERS

Elders:
Ravensong - Shapeshifter and Orator of the Ancient Forest
Borus - Gnome and Care Keeper of the Ancient Forest
Aczartar - Head of the Elders
Mendalese - Head of the Healers
Tenor - Keeper of the Forest's chronicles and Orator of the Ancient Forest
Aarus - Sage and Seeker of the Ancient Forest
Effley - Head of processing for entry into the Karrian Galaxy

Royal Family:
Noble - Scarab King
Princess Hana - Daughter of the Scarab King and adopted mother to Sarah Starbright
Princess Atalia - Principal Commander of the King's Legions, also known as the First, and daughter to the Scarab King
Prince Drake - Wielder of the Emerald Sword, Commander of the Winged Warriors (Fireflies, Dragonflies, and Fairies), and son to the Scarab King
Bronte - Second in command to the Winged Warriors
Sarah Starbright - The Starchild, born of Princess Atalia in *Atarashara*

Guardians of the Starchild:
Wisteria, Bohn, and Sabrae - Witches
Sir Perity - Warrior of *Atarashara*, also known as Perry
Matharzan-Ariebe - King of the Were-Griffins
Eblie, Sheblie, and Tazor - Gargoyle brothers
Silverspear - King of the Equines

Gyrangers:
Graziel - Gyranger Queen
Banzen - Gyranger shapeshifter posing as Mrs. Winterly
Straeger - Principal Advisor to the Gyranger Queen

Shadow Forest:
Aniese - Youngest daughter of Elder Aarus and ruler of the
Shadow Forest
Commander Baire - Lead Commander of the Shadow Forest army
Lewna - Firefly and member of the Shadow Forest army
Kaiten - Firefly and member of the Shadow Forest army

Others:
Dineah - Oracle and Song Bearer of the Ancient Forest
Atarashara - 'the field of unlimited possibilities'
Ourelia - Eldest daughter of Elder Aarus
Kerri - Wife of Elder Aarus
Monserat - High Priestess of Oorse and teacher of the mysteries of
Atarashara
Mrs. Gibson - Teacher at McGregor Junior High

PROLOGUE

A Song Bearer Is Born

Dineah sat underneath the leaf, careful not to disturb it and risk being doused by the droplet of water that balanced precariously above her. She had been sitting here for hours, listening to the vibrant inner life of the Forest, and waiting. For what, she didn't know. She just knew that something was coming; something that filled her with a terrible sense of unease. She hated the uncertainty and tension that preceded the foretelling. She could feel its presence standing quietly over her shoulder, trying to align itself with her for the message to manifest. It was often this way.

It would start with a feeling that she wasn't alone, that if she sat quietly and cleared her thoughts, she would hear the subtle voice that sounded so much like her own. She had come to accept this over the years – the ideas and images that came unbidden into her mind. As a young Firefly, she hadn't known what to do when the quiet messenger beckoned. Now she knew that she must listen.

Dineah Firefly was the Oracle of the Ancient Forest. The Elders called this a sacred gift, bestowed by the Great Mother. Dineah knew that she should feel grateful to have been chosen out of everyone in the Forest, but sometimes she secretly wished otherwise. She would never voice these thoughts out loud for she was more than aware that the foretellings were as crucial to the survival of her kind as water was to the roots of the Guardians, the giant trees that protected the Forest and had since the beginning of time.

She heard the wind moving through the Forest and knew that it was gently caressing everything that it touched. It announced its arrival by tickling her arm, and then teased her by creating a whirlwind of leaves that resembled her, but with eyes and cheeks that were outrageously exaggerated. Dineah began to giggle. Forgetting about the droplet of water above her, she leaned against the stem of the leaf, screeching as cold water splashed down on her. She could hear the wind laughing at her and knew she looked comical; her wispy, short brown hair and tiny translucent wings plastered to her small frame. Smiling, she shook the water from her body. Fireflies were not known to stay wet long. Well, at least now she wouldn't have to fly through the mist for her morning bath!

The wind was her longtime friend and companion. It often accompanied her while she travelled. She sensed that it too felt uneasy. For a brief moment, she was comforted that she wasn't alone in her feelings. This thought vanished quickly. If the wind was sensing the unease, then its magnitude must be startling. Except for Elder Aarus, Dineah's sensitivity for foretelling was greater than anyone else in the forest.

Gasping suddenly, she felt her body go rigid as indiscernible images flooded through her mind's eye and filled her with dread. At that moment Dineah knew that a drastic change was coming and that her life and the lives of all within the Forest were about to be altered forever. Dineah was not a naïve Firefly by any means. She knew that the cycle of change was necessary to release the old ways of life to allow for the new. These teachings were intrinsic to the stories she had listened to every night of her life in the Sacred Grove. They were central to the beliefs of those who dwelled within the Ancient Forest.

Dineah began to shiver uncontrollaby. The wind instantly created a blanket from fallen flower petals to wrap around her slender body, but she continued to tremble, her glow light erratically fading in and out. Without warning her head jerked back and a high-pitched keen forced itself from her lips. Dineah had no control over the primitive wail that poured out of her. She intuitively knew that it was a cry of danger – a warning of great peril. Dineah feared for the Forest. Could they possibly be ready for what was coming?

The sound continued, engulfing her like a flame, making it hard to breathe or think. Higher and higher it soared, shaking her frail body as its urgent cry for action filled the Forest. As startled creatures scurried to burrow into their dens, the natural, vibrant sounds of the Forest abruptly halted. The Elders of the Forest moved quickly toward Dineah, only too aware of what the cry was, and shocked at its intensity. A messenger was sent to tell the Scarab King to attend, immediately.

The land itself appeared to move as the roots of the oldest and most resilient trees of the Forest writhed underneath the ground, awakening and responding to what they knew was a battle cry, a war song that had called them over the millenniums. These formidable giants - the Guardians - were the sentinels, the fighters of the Ancient Forest, a Forest in turn that was the port of entry and protector of the Karrian Galaxy it inhabited. They were not afraid, as it was this very cry of urgency that allowed them to move again after so many years of dormancy. They existed solely for the war song and for protecting the Ancient Forest each time it was in its most significant time of need. Although they did not yet know who the song had chosen as the Song Bearer, they were already unequivocally tied to the singer; the carrier of the sound that pierced their very roots and moved them to action. They proceeded through the Ancient Forest, making their way toward the Song Bearer.

Dineah's body struggled to sustain the keen that moved from the depths of her soul into the now silent Ancient Forest. She was unaware that Fairies, Fireflies, Dragonflies, Elders, the

Scarab King and the Legion - the King's guard - had gathered beneath the canopies of the Guardians and now encircled her. Nor was she aware that the age-old giants had begun to sway back and forth, creating a song in response to her war cry.

The Guardians now knew the identity of the Song Bearer. They also knew that she was too far gone and that it was up to them to bring her back before her light burned out and she died. They could not allow this to happen, for her survival was paramount to what lay ahead.

The Fireflies listened to the song of the Guardians and slowly took it up, as did all who encircled Dineah.

> "We hear you, Song Bearer; the time is near,
> When war and struggle will be here,
> Come back to us, and lead us on,
> Singer, of the war song."

Dineah's awareness slowly and painfully returned to her body as she listened to the chant that was her lifeline. Her head ached, and it hurt to breathe, for each inhalation of air burned her parched throat. Oh, how she needed nectar! Turning her large brown eyes to Aczartar, head of the Elders, she tried to speak but found herself falling into darkness. She was vaguely aware that Aczartar was calling for help, but had no idea that her friend, the wind, had barely caught her before she collapsed. Nor was she aware that Mendalese, the Elder of healing, had gathered a semi-circle of his students, directing them in his calm, quiet manner to link their energy with his. His arm raised and abruptly fell as a shaft of light filled the Forest, encircling the healers and Dineah within. The healing of her emaciated body had begun barely in time.

The Guardians hummed a deep bass melody of joy and

anticipation that vibrated through their trunks, causing their leaves to rustle. The Song Bearer was safe; the tides of change were in motion. The giant trees knew that darkness was coming, but they were not afraid, for the Song Bearer had survived the birthing of the war cry. They knew that the singer would endure tremendous hardship, but she would not have been chosen if she could not succeed. The Guardians were free again after years of waiting and were ready to fight beside her as they had done with each Song Bearer, in age after age.

CHAPTER 1

After Years of Searching

Sarah sat at the desk in her bedroom attempting to focus on her homework, but with little success. Sighing, she pushed her textbook aside. Grabbing her journal, she began to thumb through the many sketches that filled it. Sarah wasn't always sure where the ideas for her drawings came from. Some, like the winged horse with the violet eyes, had come unbidden in her dreams, demanding to be birthed into form through her art. Others reminded her of nature spirits; twig-like creatures covered in moss and leaves, with eyes that twinkled like stars on a clear summer night. Some even had human bodies with animal heads. No matter their origins, they all had one thing in common. Eyes filled with *awareness* and *intelligence*.

Letting her gaze wander about the room she was struck by the numerous pieces of paper that covered the walls – papers filled with sketches of Fairies, drawn in all shapes and sizes. Similar drawings filled her notebooks and journals. How often they had kept her company during the many times she had felt lonely.

Her substitute teacher, Mrs. Winterly, had called her aside in class today and suggested that she spend less time drawing imaginary things and more time finishing her homework. She didn't know how to tell Mrs. Winterly that the pictures were not make-believe. Deep down inside, Sarah knew that they were real. Often at night as she was falling asleep, she would see pinpoints of light floating in her room. Sarah told herself that they watched over her while she slept. This thought made her feel safe.

She had wanted to tell Mrs. Winterly about this but found that she couldn't. She had been more open with her former teacher, Mrs. Gibson, a kind and gentle woman who had been encouraging of Sarah's talents and imagination. But Mrs. Gibson had disappeared two weeks ago without explanation. Sarah had felt uncomfortable with Mrs. Winterly from the moment they had met. On more than one occasion, Sarah had caught the substitute teacher staring at her with an odd expression on her face. Sometimes Mrs. Winterly smelled so foul Sarah had to cover her mouth with her hand. She wondered how the other students did not notice.

Sarah cringed as her thoughts returned to her afternoon class. Mrs. Winterly had stood in front of the students, droning on about the need for them to be more responsible *while staring directly at Sarah*. In short, she had been telling Sarah to grow up. Sarah had felt like saying that not only did Mrs. Winterly's breath stink but that she was a smelly, creepy, old lady. At times Sarah swore she could almost see pinchers protruding from Mrs. Winterly's mouth.

Sarah had taken a deep breath to calm herself. It was then that she had noticed movement by Mrs. Winterly's ear. Leaning closer, Sarah had started as she had realized what was sitting on Mrs. Winterly's shoulder. *A pixie, feigning wide-eyed innocence.* Sarah had tried to look away, but it was too late. The pixie had caught her eye and winked, a feral grin spreading across its face. Sarah had known immediately that the situation was about to become bad ... *very bad.*

Mrs. Winterly had noticed Sarah's eye movement and had stepped forward, her gaze narrowing. *What is it, Sarah,* she had demanded in a voice that had made Sarah's stomach clench. Mrs. Winterly had moved even closer, reaching her hand out as if to touch the girl.

Sarah had leaned back in her desk, trying to distance herself from Mrs. Winterly, and the pixie who was becoming increasingly mischievous. Not only was she mimicking Mrs. Winterly's actions, but she had placed her index fingers inside her mouth, stretching it into unbelievable shapes that shouldn't have been possible.

Sarah couldn't help herself; she had begun to laugh. Mrs. Winterly had become furious. Sarah had watched in horror as her teacher's face had turned a deep red and a foul smell had filled the space between them. Grabbing her journal and packsack, Sarah had run from the room, leaving the enraged teacher yelling at her to be on time for class the following morning. It had been a horrible day!

Sarah was not like other kids her age. In fact, she wasn't like most people, for she could see things that others could not. While walking in the park last week, she had met a short, plump gnome with large red cheeks. An oddly-shaped, brightly woven hat had balanced precariously on his head, speaking into the gnome's ear as he strolled. While the gnome's long grey hair had floated wildly around him, his moustache had grown horizontally from the sides of his mouth, only to fall abruptly to hang by his knees. All of this she had seen, in addition to his forest-coloured tunic of greens and browns, and the swaying vines and leaves that had bulged out of the top of his boots and wound upward around his arms and shoulders. He had undoubtedly stood out … to her! Sarah had quickly looked around to watch other people's reactions and sighed as she realized that no one else could see him.

The gnome had stopped in front of her and bowed deeply, speaking in a melodious voice.

G'day, me lady, he had said. The hat had tipped forward, also acknowledging her.

Good morning, ah … Sir Gnome, she had responded, not exactly sure how to address him.

He had beamed approval at her acknowledgement.

Sarah had felt strangely peaceful in his presence.

Well done, young lady, ye could also address me as Elder Gnome or Elder Borus, for I am one of the Elders of the Ancient Forest.

Sarah had nodded as if understanding what he was saying.

This response had also seemed to please him for he had continued to speak.

Could ye point me to the Cedarwood Grove? We need to be gettin' back to the Ancient Forest.

Sarah had not known where the Ancient Forest or the Cedarwood Grove was, but she knew that the parks located within Brendondale's city limits contained orchards of magnificent trees whose branches filled the sky. As she had given directions to what she thought might be the Cedarwood Grove, she had noticed that the vines and leaves had reached out to her. The hat had also bent downward until its tip was eye level with her.

Ah, it had said. *I know who you are!*

The gnome had bowed deeply again, departing before she had a chance to ask the hat what it had meant. She was certain she had heard it whisper, *Fare thee well, Sarah Starbright.*

Chapter 1

Today when she was walking home from school she had met three girls slightly older than herself, and dressed in dark tights and bulky sweaters. They were holding hands and laughing as they walked. Immediately after passing them, something struck her in the back. Turning around, she saw that they had stopped to stare at her. One of them, with unruly auburn hair, had a discerning look on her face. Suddenly their appearances transformed, their faces becoming ageless as their clothes changed to robes of shifting greens and blacks.

Sarah knew without question that they were witches. She also recognized by their stance that their action was meant to be provocative. Sarah's mother, Hana, had always taught Sarah not to seek out confrontation, but also not to fear it.

Without pause, Sarah reached down and grabbed a pebble from the ground, flinging it in the same way that she would have thrown a skimming stone over water. Sarah had a strong throwing arm. She knew that whoever felt the impact of the pebble would be sore. She watched the small rock speed toward the tiniest witch and instantly regretted her impulsiveness as she realized that it was going to hit the woman square in the forehead. With incredible quickness, the auburn-haired witch reached out and caught the stone before it made contact.

Sarah tensed, uncertain what would happen next.

A smile spread slowly across the face of the auburn-haired witch. The witch who would have borne the brunt of the stone squealed with delight, clapping her hands quickly together and winking at Sarah. As two of the women waved goodbye and turned to walk away, the auburn-haired witch continued to stare at her before curtly nodding her head and turning to join the others.

Sarah knew that she had just passed a test. What she was unclear about was what the test was, and why.

She had told her mom about this. Well, her adopted mom. Sarah knew that Hana was not her biological mother. Hana had always spoken openly about this while providing a home filled with love, where Sarah could talk openly about her unique abilities. Hana never doubted Sarah, for she too had the sight, the skill to see what others could not. Sarah was grateful that they shared this ability, although she did not think deeply upon the coincidence of it.

At times, Sarah would pretend that her biological mother was a brave warrior princess who commanded armies, and whose commitment to a more significant cause did not allow her the luxury of raising a daughter. Sarah knew this daydream was idealistic, even ridiculous, but without it, she could not bear the pain of knowing she had been given up for adoption *… been given away.* This thought brought a sense of loneliness that she could not share with anyone, not even Hana.

Well, almost no one. There was always Perry, her orange-coloured cat. As if being summoned, Perry called out and then waited for Sarah's response as he aligned himself with her location. Perry was unable to see because he had been born without eyes. His lack of eyesight did not stop him from getting around or from being as playful and energetic as other cats. In Perry, Sarah had found a friend; someone she could talk to about anything. She gathered him from the window sill, setting him on her lap before picking up her pencil to finish her homework.

Perry immediately jumped onto her desk, placing himself where her hand was poised.

"How do you do that, Perry?" laughed Sarah. "You can't see!"

He pushed at her pencil, demanding that she rub first his ears and then his chin.

Perry was good for her. Whenever she became too sombre,

he would interrupt her thoughts and demand her attention. He seemed to know when she was having a bad day.

Sarah looked longingly at her keyboard. She considered playing it but knew that it was time to go to bed. It was late, and she had an early morning class with Mrs. Winterly, who she was not looking forward to seeing.

Music helped Sarah release the many feelings that resulted from being a loner and someone who others avoided because she was different. Sarah's classmates were outgoing and enthusiastic about school, but they did not include her in their circles of friendship.

Sarah placed Perry on the bed and slid under the sheets, shutting off the lights. It was not long before he crawled under the sheets and curled up around her feet, purring loudly. Sarah fell asleep so quickly that she did not see the pinpoints of light that entered through the open window and took up guard on the four posts of her bed.

~

Even from under the covers, Perry had sensed the presence of the lights the moment they entered the room. Perry did not perceive his surroundings in the usual sense. Although sightless, he interpreted the world as swirls of energy and colour through the whiskers and the hairs of his body. Like tiny antennae, they alerted him to the smallest movement or sound. He knew that the pulsating masses of golden, sparkling light were here to protect Sarah, allowing him to take his leave and patrol the neighbourhood. Sarah was Perry's only focus in life, for he had been created solely to keep her safe and unharmed. Perry loved Sarah deeply.

Emerging from under the covers he turned to the light closest to him and greeted it with a rumbling *prrrraaaaaaa* from deep within his throat.

"Good evening, Sir Perity," said the tiny Fairy. "All is well with you, I hope?"

Perry squeezed his hollowed eyelids gently, nodding his head once in response.

"Please take your leave," said the Fairy "and trust the child into our capable hands for the next few hours. We arrived without issue, though you must know that there is a sense of unease in the Ancient Forest. We have been told to be particularly watchful this eve."

Perry's demeanour changed quickly at this news. The rumble in his throat turned to a low growl, and his tail twitched in agitation.

Focusing on his whiskers, Perry honed the inner sight that allowed him to navigate his surroundings. Jumping off the bed, he walked straight to the window. Leaping through, he scaled down the nearest tree to begin his nightly rounds.

The Fairies knew that Sir Perity would patrol both the perimeter of the house and the neighbourhood, reporting anything irregular.

$\sim$

Mrs. Winterly had left school immediately at 3:30, forgetting that she had agreed to meet and assist two students with their English assignments. Her mind was no longer on teaching, not that she had ever been a teacher. Her knowledge had come from memories she had forced from Mrs. Gibson's mind before placing her in a semi-comatose state and locking her in the basement of her own house. Mrs. Gibson had shown great strength in resisting the mental probing that Mrs. Winterly had subjected her to. Gyrangers were renowned for their ability to wreak havoc on and control the minds of others.

Mrs. Winterly, whose real name was Banzen, was one of the most skilled Gyrangers of her race. She was enjoying Mrs. Gibson's resilience, for it allowed her more time to drain the life-force from the old lady. Nonetheless, Banzen looked forward to the day that Mrs. Gibson would be consumed entirely, leaving a mindless, withered husk in her wake.

Hurriedly unlocking the front door of Mrs. Gibson's house, Banzen let herself in before the neighbours could strike up a conversation. One, in particular, was overly curious about her cover story as Mrs. Winterly. Banzen would have gladly eliminated the irritating human but knew better than to draw unwanted attention to herself.

Banzen's appearance began to change the moment that the door closed, followed by a foul odour that filled the room. Moving further into the entrance of the house, she froze as she heard sounds coming from the basement. Mrs. Gibson was kicking the walls of the room she was imprisoned in below. How had the old lady untied her feet?

"Mrs. Gibson," crooned Banzen. "You think someone other than me has entered your home because of the early hour. You are trying to attract attention. What a bad, bad idea. I will have to punish you."

A sinister smile spread across a face that was still in the last stages of transforming from the human Mrs. Winterly to a distinctly non-human, insect-like creature. In the space where once stood a middle-aged woman of medium height, was now a six-foot-tall being, covered in a black cloak that fell to the ground. Its face was angular and pointed at both the tip of the head and the chin, and a series of pinchers protruded from its mouth.

As Banzen's thoughts returned to the events of the day, her pinchers clicked rapidly in excitement. She was quite convinced that she had located the Starchild, spoken of in the Gyranger prophecy; a prophecy that every Gyranger knew within their collective memory.

For it was spoken that a magical girl child of the stars would be birthed from manifested need, raised by nobility in a human world, but not born of humans. The Starchild would assuredly cause the downfall of the Gyranger race unless captured during the window of her thirteenth year and her magic turned against the light. Once changed, the child would lead the Gyrangers, raising them to a level of control and power unheard of in their history.

It was the dream of the Queen Gyranger thirteen years earlier that had alerted the Gyrangers to start searching for the girl. The most proficient and lethal of the Gyranger shapeshifters had been sent out to infiltrate the planets of the Karrian Galaxy, targeting worlds that were inhabited by humans. For years they had searched, never finding the young girl who was foretold to destroy them ... until now.

Banzen was sure that Sarah was that child. The Gyranger had immediately felt a strong sense of magic upon arriving at Brendondale, tracing it to McGregor Junior High where she had found a child named Sarah Starbright enrolled as a grade seven student. Disguising herself as a student for several days had allowed Banzen not only to locate Sarah but also to witness the close relationship between her and Mrs. Gibson. It had made Banzen's next move very easy. Abducting Mrs. Gibson in her own home and stealing her memories had been effortless. Using a small amount of mind control on the principal of the school had secured the insect-like creature a role as the substitute teacher, Mrs. Winterly. Watching Sarah for the last couple of weeks and then witnessing her ability to see the insolent pixie earlier that day had confirmed the child's gift of sight.

These happenings were not all that had alerted Banzen. Most notably, she was unsettled by her lack of control when close to Sarah. Not only was it harder for Banzen to maintain her shifted human shape, but the child's magic mesmerized the Gyranger, making her want to grasp the girl and drain the life-force out of her.

Banzen was mildly concerned that the child's family was said to consist of a single mother, raising Sarah by herself. She did not believe that it was an ordinary family but trusted in her ability to handle whatever circumstances arose.

Banzen's pinchers continued to click in anticipation. If her assumptions were correct, she would forever be known as the Gyranger who had located the Starchild. This achievement would elevate her status and cement her name in the history of their race. Her future would be secure. Opening a mind link, Banzen telepathically sent the message that would alert the Gyranger Queen, ensuring the arrival of additional Gyrangers to Brendondale shortly.

Banzen smiled as she thought of the child's family. They did not stand a chance. The thought of fighting and killing caused the deadly venom in the Gyranger's pinchers to spontaneously secrete. She unlocked the basement door and went downstairs to deal with poor Mrs. Gibson.

CHAPTER 2

Exposed

It was two o'clock in the morning when Sarah sat bolt upright in bed, breathing hard and filled with a sense of dread. She had heard something in her dream; a sound of such anguish and pain that it tore her apart and left her feeling vulnerable and exposed. Was it a song of forewarning? A cry for help? A call to action? What of the singer? Who was she and what had caused such a desperate sound? Whatever it was, Sarah knew that she could not ignore it.

She continued to feel cold fear in the pit of her stomach. She knew with certainty that the singer was not from this world; that the urgency of the sound had spanned worlds, crossing into her own. The primordial nature of the song tugged at Sarah, teasing her memory to recall it. She could feel the vibration of it inside her as if it made up the very molecules of her being.

Sarah's worry for the singer left her with an overwhelming sense of helplessness. She considered waking her mom to tell her about it but decided not to rouse Hana at this late hour.

So immersed was Sarah in her thoughts that she did not

notice the four pinpoints of light that had shot out the open window. Had she looked out into the night and focused her vision, she would have witnessed an incredible sight. The four lights had grown and expanded into a translucent, impenetrable dome that surrounded her and Hana's home, pulsing with a vibrant life-force.

～

Hana stood by the living room window staring out at the night sky. She knew the energy shield was in place. She had felt it erupt into existence. It did not scare Hana. As Princess and daughter of the Scarab King, she was not easily scared. She had expected this day to come. She knew that the haven she had created for Sarah would not last forever; that one day it would be challenged, perhaps even shattered. But she, like Sir Perity, or Perry as Sarah called him, had made a promise. She sighed and spoke aloud to herself.

"You can choose your friends, but you cannot choose your family. Do not make me regret my promise, dear sister."

They had kept Sarah safe and hidden for thirteen years. Dear, sweet Sarah, who had so much magic in her that Hana marvelled at how she could live through each day seeing things that no one else could, yet still cope in the human world.

Hana knew that things were about to change. She too had heard the war song. She fleetingly wondered who it had chosen as the Song Bearer. The keening wail made Hana's heart pound with longing and anticipation. She, like the Guardians, had lived a long time and was pulled by the song. It moved the blood within her veins, taking all of her willpower not to open a portal and immediately return with Sarah, to her homeland, the Ancient Forest.

Calm yourself, she thought, irritated at not being able to contain the intense emotions the sound had created in her. She was too well-trained to feel this out of control. Now that the wheels were in motion, the time for action would be soon enough. At this moment, she needed to ensure Sarah's safety and wait for further orders from the First, her father's Principal Commander, and her sister.

She caught a flicker of movement, recognizing the orange tail that moved underneath the low hanging cedar tree. She knew that Sir Perity had purposely paused long enough for her to be able to see him. She counted her blessings for the many years of his presence and commitment as Sarah's confidant and protector.

Hana suddenly snapped to attention, her years of training kicking in. How foolish of her! So wrapped had she been in her thoughts that she had not noticed the air in the room begin to thicken and become foul smelling. But that was impossible! The Fairy shield was impenetrable from the outside.

Through the window, she saw Sir Perity turn his gaze toward her and let out a screeching wail that filled the night air. The lights of the four Fairies grew as they sped to the house at supernatural speed. Hana knew without question that Sarah was in danger; a danger that had somehow entered the house before the shield had gone up.

Hana turned to run up to Sarah's bedroom, never seeing the dark shadow that reached out and grasped her around the neck, violently snapping her head backward while slowly lifting her into the air. She kicked out wildly, unable to make contact with the Gyranger or release the choking hold around her neck. She knew that if the vile creature destroyed her, Sarah would be defenceless upstairs in her room. Hana also knew that the creature's mere touch of her body had set alarms off throughout the Ancient Forest. She was counting on this to save her life and keep Sarah safe.

The Gyranger continued to crush Hana's windpipe, relishing in the slowness of the death and in watching the light fade from her eyes. It had not expected to find one of the Scarab Princesses as the guardian of the Starchild. It was exceedingly pleased, for it would be rewarded richly for destroying Princess Hana. Her very link to the Ancient Forest made her a hindrance to their race.

So consumed was the Gyranger that it was unprepared for the blur of orange fur and exposed claws that flew through the air, tearing into the ear and skin on the side of its face and leaving bone exposed. Nor did it anticipate the pain that exploded in its head as the Fairies drove their spears deeply into its eyes, robbing the creature of sight forever.

As portals of light opened into the room, Hana barely noticed the masses of Fireflies that spilled through the doorways, densely swirling around the nose and mouth of the Gyranger to block its air passages. Her oxygen-deprived brain did register the droning sound of the Dragonflies which meant that the Prince, the leader of the Winged Warriors and the bearer of the Emerald Sword, had arrived. Sarah *would* be safe! As Hana's life-force prepared to leave her body, time seemed to slow down, filling her with an overwhelming sense of sadness. She would not live to witness Sarah's destiny as foretold thirteen years earlier; a foretelling of which few were even aware.

Dropping Hana's lifeless body to the floor, the now blind Gyranger stretched out its hands. Bolts of laser-thin light shot from the tips of its fingers.

Dragonflies carrying armed Fairies moved quickly out of range of the lethal beams of light, only to renew their attack at the Gyranger's head, and assist the Fireflies. They knew that the winged armies could destroy a creature such as the Gyranger, but it would mean risking many of their own in the process. Instead, they chose to confuse and overwhelm the hideous creature. They would wear it down for the one person who could readily eliminate it.

Everyone but the blind Gyranger saw the Prince emerge from the portal, bearing the legendary sword that shone of emerald green light. Without breaking stride, he raised the blade toward the creature while crying out ancient words in the Scarab tongue. A burst of green light shot from the sword, striking the Gyranger bluntly in the chest, and causing it to hover, suspended in the air.

Again the Prince cried out while turning the blade clockwise. Instantly the lifeline between the creature's body and spirit was severed. A moment later, the Gyranger shuttered as a ghost-like semblance of itself detached and floated upward, evaporating into nothingness. Its body crumbled, dissolving into ashes.

Turning, the Prince gasped, for Princess Hana's body lay on the floor, her neck twisted and crushed. He knew better than to get in the way of the Fireflies who had immediately moved to cover the Princess's still form like a blanket. These small beings of light, also known as the Ancient Fire Carriers, had healing abilities. There was only a small window of time to draw Hana's spirit back to her body.

One shrill, unified call went out as the lights of the tiny healers began to pulsate, filling the room with a hot, bright light. Only these extraordinary beings could reverse the damage done to the Princess's body and spirit.

The Prince was forced to turn his head away and cover his eyes with his raised arm. He continued to wait, scared and impatient. As the light finally dulled and levelled off, he could see that the bones of Hana's throat were no longer crushed.

Chapter 2

The bruising around her neck quickly diminished and then completely disappeared. Colour slowly returned to her face, as her breaths deepened and became regular. Prince Drake knelt beside his sister, worry embedded in the lines of his weathered forehead. He touched his fingers to her cheek. What would he have told their father if Hana had not lived?

"Hana, wake up," he said with urgency. "Please, Hana – WAKE UP!"

Hana slowly opened her eyes and looked at her brother, Drake. She was having trouble focusing. What had happened? The memory of the Gyranger returned, and panic engulfed her.

"Sar …?" She tried to speak but began to cough.

"Do not worry, Hana," said Drake, "Sarah is safe. She has no idea what has taken place here. The Fireflies have already taken up guard around her room, and the Dragonflies and their Fairy riders are surrounding the house. Atalia and the Legions have just arrived. There will be no further attacks here tonight."

Hana closed her eyes and let herself rest. She knew that the healing energy of the Fireflies would have its best effect after she slept. She felt Drake lift her and carry her to the bedroom. The house was once again safe, guarded by both her brother and sister and their armies. A distant thought passed through her tired mind.

How long has it been since the three of us were together?

Hana could hear the murmured voice of Drake speaking with the First, their sister, Atalia. Hana knew that she would be angry with herself in the morning for not recognizing the signs of danger earlier. For tonight her depleted life form did not have the energy to chastise herself or to make total sense of what had occurred. She fell into a deep sleep and dreamt of being held by the gentle roots of the Guardians, whose deep bass tones filled her with comfort and peace.

CHAPTER 3

The Past Catches Up

Atalia quietly opened the door to Sarah's room and stepped inside, passing through the guard of Fireflies lined up and down the hallway. Although members of the Legion had arrived and taken up position, she would not have the Dragonflies or the Fireflies step down. She was only too aware of their allegiance to the Scarab King and always strove to respect and foster that relationship. She also knew from years of fighting alongside them that they were fierce and formidable and that they would protect the Royal Family with their lives. It was their speed and an instinctual battle sense that had spared her sister's life tonight, for they had moved en masse the moment the alarms had sounded in the Ancient Forest. No one, not even her legendary Legions could relocate and attack as quickly as the Winged Warriors. Without them, she would have lost Hana. That thought, she could not bear.

Atalia stood by Sarah's bed and looked down at the child she had created thirteen years earlier. Few knew that she was Sarah's mother, if that was the proper title. Even fewer knew how Sarah had come into existence. Hana did, of course. She had figured it out. Atalia had come to accept this for she trusted Hana with her life.

Atalia also knew that it was best that others assumed that Sarah had been born into a family that had identified great potential in their child based on her astrological chart at the time of birth. It was not uncommon for the Royal Family to foster babies identified with such possibility so that their gifts were cultivated and used for the highest good of the Forest. This explanation was commonplace and did not cause speculation. To reveal the truth would mean disclosing what Atalia had done, something that was unfathomable, even for a Princess. It also endangered Sarah. There were those who would seek to harm Sarah as a means of striking at Atalia or try to destroy the girl once they understood what she was.

Atalia thought back to that night thirteen years ago. As the First, she was known for her undeniable logic and her uncanny precision in making split-second decisions in battle. They called her brilliant, cold, ruthless. Those closest to her knew differently, but she played upon this perception for it kept her enemies wary and unsure. The Legions knew Atalia to be fair, yet demanding with uncompromising standards. She had never failed them and on more than one occasion had seen them through battles where they should not have survived the odds. It was whispered by some that the Goddesses of war favoured Atalia and that they walked with her in combat. Some even said they had seen the spirits of old warriors surrounding Atalia in the midst of battle – that yet after death she continued to demand and obtain their allegiance. In short, the Legions trusted Atalia unquestioningly, and they followed her wherever she led them.

Atalia was more than aware of the allegiance of both the

Legions and the inhabitants of the Ancient Forest, which was why she struggled with the actions she had taken so many years earlier. How could she have made one of the most critical decisions in her life based on emotion and a premonition? Atalia never let her emotions rule her, and she most certainly did not have the foretelling. So why had they both governed her on that evening?

Sarah was the result. Beautiful, magical Sarah. Was it so wrong what Atalia had done?

Oh stop it and take responsibility for your actions, she thought impatiently. *You sealed your fate when you passed through the sacred threshold.*

Atalia did not have to remind herself that this particular threshold was only safe to pass through if the proper rites of passage were practised and found acceptable. Atalia cringed as the last thought moved through her mind.

The threshold or doorway led to a consciousness known in the Fairy language as *Atarashara*. In the Scarab language, this translated to *'the place of all births'* or more commonly, *'the field of unlimited possibilities'*. It was located in the densest woods of the Ancient Forest and was as old as the Forest itself.

Atalia could not admit the truth about her actions to others, for what she had done was unspeakable. Crossing the threshold without proper preparation and ceremony went against the very laws of her people. *Atarashara* was made up of pure magic, pure potential, and limitless opportunity for manifestation. It was a direct connection to the Great Mother. Only a fool would enter the sacred space without proper reverence and humbleness.

So how could Atalia explain that *Atarashara* had called to *her,* pulling *her* forward with an intensity of emotion that she had never experienced in her life? And how could she admit that her response had been utterly irresponsible? That she had passed through the threshold without question, without consulting any of the Elders, without notifying any of the Royal Family, and without performing the sacred rituals that were necessary for one's safety. On that night she had not known if she would even be allowed to return to the Forest … and she had not cared.

But there was more. For in the moment of entering *Atarashara*, she had seen visions of the future of her people that to this day played out in her mind's eye and chilled her heart. She had witnessed a time when the inhabitants of the Ancient Forest would lose themselves, having no recollection of who they were, or their ancestors before them. They would no longer know the songs and stories that sustained the giant Guardians, and ultimately the delicate balance that the Forest played as the gateway and safe-keeper of the Karrian Galaxy. During this time they would lose all hope and would need something to will them to live. Their very existence would be at risk.

Atalia had been terror-stricken. She had squeezed her eyes shut as hot tears had streamed down her face and panic-filled thoughts had raced through her mind.

These images cannot be happening! I do not want to know the future! Why in the Great Mother's name have I come to this place and compromised values and beliefs so dear to me?

As a kaleidoscope of emotions had continued to surge, Atalia had heard the inner voice that she counted upon when faced with immeasurable odds. She had welcomed it like an old friend as it had firmly pushed her feelings aside and began the process of strategising and considering all options. Further and further it had forced the emotions down, placing them in a room in her heart and firmly latching the door. She had known that she would not forget them. She just could not be ruled by them at that moment. She had needed a cool head for her brilliant mind to track and systematically compile the information she had observed.

Those who knew Atalia well would have recognized the lifting of her chin and the squaring back of her shoulders that was characteristic when she had made a decision.

Opening her eyes, she had thought to herself, *Options! What are my options? Think! I am in Atarashara – 'the field of unlimited possibilities'.* Taking advantage of the portal's magic she had closed her eyes again and concentrated. Focusing on the fate of the Ancient Forest, Atalia had released a heartfelt intention, determined to change the course of the future, or at the very least, assist the Forest with what was spiralling its way. She recalled the invisible presence that had moved through her body. She had known instantly that her intention had somehow altered the outcome of the visions she had seen.

Slowly opening her eyes, she had drawn her breath in sharply. Floating in the air in front of her had been a baby, a girl child, with celestial bodies of golden stars, moons, and planets rotating around her tiny form. Not only was this child a product of *Atarashara*, the infinite ocean of possibilities, but she was also *pure magic!* Atalia had felt the magic from where she stood and had known that this child would help the Ancient Forest when they were in their darkest hour.

Sarah Starbright, had whispered a voice in her head. *Atarashara* had given her one more gift – the child's name.

Although in shock, Atalia's strategic mind had still recognized that bringing this child back to the Ancient Forest would raise too many questions. The magical force that emanated from Sarah was staggering. It would not be long before those in the Forest came to sense her presence, making it increasingly harder to keep secret. Atalia had also known that her position as Principal Commander of the Legions would not allow her to raise Sarah or adequately protect her. She had spoken these thoughts out loud.

Hana, Princess Hana, had whispered the voice of *Atarashara.*

Atalia had still known that Sarah was going to need more protection than Hana could provide. Enlisting too many of the guards that served the Royal Family would draw unwanted attention to Hana, and ultimately to Sarah.

Atalia had not known if *Atarashara* would assist her a second time. Calming her mind, she had set the intention to ensure the safety of both Hana and the child. She had waited, but nothing had happened. Atalia had become discouraged. Exhaustion had begun to creep in, forming cracks in her thin veneer of self-control. Once again she had felt the whisper of *Atarashara* stroke her mind. A gentle heaviness had settled over her, emptying her of thought and purpose.

Atalia's next memory was of standing at the entrance to Hana's wooded home in the Ancient Forest, clutching tightly to the bundle of disarrayed cloths that held the Starchild. She had not recalled gathering up Sarah Starbright or leaving the portal.

Atalia had stared at Hana, wide-eyed and silent as Hana had gently guided her inside the house, lifting the undisclosed Sarah from her arms.

Hana and Atalia had been each other's allies since childhood. The bond they shared went beyond a physical closeness. They could feel each other's emotions and know each other's thoughts, even when separated by distance. Atalia knew that even before her arrival, Hana had sensed something was wrong. At that moment, Atalia had not given Hana the luxury of a proper explanation. Words had tumbled out of her, laced with an edge of hysteria.

You must take her, Hana! You must raise her as your own! We cannot afford for her to die! She will save our people and all the beings of the Ancient Forest, but she must be hidden away until the time is right. Guard her, Hana! Promise me that you will keep her safe! I have done what I can. I have also done something that is unheard of and forbidden, sister, but I had to … I had to for the good of our people. This child is vital, Hana! She is pure potential, pure magic. Sarah Starbright must be kept alive at all costs. I will make arrangements for you to take her to the human world on the planet Earth and keep her safe until the time is right!

Hana had stood in stunned silence as she had listened to Atalia's unspoken thoughts and learned of her actions.

Atalia had cringed as Hana's thoughts had pulsated back through their bond.

What in the name of the Great Mother were you thinking? How is it possible that you breached the threshold and entered Atarashara? And survived? Why do you fear that our people are in grave danger?

But Hana had not asked these questions out loud, and at that moment Atalia had loved her more than at any other time in their lives. It had spoken to the closeness of these two sisters and how well they knew each other. For the simple truth was that Hana knew that Atalia would not have acted in the way she had unless the circumstances were dire. Even so, Atalia recalled watching Hana struggle with the shock of it all; almost dropping the bundle that she had lifted from Atalia's arms.

Atalia had slowly lowered herself to the floor, holding her head in her hands and finally releasing the pent-up feelings that she had kept at bay. She had felt Hana's heartbreak at watching this uncharacteristic display of raw emotion and recalled her sister moving forward to comfort her … but then stopping. Slowly lifting her head Atalia had watched Hana stare at the bundle that she held. It had begun to move. Slowly peeling away the layers of cloth, Hana had gasped upon finding the golden girl child, *the child whose magic sparkled like sunlight on a quiet pond of water.*

Atalia had known that Hana's world had altered at that moment, for she had felt the change within her sister. Hana had witnessed the magic of the child and now understood the need to protect Sarah at all costs.

It was then that they had heard the scratching sound at the door. Someone or something was outside. Hana had touched Atalia's shoulder, motioning for silence by placing her finger on her lips and then pointing at the back door.

Atalia had collected herself immediately and rose from the floor. Adrenaline had moved through her body as she had pulled a dagger from the calf of her boot and silently left through the rear exit to circle the house. She had moved into position at the front of the house at the same time that she had felt Hana focus her mind and create an invisibility shield around herself and the child.

Without warning the front door had begun to open. There had been no time to extinguish the tiny balls of light floating in the room.

Atalia had moved closer to the front door ... and then stopped. She had felt Hana's surprise through their bond. She knew that it had taken a moment for her sister to register the presence at the base of the stairs. There, sitting with remarkable composure had been a small orange feline-looking creature – *a cat!* The only cats Atalia had ever seen live were in the human world. Atalia had known that Hana had not been comforted by the odd expression on Atalia's face or by the fact that she had taken no steps to restrain the creature.

Atalia had watched the cat rise and enter the house with a sense of unexplainable familiarity, walking directly to where

Hana stood with Sarah. Once again Atalia had felt Hana's shock. She had understood why. Not only had the cat been able to detect Hana and Sarah through the shield, but the animal was blind – it had sunken holes in its head where its eyes should have been.

As the cat had moved through the invisibility shield and rubbed against Hana's leg, Sarah had begun to coo and squirm. Guided by Sarah's response, Hana had released the hidden wall of protection. Cautiously bending down, she had allowed the unusual looking animal to stick its head inside the cloths. The cat had immediately let out a *prruuuttt*, rubbing its head against Sarah's hand.

Atalia had still not spoken, for she had been trying to absorb the words she had heard in her mind before the tiny animal had entered the house.

My name is Sir Perity. I am here to protect the Starchild and will be leaving with her and Princess Hana.

Atalia had been flooded with relief as she realized that *Atarashara* had heard her final request. At that moment she had not questioned the size or shape of Sarah's guardian, even if it was a blind cat. She merely trusted what had she had manifested in *Atarashara* and what had subsequently arrived at Hana's doorstep. Knowing that plans had needed to move forward quickly, she had readied herself to leave … and then stopped.

Silence had hung in the space between the two sisters. Atalia had closed her eyes and turned her face away from Hana. She had struggled to come to terms with what she was about to do. Slowly turning back, she had begun to speak, her eyes filled with compassion and sorrow.

I am so sorry, Hana, for what I am doing to you. You must believe in me. Trust me, and always know how much I love you.

Chapter 3

Hana had smiled sadly back, only too aware of the burden that Atalia felt in the role that their father had thrust upon her. More than anyone, Hana knew of the inner battle that Atalia struggled with when having to exert her role as the First, over those she loved.

Atalia had watched as Hana sighed and shrugged her shoulders, speaking words that had etched themselves in Atalia's heart.

I do not understand, but I have always trusted you, Atalia. You know that. And I will continue to believe you in this matter, though I will not lie and say that I am pleased with having to uproot my life overnight. I too feel an overwhelming need to protect this child, and so it will be done. I understand that Sir Perity is Sarah's protector. I am not clear how he will play out that role, but I have a strong sense that he is not quite what he seems.

Hana's gaze had turned to the small, orange animal that had been busy cleaning his ears. Opening his mouth in a wide yawn, he had shown off an impressive row of sparkling white teeth. He had then collapsed on his side, using his front paws to draw his tail forward to clean.

The two sisters had stared at him and then looked at each other, each raising their eyebrows at the same time. They had both started to laugh, Hana rolling her eyes at the same time that Atalia had covered her face with her hands. For a brief moment, they were young girls again, carefree and light-hearted. Atalia had committed the moment to memory. There were too few instances like this since she had become the Commander of their father's Legions.

As the intimacy of the moment had come to an end, Atalia had known what needed to happen next. Slowly dropping her hands to her side, she had lifted her chin and squared back her shoulders. Atalia, the First, had spoken the next words.

Pack your belongings, Hana. I will call upon my most trusted guards to accompany you on your journey tonight. Prepare to leave with Sarah and Sir Perity.

She had watched as Sir Perity had turned at the mention of his name as if aligning himself with where she stood. With one last lingering glance she had departed, hearing Hana's response through the bond, like a whisper in the night.

I will always love you too, Atalia; you know that ...

Atalia pulled her focus back to the present. She watched the blankets rise and fall as Sarah slept, completely unaware of what had transpired earlier that evening. Atalia still marvelled at how Hana and Sir Perity had kept Sarah safe, and her magic hidden all these years.

Atalia knew that Sarah was crucial, a key to the future of all life within the Ancient Forest. Over the years she had wanted to explain better her actions of that night to Hana, except she could not voice to someone else what she still did not understand herself. It was as if she had been made to enter *Atarashara* and manifest Sarah. Atalia knew deep within herself that there was a truth to this that she was not yet able to accept. The thought of *'the field of unlimited possibilities'* manipulating her in this way, terrified Atalia. It was too much to comprehend, for *Atarashara* did not interfere or direct the lives of those within the Ancient Forest.

CHAPTER 4

The Meeting in the Sacred Grove

Aarus sat on the floor of the simple hut, resting, his legs tucked beneath him. Aarus was the most senior of the Elders and old, like the Guardians. Limp, stringy, grey hair hung down around his small, sinewy body. His hollowed-out face contained one eye of grey with flecks of yellow, and another of startling opaque blue that looked not to the outer world, but into the inner world of spirit. At first glance, one could have mistakenly thought that he was frail and worn, but those dwelling in the Forest knew that the old Sage was more powerful than the King's mightiest warriors. Aarus was a Seeker. He could travel between the worlds to see glimpses of the past, present, and future. He was highly revered, for he played a vital role in the equilibrium that permeated the Forest and ultimately the Karrian Galaxy it inhabited and protected.

One hand rested on Aarus's knee, palm facing upward. The other held Jiapiz, the crystal that he used when journeying from his body. He was barely aware of the burning sage that floated in the air, or the muted sounds of the outer world that snuck through the dense fabric of his hut. He knew that two Fireflies guarded the entrance to his home, ensuring that he would not be disturbed.

Aarus's attention was in the hidden realms. He soared upward, shifting his focus to the past, and then watched as the images flipped backward in his mind as if on rewind. When they finally slowed he knew that he had arrived at the beginning. He had seen the forming of the Universe on more than one occasion and was humbled each time anew. It began with bursting, swirling masses of colour and energy that went on to birth whole galaxies, solar systems, stars, and planets. Every piece of creation proudly represented itself by a single tone, marking its unique presence. Together the sounds and vibrations played like a full-blown symphony where each voice added to the greater whole. The sacred song of creation always brought tears to the eyes of the Sage, overwhelming him in its beauty. He knew that upon returning to his body, his face would be damp.

Briefly, Aarus allowed himself to reflect on one other point in the history of time that could bring tears to his face; a time that had been both the most fulfilling and yet most heart-breaking in his long life. This experience he did not speak of to others, though those in the Forest were aware of his loss. They also knew that Aarus had never loved as profoundly since. Refusing to allow himself any more time to think upon it, Aarus focused his mind again on the task at hand.

As history played forward, he observed the birthing of the Karrian Galaxy, the Ancient Forest, and *Atarashara*. It was at this time that he too had been born. He, like each of the Elders, knew that the Forest was not only the port of entry into the Karrian Galaxy but also its guardian and the first line of defence. Throughout the ages, the Ancient Forest had been challenged, fighting battle after battle. Always, the Song Bearer, the giant Guardians, and the Elders had banded together to successfully overcome the forces of darkness that sought to compromise or even obliterate the sacred gateway that the Forest was, and take control of the Karrian Galaxy. The Sage knew that the cycles of dark and light would play themselves out until the end of time. But he, too, had heard Dineah's song last night. He knew that the Forest and its inhabitants were in for troubling times, for something was different this time. In fact, something was *incredibly wrong*.

Never had the Song Bearer's song contained such turmoil and uncertainty. Never had the singer almost been destroyed in the process of delivering the song, and never before had *Atarashara* interjected, producing a Starchild of staggering potential and unimaginable magic.

He knew of the child, Sarah Starbright, and her true origins, for he had been journeying out of his body the night Atalia had entered *Atarashara*. Aarus knew that the *'the field of unlimited possibilities'* was unforgiving. To pass through the portal without proper reverence or protecting oneself with ritual meant certain death. And yet the portal had allowed Atalia entrance without taking her life. Aarus could only speculate why this had happened, but he was certain it had something to do with the Starchild. He had felt the child's magic the moment Atalia had emerged from *Atarashara*, carrying the cloth bundle in her arms. Aarus had then allowed his spirit to follow her to Princess Hana's home where he witnessed what occurred next.

So intrigued had Aarus been by what he had seen that he had then journeyed into the future. The images had been oddly sparse, his vision seemingly impeded. Even so, it had become clear that Sir Perity, the orange cat who had also been created by *Atarashara*, was crucial to the existence of the Starchild. Not only was this strange little creature a shapeshifter but it also carried an unusual amount of magic.

Why had *Atarashara* interfered? This involvement was unprecedented! What did *'the field of unlimited possibilities'* know that others could not be privy to, *including Aarus himself?*

Aarus brought his attention back to the present. He was journeying today because Dineah, the Song Bearer, was not recovering as she should have. In fact, she was steadily declining. The war song had damaged her tiny body, impacting her ability to heal. As a result, her firelight had diminished and was barely glowing. As the singer of the song, Dineah's survival was crucial to the success of the Ancient Forest in the upcoming battle. Aarus needed to understand why she was ill.

Aarus was aware that on the same night that Dineah had birthed the war song, an attack had been made on Princess Hana, and ultimately on the young girl, Sarah. Aarus decided to explore the events of that evening.

Moving his attention back in time, he slowed at the moment that four pinpoints of light entered the upper window of a house on Fairy Lane in the city of Brendondale. Shortly after that, he observed Sir Perity depart through the same window. Nothing seemed out of the ordinary until … Aarus paused his attention, rewinding the images to review them again. At the moment that Dineah had channelled the warning wail, Sarah Starbright had awoken in distress. *The Starchild had heard the song from the planet Earth!* This awareness was highly unusual given her lack of training. It also affirmed Sarah's innate connection to the Ancient Forest as a child of *Atarashara*. Her instinctual abilities were much stronger than Aarus would have thought possible.

Aarus felt a familiar feeling and honed his attention to

receive the channelled information. Suddenly he knew with unwavering certainty that Sarah could expedite Dineah's healing as well as her ability to carry on as the Song Bearer. Aarus was astounded! Never before had the song chosen both a singer *and* an ally to the singer.

Aarus's suspicions were confirmed. He would not have the luxury of drawing upon previous experience, for nothing about the present danger barreling toward the Forest was going to be similar to what they had known before. Resigned to this revelation, yet renewed by his insights, he set his intention to return to his hut. Aarus's spirit at first hovered and then gently drew back into his body. After a moment, he whistled one, short call. The two Fireflies guarding his hut entered, suspending themselves in the air on each side of his head.

"Tell Elder Aczartar to call the Council and the Guardians together in the Sacred Grove, immediately. I have news that can help the Song Bearer heal."

Bowing deeply, the Fireflies left the hut.

∾

Once the Elders and the Guardians had gathered, Aarus relayed his observations, and belief that Dineah's healing was dependent upon the young girl, Sarah Starbright. The Elders were aware of Sarah's existence as an adopted member of the Royal Family and that she was being raised away from the Ancient Forest by Princess Hana. For the first time, Aarus disclosed the full story behind Sarah's lineage and Atalia's part in manifesting her in *Atarashara*. He also shared Sarah's upcoming role in the survival of their people and the Ancient Forest, based on what he had heard Atalia tell Hana. Silence fell as those present were not only stunned at this news but also at the violation of laws that had taken place. Even the Guardians appeared to be shocked into complete stillness.

Aarus allowed for the silence, giving everyone time to integrate his words. As he looked around the circle, he knew that the Elders were unsettled. The Council was acutely aware of the grave, yet undefined danger that was upon them, and they had all agreed that the urgency of Dineah's song was very different from previous war songs. But they were not prepared for what Aarus had just revealed.

"There is more, isn't there, Aarus?" asked Elder Ravensong in his high, reedy voice, his head swivelling from side to side as he looked at Aarus first out of one eye, then the other. "What else did your journey reveal?"

Aarus was not surprised that Ravensong was the first to break the silence and ask a question. Ravensong was one of two Orators of the Ancient Forest. He was always quick to spot a story to weave into those he and Elder Tenor told every night in the Sacred Grove. Known for his ability to shapeshift between a raven and a human, he currently occupied his bird form from the shoulders up, his intelligent eyes a bright yellow within the rich, black silkiness of his feathers. The rest of him appeared human.

Ravensong was fearlessly inquisitive. Some of the Elders even considered him reckless. Aarus knew this was not so, for Ravensong's intrinsic need to stir up magic made him legendary in helping the Council find solutions to their problems.

Ravensong was excited by Aarus's pending news for wings suddenly appeared on his back, and his legs changed from human to bird. Aarus doubted that the Elder was even aware that he was visibly shifting back and forth.

Taking a deep breath, the Sage delivered the news that he had received through the channelling.

Chapter 4

"Dineah needs Sarah for her role as the Song Bearer to come to fruition. This information is unprecedented. Never before have we known the war song to choose both a singer and an ally, *and* never before have we known *Atarashara* to intercede in an impending battle."

Aarus's next words were like a bombshell.

"What this means is that Sarah Starbright, birthed in *Atarashara* through Princess Atalia, for reasons we do not yet understand, will play a crucial role in the survival of the Song Bearer, the Ancient Forest and ultimately, the Karrian Galaxy."

The Council erupted into loud voices, clamouring to be heard overtop each other.

The Guardians reacted by rocking their giant trunks back and forth, causing their branches to creak and leaves to twirl.

Aarus tried to speak; his voice lost in the uproar. Looking to Noble, the Scarab King, he bowed his head slightly.

Noble stood slowly, his presence massive. He commanded silence in a deep baritone voice. Very seldom did the King exert his power within what could be considered a circle of equals, but tonight he, like Aarus, could see that the Council was uncharacteristically reactive. Understandably so! Underneath his calm demeanour, Noble was also profoundly shocked by what Aarus had shared, starting with the actions of his daughters.

As the noise subsided, Aarus stood to the height of his tiny frame, speaking calmly to both the Council and the Guardians.

"Brothers, I do not understand why *Atarashara* has chosen to interject and create the child of magic, Sarah Starbright. Although I cannot be certain, I believe that *Atarashara* was responsible for summoning Atalia to it on that fated night. I do know for certain it allowed her to come and go without harm. For some reason, *'the field of unlimited possibilities'* has chosen to have an active role in combating the danger that will undoubtedly fall upon us now that the war song has sounded. *Atarashara's* involvement is unheard of in the history of our battles. Brothers, we fight this fight as if for the first time. Nothing about it will be like what we have known in the past."

Silence ensued until broken by Elder Borus, a stocky looking gnome wearing an unusually shaped hat named Felix.

Aarus slowly let out his breath. Borus's viewpoint was sorely needed at this critical point.

As the Care Keeper of the Ancient Forest, Elder Borus always stopped to touch an ailing plant or tree, or to listen to the voice of a Fairy or Firefly as he and Felix bounded through the Forest. No matter was too small to demand his unwavering attention. Trusted by all, it was common to see tiny creatures riding on his shoulder or hanging from his moustache. Vines and leaves often bulged out of his boots and pockets, choosing to accompany him as he walked. Everyone wished to spend time with the gnome and his talking hat. Borus's grounding presence often played a role in calming the Council.

"Felix and I 'ave met the lassie, Miss Starbright," he said in a soothing and lyrical voice, his eyes sparkling, and his cheeks flushed and bright.

Felix nodded in agreement and then leaned forward, whispering into Borus's ear. The gnome nodded his head in agreement and continued to speak.

"Brothers, ay, it is true – her magic is so strong, tis like a beacon in the night."

Aarus watched as the Elders sat, mesmerized by Borus's words and by the music in his voice. Aarus often saw notes accompanying Borus's words, floating and shimmering before they faded away. Aarus knew that if anyone could recognize Sarah's potential, it would be Borus, for he too exuded magic.

"I realize that we 'ave only met Sarah Starbright briefly, lads, but both Felix and meself already believe in her ability to help the Song Bearer heal and fulfil her role."

Again, Felix nodded in agreement.

Borus then turned his gaze to the Scarab King, and his voice softened, forcing some of the Elders to lean forward to hear.

"She is a fine young lassie, raised well by ye own Princess Hana, ye Majesty. Ye need to know that Sir, and be proud."

To accentuate his next words, Borus raised his eyebrows, projected his voice, and made direct eye contact with each of the Council members as he spoke.

"What all of ye need to know is that she has potential like nothing I have yet to see in me lifetime. *She is pure magic!*"

Borus let his words sink in as he nestled deeper into his chair, folding his large hands across his ample stomach and staring serenely up at the Guardian closest to him. The tree responded by bending its trunk toward the Elder. Chuckling softly, Borus fondly patted its weathered bark.

It had worked. Elder Borus's words had struck home. Aarus breathed an inward sigh of relief as the Council drew together and began to strategize. They unanimously agreed not to disclose Sarah's true identity yet. They also discussed punishment for Atalia's actions, but their hearts were not in it after hearing Borus speak, and knowing that Sarah Starbright was to play a significant role in saving their people. Ultimately, the Scarab King needed to talk with his daughters. Until then, no decisions would be made.

Noble had been purposefully quiet throughout the Elders' discussion, not wanting to sway their decision-making. Inwardly, he continued to be shocked at Atalia's actions, only too aware that she could have died in *Atarashara*. For now, he would give her the benefit of the doubt, for it was his trust in her impeccable judgment that had led to her appointment as the First, head of the Legions. The King intrinsically knew that something of great urgency had moved both of his daughters to take such enormous risks. Not realizing how much his next actions were like Atalia's, he chose to put the matter from his mind. He could not come to any conclusions until he had talked with her. Taking a deep breath and squaring back his shoulders, Noble returned his attention to the matters at hand.

The Elders continued their discussion for several more hours, ultimately agreeing that Dineah and Sarah would meet. Elder Mendalese, as head of the healers, and Elder Aarus would transport Dineah to the planet Earth while ensuring that the energetic connection between the Song Bearer and the Guardians remained intact. Maintaining this tie was paramount to their relationship and the well-being of the Ancient Forest.

As the night air cooled and the golden-horned owl hooted three times, the meeting drew to a close. The Elders departed from the Sacred Grove.

Aarus stayed longer, resting within the sanctuary of the Sacred Grove with his old friends, the Guardians, and letting their energy permeate his weathered body. Even though the Elders had agreed, Aarus knew that there was some risk in having the Song Bearer reach out to someone as unknown as the Starchild. Although born of *Atarashara*, Sarah had not grown up in the Ancient Forest. She did not know the Forest's true identity, or for that matter, he doubted that she yet knew of her own. Even so, Sarah Starbright was clearly going to play a crucial role in how the Forest's never-ending story unfolded.

Aarus also knew that there was more here than met the eye and that it was necessary to watch for signs that could alert him to the Great Mother's plan. He recalled other times when the very fabric of existence had hung tenuously on a string – this was not new to him. But something was different this time. For the first time in his long-standing relationship with the Guardians, he could tell that they felt disquieted. Aarus was also uneasy, for he was uncertain about the future. Twice now in journeying forward in time, he had seen several possibilities. One that deeply troubled him was darkness, emptiness, as if all life ceased to exist. He did not understand what it meant, for no matter the outcome of the never-ending struggle between dark and light, he had always believed that something would remain.

Aarus thought longer on this, finally making a difficult decision. It was not his practise to summon otherworldly beings into the Ancient Forest without the Council's knowledge. He knew that some of the Elders would vehemently disagree with what he was about to do. There was history with this individual.

He spoke his thoughts to the Guardians who communicated long among themselves and finally consented. Aarus did not miss the shiver of alarm that moved through their leaves, or the roots that writhed underground briefly before settling.

"Thank you, my old friends," he said gently, knowing how difficult his request was for them. Closing his eyes, Aarus allowed his mind to span out beyond the Forest, telepathically sending forth a summoning. He sat, and waited.

It was not long before the wind moved through the leaves of the trees, whispering that a new presence had joined the Forest. Aarus could feel the wind's uncertainty and tension, for it remembered the visitor from long ago and was more than aware of the power and danger of this being. He calmed the wind, asking that the winged guards of the Ancient Forest not be alerted. He had agreement from the Guardians and needed this exchange to be private, at least for the time being.

Aarus stood and turned his body in the direction from which

the wind had come. He groaned, standing as tall as his slight three-foot frame would allow. He did not miss that the tree roots of the giant sentinels closest to him shaped themselves into a chair resembling a throne. Aarus felt humbled by the gesture. He knew that this was a demonstration of respect for him, as well as to imprint his status upon the pending visitor.

Aarus raised his hands in the air, crying out words in a language that only the Guardians would understand. In doing so, he set a spell of protection. He needed to safeguard the being that was approaching, for the Forest would instinctively protect itself and capture or destroy what was about to enter the Sacred Grove. He watched as the majestic seven-foot-tall creature stepped forward from the trees, walking in long, measured strides that portrayed no fear or hesitation. Aarus felt his world settle just knowing that the being had answered his call despite the risk of it being here.

The Guardians drew still, their boughs filled with tension.

Aarus knew that their protectiveness of him could cause problems here tonight. As the creature came to stand in front of Aarus, they stared at each other without flinching.

The Guardians at first rigid began to bend ominously toward the visitor.

Suddenly the Were-Griffin dropped to one knee, bowing with a curt nod of his head. He continued to keep his head down as Aarus stood with arms outstretched, speaking the formal words of greeting that would allow the Guardians to relax.

"Welcome, King Matharzan-Ariebe," Aarus said formally. "You are welcome and safe here tonight as a guest of the Ancient Forest."

The Guardians' leaves fluttered as if letting out a sigh of relief. The night sounds returned to normal as the tension of a moment ago was gone.

Having completed the formalities, Aarus moved to embrace the Were-Griffin in a hug. No one but these two men knew of the depth of friendship that existed between them. Aarus's voice was now gentle and filled with affection.

"Thank you for answering my call, Matharzan. You come to me in my hour of need."

The Were-Griffin looked at the Sage, noting that his face looked haggard as if he lacked in sleep. Matharzan felt unease, for he knew that Aarus's decision to summon him would only be under dire circumstances. Alarms began to sound in the back of the Were-Griffin's head. He kept his thoughts quiet, allowing the Sage to lead the dialogue. He did feel some agitation though about being summoned and decided to voice it.

"It has been long since we have talked, Aarus. I don't need to remind you that you take great liberty in calling me forward this way and risk both of us in such a bold gesture. Times have changed from what they once were, and many in the Forest do not consider me an ally. That still grieves me," he said in a softer voice, "for it was not always so."

Aarus said nothing, only nodding his head slowly up and down. His eyes filled with compassion, quickly followed by worry.

Matharzan's flare of frustration instantly dissolved as he witnessed Aarus's distress. The Were-Griffin recalled why he had once before followed this gentle Sage with unwavering loyalty, and knew that he was likely about to do it again. Sighing, he removed his cloak from his shoulders, flexing his wings once before neatly placing them back in place. Folding the coat, he put it on the ground, settling himself down on top of it. Looking up at Aarus, a wry smile appeared on his face. In a kinder, yet still gruff voice he began to speak.

"Well old friend, tell me what it is. What has moved you to take such extreme measures, for I highly doubt that the Council is aware that I am here?"

Matharzan's right eyebrow rose in speculation as he finished speaking.

"Ah yes, extreme measures – that is a good way to put it, Matharzan. I apologize for taking advantage of an old and dear friendship, and I know that our paths have not crossed for many an age."

Aarus paused as sadness passed over his face.

"I also know that our history goes back further than time itself and I trust no one more than you. Matharzan-Ariebe, King of the Were-Griffins, I seek your assistance on a matter of great importance."

With that Aarus nodded at the Guardians, whose boughs moved atop them, allowing no creature big or small to eavesdrop on their conversation. Aarus and Matharzan spoke further into the night. More than once Matharzan sat stunned into silence as Aarus relayed events both past and present. Finally, the Sage and Were-Griffin stood, grasping each other's forearms to solidify their pact. The winged giant then bowed at the tiny Sage before stepping back into the trees and departing.

As Aarus watched the Were-Griffin take his leave, he now felt safe to rest and sleep. He did not know what the outcome of his intervention would be. He had not been confident that Matharzan would even agree to his request. Aarus only knew that he had set something in motion, and if anyone could fulfil this quest, it would be Matharzan. Aarus sighed as fatigue settled over him. He called for the Fireflies to assist him back to his hut.

CHAPTER 5

Unlikely Allies

Sarah did not go to school the next day. She had not slept well through the night, troubled by the haunting wail that had continued to play itself out in her mind. Sarah desperately needed to talk to her mom. Upon entering the kitchen, she found her Aunt Atalia instead. Surprise at her aunt's presence, followed by bitter disappointment flooded through her when she was asked not to bother Hana who was unwell and resting in bed.

Sarah wondered if her mom's illness was due to the unnerving sound of last night. Tears filled her eyes as she mumbled to her aunt that she too was unwell and wanted to stay home. Sarah turned her back so that Atalia could not see the tears sliding down her cheeks. She needed so badly to talk about what had happened during the night but did not feel that she should discuss it with her aunt. Atalia's brusque and to-the-point personality was not as approachable as Hana's.

Atalia was relieved at Sarah's request to stay home and was so quick to agree that Sarah gave her a quick sideward glance through narrowed eyes.

Way to go Atalia, she thought to herself, *now she knows you are hiding something.*

Atalia quickly shifted the topic, suggesting that Sarah return to her room where a warm breakfast would be brought to her. There was no response. Atalia looked closer at Sarah, and for the first time saw the tear tracks on her face. Barely hiding her frustration she sighed, speaking in a gentler voice.

"She is resting quietly in her room, Sarah. Go join her, but I would ask that if she is sleeping that you do not disturb her until she awakens."

Sarah smiled, giving her aunt a quick hug before running upstairs and quietly opening the door to Hana's room. Looking toward her bedroom, Sarah let out a soft whistle, waiting for Sir Perity to join her before closing the door. Crawling under the covers, Sarah was careful not to wake her mom, who was still asleep. Feeling better now that she was close to Hana, Sarah promptly fell asleep.

Sir Perity curled up beside her, purring loudly.

~

Sir Perity was glad that Sarah had stayed home today, for the Gyranger's attack the previous evening had made it clear that the Starchild was no longer safe to be on her own. Sir Perity had no idea how Sarah's location had been found out. For thirteen years they had successfully kept her hidden. Now, that sanctuary was shattered. Protecting Sarah would require new strategies and the help of others.

Sir Perity had observed the Prince, along with the Dragonflies and Fireflies, leave in the early morning hours, after determining that another sudden attack was unlikely. The Legion had been instructed to stay, albeit at a distance, and Atalia had taken up command from within the house. Knowing that Sarah was well guarded had allowed Sir Perity to venture out tonight to watch for signs that would alert him to the Gyrangers' next moves. Sir Perity believed that it would not be long before they struck again.

Although he did not typically travel this far from the Starchild, Sir Perity's instincts drew him to the banks of the Sparry River on this warm summer eve. Upon arriving at the water, he sat down and lifted his head toward the night sky, patiently waiting. It was not long before his keen senses felt a change in the air.

Thick, spiralling energy began to take shape, followed by a tearing sound that birthed a form in its aftermath. A deep growl emerged from Sir Perity's throat at the same time that his hollowed eye sockets opened into thin slits, revealing glowing lights within. He waited, crouched down in the tall grass, his tail twitching in agitation. He was prepared to do whatever needed to be done to protect his charge, Sarah Starbright.

≈

The song of the crickets filled the evening air; the insects' presence hidden in the tall grasses and reeds that lined the Sparry River. Suddenly, the water bubbled and foamed as the consciousness of *Atarashara* infused the river that flowed through Brendondale City. Carried along by the water into the heart of the city, *'the field of unlimited possibilities'* now bore witness to the sounds of nightlife – human laughter, the screeching of tires, police sirens, and the loud thumping bass of a car stereo. As the river and *Atarashara* moved further away from the downtown, the drone of traffic diminished, replaced by the cry of the night owl, the sound of the wind gently rustling the tall grasses, and the music coming from the camps of the gypsies located on the outskirts of the city limits. *Atarashara* liked what it heard in the music of the gypsies for they acknowledged the old ways; the days when humankind respected and remembered their relationship with the Great Mother.

Atarashara's keen awareness sensed the four pinpoints of light that were guarding the Starchild in the house on Fairy Lane. It also was aware that one of the inhabitants of that same house – a creature well known to *Atarashara*, had made its way to the water's edge. It watched as Sir Perity gingerly chose his way, stopping near the reeds and lifting his face to the evening sky … waiting. *Atarashara* also waited, trusting the instincts of the guardian it had created.

It was at that moment that the night sounds abruptly came to a stop as a disturbance briefly pulsed through the air. *Atarashara* saw Sir Perity drop to the ground, the hair on his back raising as his tail swished back and forth in agitation. '*The field of unlimited possibilities*' also sensed the disruption, followed by a tearing sound as if the veil of reality was being torn apart … and then closed again.

Before, the river bank was empty. Now it hosted a creature of incredible size, its nose a beak, its eyes beadlike and brilliantly yellow. It crouched as still as stone with its fingertips touching the ground, poised like a sprint runner ready to launch forward. The bulge underneath its black cloak moved slightly as the creature lifted and adjusted its mighty wings. It continued to keep its upper body adjacent to the ground, swivelling its regal head deliberately back and forth. Slowly, the creature rose, turning in a full circle … as if searching.

Atarashara watched … and waited.

Chapter 5

⌁

King Matharzan-Ariebe crouched with his fingertips on the grass, tense and alert. Taking a deep breath, he felt his body align into the earth plane. Continuing to stay low, he flexed his wings, drawing them closer to his back. Moving his head slowly back and forth he allowed his senses to span outward. Convinced that he had not been followed, Matharzan stood to his towering height of seven feet. As he turned in a full circle, he viewed the city that spread out before him.

Matharzan fingered the pebble that was in his pocket. It was gifted from Aarus; a honing stone that would guide the Were-Griffin to Princess Hana, the Starchild, and her guardian. Matharzan did not understand how a blind cat could be a guardian, but it was not his to question *Atarashara*.

The Were-Griffin focused his thoughts into the pebble until Princess Hana's presence was perceptible. He moved forward, drawn by an invisible force. He had few hours of the night left and wanted to find the Starchild before dawn.

It was only then that Matharzan understood his mistake. Anger coursed through him as he realized that he was not alone. Readying himself for the fight that he knew was about to occur, he threw his dark cloak aside and freed the wings that were his greatest weapons.

⌁

Sir Perity crouched close to the ground, growling deeply as every hair on his body warned that grave danger had transported onto the earth plane. A Were-Griffin! He could try to kill it in his cat form, but instinct screamed at him to shapeshift. Overwhelmed by the imminent danger, his body fought to take control and shift itself. Sir Perity surrendered, putting his head between his forelegs and stretching out his spine and tail. It was during this time that he thought he felt the veil of reality tear again. Lost in his transformation, he could not be sure.

The small orange cat was gone, replaced by a two hundred and fifty pound tiger of rippling muscle and strength. Sir Perity flexed his razor-sharp claws, creating deep furrows in the earth. He lifted his head slightly to make room for the fangs that protruded from his mouth and extended down to the ground. His eye sockets, no longer sunk inward, pulsated with the piercing golden light of his birthright. Sir Perity could see! The guardian of the Starchild was now present in his full capacity, deadly and unstoppable.

Sir Perity watched the Were-Griffin turn in a full circle. He was not pleased to see the creature stop and focus its attention in the direction of the house on Fairy Lane. Nor did it elude him that the Were-Griffin's path would lead to the spot where the great cat hid. When the creature unveiled its mighty wings, Sir Perity knew that it had marked his presence and was preparing to fight. Sir Perity flexed his razor-sharp claws. He too was ready.

Sir Perity's senses suddenly grew taut as he realized that he and the Were-Griffin were no longer alone. Swinging his massive head back and forth, he searched. Only then did he see the two Gyrangers advancing in plain sight toward the Were-Griffin. Sir Perity growled in frustration. Something was wrong! Gyrangers were shrewd and cunning. They would not fearlessly provoke a Were-Griffin, unless … Sir Perity's head snapped up. He scanned the area again. Gyrangers would only act this boldly if there were more of their kind present. Sir Perity realized that he *had* heard the veil tear a second time.

He wondered how many of the insect-like creatures were at the riverside.

The Gyrangers had either followed the Were-Griffin or detected its arrival to the earth plane. This meant that there would likely be another attack on the house at Fairy Lane. Why were both the Were-Griffin and Gyrangers interested in Sarah? Were they in league together? Sir Perity doubted it, as he saw the Gyrangers separate to relocate on each side of the Were-Griffin. They were moving in for a kill.

Sir Perity realized that neither the Were-Griffin nor the Gyrangers were aware of his presence. Releasing the tension from his haunches, he positioned himself to wait and witness the battle that was about to take place. He would eliminate whoever survived.

It was then that Sir Perity saw the third Gyranger out of the corner of his eye. He could barely make out the shape of the creature for its dark robe was virtually impossible to detect against the evening shadows. It silently approached the Were-Griffin from the rear, floating soundlessly over the ground and leaving a trail of shrivelled and decayed grass in its wake.

Sir Perity's instincts had been correct. The two Gyrangers approaching the Were-Griffin were a decoy for the third creature to attack from behind. One bite from the rear Gyranger's deadly poisonous pinchers would render the Were-Griffin easy prey for the three insect-like monsters. The Were-Griffin stood no chance, *and* Sir Perity would be left to fight the remaining adversaries. He crouched lower, a menacing growl escaping from his throat. His eyes began to glow brighter.

Sir Perity knew that the Were-Griffin was about to die. He also knew that with three Gyrangers already present, more would likely follow. It was essential that he stay alive to alert Atalia and the Legion of the danger that had arrived at Brendondale.

He watched as the Were-Griffin slowly lifted its muscular frame, stretching out its enormous bat-shaped wings to make full use of the razor-sharp claws located at the bottom of each wing's sections. Sir Perity saw the creature step forward to meet the approaching Gyrangers, utterly unaware of the death trap it was in and the predator soon to attack it from the rear.

Time slowed down as Sir Perity watched the Gyranger leap through the air, launching its deadly assault. Sir Perity also sprung forward at that moment, not aware of the decision he had come to until he collided in the air with the Gyranger. Snapping its neck, he threw the dead creature to the side. As Sir Perity landed, he squared off with the Were-Griffin. Looking into its eyes, he saw surprise followed by dawning recognition. They continued to stare at each other in strained silence, the seconds stretching out.

Glancing at the advancing Gyrangers, Matharzan turned his attention swiftly back toward Sir Perity.

"I am not your enemy, guardian of *Atarashara*. I am here by the counsel of Elder Aarus of the Ancient Forest and because of the Starchild. You must trust me, or we are doomed! We do not have time to ponder this! *Will you fight alongside me guardian?*"

Sir Perity bared his fangs, having difficulty registering the Were-Griffin's words. Now that they stood only feet apart the instinct to kill was overpowering. Every fibre of his being screamed to destroy the danger in front of him. Sir Perity's adrenaline-driven mind heard *Atarashara* cry out.

KILL THE GYRANGERS OR ALL WILL BE LOST!

But it was too late. Sir Perity had already launched himself toward the Were-Griffin, his fangs bared and claws outstretched. He barely had time to change his focus to the black shadow growing around the Were-Griffin's shoulder.

Matharzan watched as the giant tiger flew through the air toward him. Spreading the lethal wings that could decapitate a foe in a single swipe, he prepared to meet the creature with resignation, but not fear. It was only the sound behind him, coupled with the shift of Sir Perity's focus that prompted the King to fold his wings around his abdomen. Tucking his head, he somersaulted underneath *Atarashara's* guardian. Coming out of the roll, he came face to face with the Gyranger that would have impaled its pinchers into Sir Perity's neck.

The Gyranger was furious that its plans had gone awry. A significant opportunity was forfeited when the orange tiger had killed its partner. It moved forward, swift and ruthless.

The Were-Griffin responded in kind, moving his great wings from side to side in sweeping motions that pushed the Gyranger backward. As the creature reached the edge of the river bank, it lost its footing. Taking advantage of the Gyranger's loss of control, Matharzan rushed forward, slicing his razor-sharp claws across its chest. The Gyranger shrieked as its severed body hit the ground, falling silent as dark blood bubbled and frothed before being absorbed into the ground.

Turning quickly to aid Sir Perity, the Were-Griffin saw the last of the Gyrangers lying lifeless on the ground. Next to the foul-smelling creature sat a small, orange cat with sunken-in eye sockets, cleaning black blood off his paws. Matharzan stared in amazement as the animal turned its face in his direction. He no longer doubted *Atarashara's* choice of guardian. He thought briefly of how close he and Sir Perity had come to risking what they were both committed to protecting.

The Were-Griffin moved closer to Sir Perity and began to speak.

"I understand who the Starchild is. I understand her role in the pending danger to the Ancient Forest and in helping the

Song Bearer to heal. I know who you are, and I am aware that Princess Atalia and Princess Hana have been keeping Sarah Starbright a secret for many years. I cannot explain why I have dropped everything in my bloody life, and bloody well agreed to protect the girl, but I have. Bloody Aarus," he muttered under his breath as he questioned the pact he had made with the Sage of the Ancient Forest. The evening was getting stranger by the moment.

"You have my word as King of the Were-Griffins that I will fulfil the promise I have made. You cannot protect the Starchild every moment of the day. You have no reason to trust me and yet I would ask that you do. I am not here to fight you, guardian. Killing each other will only leave the child and her Princess mother vulnerable. I have more to explain, but I feel the need to proceed to the house on Fairy Lane as quickly as possible. I will explain further once we are with Princess Hana. There is little time left in the evening, and the sooner we can gather together, the better."

Sir Perity continued to focus his head in the direction of Matharzan's voice. Suddenly he stood and walked toward the Were-Griffin, wrapping his body and tail around the giant King's leg while purring loudly. A moment later he stepped away, proceeding toward Brendondale City and the house on Fairy Lane. When the Were-Griffin did not move, he stopped and turned his head as if waiting.

Matharzan understood that he was to follow. Gathering his cloak and placing it about his neck, he walked toward the cat. He did not question the fact that the cat was blind. Nothing about this animal was ordinary. Once again he considered how he had barely missed being the target of Sir Perity's wrath.

Stepping up to Sir Perity, the Were-Griffin bent down, lowering his shoulder in invitation.

Taking a moment to focus his senses, Sir Perity quickly accepted Matharzan's offer. Purring loudly, he nimbly jumped up, settling in between the Were-Griffin's shoulder and the upper ridge of his wings.

As King Matharzan-Ariebe walked away with the small, orange cat, Sir Perity, on his shoulder, the unlikely partnership of the two guardians began – one appointed by *Atarashara*, the other by the Sage of the Ancient Forest.

~

*A*tarashara observed the unspoken pact between the giant Were-Griffin and the guardian it had created. '*The field of unlimited possibilities*' had counted on Aarus acting independently of the Council and taking steps to secure the future of the Ancient Forest. It was pleased with Aarus's choice of protector. As the consciousness of *Atarashara* released itself from the Sparry River to return to the Ancient Forest, it knew that danger was imminent, but the Starchild was safe.

CHAPTER 6

Pledges of Allegiance

It was well into the early morning hours as Matharzan, with Sir Perity on his shoulder, walked in silence back to the house on Fairy Lane. Nothing in their demeanours reflected the previous animosity that had almost caused them to destroy each other. Both were alert to their surroundings yet lost in their thoughts.

As they walked, the moonlight shone down on a cloudless night, lighting the flat grasslands and making it easy to detect movement. The sounds of the countryside receded as they entered Brendondale's city limits, replaced by the hum of street lights, and the occasional sound of a siren.

It was at this time that Matharzan heard another sound. Numerous muted footsteps echoed lightly through the darkness. Turning his head quickly to peer down a side alley, he saw a flash of silver. He knew that Sir Perity had also picked up on it. Even though the guardian's head faced forward, his ears flickered toward the sound. Sir Perity did not seem concerned. In fact, his purr had become louder.

As the light of dawn began to manifest, they turned onto Fairy Lane. Matharzan was stunned at the amount of magic that permeated the home where the Starchild dwelled. He wondered how Sarah had been kept a secret for so long. Anyone with the ability to detect magic would know of her presence. The Were-Griffin had a feeling that she was not as anonymous as the inhabitants of Fairy Lane assumed.

Matharzan felt Sir Perity crouch low on his shoulder. He saw the hair on the cat's back rise at the same time as a low growl emerged from its chest. Matharzan quickly looked around, noticing the pinpoints of light that moved in and out of the bedroom window on the second floor. His sensitive hearing also detected the breathing of what could only be members of the Legion, placed strategically around the house. What was irritating the small cat?

Sir Perity's tail twitched in agitation as he stared at the gable of the house. Following his gaze, Matharzan could see nothing beyond the three gargoyles perched on both corners and at the centre front peak of the house. When the middle gargoyle looked toward them and grinned, revealing a mouthful of very pointed fangs, he understood Sir Perity's reaction. These creatures were not ornaments of the house – they were *real*.

Sir Perity was irritated. He knew that Atalia's guards were protecting the house. He could feel their presence as he neared the home and in his way, pinpoint each of their locations. He also knew that someone had been paralleling their movements since they entered the city limits. He sensed who it might be and was pleased with the possibility. But he was not happy about the three short, squat, winged statues that sat on the roof of the house staring straight ahead as if marble. He knew that Sarah was familiar with them but still did not like their proximity tonight. He wondered why Atalia and the Legion had allowed them to stay. Deep inside, Sir Perity already knew the answer. They were here for Sarah. Even so, he was still agitated, continuing to growl as he accompanied Matharzan up the walkway to the house.

The middle gargoyle immediately broke his stance and bowed his head respectfully. "My name is Eblie," rasped the creature in a gruff voice.

With those words, the gargoyle lifted his wings in the air gracefully and bowed his head.

"Please don't be alarmed – our unannounced presence is not meant to be disrespectful, Sir Perity. We have come to offer our services to the child living in this house. All magical creatures living in Brendondale have felt the Gyrangers manifesting onto the earth plane in the last twenty-four hours. Word has spread that they are here to harm the girl. Many of us have come to know her in the time she has lived in our city. She has always treated us kindly and with respect. *We will not let the Gyrangers harm her.*"

Eblie spoke the last words as a snarl. In a quieter voice addressed to those closest to him he added, "And she does not ignore our existence."

Matharzan watched the gargoyle on the right nod his head so emphatically that he almost lost his balance, scrambling to stay on his perch. The creature then broke into a feral grin, accompanied by wild snickering that became muffled when he dropped his head to his chest and hid it in his armpit.

Eblie briefly looked at the gargoyle with concern before continuing.

"To my left is my brother, Sheblie, and to my right is my other brother, Tazor."

Sheblie bowed as elegantly as Eblie. All eyes then turned to Tazor who was still struggling to maintain his composure.

His snickering suddenly erupted into noisy and unrestrained laughter.

Sir Perity and Matharzan stared in shock.

"Wonderful!" exclaimed a woman with auburn hair who had emerged from the nearby bushes. "A mad gargoyle! There simply aren't going to be boring times with the lot of you, are there!"

The gargoyle continued to laugh hysterically, barely hanging onto its post.

Sir Perity and Matharzan's attention shifted back and forth between the crazed creature and two more witches who had just stepped forward to join the first. Each wore long black cloaks.

The first witch spoke again. "Well, it's about time you got back, cat! The fabric of our plane was torn apart hours ago. Our alarms have been going off all night. We were starting to wonder if you were going to return. And who is the big bird ... uh ... man ... um ... dear Goddess, is that who I think it is?"

Her voice trailed off as she stared, her mouth ajar.

Sir Perity's hair rose on his spine as a grating howl built in his throat. Jumping from the Were-Griffin's shoulder, he released a roar that drowned out Tazor's laughter. He was tired of the intruders and their disrespect!

Both the gargoyles and the witches froze, shocked at the sound that had come from the tiny cat.

The front door of the house swung abruptly open. Atalia stepped out, fury filling her face. Looking at Sir Perity, she spoke in a frighteningly quiet voice.

"Now that you and that hyena-crazed winged bat have woken up the entire neighbourhood and risked exposing us, what are you going to do? Get inside, *immediately, all of you!*"

No one but Sir Perity was able to tolerate the look that Atalia turned on them. Each quickened their pace as they passed in front of her, including the gargoyles that either gracefully flew, or in Tazor's case, slid down from the roof with wings flapping uncontrollably and claws dismantling shingles upon the way.

Inwardly Matharzan tensed – a reflex reaction. He was more than familiar with the fabled First. As she turned her full attention on him, he found it difficult not to unfold his wings in a defensive stance. They stared at each other. Finally, Atalia spoke in a low, but dangerous voice that only the Were-Griffin could hear.

"Matharzan-Ariebe, King of the Were-Griffins. It is a long time since we have met. Your presence is of great surprise to me." Pausing, she emphasized her next words through gritted teeth. "I am sure your story will be interesting."

The Were-Griffin could smell the fury rolling off of her. He was more than aware of the First's character and reputation and for the second time wondered if he had chosen wisely in taking on this fight. Raising one eyebrow, he decided to test his authority. Knowing the power of his gaze, he stared at her without comment. Atalia did not flinch. Matharzan slowly raised the other eyebrow in surprise. This woman evidently hadn't changed since the last time they had met. *A worthy foe,* quickly passed through his mind as he slowly bowed his head in acknowledgement, and entered the house, ducking so as not to bump the doorframe.

Atalia's gaze never wavered as it followed him into the house. Nor did her anger lessen when she saw a grin spread across his face.

Suddenly a challenging neigh was heard from the street as a regal, silver-winged horse moved like mercury from out of the shadows. It sped past Atalia before she could close the front door, and gracefully came to a stop in the living room ... but not before forcing one of the witches to jump over the couch to avoid being stepped on. Its majestic wings clipped the light fixture at the front door and caused the coat rack to topple over.

Tazor began to laugh again, bending over and clutching his pudgy stomach with both hands.

Others struggled not to join him, but Atalia's stony face and formidable presence commanded silence. Tension permeated the silence that hung in the room as she slowly moved toward the horse; her approach graceful, yet lethal. No one knew that upon looking in the creature's luminous violet eyes, Atalia found herself staring into an ocean of liquid peace and calm, where anger ceased to exist. As her fury dissolved, she reached out to touch the velvet nose of the beautiful animal. Startled at both her feelings and actions, she pulled her hand back, but not before her brilliant mind pieced together who stood in front of her.

Atalia's heart hammered in her chest as she tried to grasp how swiftly things were changing. First, the King of the Were-Griffins, and now the legendary winged Equine King, Silverspear, was in this living room. Both beings were from planets within the Karrian Galaxy that the Ancient Forest protected. Moving her hand forward again, she touched the soft velvet muzzle of the King and bowed her head respectfully before slowly stepping back. Turning, she made eye contact with everyone in the room. Apprehension filled her. Atalia already knew the answer to the question she was about to ask. Even so, she needed to hear it from each of them.

No one spoke. In fact, the only sound in the room came from Tazor who was looking wildly about while snickering and breaking into subdued spurts of laughter. Sheblie and Eblie crowded beside him, their faces filled with worry. Each took turns nudging and motioning him to silence. Glancing at each other, they bleakly shook their heads.

In a voice that would have made seasoned fighters uneasy Atalia asked: "Why is each of you here?"

Unprepared for the cold bluntness of the question, no one responded.

Atalia looked around the room, holding the gaze of each being. Although many bravely held her stare, no one answered. Then she looked at the little gargoyle who struggled with self-control and whose eyes were splayed out in different directions. It was he who responded first, snickering between the words.

"I … Tazor … what … your name?"

Laughter peeled through the room. Everyone turned to look at the woman who had descended the stairwell and was enjoying the moment. Atalia stared at her sister. Hana had obviously been watching the chaos of the last several minutes. She wondered if Hana, like the gargoyle, had gone mad. Atalia quickly dismissed the thought as she realized that her sister was strategically trying to diffuse Atalia's growing anxiousness. The feelings through their shared bond confirmed this.

"Yes, Atalia," said Hana, grinning. "What is your name and by the way, who are you?" She started to laugh again, not even attempting to control herself.

Tazor knew he struggled with darkness and that at times his affliction disappointed his brothers, who loved him dearly. But he was brave and dedicated, and he had never let them down in times of need. He was not prone to registering subtleties and nuances as others could, but he knew the answer to the question that the very grumpy lady had asked. Before he could answer it though, he thought it only polite to introduce himself, as his brother Eblie had done earlier. And so Tazor unknowingly asked one of the most legendary leaders alive in the Karrian

Galaxy, to identify herself – a leader who was well known to every other being in the room. He was aware that someone had started to laugh, but that didn't bother him. It didn't sound unkind, and he was used to people snickering when he talked. He struggled not to join in as he loved to laugh but knew how quickly he could lose control. He focused all his attention on holding himself together. He was mostly successful ... well, except for the eye that started to drift inward toward his nose.

Atalia's focus was drawn away from Hana when she felt a tap on her foot. Squatting squarely on the ground in front of her with his wings folded neatly on his back was the crazed gargoyle. He stared up at her with wide, trusting eyes, while continuing to poke her with his claw. She noticed that one eye focused directly on her, while the other pointed inward toward his nose. She could see that his earlier behaviour had subsided. Atalia sensed the creature's innocence and was struck by his courage, for she knew how intimidating she was.

Atalia instinctively knew that everyone in this room was here because of Sarah. She would be a fool to ignore the obvious. Not only had Sarah's magic been discovered, but somehow each of these beings had bypassed the superiorly trained Legion members set around the house. Inwardly she sighed as she reminded herself for the hundredth time that they were working with a child born of *Atarashara*. Nothing should have surprised her. Squaring her shoulders back and softening her voice she responded to Tazor's question.

"I am Princess Atalia, daughter of the Scarab King of the Ancient Forest, and Principal Commander of the King's Legions. I am also known as the First. I am here to guard Sarah Starbright and her mother, my sister Hana, and seem to be miserably failing given the fact that every one of you has eluded the guards set around this house and are standing here in front of me." Taking a deep breath, she said brusquely but not unkindly, "Now tell me, why you are here, Tazor Gargoyle."

Tazor smiled at the formal acknowledgement of his name, unaware that both of his eyes were now firmly lodged in the lower regions near his nose. He looked hopelessly cross-eyed. He answered humbly, bowing at the end of his response.

"We here to protect friend, Sarah, 'cause that what friends do. Me and my brothers - Eblie and Sheblie - offer service, Lady … Princess … First … Atalia."

Tazor's eyebrows etched higher as he added each name. He was unsure of how to address a Princess and the Commander of the King's army, but he was trying his best.

Eblie and Sheblie also bowed at the end of his response. At that moment they were more proud of their little brother than ever before.

"Why are you here to protect me?" asked another voice.

Everyone in the room turned to look at the slightly built thirteen-year-old girl standing at the top of the stairs in pyjamas, and holding what appeared to be a journal to her chest. Wavy, sandy-blond hair framed an oval face with bright blue eyes that shone with starlight.

"Wow," was all she said as she looked at everyone in the room.

Sarah recognized the three witches and raised her hand in greeting. Two of them broke into smiles and waved their hands vigorously back, stopping the moment that Atalia turned to look at them. She also recognized the three gargoyles that frequently accompanied her to school. The one named Tazor often got nervous when she spoke to him, stammering and hiding his head under his wing. That didn't bother her though. In fact, she found it quite endearing. She thought he might have a crush on her. She did not know the bird-like man standing near Sir Perity, nor the majestic silver horse that took up much of the space in the living room. She did notice that they both had wings.

"Tazor, why are you here to protect me?" she asked again.

Sarah pulled her journal closer to her chest, unconsciously protecting herself.

Atalia started to interject but decided to let the moment play itself out. Opting to remain silent she allowed the gargoyle to answer.

"Cause Gyrangers want to harm you. I no let that happen, Sarah. I a good friend and loyal. Me and my brothers guard and protect you, okay Sarah? Okay?"

Tazor stared at Sarah, enraptured. As the words had left his mouth, he knew that his life purpose had been made clear to him. In his mind, he pledged his heart and soul to the girl child standing at the top of the stairs.

Sarah stood in stunned silence. She did not know what Tazor was talking about and yet the sincerity within his words touched something deep within her. She felt moved to acknowledge what he had said. Words spontaneously flew from her mouth, stated with conviction and formality.

"I accept your offer, Tazor, Eblie, and Sheblie Gargoyle, as guardians to protect my life and to ensure that no harm comes to me. As my guardians, may your well-being be watched over and shielded from harm."

Sarah quickly looked around the room. Her Aunt Atalia was watching her with fierce concentration. Sarah felt bewildered. How had she known what to say? From where had the words come? Gathering herself, she moved down the stairwell past her mother and closer to the little gargoyle who continued to gaze intently at her. Well, at least with one eye – the other seemed to have shifted again and was now looking at her Aunt Atalia. The creature shuffled up to her and bent forward, gently placing the side of its face on her foot. Sarah could see that tears coursed from its eyes. She did not know that no one had ever listened or believed in Tazor's worth in the way she had just done.

The focus remained on the gargoyle that in front of all present, had vowed his life to protect the Starchild. At that moment, everyone saw beyond Tazor's madness. They understood and felt the same yearning to protect Sarah.

Walking over to Tazor, Hana picked up the pudgy creature from on top of Sarah's foot. Hugging him warmly, she wiped his tears away. Tazor, at first shy, began to grin. Turning beet red, he tucked his head under his wing, snickering and talking to himself.

"Don't worry, Mom," whispered Sarah, "he'll come out in a little while."

Hana placed Tazor back on the floor.

"I too pledge my guardianship to Sarah Starbright," said Matharzan. "You have my word as King of the Were-Griffins that I will fulfil the promise made earlier to Elder Aarus of the Ancient Forest to keep you safe, Sarah. I know who you are, Starchild, and am aware of your role in the survival of the Forest. You do not know me and have no reason to trust me, but Princess Atalia and Princess Hana will undoubtedly understand the ramifications of Aarus appointing me as guardian."

Looking at both Atalia and Hana, he continued. "Sarah's identity has become known to the Council, as well as the truth behind her origins. Aarus has also foretold a connection between Dineah, the Song Bearer, and Sarah Starbright. I am sorry that you are finding out the information in this way, but the recent attacks and discovery of Sarah's safe place have made her protection and security an urgent priority. Princess Atalia,

Aarus needs to speak to you immediately upon your return to the Ancient Forest, as does your father and the Council of Elders. I am aware that I have made a bold step by sharing these words in front of all present, but only hours ago, Sir Perity and I fought Gyrangers down at the river. They are coming for the Starchild. Look around you, First. Magical beings have gathered in this room. I believe that it is in your best interest to accept all the resources available to protect Sarah's life, and ultimately the life of the Song Bearer."

Both Atalia and Hana could feel their world falling through cracks that had opened beneath their feet. They had known this day would come, but neither had anticipated it in this way. And Sarah, poor innocent Sarah! They had taken no steps to prepare her for what she was hearing. As Hana turned toward the girl, she saw something in her daughter's face shatter. Her world would never be the same after last night, and by what she was witnessing in their living room this moment. Hana unconsciously moved her arms toward Sarah as if to gather and keep her safe. Sarah took a step backward.

"Mom?" she asked, a puzzled look on her face.

A cold fear settled in Sarah's stomach as questions raced through her mind.

What is a Starchild? What truth behind my origins? Who is coming for me? What Ancient Forest is the Were-Griffin referring to, and who is Dineah?

Sarah suddenly recalled the haunting wail she had heard last night. Fear continued to consume her, making it hard to concentrate. Her next words burst from her mouth.

"What is he saying? What Ancient Forest? Who is Dineah? Why does he keep referring to you and Aunt Atalia as Princesses? *I have a grandfather who is a King!*" Sarah's voice rose, becoming shriller as she asked each question.

Hana's arms fell back to her side, her eyes filled with sadness and tenderness. Her response was direct and did not allow for argument.

"There is much to tell you, Sarah, which your aunt and I will do immediately after this meeting is over. I promise! In the meantime, it is crucial that you accept the offer of guardianship that King Matharzan-Ariebe has offered. Please," she said more gently, moving toward Sarah who looked pale and confused.

Atalia did not intervene. Her thoughts were too focused on what she had just heard Matharzan say. Inwardly, she was furious at the Were-Griffin for disclosing years of hidden information in front of everyone, and yet there was truth in what he said. Atalia had to trust in the synchronicity of the odd but significant beings that had materialized this evening to protect Sarah. She drew her attention back to the girl.

Sarah looked at the seven-foot-tall Were-Griffin that stood in front of her with massive wings that could simultaneously envelope many of them in the room. He was gruff and somewhat cold and yet somehow she knew herself to be safe in his presence. Feeling the need to test him, she did so in true teenage fashion.

"Can I call you Grif?" she asked while looking directly into his brilliant yellow eyes.

Atalia gasped, and Hana's mouth dropped open. Her child had just addressed the King of the Were-Griffins in the most disrespectful way possible.

The Were-Griffin knew that his presence was formidable, but he did not see any fear in the steady gaze that Sarah levelled at him. Nor did he sense disrespect. Instead, he recognized the need for a young girl to establish control in an environment that had quickly become devoid of it. Matharzan did not know much about teenagers, but he sensed a spirit in Sarah that held tremendous potential. Without losing eye contact, he slowly nodded his head up and down. At the same time, a smile curved around his mouth.

"Grif, it is," he said in a deep resonate voice, as his massive wings unfurled and then folded in upon themselves.

Sir Perity purred even louder.

"Well then, Matharzan-Ariebe, King of the Were-Griffins and hereafter known as Grif, I accept your offer to protect my life and to ensure that no harm comes to me. As my guardian, may your well-being be watched over and shielded from harm."

Sarah's voice faltered at the end. Once again the words had come unbidden from within her. Unable to fully comprehend what was happening, she pushed the thoughts from her mind. In a voice filled with wonder she cried out, "Grif, do you fly with those wings, because they're like, *huge!*"

Again Atalia cringed at the directness of the question, while Hana simultaneously bent her head forward, placing her hand over her eyes. Once more, a smile pulled at Matharzan's mouth, and he nodded his head slowly up and down in response.

"Radical," said Sarah. For a brief moment, a wildish grin transformed her face, replacing the sombre, uncertain expression of a second ago. One last time the smile crossed her face as she thought, *a flying birdman, go figure!*

"Well, I guess it is our turn," said the oldest of the three witches. Her auburn hair twisted wildly around her head, offsetting the emerald green of her eyes. "My name is Wisteria. This is my sister, Bohn, and our cousin on our mother's side, Sabrae."

Sarah recognized all three witches from the day she had thrown a pebble at them – after they had thrown one at her, of course. Bohn shared Wisteria's eyes, but her hair was as black as night. Both of them were strikingly beautiful. Sabrae, far less attractive, had sandy hair with freckles on her nose which crinkled when she smiled. Sarah felt most drawn to Sabrae whose gentle eyes sparkled with humour.

Wisteria continued.

"We have been aware of Sarah's presence for some time now. As witches, we are sensitive to magic and Sarah is filled with it. Not only have our paths crossed on occasion, but we have been known to keep an eye out for her. In some ways, we consider her a sister, so we take it upon ourselves to cover her back."

Wisteria shrugged by way of explanation.

"We don't fully understand what is going on here. We only know that Gyrangers are teleporting onto the earth plane and witches have a terrible dislike for Gyrangers, especially when they are after one of our own. We have ways of dealing with them that are …" Wisteria paused as a fierce look crossed her face, "… unpleasant."

Turning to the Were-Griffin, she said, "You are lucky, King Matharzan-Ariebe. Had our protective measures been put in place before your entrance to the earth plane, your arrival to Brendondale would have been fatal. It would have saddened us deeply to have harmed you. Because your presence was followed so closely by Gyrangers, we incorrectly assumed you were one of them."

Sir Perity growled deeply in his throat as he recalled the successions of events that had occurred at the river.

"Any other Gyrangers that crossover will be enveloped in flames as they pass onto this plane. We can't keep these defences up indefinitely but can promise you forty-eight hours. We hope that is long enough for you to decide what you are going to do with Sarah, now that her location is known."

Chapter 6

"Sisters," continued Wisteria in a commanding voice, "let us speak our pledge." Simultaneously Wisteria, Bohn, and Sabrae joined hands and raised them as they intoned:

"By the power of three, we pledge guidance to thee,
To protect and keep safe, we as sisters embrace,
We command air and fire, make a shield for this child,
Keep her out of harm's way, both through night and through day."

As the last words left their mouths, Sarah felt warm air move about her and settle. She flexed her shoulders and her neck. The protective shield flexed with her. It felt good.

As they lowered their arms, Wisteria spoke. "Our magic has marked you, Sarah. Wherever you are, near or far, we will sense if you are in danger and will protect you as best we can. We ask for one last thing to assist us in lending our power from afar. Will you give us a tiny drop of your blood to be placed in amulets around each of our necks?"

"No!" said Atalia, Hana, and Matharzan simultaneously. The Were-Griffin's wings rose from his shoulders.

Sir Perity did not move, but his body was taut. He alone was aware of *Atarashara's* presence in the room. Something of great significance was taking place.

"Yes," said Sarah in a voice that sounded foreign even to her. She did not fully understand why she needed to agree to this, but simply knew that she must. Turning to look at Hana she said, "I am sorry, Mom, but you have to trust me on this."

Hana paused for a moment before dipping her head in agreement.

Sarah was reminded of Hana's unending faith in her. The anger and upset she was feeling toward her mother and aunt lessened.

Sarah intrinsically knew that in agreeing to this request, something had changed. Sir Perity confirmed her feelings by moving toward her and rubbing against her leg. Next, he head-butted each of the witch's legs to signify his agreement and acceptance of their blessing.

"That is wise, child," said Wisteria, a contemplative look on her face. "For the decision would have held no power if made by anyone other than yourself."

Atalia kept her counsel. She had seen and recognized the sudden surge of strength in Sarah when she had stood her ground. Once again, Atalia was reminded that the magic of *Atarashara* ran through the Starchild's blood. Atalia guessed that in very little time, there would be more instances where Sarah would make decisions with the same sense of command and authority she had just displayed. She continued to watch the child she had created, strategically assessing the girl's strength and intuition. She was pleased. Sarah was doing well.

Matharzan had also pulled back, his vast wings refolding upon his back.

Sabrae knelt in front of Sir Perity.

"We apologize if we were disrespectful earlier. We ask that you accept our apology and hear our commitment to safeguard and protect Sarah. What is your formal name, dear one?"

Sir Perity placed his head in Sabrae's hand, letting her rub his chin.

"Perry," said Sarah. "He's my cat and my best friend."

"He is also known as Sir Perity," said Hana. "That is his formal name. He has been Sarah's guardian since she was born."

Sarah once again looked at Hana questioningly. Hana smiled tenderly, taking the girl's journal from her arms and placing it on the coffee table. Hana then wrapped her arms around Sarah, holding her tightly and whispering in her ear. Sarah relaxed into her mother's embrace.

Wisteria waved her hand briefly, producing three shining amulets on black chains that floated in mid-air. Bohn repeated the motion, generating a silver knife. Sabrae took the blade from the air. Reaching for Sarah's right hand, she turned it palm upward at the same time that Wisteria lightly grasped the girl's chin and locked eyes with her. With one quick movement, Sabrae cut Sarah's palm. As drops of blood fell, the amulets moved forward in succession, holding their place until full. They then flew to each witch, drawn by the chains that at first unclasped and then re-latched themselves around the women's necks.

Moving for the first time since entering the house, the winged horse stretched its elegant neck and breathed warm air over Sarah's hand. Instantly, the wound was healed.

Touching Sarah lightly on the shoulder, Hana motioned in the direction that the three witches stood.

Once again Sarah intoned the words that instinctively came from within her.

"Wisteria, Bohn, and Sabrae, I accept your offer to protect my life and to ensure that no harm comes to me. As my guardians, may your well-being be watched over and shielded from harm."

The witches simultaneously released sighs as if they had been holding their breaths. Sabrae leaned forward to pull Sarah close to her and envelope her in a hug. Letting the girl go, she whispered, "I have always wanted to know you better, child." Gently stroking Sarah's hair, she stepped back beside her sisters. Bohn grinned from ear to ear, while Wisteria watched her appraisingly, but not before offering a smile that lit up her face.

Sarah then turned her attention to the winged horse.

Reaching up and taking its majestic head into her hands, she stared into the depths of its violet eyes. Immediately, she found herself wrapped in a shroud of peace and calm. As the fear and uncertainty that had bubbled at the edge of her mind dissipated and dissolved, a blossoming light spread through her mind's eye. She knew that the animal was about to speak to her telepathically. Out of the corner of her eye, she saw Sir Perity also lift his head and stare at the horse. She wondered if he too would hear what was about to be said.

And now it is my turn, Sarah Starbright, said a voice that whispered across her mind, leaving streaks of rainbow hues and fragrances of rose petals. *You have seen me in your dreams Starchild, and I have watched over you from afar. We are already connected through the pictures you have created of me and through the magic that flows through your music. I come from a planet that abounds in magic. We are drawn together because of the magic that we share in common.*

The horse turned his massive head toward Sir Perity. The small cat bowed in response.

You knew that I followed you tonight, didn't you, Guardian?

Yes, I did, answered Sir Perity. *I could feel your presence as you kept step with us.*

Sarah's mouth dropped open. She had never heard Sir Perity speak, or even presumed that he could. *You can talk too, Perry?*

Sir Perity turned his head toward Sarah, squeezing his hollowed eyelids in response.

Sarah felt overwhelmed by all that was happening.

Well, why didn't you speak to me before tonight?

I speak to you all of the time, sweet Sarah. You hear me through your other senses.

Sarah knew what he said to be true. She always sensed what Perry was thinking, and he seemed to be able to guess her every mood. Her thoughts were interrupted as the winged horse continued to speak. She knew by the reactions of those nearest to her that the animal was speaking telepathically to everyone.

My name is Silverspear. I am King of the Equines. I come from a place of mystery and light and can quickly move from one world to another. I have sharp hoofs that can beat any enemy who tries to harm Sarah and mighty wings that can fly her to safety.

Turning to look directly at Sarah, he continued.

I offer myself to guard and to carry you, Sarah Starbright. It is in the music that I can hear your voice. If you are in danger, merely sing my name, and I will come. These words are my pledge to you. Do you accept?

Sarah stood in stunned silence as she tried to make sense of what she had just heard. All the years of dreams, all the years of feelings that had birthed themselves into drawings that covered the walls of her room. Understanding flooded through her … *they were real!* A sense of wonder filled her mind as she slowly placed her forehead on Silverspear's broad nose and answered through the telepathic link.

Thank you, Silverspear. I accept.

Sarah then proceeded to intone the same words of binding that she had with the other guardians in the room. She noticed that in Silverspears's company she felt safe and sure; like no harm could come to her.

Scooping Perry into her arms, she moved back to stand in her mother's embrace, looking at all of the beings in the room who had promised to protect her. She didn't know what a Gyranger was or why she needed protection. She didn't understand what *Atarashara* was, and yet the name sent her blood singing. What she knew was that her mom and her aunt were Princesses and that she had a grandfather who was a King.

She was overwhelmed, upset, and excited at the same time. She wasn't the only one in awe of what had transpired this evening. She watched Wisteria nudge Bohn, motioning her to close her mouth. That brought a small smile to Sarah's face.

Atalia knew it was time to take charge. Drawing upon her commanding presence, she began to speak.

"I have heard each of you pledge your guardianship to Sarah. I too accept your words and in my role as the First, and as the daughter of the Scarab King, I bind you to the promises you have made this evening. I do not take for granted that you were all drawn here at the same time. Every cell in my body tells me that you will each play an important role before all is complete. We need to discuss how to use your unique skills, but even more importantly, I need some time alone with Sarah and my sister. The sun has already risen. We will reconvene in a few hours. In the meantime, Wisteria, take charge of everyone in this room and settle them. We are in debt to you, Wisteria, Bohn, and Sabrae for buying us time to plan our next steps. Because of your foresight, Sarah is safe for the next forty-eight hours."

Atalia noticed that Tazor had fallen asleep on Sarah's foot, and was gently snoring. Picking up the tired gargoyle, she turned around to look up at the Were-Griffin. *The hugely controversial Were-Griffin, and guardian as newly appointed by Elder Aarus!* Anger coursed through her, followed by fear. The time had finally come to account for her actions thirteen years earlier. Aarus, the Council, and her father had found out the truth.

She was aware that she had been curt with Matharzan earlier and that there was a need for redress. Atalia had a fearsome temper. She knew how imposing she could be. She was also the first to be accountable if she was in the wrong. Giving the Were-Griffin direct eye contact, she opened herself to criticism for her earlier behaviour. Matharzan did not challenge or lessen her stature in front of the others. As much as his company displeased her, Atalia still knew that she stood in the presence of a King. His steady, powerful gaze held her own, empty of anger or judgment. She could feel the strength that radiated from him. Aarus had chosen well.

Gently holding out the gargoyle as a peace offering, she raised her eyebrows slightly. Matharzan responded by gathering Tazor in his arms while bowing his head slightly, a small smile playing on his lips. Atalia knew that a compromise had been reached between the two of them, and left it at that.

The Were-Griffin motioned for the other two gargoyles to mount his shoulders. Eblie and Sheblie were awed by the giant King's invitation. Once seated, they shyly glanced at him out of the corner of their eyes, their faces flushed in excitement.

Still preoccupied with her thoughts, it took Atalia a moment to realize that everyone had turned their heads to look at Sarah's journal. The book was moving jerkily about on the coffee table, the front cover flapping up and down. As Sarah stepped toward the journal, Hana quickly grabbed her by the shoulders to stand in front of her. The three witches also took up protective stances. Atalia reached for the knife that she hid in her boot, shifting her body closer to the journal in a defensive pose.

The journal abruptly stopped moving ... and then without warning, the cover flew open.

CHAPTER 7

Trial by Initiation

Dineah lay wrapped within the bed of leaves and moss that was her bed. Her head ached, and her lungs burned as if they were on fire. Elder Mendalese had barely left her side since she had collapsed. Her mind still struggled to comprehend what had happened. As a young Firefly, she had received the appointment as Oracle of the Ancient Forest. That role she had come to accept. *But, the Song Bearer!* What was worse was that she knew it to be true. She just knew, somehow, for she could sense the Guardians in a way that she had never before. Even now she could feel the bass rumble of their presence. She could also sense their disquiet and their concern for her.

Elder Mendalese had said that her healing was taking longer than previous Song Bearers. Dineah knew deep inside that something wasn't right, for her body was struggling to recover. It was as if she was burning up. Even now, her friend the wind was moving about her, stroking Dineah's brow and fluttering her tiny wings.

Her glow light had acted strangely since the war song had

moved through her. At first erratic, it now burned continuously, adding to the heat of her petite body. Dineah knew that as the Song Bearer she had to heal. Anything less would be catastrophic to the welfare of the Ancient Forest. But she wasn't improving – in fact, she was getting worse.

Dineah could hear the murmur of low voices. Turning her head, she saw Elder Mendalese and Elder Aarus, deep in conversation. She was not surprised when Elder Aarus turned to look at her even though she had not made a sound. It was as if he could read her thoughts. She watched as the Elders moved to stand beside her. It was Elder Mendalese who spoke first, his voice gentle.

"Dineah, Elder Aarus as Sage of the Ancient Forest, has journeyed to the world of spirit to understand how to expedite your healing. He has determined that the healers of the Ancient Forest have done all they can. To allow you a full recovery, we must send you to the planet Earth."

Elder Mendalese exchanged a look with Elder Aarus.

Dineah could sense the uncertainty in it. She closed her eyes to focus on Elder Mendalese's voice, but anxious thoughts coursed through her mind.

The healers of the Ancient Forest couldn't heal her? That was impossible! Why were they going to send her away from the Ancient Forest? What about her energetic bond to the Guardians? Would it be compromised?

The Elder's next words drew her attention back.

"... her name is Sarah Starbright. She lives on the planet Earth with Princess Hana. You will be leaving shortly. Dineah – it is imperative that you find Sarah. She will help you to heal fully. Do you understand what I have said to you? We will ensure that you arrive as close to the Starchild as possible, but you have to take the next steps – you *must* seek her out.

The Guardians will continue to support you from the Ancient Forest – the connection you have with them will stay intact.

"What do I do once I have found her?" murmured Dineah, her eyes still closed. Realizing that no one had replied she opened her eyes and watched as Elder Mendalese glanced at Elder Aarus. This time there was no mistaking the apprehension on Elder Mendalese's face. Turning to look at Elder Aarus, she noticed the serene composure of the Sage. He stared back at her, his eye of opaque blue even more startling than usual. Gently cupping her bed in his weathered hand, he raised her to his eye level. As he spoke, she felt the warmth and surety of his words.

"You will need to ask her, Dineah. Trust me in this. Now close your eyes as we prepare you for travel, child."

As Aarus spoke, calmness spread through Dineah's body. She did trust him, explicitly. Closing her eyes, she was not aware that she had drifted off, or even moved from the softness of her bed until she awoke in a very confined space.

Panicking, she instinctively struggled to break free. Using her wings, she repeatedly thrust upward, shooting into softness that expanded with the impact of her movements. As she rose higher into the opening, she found yet another barrier. Repeating the same actions, she felt it start to give way before falling back on top of her. Resting briefly, Dineah tried again, using all her strength to give one last push. She watched the obstacle that had impeded her move upward and fall away.

Dineah pulled first her wings, and then the rest of her body through the opening. She was utterly drained and could barely stand. Swaying slightly, she looked down to steady herself. Dineah gasped! All about her feet were pictures of Fairies, in all shapes and sizes. Drawing her gaze upward, she realized there were others present, many of whom she did not know. She wrapped her arms protectively around herself. It was then that her eyes fell upon the First. Relief flooded through Dineah. Remembering the urgency of Elder Mendalese's words, she began to speak.

"My name is Dineah," she said in a small voice. "I am the Song Bearer of the Ancient Forest."

She thought she heard someone gasp. Dineah watched the First take a step back. It was then that she saw the young girl with the sandy-blond hair. Dineah shook her head to clear her vision. Had she just seen stars shining through the girl's eyes?

"I need to find Sarah Starbright. I need her help. I need ..."

Dineah was overwhelmed with despair and fatigue. She had tried so hard but could not go any further. As she lost consciousness, she knew that she had failed the Ancient Forest.

∽

Matharzan watched the witches and Princess Hana protectively surround the Starchild while the First took a defensive stance in front of the journal. Preparing to step in, the Were-Griffin stopped when he saw Sir Perity's calm demeanour.

Suddenly the cover of the journal flew open. Protruding from a page covered with drawings of Fairies was an oval-shaped head with large brown eyes and wisps of light brown hair. The tiny being continued to push upward out of the paper, freeing her wings and glow light. Swaying back and forth, she wrapped her arms around her body. It was only then that she looked up at those around her.

Atalia recognized the Song Bearer immediately and noticed that she looked far too frail. The First stepped back, releasing her defensive stance.

"My name is Dineah. I am the Song Bearer."

Hana gasped.

"I need to find Sarah Starbright. I need her help. I need …" The sentence was left unfinished as the fragile Firefly's eyes rolled to the back of her head and she crumbled into a heap on the page.

Sarah's world ground to a stop as she realized who stood in front of her. *The singer of the sound she had heard last night.* Sarah instantly knew that something was very wrong with Dineah. She could see the Firefly's spiralling energy of life-force leaving her body. The Song Bearer was *dying*.

Sarah turned quickly to Hana, panic in her voice.

"We must help her, Mom; she is dying."

Looking at the others in the room, Sarah's overwhelmed mind registered how everyone stood as if paralyzed. She then watched as each of them slowly turned their gazes upon her. Atalia's next words pierced her soul.

"You are the Starchild, Sarah, born from a place of unlimited magic. You know of what I speak! Look within! What are *you* going to do, Sarah Starbright? The Song Bearer has summoned your help in this moment of need."

Atalia knew that her words were harsh and unfair. The girl had no understanding of her true lineage or that she was even the Starchild. Atalia was taking an enormous gamble with how hard she was pushing Sarah, but there was no time to initiate the girl into her power gently. The Song Bearer *could not die!* Atalia grasped Sarah by the shoulders so that they were eye to eye.

"I believe in you, Sarah. Listen from deep within yourself. Dineah needs your help! You already know how! The wisdom is in you! *What will you do?*"

Sarah felt the blood rush from her head as time slowed down.

She was terrified! She did not understand what she was being asked to do. Thinking back to the previous evening, Sarah drew upon the memory of the song. Letting it fill her mind, she embraced its chilling need. Turning to look at the fallen Firefly, Sarah realized that her Aunt Atalia was right. Deep down inside, she had already known last night – she just had not wanted to admit it to herself. She *was* connected to the song, *and* to this tiny being in front of her. A sense of calm spread throughout Sarah.

Sarah felt her arms move upward in the air as if driven by an unknown force. As she spread her hands up and over the Firefly, she sensed that Dineah's heart had stopped beating. Sarah opened her mouth, releasing a piercing tone that spiralled upward from her lungs and emerged from her throat. The vibrations of sound hit the body of the Firefly, like waves pounding against a shoreline. At one point, Sarah felt Dineah's heart begin to beat again. At another point, she knew that the Firefly's life-force was returning to its compromised body. And finally, when Dineah had shifted into a state of deep, healing sleep, Sarah allowed the sound to recede and eventually stop.

Reaching for the Song Bearer, she protectively cupped the tiny being in the palm of her hand. Peace and tranquillity now enveloped Sarah. As she turned to face her mom and aunt, her eyes were no longer innocent or unknowing. Nor were they Sarah's eyes, for thousands of stars shone through them.

A soft presence brushed across the minds of everyone in the room. Atalia immediately recognized the consciousness that had spoken to her thirteen years earlier on a night that had changed her life forever. She knew who now spoke through the Starchild it had created.

"What is she going to do Princess Atalia? She is going to protect and guard the Song Bearer as carefully as each of you has promised to

protect her. You have given your word guardians – do not fail!"

As *Atarashara* caressed the minds of everyone one last time, it left Sarah's body.

"Mom," she said in a quiet voice as of awakening from a deep sleep. "I heard what the voice said."

Hana was beside her instantly, stroking Sarah's hair at the same time that she covered Sarah's hand that held the sleeping Firefly.

"Come, Sarah, it is time for us to speak. We also need to make a bed for the Song …"

A knocking at the door interrupted Hana. The first Lieutenant of the Legion entered the house and strode toward Atalia to speak with her privately. A moment later, two more guards crossed through the doorway, partially carrying an older woman between the two of them. The woman looked tired and worn. Her dress was stained and torn, and her feet, bare. Dried blood spotted her arms and neck, and bruises wracked the parts of her body that weren't covered by clothing. She tried to lift her head and view the room, but the lenses of her glasses were shattered.

"Mrs. Gibson," cried Sarah as she quickly passed Dineah to Hana, and ran toward her former teacher. "Mom, it's Mrs. Gibson, my …"

The room erupted. In one quick stride, Matharzan placed himself between Mrs. Gibson and Sarah, spanning his wings to create a barrier. At the same time, a guard stepped in front of Mrs. Gibson. Faster than anyone was Tazor who instantly left the Were-Griffin's arms to hover in front of Sarah's teacher. Eblie and Sheblie circled nearby, teeth bared and ready to attack.

Tazor's next words were clear and concise, with no trace of madness.

"I know this one. She gentle and kind. She Sarah's teacher. But what wrong with you, friend of Sarah? Why you smell so bad? You smell like a ... *Gyranger!*"

Growling, he bared his teeth as the hair on the back of his neck raised. Eblie and Sheblie also began to growl.

"Wait," commanded Atalia. "Speak," she said to the guard. Bending his head close to Atalia, he spoke quietly, but urgently. Atalia peered over the guard's shoulder toward Mrs. Gibson who was struggling to stand. If the guard's facts were correct, then it was a miracle that the woman was still alive. Atalia had to be sure this wasn't a trap.

"Well done, Tazor Gargoyle. Now stand down and return to your brothers."

Although Tazor obeyed Atalia's command, he was upset by Mrs. Gibson's presence. As he returned to the Were-Griffin's shoulders, a low rumble continued to sound from his chest. He watched Sarah protectively.

Atalia turned her gaze to Silverspear.

"King Silverspear, we need to ensure that this woman speaks the truth. Please."

As Silverspear moved toward Mrs. Gibson, the guards positioned her so that she was head to the head with the regal animal.

"Remove her glasses," commanded Atalia.

Mrs. Gibson's eyes widened in surprise as she stared at Silverspear. She began to cry, sobs wracking her body.

"Yes," she cried in response to a question that only she could hear. "I am here to protect Sarah! They are coming to take her! They will hurt her! They are monsters! One of them has tortured me for weeks to get closer to her. I am here to warn you!"

Silence ensued as Silverspear continued to speak with Mrs.

Gibson. He then turned his gaze back to Atalia, creating a mind link so that everyone in the room heard his next words.

She is pure of heart and strong of spirit. She is here to aid the Starchild. She has been captured and tortured by a Gyranger who has been posing as a teacher from Sarah's school. We are fortunate that Mrs. Gibson's love of Sarah enabled her to withstand the mental and physical anguish she has undergone. Not all could have endured such pain. Mrs. Gibson must come with us. She is no longer safe now that the Gyrangers have marked her, and she will not be able to withstand their torture if they find her again. Her presence, if not protected, is a risk to the safety of the Starchild. I will restore her body for she is in terrible pain. Her mind also needs healing for it is injured, but there is not adequate time to do that right now. She must go to the Ancient Forest where Elder Mendalese can tend to her. Princess Atalia, I will leave that responsibility to you.

Of course, said Atalia through the mind link. *It will be a priority.*

With that, Silverspear returned his gaze to Mrs. Gibson, who stood as if in a trance. Moving closer, he placed his muzzle against her forehead, expelling a breath of air that made her gasp. Suddenly, Mrs. Gibson's head jerked back, and a shudder ran through her body, causing her arms to splay outwards and dangle. She stayed this way for several seconds, breathing in staccato-like pants that wracked her body.

Sarah helplessly watched, devastated that she had caused this woman's pain. Slowly Mrs. Gibson's body returned to its natural posture, and her breathing deepened. Sarah saw that Mrs. Gibson's bruises were gone. Moving around the Were-Griffin's wing, Sarah ran to embrace her teacher. Mrs. Gibson hugged her fiercely in return. Finally releasing the girl, she continued to grasp Sarah's arms, squinting, while looking her up and down. Relief filled her face.

"My dear child, you are safe. I have been so worried about you."

Her voice cracked at the same time that tears welled up in her eyes. Stepping back from Sarah, she looked around the room. As her compromised eyesight took in the odd assortment of beings standing in front of her, she shook her head as if to clear her vision. Turning to look at Sarah, she opened her mouth, but no words came out.

Sarah quickly grasped one of Mrs. Gibson's hands. Hana also stepped forward and took hold of the other.

"You are one of our family now, Mrs. Gibson," said Hana. "Be welcome. I am afraid that you cannot go back to your old life. You will have to come with us and leave everything you have known, behind. I am sorry to ask this of you, but there is no other way."

Mrs. Gibson could not be said to be faint of heart. She stared at Hana for only a moment before bravely shrugging her shoulders.

"My world changed three weeks ago when that hideous monster captured me – what you call a Gyranger, I believe. I do not understand what is happening here, but if that creature is after Sarah, then I will do whatever is within my powers to protect her. I would not wish on anyone the pain I have experienced. Particularly not this gifted child whom I care so dearly for."

Taking a deep breath, Mrs. Gibson fell silent. Despite the healing by Silverspear, her voice quavered, and fatigue lined her face.

"Wisteria," said Atalia. "Attend to Mrs. Gibson's needs. She must have food and a warm bath before she goes to bed. King Matharzan-Ariebe, you will begin working to launch an immediate attack on Mrs. Gibson's house. Prince Drake and his army will accompany you. You must capture the Gyranger! Let's hope that Mrs. Gibson hasn't inadvertently led the creature to this home."

Turning to the Lieutenant, she continued to give orders.

"Double the guards around the house and update them on what has transpired here tonight. Have a report relayed to my father and the Council with a request that Prince Drake and the Winged Warriors attend as quickly as possible."

Atalia was interrupted by someone clearing their throat.

"First," said Wisteria.

Atalia turned to look at the witch.

"I believe that Mrs. Gibson's ability to escape from the Gyranger may not be coincidental. It is possible that when the wards were set to kill Gyrangers passing onto the earth plane, that they extinguished the creatures that were already present. Mrs. Gibson, how is it that you were able to break free from the Gyranger?"

At first hesitant to answer the question Mrs. Gibson then responded in a quiet voice. Her face paled as she recollected what had occurred.

"I think the Gyranger was going to kill me. She was angry because I had gotten my feet free and was kicking the bed railing. She untied my arms and was dragging me from the bed when I accidentally kicked her. She became enraged, shrieking at me. She said that I had finished my usefulness and that she did not need me anymore. I believe she was going to hurt me with those awful things that protruded from her mouth. Suddenly, she threw back her head and screamed. I will never forget that horrible sound."

Mrs. Gibson began to cry, but she continued to speak.

"She became engulfed in flames and then disintegrated into *nothing* – right in front of me! I think that I lost consciousness and fell to the floor. When I came to, all that remained of her was a pile of black ash. I forced myself to stand and find my way to this house. I don't know how I made it here," she said quietly, lost in thought. "I vaguely remember lights circling me and then these men surrounding me."

"It is as I thought," said Wisteria. "First, the Gyranger is dead. I am sorry that the creature is not available for questioning, but at least it cannot harm Sarah."

"That may be so," said Atalia, "but how many other Gyrangers were notified about Sarah's existence before it died?"

Silence filled the room. Even though Atalia stared at Wisteria, it was clear that her focus was not on the witch. Finally, she nodded her head, having come to a decision.

"Regardless, I want the remnants of the Gyranger. Until we have them secured, I will not be comfortable knowing that they could be used as a homing device by other Gyrangers as they teleport onto this planet."

"Not unlike the pebble I received from Aarus that led me to Princess Hana and Sarah," said Matharzan.

Atalia looked at him in surprise for she hadn't known of this. It made sense though – how else could the Were-Griffin have located them. She continued to speak.

"Wisteria has apprised us that we have forty-eight hours of grace. After that, we can assume that the Gyrangers will be teleporting en masse. Search Mrs. Gibson's house immediately. Upon gathering the remains, report back to me."

Matharzan nodded his head in agreement as did the Lieutenant.

Bowing her head quickly at the Were-Griffin, Atalia turned away. Walking to where Hana and Sarah stood, she put her arms around them both. It was time to talk to Sarah.

Only those standing closest to Mrs. Gibson saw Sabrae gather the eyeglasses that the guard had removed from the older woman's face. With a brief movement of her fingers, the lenses became whole at the same time that the frame returned to its original shape. Sabrae tenderly brushed aside Mrs. Gibson's dishevelled hair before placing the glasses back on her face.

"Mrs. Gibson, I am Sabrae, and these are my cousins, Wisteria and Bohn."

Both Wisteria and Bohn smiled at the teacher.

"You are safe with us," said Sabrae. "Come, it is time to tend to your needs."

Mrs. Gibson touched the glasses with a look of awe as she allowed the three witches to escort her out of the room.

CHAPTER 8

Secrets Revealed

Atalia, Hana, and Sarah remembered the next conversation for the rest of their lives, but in very different ways. For Atalia, it was the first time she had spoken aloud the full events of the fateful night thirteen years ago. It also allowed her to release secrets that had been held inside for too long. For Hana, it was the first time that she fully understood what had transpired, though she had pieced a lot of it together herself. Hana was stunned at the enormity of what Atalia had carried for so many years. For Sarah, it was about learning of the existence of the Ancient Forest, the lineage of her mom's family, and realizing that she originated from a place of magic called *Atarashara*. She was so overwhelmed that she mostly sat in stupefied silence. One thought did make its way through her numbed brain.

I was never really given up for adoption.

For the first time in her life, Sarah felt the band around her heart release, dissolving the sense of abandonment that she had carried for so many years. The rest would take time to absorb. For now, she lay quietly on the bed in her mother's arms, listening to Hana and her Aunt Atalia talk.

She wondered whether she should be angry at her mom and aunt, but found that she wasn't. She understood the sacrifice that had been made by both of them to keep her safe. For thirteen years, Hana had lived away from her birth home and family to ensure Sarah's protection. Her Aunt Atalia had risked her very life, not to mention position and reputation, for the good of the Ancient Forest and the Karrian Galaxy. Both sisters had carried her secret, keeping it from others whom they loved and trusted. Sarah could not believe what they had endured for her.

Sarah had no idea what a *Starchild* was. That thought made her think of Dineah, who was sleeping inside the flower that Tazor had brought in from the garden. Pulling the petals aside she could see the tiny Firefly deep within, her head resting on her arm and her wings tucked neatly behind her back. Dineah's breathing was sure and steady, as was the pulse of her firelight or glow light, as her mother called it. She was no longer fragile. Sarah felt linked to Dineah – something that had occurred in the course of the healing. It was almost like she could feel a piece of the Song Bearer within her mind. She wondered if Dineah would also be able to sense her.

Sarah knew that they would be leaving for the Ancient Forest shortly. It meant leaving behind her life as she had known it. Strangely enough, she was okay with that.

Once again she thought of the many figures that she had spent her life drawing. *They were real!* It was this and this alone that helped to cement the reality of what was happening. Even when she hadn't truly understood her identity, she had somehow manifested magic all around her through her art, her music and through the supernatural creatures that she had attracted. Sarah *knew* she was of *Atarashara*. Since 'the *field of unlimited possibilities'* had manifested through her, she had become aware of its constant presence in her body. She snuggled closer to Hana, still needing to know the surety of her mother's arms. That would never change.

Sarah found herself being pulled into a much-needed slumber as her mother stroked her hair and hummed a lullaby in her ear. Although she vaguely heard the voice of her aunt, she was too tired to register what Atalia was saying.

"It is finally time, sister," said Atalia. "We have done what we could – it is now up to Sarah, *Atarashara,* and the Song Bearer."

Hana did not respond, only nodding her head up and down as she continued to hum into Sarah's ear. Hana knew that both she and Atalia had to account to the Council and their father, the King, for their actions. She could feel Atalia's anxiety through their bond. Looking at her sister, Hana gently began to speak.

"It is time to let your secret come into the open, Atalia. We have carried it for many years, you and me. We have never been fearful or unwilling to be accountable for our actions. We will not back down for what we did. No matter what happens to us, Sarah will be safe. Aarus has ensured that, by appointing Matharzan as Sarah's guardian. We have to trust that everything we did was for the greater good. Hopefully, the Council will also see it that way. If not ..." Hana shrugged her shoulders before turning to gaze down at the sleeping Sarah.

"Look at her, Atalia, look at how beautiful she is! You and I both know what this child is! I will not apologize for what we have done. Now, come sister, lay down beside us and allow yourself an hour of sleep." Hana smiled to take the sting out of her next words. "Anyway, we both know that all chaos is soon going to break loose."

For a brief moment, a whisper of a smile crossed Atalia's face as she shook her head back and forth.

"I need to oversee what is transpiring downstairs. Drake and the Winged Warriors have already arrived; I can feel their presence. I am glad that they will be with the Legion as we prepare to return to the Forest. I am not taking any chances."

Leaning over, she grasped Hana's arm tightly before striding out of the room.

Hana felt tears well up in her eyes. Such a display of emotion was uncharacteristic for Atalia. Even though her sister appeared composed and sure, Hana knew that the events of the evening had shaken her. Thirteen years was a long time to anticipate how one's actions would be interpreted. Sighing deeply, Hana allowed herself to reflect on the last twenty-four hours. A lot had happened, including her death and revival. Unconsciously she rubbed her neck where the Gyranger had crushed her windpipe.

Hana reviewed the sequence of incidents that were propelling them forward at an unnatural speed. After years of being successfully hidden, Sarah's whereabouts had been located by the Gyrangers. Aarus had discovered Sarah's real identity and taken it upon himself to send a guardian to protect her, a guardian that Sir Perity could have mistakenly destroyed, and who was one of the most controversial beings in the history of the Ancient Forest. The main floor of the house teemed with magical creatures that had pledged oaths of fealty to ensure Sarah's safety ... *including a gargoyle whose state of mind hung from a thread.* The Song Bearer had narrowly escaped death, thanks to Sarah who had instinctively tapped into her birthright, *Atarashara,* and saved Dineah's life. Hana's thoughts returned to Tazor, the gargoyle who struggled to contain his sickness. Her sixth sense told her that he was going to play a more significant role than anyone could imagine.

Hana knew that it was time for them to return to the Ancient Forest. Things were rapidly spiralling out of control, and there was a need for Aarus's, as well as the Council's, guidance. She also wanted to feel the safety and sanctuary of the Guardians again. She was ready to return home, no matter the outcome of her and Atalia's actions. Closing her eyes, she allowed herself and the exhausted Sarah an hour of sleep, but not before stroking Sarah's hair one last time.

$\sim$

Prince Drake and the Winged Warriors transported to Brendondale immediately upon receiving Atalia's message. The Prince and his army went to Mrs. Gibson's house with King Matharzan-Ariebe, leaving the Legion and Sir Perity to guard the home on Fairy Lane. Although Prince Drake and the Were-Griffin had not worked together in many years, the outcome of their combined strategic minds was spectacular. The search of Mrs. Gibson's house was carried out swiftly and with relentless precision.

The Fairies encircled the house, creating a shield of illusion and a sound barrier. It was important that the neighbours be unaware of what was about to happen. Moments later, Fireflies dispatched a sonic burst of heat that shattered every window in the house. If additional Gyrangers had teleported into the house, the combustion created by the Fireflies would stupefy, if not utterly destroy them. Dragonflies with Fairy riders acted next. Infiltrating the home, they moved from floor to floor in impressive aeronautic manoeuvres so as not to be susceptible to the laser beams of any Gyrangers who may have survived. Upon establishing that there were no additional insect-like creatures in the house, Prince Drake and the King began the search for the remains of Mrs. Winterly. Once located, the Were-Griffin took control of the ashes.

Before leaving, the Prince ordered the Fireflies to burn Mrs. Gibson's home. The Gyranger known as Mrs. Winterly had utterly desecrated the space in the time it had lived there. Putrid slime covered the furniture, and a horrid smell permeated the house. If police searched the premises, they would have questions. Let them speculate that Mrs. Gibson had died in the fire, even if they were not able to find her body. Upon returning to Fairy Lane, the ashes of the Gyranger were immediately transported to the Ancient Forest and destroyed.

CHAPTER 9

The Shield of Protection

Wisteria, Bohn, and Sabrae knew that vast numbers of Gyrangers were trying to teleport onto the earth and more specifically to the city of Brendondale. Each attempt felt like a blow to the shield the witches had set in place. Wisteria had telepathed urgently with other covens for assistance in expanding the protection to cover a larger area. Gyrangers could just as quickly teleport in at a distance and travel swiftly over land. It was essential that no place near Brendondale was safe for entering the earth plane.

Wisteria was shocked at the persistence of the insect-like creatures. It could only mean two things – that Mrs. Winterly had alerted her race before dying, and that they knew the true identity of Sarah. By now the Gyrangers had to realize what would happen when they passed through the shield. Wisteria knew it was a grisly death. The recipient was doused in an excruciating electrical current that rendered it inoperable before being enveloped in flames. The fact that so many continued to try to gain access concerned Wisteria, as did the evident fatigue it was causing the witches. She had promised the First two days, but wasn't sure if that was any longer possible. The witches were only into their twenty-fourth hour, and they were tiring. Wisteria was aware of the enormous numbers of Gyrangers that existed. The Queen of the Gyrangers appeared to have no qualms in sacrificing members of her race.

Wisteria looked at her sister and cousin. Both returned level gazes, but she knew better. She could see the strain that maintaining the shield was having on them, not only by the tightness around their mouths but in the pressure around their eyes. It was not good. As the creators of the shield, any attack was felt first and foremost by them. Secondary witches had linked in to add strength and support, but they did not experience the same degree of buffeting. Tapping into the mind link that allowed her communication with the other covens, Wisteria framed a single word in her mind and sent it out.

Help!

Instantly, the strength of the peripheral witches poured through the shared link. It filled the Brendondale witches, reducing the pressure that physically weighed on them like a heavy blanket. Taking the hands of Sabrae and Bohn, Wisteria guided them over the large black tourmaline and smoky quartz crystals that sat in the centre of the floor. As they transferred their energy into the gemstones, she watched it shoot up through the ceiling of the room, flowing directly into the massive shield above them. She could allow them all a much-needed break, knowing that the crystals were capable of maintaining the channel for the short term.

Standing, she put her hands on her hips and stretched forward, trying to lengthen her back which was sore from sitting for so long. It was then that she noticed the figure leaning against the far wall, shrouded in the shadow of the room. He was lean and well-muscled, with a sword belted around his waist that radiated a green glow.

As lethal as a cat ready to pounce, crossed through her mind.

Wisteria immediately knew who this was. There existed only one Prince Drake, Commander of the Winged Warriors and the Wielder of the Emerald Sword. His reputation was as legendary as his sister, the First, and the stories she had heard about his physique and attractiveness were entirely accurate. He continued to lean against the wall, arms folded and one foot crossed over the other. The word, *lethal,* kept playing through her mind. She was glad they were allies.

Without preamble he uncrossed his foot and arms, standing erect.

"How many, Lady?"

"Far too many," she responded swiftly, surprised by the fatigue and anger in her voice. "They are attacking our shield in droves and trying to wear us down. We are fortunate to have the other covens, or we would have broken by now. As it stands, the sooner we can move, the better."

She hadn't meant to say that much and was surprised at what had blurted out of her mouth. So were Bohn and Sabrae based on the looks they directed at her.

Wonderful, she thought. *Put a good-looking man in front of me, and my mouth takes on a life of its own.*

Wisteria knew that her thoughts were unfair. Fatigue and uneasiness were taking a toll, and she was having a hard time coming to terms with the vast numbers of Gyrangers who had already expired. The implications were staggering. What if the shield broke? Did they have the resources to withstand the attack that would undoubtedly come, be it here or where they were taking Sarah? Not known for being shy or necessarily diplomatic, she was as forward with the Prince as he was with her.

"We need to move and move soon. I cannot promise how long we can sustain the shield given the unrelenting attacks. What does the First have planned?"

"We can move immediately and quickly if we have to. Some of the Winged Warriors and Legion members have already transported back to the Ancient Forest. If the shield breaks, those of us remaining, including the Starchild and Princess Hana can relocate instantly. Once in the Forest, the Gyrangers are incapable of harming us."

"What are we waiting for?" asked Wisteria, worry creasing her forehead.

"A thirteen-year-old girl who is being asked to pack up her entire life in a couple of hours." Drake smiled to take the sting out of his words. "Trust me, we are all on high alert and are not taking this lightly. Our Council is monitoring this from afar. Even with the constant onslaught of attacks, they believe that we are still within our window of safety. The Guardians of the Ancient Forest are also lending their protective energy to us."

"The Guardians!" exclaimed Wisteria in surprise.

"Their connection to the Song Bearer allows for this, Lady," said Prince Drake. "Dineah Firefly is here in Brendondale, as is Princess Hana who was born and raised in the Ancient Forest. As a result, the Guardians can extend their power, albeit, not as forcefully as in the Ancient Forest. As capable as you and your covens are, you are not doing this alone. If you concentrate, you will sense their presence."

Wisteria knew he was right. She had felt it as a thick, pulsating undercurrent, before transferring the shield to the crystal. Her witch sense confirmed that a vibration of that depth could only be coming from trees as ancient as time itself.

She focused inwardly, allowing their strength and steadfastness to spread through her. Immediately, the fatigue and tension of only moments earlier was gone.

Taking a deep breath, Wisteria turned to look at Sabrae and Bohn. Both of them stood with their eyes closed. She could tell that they too had connected with the vast reservoir of energy emanating from the Guardians. Bohn's face was turned upward, while Sabrae, as usual, had a smile on her face. A moment later, Sabrae opened her eyes. Walking over to Prince Drake, she touched his arm.

"Thank you for telling us that," she murmured, before returning to position herself in front of the crystal.

"Take more time, Sabrae and Bohn," said Wisteria. "Drink some water and eat something before we begin again. Bohn, can you take a moment to check on Mrs. Gibson please?"

"Did someone say my name?" a cheery voice asked from the hallway. A moment later, Mrs. Gibson entered the room bearing a tray of sandwiches and drinks. "Oh, hello, Prince Drake. I brought food for you. Oh and you too, girls," she said as an afterthought.

It seems that I am not the only one who loses her senses when a good-looking man is near, thought Wisteria.

"Now, it is time for you to eat," Mrs. Gibson said in a firm voice. Looking at each of the witches, she continued. "You cannot protect us if you don't sustain yourself. Come, quickly! I don't want to think that my culinary talents have been in vain."

No one pointed out that her culinary talents were tuna sandwiches and dill pickles.

"Isn't he handsome," whispered Mrs. Gibson, nudging Wisteria as she handed a sandwich to the Prince, and speaking as if he were not standing right in front of her.

"Handsome," responded Wisteria dryly.

Prince Drake looked over Mrs. Gibson's head at Wisteria, and grinned as he winked at her. He was enjoying the attention.

Mrs. Gibson had responded well to the physical healing that she had received from Silverspear. She was back in full teacher mode. It was clear that she liked being in charge and directing people. Everyone had been tolerant of her over exuberance because it was precisely that. Terrible things had happened to her mind at the hands of the Gyranger. Mrs. Gibson was still very wounded. If being busy and a little too cheerful was how she handled it, no one pointed it out.

Wisteria could see that the poor woman was troubled. At times she would catch the former teacher staring at the wall, her eyes sunken inwards and her face shallow and grey. Bohn, as the most skilled healer of the three witches, had done what she could to further restore Mrs. Gibson's mind. Wisteria knew that Elder Mendalese would work with the teacher upon her arrival to the Ancient Forest.

Wisteria accepted a sandwich and a bottle of water from Mrs. Gibson. Wisteria was not prone to demonstrations of emotion like her cousin Sabrae, but she took Mrs. Gibson's hand nonetheless and squeezed it.

"Thank you for lunch, Mrs. Gibson."

Mrs. Gibson responded with a quick smile, but then unexpectedly burst into tears. Sabrae went quickly to her side. Wisteria was surprised to see that it was Prince Drake who instantly gathered the older lady in his arms, holding her silently and patiently while she cried. In a short while, she pulled herself together, wiping at her face and the wet stains on the Prince's shirt. She was embarrassed by her outburst.

"Can't ... seem to ... hold .... myself together," she said between sniffles and stifled sobs. "It just ... comes ... out of nowhere and ... pours out of me."

"Then you must let it out, Lady," said the Prince, his voice gentle.

"You must ... think ... I'm a silly ... old ... lady," said Mrs. Gibson who was still struggling not to cry, more tears streaming from her eyes.

"Mrs. Gibson – anyone who could withstand the torture of a Gyranger is neither silly nor lacking in courage. Your strength and endurance kept the Gyrangers from my niece, Sarah Starbright. Believe me when I say that the Royal Family will never forget what you endured for us. Do not underestimate yourself, for few would have lived through what you did."

Mrs. Gibson was pleased with the Prince's words but embarrassed by her lack of control. She kept her gaze downward, refusing to look at the Prince or the three witches.

Once again the prince interjected.

"Now, Lady, would you please pass this famished Prince another sandwich before he faints from starvation."

A smile spread across Mrs. Gibson's face as she handed him the plate of sandwiches. Patting the Prince on his shoulder, she said, "You're a good boy."

Turning, she left the room, her head a little higher than a moment earlier.

"Well done, Prince Drake, thank you for that," said Sabrae. "Does she know about her house yet?"

"Yes, we have told her," said the Prince. "She was very stoic. Nonetheless, it is one more thing for her to grapple with at this time, unfortunately."

Nodding her head in understanding, Sabrae opened her mouth to speak. She was interrupted by Bohn, who had abruptly turned toward the crystals.

"Wisteria," said Bohn, urgently. "The crystals! We need to return to our vigil, immediately."

Without comment, the three witches reconvened in front of the gemstones. Reclaiming the current of energy they had channelled into it, they tapped back into the shield. Their furrowed brows and focused concentration instantly alerted the Prince to the magnitude of forces buffeting them.

Kneeling beside them, he spoke.

"Remember the Guardians! Draw upon their powers! They are working with you!"

Straightening, he walked to the wall to continue his watch over the three women who were keeping the Gyrangers at bay. His mouth tightened as he witnessed the toll it was having on them. The Emerald Sword blazed in its sheath, fed by the resolution it could feel from the Prince.

CHAPTER 10

Preparing to Leave

Dineah gradually awoke as if emerging from a long-drawn-out dream. With her eyes still closed she stretched slowly, releasing muscles held in position for too long. Turning onto her stomach, she fluttered her tiny wings. Why was she so stiff and sore? As she attuned her senses, her delicate nose recognized that there was nectar nearby. Smiling, Dineah opened her eyes and shot upward ... only to be stopped short by the closed flower petal that had safeguarded her as she slept. Looking at it more closely, a sense of worry began to gnaw at her. Where was she? Why did she not recognize the flower walls that surrounded her?

Memories flooded Dineah's mind, causing her to shudder. She recalled how drained and lethargic she had felt after the war song had surged through her. From that moment forward, she remembered little of her illness except for the shock she had experienced when Elder Mendalese had said that the healers of the Ancient Forest could not cure her. She recalled his words.

Dineah, Elder Aarus as Sage of the Ancient Forest, has journeyed to the world of spirit to understand how to expedite your healing. He has determined that the healers of the Ancient Forest have done all they can. To allow you a full recovery, we must send you to the planet Earth.

Dineah still recalled the ambiguity in the Elder's voice. At the time she had not understood the seriousness of the situation. Now she realized that it had to have been urgent, for it was incredibly risky for the Song Bearer to leave the Ancient Forest. If the energetic bond between the Song Bearer and the Guardians of the Ancient Forest were to break, it would leave the Forest utterly vulnerable and open to attack.

Dineah remembered agreeing to travel to the planet Earth to meet with a young girl named Sarah Starbright. She had panicked upon waking and finding herself in a tightly confined space. After a number of attempts, she had succeeded in pushing her small body through an opening. Looking up, she had realized that other beings were present, and had been flooded with relief when she saw the First. It was then that she saw the sky-blue eyes of the young girl ... *the eyes that sparkled with starlight.* Dineah thought that she had said her name aloud before losing consciousness.

Dineah looked around her again. Where was she? Had she accomplished what Elders Aarus and Mendalese had asked her to do? Had she found Sarah Starbright? Dineah's thoughts were interrupted by a sound above her. Looking up, she watched as the flower petals separated. A large brown eye stared down at her before involuntarily floating down toward the owner's nose.

"Hello, little Dineah Firefly and honoured Song Bearer," said a gravelly voice. "Welcome to Sarah's home ... for a while, anyway."

The eye withdrew from the opening, and the creature started

to snicker as if he had said something funny. A moment later, a loud outburst of laughter startled Dineah, making her wonder if the being had gotten into some fermented nectar. The eye appeared again. This time it maintained direct contact with Dineah.

"I so sorry. Sometimes I no able to stop myself. The laughter, it comes out of me like ..." Tazor struggled to find the word that could describe his condition. "... bubblies. Yes, that a good word."

Dineah could hear the amusement in his voice.

"You understand what I mean?" asked Tazor. "I no hurt you ... I just laugh sometimes when my brothers say, TAZOR, NO LAUGH!" Tazor withdrew again.

Dineah could tell that disappointing his brothers was upsetting for the odd little being.

Suddenly the eye was back again.

"But Sarah believe in me. Me and my brothers are her guardians. We guard you too, because you the Song Bearer and a friend of Sarah's. But forgive me. I forgot to ask. How you? You slept well, Song Bearer? You look better now that Sarah heal you."

Relief flooded through Dineah as she registered the creature's words. She *had* found Sarah Starbright and completed her mission! Elder Aarus had been right! She had needed to come to the planet Earth to be healed by Sarah. A feeling of joy infused Dineah. Fluttering her wings, she arose from inside the flower, her glow light pulsating in steady rhythms. Flying toward what she recognized to be a gargoyle, she landed on the end of his broad nose. His eyes crossed as he looked at her.

"By what name shall I call you, guardian?"

"Tazor, Tazor Gargoyle, but you can call me just Tazor. My brothers are Eblie and Sheblie. Their names rhyme, but mine, no."

High-pitched laughter burst from Tazor. He tried to stop it by clapping his paw over his mouth which only caused his left eye to drift toward the ceiling.

Dineah broke into a grin, causing her glow light to brighten. As unusual as he was, there was something about Tazor Gargoyle that she liked. Gently reaching upward she grasped the eye that had drifted and returned it to the bridge of his nose.

"Why do your eyes float away, just Tazor?"

"Because they loose," grinned Tazor, "like my mind."

Dineah started to laugh so hard that she rolled backward off of Tazor's nose, only to be caught by his outstretched paw. Tazor began to laugh too. His attempts at self-restraint quickly spiralled out of control. In short order, hyena-crazed yips filled the room. He hadn't had this much fun in a long time!

The door to the room burst open. Sarah, Hana, and Matharzan filled the doorframe. Eblie and Sheblie hovered in the air over the Were-Griffin's shoulders, worry filling their faces.

"What in the Great Mother's name is going on here?" demanded Hana.

Dineah and Tazor were not aware that anyone had entered the room, so lost were they in the joy of the moment. Dineah had not flown since becoming ill and was enjoying pushing her tiny body to its limits, zipping around the room so fast that streaks of zigzagged light followed in her wake. Tazor, on the other hand, was elated that he had someone to fly with who wasn't trying to restrain him. Rolled up like a furry ball, he bounced from wall to wall, occasionally hitting the bed before relaunching himself. A smile split his face.

Hana shook her head and folded her arms over her chest, aware that both the Song Bearer and gargoyle needed to expend some pent-up energy. Looking at the Were-Griffin, she saw his typically stoic face transformed into a grin. *He was enjoying the show!* Eblie and Sheblie chattered behind her, distressed by their brother's behaviour. Sarah, on the other hand, had started to laugh and was clapping her hands together as she bounced up and down on the balls of her feet. It wasn't long before Hana fought to keep a smile from her face.

Touching Sarah on the shoulder, she mouthed the words, "Handle this, Sarah, and then get back to packing." Moving around the Were-Griffin who continued to enjoy the entertainment, she left the room.

Throwing her head back, Sarah let out one beautiful high-pitched tone. Dineah instantly halted in mid-air, almost colliding with Tazor who zoomed by, stretched out like a flying squirrel. As he hit the wall and slid ungracefully to the floor, silence filled the room.

Dineah immediately recognized the young girl who stood in the doorway.

"Sarah?" she asked, aware for the first time of a presence in her mind.

"Yes, Dineah, it is me," said Sarah.

I can feel you ... in my head ... somehow, said Dineah through the mind link.

I know. We must talk ... alone, responded Sarah.

Awkwardness hung between the Firefly and young girl, neither sure what to say. Finally, Sarah broke the silence, her words tumbling out.

"I am so glad you are awake, Dineah. How are you feeling? Well, you must be well considering how you are, uh ... flying around. Anyway, we have lots to discuss. I want to know more about the song you sang. Well, war song is what my mom called it, but we have to wait until we leave Brendondale. My mom says that I have to pack as quickly as possible because we may be leaving within hours. I can only take things that are very special to me but ... *everything is special to me!*" moaned Sarah.

Matharzan's eyebrows rose as he listened to Sarah. His mouth curved into what was becoming a predictable grin when she spoke.

Indignant at the Were-Griffin's response, Sarah exclaimed, "It's not very easy you know, Grif."

"Mm-hm," was his only response, spoken in a deep, resonant voice.

Dineah relaxed as she listened to Sarah, her earlier discomfort gone.

"Maybe I can help you," she said shyly. "I could ride on your shoulder and encourage you. But first, I would like some nectar. I am sure that I smelled some when I woke up."

"Oh, my gosh," gasped Sarah, her hands covering her mouth. "The nectar! Tazor, did you show Dineah where the nectar is? It was sent all the way from the Ancient Forest with my ... Uncle Drake."

Sarah paused. It still felt odd to say that she had an uncle.

"Anyway," she continued, "it came from some old guy whose name I can't remember."

Dineah began to giggle. "I think you mean Elder, not old guy. It was probably Elder Mendalese. He helped me to find you."

"Oh," said Sarah sheepishly. "Let's make that our little secret," she said, casting a meaningful glance toward everyone in the room.

Tazor gathered himself from the floor to bring the nectar to Sarah. He knew that his earlier behaviour had grown out of control. Struggling to contain the laughter that still threatened to bubble up, he focused on her blue eyes.

"I found the Song Bearer, Sarah. I protect her like you said me to. I do okay?" he asked, uncertainty in his voice.

Sarah considered pointing out that Dineah had never been lost, but knew that berating the little gargoyle would not help anything.

"You were a little wild, Tazor, but it is okay because I think you helped Dineah feel better."

Tazor smiled hesitantly but then broke into a huge grin when he looked at Dineah who was giggling and vigorously nodding her head up and down. Plucking Tazor out of the air, Sarah gave him a quick hug before handing him to Matharzan. The Were-Griffin placed him on his shoulder with the other gargoyles. Eblie and Sheblie crowded around Tazor, glad to have their brother near.

"Please eat, Dineah, and then help me choose what I need to bring to the Ancient Forest. My mom says that we barely have a few hours before we leave. The longer we stay here, the more dangerous it is. Will you help me?"

"Of course," said Dineah.

It was not long before Hana's prediction came true and *all chaos did break loose.* In the end, Sarah went to the Ancient Forest with nothing but the Song Bearer and the backpack on her back.

CHAPTER 11

Destruction

She floated freely, vaguely aware of the parameters of her body. It seemed like such a long time since her mind had initiated new thoughts. It was too overwhelmed by the recurring memories that allowed her no rest. She had tried to be diligent, striving to keep her wits sharp and ready for the moment when she would escape; a moment that she had anticipated for many years. She didn't dwell on how long ago her life had changed. It only reminded her that her family, betrothed, and everyone dear to her believed her to be dead. But she would not forget – no, she would always remember that she had been captured and taken against her will.

Maintaining a sense of her physical body had grown harder as the years had passed. She knew she was in a comatose state, brought on by forces outside of her control. She also knew that her body's health was being regulated and observed. By whom or what she wasn't sure. Well, that wasn't exactly true. She was aware of at least two beings that were responsible. Both of them repelled and filled her with rage whenever she felt their presence in the room. At least she still had her feelings; pent-up, repressed years of smouldering anger. She was a warrior's daughter. She would have her revenge ... someday. Her father would have chastised her for those thoughts but she no longer cared. Her husband-to-be would have understood.

In the meantime, she *would not* surrender. It was not in her nature to easily submit. Like so many times before, she tried to project her consciousness outward to make contact with her kind. As usual, something blocked her. She had struggled for years to reconnect with them.

Over time her captors had done tests on her – painful procedures and experiments that had felt like she was being torn apart and rebuilt. She knew why. She had special abilities that they wanted. Particularly the small, cruel woman who often stood in the chamber silently staring at her.

She wondered how much these experiments had changed her. She had no way to find out, while in her cocooned state. She knew that they had extracted her unique genetic makeup and implanted it into the woman. It was during this time that the woman's identity had become clear. Actually, not a woman – a foul creature that could shapeshift into human form.

Her heightened sensitivity had skyrocketed during the implants and in time she had sensed the woman's presence, even when they were apart. Worse than that, she had started to feel the woman's desires, and know her thoughts and memories. They were hideous! Unspeakable! Although repulsed by this new found awareness, she had used it to her advantage to familiarize herself with the creature that had stolen her life. As she had come to understand the woman's nature and weaknesses, she had channelled memories and thoughts of her own to disquiet and throw the foul being off balance. She had also helped the woman learn to project her consciousness outward from her body, skillfully attaching her awareness as a silent companion. She may be captive, but she was not helpless.

She could feel rage coursing through the woman. Striking to unsettle the malicious creature even further, she projected a memory; something she knew the woman incapable of – love. Preparing herself for the response, she focused her mind … and waited.

∿

Graziel, the Queen of the Gyrangers was furious. It was at times like this that she saw the limitations of the insect-like creatures that she commanded; most notably, their inability to think independently without her direction and leadership. Her brilliant mind was known to strategize and battle plan better than any in her race. It was this influence, coupled with the constant expansion of their numbers, which kept the Gyranger nation prolific and a threat to others.

Over the years Graziel had made changes to the race's genes that had increased their ferocity in battle. In addition to the deadly venom situated in the Gyranger pinchers and the ferociousness of their swordplay, they could now discharge rays of laser-thin beams from their fingertips that were lethal upon contact. She had created a super race, *and yet the shield protecting the Starchild was still unbreached.*

Standing abruptly, Graziel sent her chair crashing backward. Violent emotions coursed through her. Turning to the closest servant, she took control of its mind, ready to vent her wrath … *except she suddenly felt dislocated from her surroundings. It was as if she were in a dream where another lifetime beckoned to her – one where light and love surrounded her; a love that was deeper than she had ever thought possible.*

The vision broke as suddenly as it had started, leaving Graziel startled and disorientated. Gasping, she stumbled toward a nearby table. The servant continued to stare at her, terrified and unmoving. Turning away from the gaping fool, she fought to control the panic building in her. These visions were becoming more frequent. They filled her with a sense of dread. She had always been able to foretell, but these images made no sense to her. Instead of predicting the future, it was as if they were showing her a past that was not her own. There had never been a time in Graziel's life that had held love. She was not familiar with the emotion, nor did she want to be, for love made one vulnerable.

The sense of loss of control refuelled the Queen's anger. Grasping the servant's head in her hands, she used mind-control to obliterate the memories of what he had witnessed, *and a great many more.* His eyes glazed over. She knew that her advisors had not noticed her confusion for they were cowering, their eyes on the floor.

Graziel knew how much they feared her, whether in her human or insect form. As a human, she was a dark-haired beauty who stood barely five-feet-tall. As a Gyranger, she was also extraordinarily striking. Regardless of what face she wore, her presence brought the most dangerous Gyrangers to their knees. They were scared of her, particularly when she was angry.

Her character was volatile by nature, particularly at the end of the cycles when she oversaw the eggs that ensured the vast numbers of their race. During these times her behaviour was so unpredictable that she would seclude herself, having food and water left in a separate compartment. She would enter the room only after her servants had gone, for too many of them had died in her presence. She did little to control her fickle, explosive nature and knew that when the rages overtook her, she was capable of anything. She felt no remorse for her character. Instead, she basked in the power that her presence evoked.

Graziel knew that vast amounts of Gyrangers were painfully dying as they teleported onto the earth plane. She did not care that they died in pain; it was not in her nature to be compassionate. She did mind the reduction of their numbers, for fewer Gyrangers weakened the empire that she ruled.

She was irritated that there had been no further word from Banzen, the Gyranger shapeshifter who had located the Starchild. The magnitude of defences protecting the child certainly gave credence to Banzen's claim. Once again the Queen reached out telepathically for Banzen's mind. She found only emptiness, which meant that the Gyranger was dead or captured.

Why were the Gyrangers unable to penetrate the shield? Who had the resources and ability to protect the child in this manner? The Queen recalled the prophecy that had come to her through a dream, thirteen years earlier. There was but a brief window of time to capture the Starchild in her thirteenth year of life and turn her magic against the light, granting supreme power and control to the Gyranger race. If not, the Starchild would play a vital role in their downfall. Since hearing of the child's whereabouts, the Queen had been relentless. She *must* find the girl. The future of the Gyranger race depended on it.

The Queen considered all possibilities. There was only one option that presented itself. To be fully informed, she must travel out of her body to the planet Earth.

She stated this to her advisors. They responded with outcries and resistance unlike any she had previously witnessed. Graziel understood why. She would have expected nothing less given the gravity of what she was proposing. If she were captured or killed, they would be leaderless, like a rudderless ship.

She noticed that Straeger, her Principal Advisor remained unusually quiet throughout the exchange. She was only too aware of his cunning nature and knew he would try to assume control if she died. Straeger was the only one of their race who truly challenged her. Graziel treasured his scheming, twisted mind, for it had allowed the capture of the woman in the adjacent chamber. Her new ability to soul travel was a direct result of the trials, tests and genetic sharing of this woman. As much as she valued Straeger's brilliant, self-indulgent character, she also hated him. She knew that the feeling was mutual

Graziel ordered her advisors to sit in a circle around her. She directed them to open their minds and create a shared mind link. Tapping into it, she anchored herself before allowing her spirit to project out of her body toward the planet Earth. It was then that she felt a tiny tremor in the mind link – one of the advisors had joined in after the fact. His insolence infuriated her. Knowing she could do nothing about it at the moment, she focused on her goal.

As Graziel's consciousness drew near the city of Brendondale, she was careful not to touch or penetrate the shield that surrounded it. She was intrigued by what she saw. Meridians of energy covered the city and surrounding areas like a grid, joined together by pinpricks of pulsating light. Slowly approaching the pulsing dots, she instantly recoiled. Anger and shock filled the Queen, followed by dawning clarity. The lights were small reservoirs of energy holding the shield together. Within each one was the presence of witches and none other than the Ancient Forest. Her race had known allegiance to the Forest long ago, but those days were gone. She now considered the Forest an adversary.

Questions coursed through her mind. Why were the witches and the Ancient Forest working together? How were they linked to the Starchild? Growing excitement replaced confusion and frustration as Graziel recognized an opportunity to wreak chaos. She would debilitate the witches who had always been troublesome to her, while at the same time, weaken the Ancient Forest.

Focusing on the grid, the Queen moved her attention along the meridians, following one pinpoint of light to the other. Her shrewd mind was searching for a weak link. Smiling inwardly, she settled in, prepared to take as long as was needed.

Suddenly Graziel tensed, certain that she had sensed another presence. Expanding her awareness outward, she probed but found nothing. Even though the moment had quickly passed, something about the presence troubled her. It had felt oddly familiar.

Returning her attention to the shield, she was delighted to discover one of the pulsating lights had dimmed. Fueled by the anger and malice that saturated her character, the Queen energetically released an intention of such power that it penetrated the shield, instantly extinguishing the light. Immediately, other dots of light blinked out as the severed links spread. Laughing inwardly, she readied herself to speed back to her body – but not before delivering one last blow. Forming another burst of toxic energy, she sent it throughout the remaining meridians. It may not obliterate the witches, but it was deadly enough to render many of them useless. It was time for battle. *The Starchild would soon be hers!*

The advisors felt a change within the mind link. Something significant had happened. One of them dared to open his eyes and look at the Queen. He blanched at the sinister smile on her face.

~

As the Gyranger Queen's spirit returned to her body, the woman disengaged her consciousness, albeit much more gently than when she had attached herself and almost been found out! Returning to her comatose form, she fought to control the emotions that threatened to overwhelm her. She had felt another presence while hovering above Earth – a presence she had not felt in years. Tears welled up in her eyes at the same time that sobs strained for release from her lungs. She stopped herself immediately. If her captors noticed changes in her body they would become suspicious.

She knew the presence that she had felt – she had tried for so many years to contact him. Closing her mind off, she drew inward. She could not let the Gyranger Queen sense her feelings.

~

"I am getting bored with this, Maren. How long will we need to keep this shield up?"

"Silence, Amy. Your chatter impacts my ability to concentrate," responded Maren.

Maren was irritated. Although Amy was the newest witch of the coven, she already demonstrated abilities that would surpass some of the senior witches. Maren was typically tolerant of Amy's constant need to question and challenge, but not today. Something about the request for aid from the Brendondale witches had her deeply disturbed. Why did creatures as evil and sinister as the Gyrangers want to teleport into Brendondale? What if they were able to? Would the covens band together and go to battle? Would the witches be exposed to the human race?

Maren knew why Amy was acting out. Holding an external mind link to support the Brendondale witches felt monotonous to the young witch whose bright mind was in need of constant stimulation. Not only did she lack the life experience to understand the significance of what they were doing, she had never been in battle or experienced the death of a fellow witch.

Suddenly the doorbell rang. Maren pursed her lips in displeasure. When it rang the second and then third time Maren decided to answer it. Although she would not usually have left a witch as young as Amy alone, Marin knew that she would only be gone a few moments. Surely, Amy could maintain the link by herself.

"Amy, I have to see what is so urgent that the caller continues to bother us. Hold the link and do not release your vigilance for even a second. I would not normally do this, but I know that you are more than capable, and I will only be gone a moment."

Maren did not believe that Amy was at high risk. More than anyone, it was the Brendondale witches who the Gyrangers would scrutinize for weaknesses.

"Yada-yada-yada," mimicked Amy, smiling as she exaggerated Maren's tone of voice. "You know I can easily do this, Maren. I won't let you down."

Maren bit her tongue. The stress of the situation was making her short-tempered. It would have been easy to snap at Amy's insolence. Leaving the room before Amy could see her face, she went to answer the doorbell which had now rung a fourth time.

Amy kept her word to Maren. As much as she challenged the older witch, she did take her responsibilities seriously. Holding the link was effortless, which is why at that moment Amy decided to text her boyfriend to tell him not to pick her up. She did not anticipate the explosion in her mind that was so powerful it physically snapped her head back, rendering her unconscious before she hit the floor.

When Maren came back into the room, she found Amy's body lying on the floor. The girl's eyes were glazed and her breathing shallow. Maren's legs buckled under her in shock.

"Dear Mother," she whispered, "they have broken through."

CHAPTER 12

Crossing to the Ancient Forest

It was the ever astute Wisteria who first felt the breach in the mind link and knew it had become compromised. But it was Sabrae, the most sensitive of the three witches, who sensed the intrusion of something dark and sinister. She knew that every witch linked to their circle was in imminent danger.

"RELEASE!" she cried, both out loud and telepathically, trying to warn the covens.

Although Sabrae and Wisteria severed their connection in time, Bohn did not. Her scream filled the house as if her very heart was being torn out. Blinded by the pain in her head, she moved without thought, bolting toward the second story window. It was only the quick reflexes of the Prince blocking her while Wisteria rendered her unconscious, that stopped Bohn from crashing through the window to her death.

Cradling the injured witch in his arms and taking two steps at a time downstairs to the main floor, Drake yelled the ancient Scarab words to open the portal to the Ancient Forest. This activation simultaneously alerted the Forest that the inhabitants of Fairy Lane were under attack, while signalling the Winged Warriors and Legion members to fall back to the house to leave the earth plane.

In the short seconds that it took to arrive at the living room, Drake realized he was already too late. Chaos reigned as the Legion and the Winged Warriors fought Gyrangers who had crashed through the front windows and were dangerously close to his sister and the Starchild. Handing Bohn to Wisteria and Sabrae, he pointed at the shimmering portal that stood in the middle of the room. Yelling at them to find Mrs. Gibson, he pushed the witches forward. Unsheathing the Emerald Sword, the Prince shouted the Scarab battle cry and launched himself into the fight.

∾

Dineah had indeed been a tremendous help to Sarah. Only a small number of bags littered the living floor filled with her clothes, books, and memorabilia. Most importantly though, was the backpack on Sarah's back that contained her journals, sketches, and her music. It also included a miniature version of a keyboard that Sabrae had with the wave of her hand, diminished in size so that it could fit into a side pocket. Sarah seemed reticent to remove the pack, so Dineah had taken up a position on one of the straps that crossed Sarah's shoulder. She was pleased to see that Tazor had placed himself on Sarah's other shoulder. The gargoyle kept peeking around the back of Sarah's head to look at the Firefly, a barely-contained grin on his face. Dineah couldn't help but return it with one of her own. She had found a real friend in the strange but funny, little gargoyle.

"I am ready, Mom," said Sarah.

"So are we, Sarah. I will let Drake and the witches know that it is time to ..."

Hana's words were cut short by a hideous scream from upstairs. A movement to the left of her vision made her look outside. Her heart began to race as she saw Gyrangers teleporting en masse onto their front lawn, Legion members and Winged Warriors fighting desperately to contain them. Hana could see it was futile. They were severely outnumbered and needed back-up. Yelling the Were-Griffin's name, she pointed outside.

Without hesitation Matharzan moved to the front door, ripping it open so violently that the hinges snapped. In a demanding voice filled with frightening authority, he said, "Gargoyles, upon your life, PROTECT THE STARCHILD."

As the Were-Griffin stepped outside, he unfurled his massive wings. Sweeping Gyrangers aside, he created space for the Legion and Winged Warriors to return to the house. A moment later, he heard a welcome roar from behind. As Sir Perity landed by his side, Matharzan turned to look at *Atarashara's* two hundred and fifty pound giant warrior. A gleam of anticipation filled the Were-Griffin's eyes as he shouted his next words.

"Guardian, will you fight alongside me?"

This time Sir Perity did not hesitate. Baring the huge fangs that protruded from his mouth in what looked to be a smile, he lifted his head, bellowing his response. They moved forward simultaneously, fearlessly tearing into the Gyrangers.

≈

Aarus was journeying outside of his body when he sensed a presence pass him through space that felt oddly warming and familiar. Shifting his formlessness, he followed it, careful not to be detected. Suddenly he pulled back, shocked to realize that the Queen of the Gyrangers was also out of her body travelling in the infinite void. Aarus withdrew further, ensuring he remained unnoticed. He was stunned! When and how had she acquired this skill? He, more than anyone, knew of the risk she was taking in being separated from her body.

Aarus considered confronting her, but instinct told him to remain hidden. They could battle in the unseen realms but the impact would be staggering to the Ancient Forest if he were to die. He was not as concerned for the welfare of the insect-like creatures. Many years ago, the Gyrangers and the Forest had known peaceful relations, until the improper actions of their Ambassador had set a series of unexpected events into motion that had severed their relationship forever.

The Queen's presence was a statement. Risking herself in this way told Aarus that the Gyranger's situation was dire. Remaining hidden, he continued to follow and watch her as she studied the network of energy lines that made up the shield created by the witches of Brendondale. He immediately understood what she was planning to do. He would have done the same himself.

Suddenly he felt the Queen's mind reach out and search for him. Aarus growled inwardly in frustration. He was too seasoned a soul traveller to have let his guard down this way. He had been so focused on watching her that he had risked being discovered, barely veiling himself in time.

Aarus knew that the Queen had returned her attention to the shield, for the mind probe faded away. Aarus noticed the tiny light that suddenly dimmed even before she did. He knew it would be only a matter of time before it became the fatal weak link. Speeding back to his body as fast as his spirit would allow, he did not wait to transfer a message to the King and the Council via the Firefly guards. Opening his mind to the Forest and amplifying his outer voice, he released the words that they had been waiting to hear.

"BROTHERS, THE BATTLE HAS BEGUN, THE STARCHILD IS UNDER ATTACK!"

❧

Sarah was terrified. She stared, her heart wildly beating as she saw members of the Legion and Winged Warriors pushing their way into the house. They were only able to do so because of the path that Grif and Perry, *who was now a tiger*, had created for them. Everywhere she looked, she saw fighting and chaos. Her Aunt Atalia and Uncle Drake fought back to back, moving together like dancers in a graceful display of swordplay, destroying Gyrangers that continued to flood in through the shattered living room window. Twice now, her mom had been blocked by Gyrangers while trying to reach her. Hana had rendered them useless through kickbox manoeuvres Sarah never knew her capable of. Tazor, Eblie, and Sheblie had banded together and were a short distance away, fighting to keep Gyrangers away from her while she crouched in the corner, Dineah tightly holding on to her shoulder.

Sarah knew that she needed to go to the shining portal, but she was too afraid to move. Slowly she began to slide up the wall into a standing position. It was then that she heard the clicking sound to her left. Fear choked her, making it difficult for her to breathe. She turned her head, transfixed by the dark shadow that was sliding along the wall toward her, unnoticed by everyone else in the room. Sarah watched as the foul creature inched closer and closer, stretching out its arms and flexing its long, thin fingers in anticipation of grasping her. She knew it was hopeless; she could not fight the Gyranger off.

Dineah, too, watched in horrified suspense. She could tell that Sarah was paralyzed and unable to think, her connection to *Atarashara* blocked by fear. The thought of her new friend suffering was too much for Dineah to bear. Remembering what Sarah had shared about each of the guardians, she flew up and shouted into Sarah's ear.

"Silverspear, Sarah, you *must* remember Silverspear. SING HIS NAME!"

But Sarah could not. She could not move and could not think. And because Dineah could feel this within the bond they shared, the Song Bearer knew that both she and the Starchild were in grave danger.

At that moment, Dineah forgot that she shared another link – with the Guardians. Through that connection, they instantly felt the threat to her. In her mind, she vaguely heard tearing sounds that preceded tree roots exploding from the soil of the Forest. *The trees were coming through the portal to protect her.* Dineah began to panic. She knew that the Guardians would stop at nothing to save her, yet crossing the threshold and leaving the Forest would kill them. Their resonant singing voices filled her head.

We come, Song Bearer, we come with speed,
We sense your fear; we feel your need,
To keep you safe is our vow,
We come, Song Bearer, we come NOW!

Their song burst through her scattered thoughts, allowing Dineah the insight she needed at that moment. Even though she knew she was taking an enormous risk, Dineah lifted her head and drew upon the mind link she shared with the Starchild. Summoning all her strength, she sang out Silverspear's name. At the same time she focused the sound inward through their mutual bond, beckoning the King of the Equines.

The air thickened, and for a brief moment, time slowed down, weighing upon Dineah like a heavy stone. Turning her head in what felt like slow motion, she watched the chaos in the room grind to a complete stop; suspended in time. Then, ever so gradually, it began to accelerate, gathering momentum, speeding forward ... until ... suddenly ... HE WAS THERE, his silver hoofs streaking through the air and slamming the Gyranger through the wall. Pushing his body up against Sarah, Silverspear became her shield, rearing and lashing out with his front and then his back legs to create a space around the Starchild.

Instantly, Hana and the gargoyles were beside the Equine King. Hana was breathing shallowly; her left forearm clutched tightly to her side. Grabbing Sarah around the waist with her right arm, she yelled at Silverspear to cover them as she pulled the terrified girl toward the portal.

"Tuck and roll," Hana yelled into Sarah's ear, as she pushed her through the archway, frantically waving Eblie, Sheblie, and Tazor to follow.

As Hana launched herself through she did not expect the claw-like fingers that grasped her from behind, pulling on her injured arm and causing her to scream in pain. Kicking the Gyranger away, she continued forward, unaware of its whereabouts. She desperately tried to yell a warning at the Ancient Forest.

∾

Chapter 12

The Scarab King stood guard at the end of the corridor that stretched from the mouth of the portal into the Forest, dressed in the magnificent iridescent colours of the Scarab armour that bore witness to his lineage. Lining the corridor were members of the Legion; alert and ready to battle. Already, the three witches and the Starchild's high school teacher had safely made it through, as had most of the Legion and Winged Warriors.

Noble appeared confident and in control. Only Aarus, who stood beside him, knew how on edge the King was. Not that Aarus wasn't tense himself. The Gyrangers had gained much quicker access to the earth plane than anyone could have anticipated, and the Starchild had not yet made it through the portal. Both men knew that the most reliable fighters were with the Starchild, and that until there was a call for reinforcements, Sarah was safe. Still, they were becoming increasingly concerned.

Aarus felt the threat to the Song Bearer at the same time as the Guardians. He reacted instinctively, only too aware of what was about to happen. As the giant trees' roots broke free of the earth, and their massive trunks moved toward the portal, he rushed to block their way, his tiny frame barely noticeable against their enormity.

"STOP!" he cried, "YOU CANNOT LEAVE THE ANCIENT FOREST!"

The trees drew to a halt in front of the weathered Sage, furious at being challenged! Their boughs bent back and forth as if buffeted by a strong wind, while their roots flew out and around Aarus ... *but they did not touch him.*

"STAND DOWN," he cried, closing his eyes and hunching his shoulders forward as he forced his will upon them.

Just as suddenly they grew still.

Aarus felt it too. The Song Bearer was passing through the

portal. Aarus watched as a young girl with sandy-blond hair and a backpack on her back, dove and rolled into existence. Not only was the Song Bearer on the girl's shoulder, but three gargoyles had accompanied her, taking up defensive stances.

Aarus then saw Princes Hana pass through. His heart sank, for she was not alone. He watched as the Gyranger stepped back and raised its sword, readying itself to strike the Princess who had stumbled and appeared to have no control of her left arm. A feeling of dread filled Aarus as he witnessed Hana raise her right arm in a defensive block, unable to gather her feet from underneath her. Aarus heard the Scarab King roar in a fury and saw a flash of silver move through the air.

～

Noble was on fire inside. Members of his armies and all three of his children were still on the other side of that portal. He had no sure way of knowing what was happening, except through updates from those who had already arrived at the Ancient Forest. Although his composure remained steady and unbroken, a rage was building inside of him, fed by fear and a sense of helplessness.

He knew instantly when the Starchild passed through the portal, for he felt her magic like a shaft of light piercing through gathered storm clouds. And then he saw his daughter, his beloved middle child, Hana, who held a special place in his heart, and who he had not seen in thirteen years. His relief vanished when he saw what had accompanied her. She was in peril. Not only was she injured and unable to get away from the Gyranger, but the vile creature had raised a sword above her head.

Fury shook Noble as he witnessed the defencelessness of

his daughter. Bellowing like a crazed animal, the Scarab King launched his sword toward the Gyranger, watching it spin far too slowly through the air. Noble knew it would not reach its destination in time. *Except he hadn't anticipated the interference of the fierce little gargoyle, who flew directly into the Gyranger's face, clawing at its eyes and distracting it long enough for the sword to impale itself in the creature's chest.* The Gyranger vaporized into thin air, its life-force no longer able to sustain itself in the Ancient Forest. The gargoyle returned to the Starchild who hugged it fiercely as she ran toward her mother.

Noble watched as members of the Legion quickly gathered Sarah and Princess Hana, ushering them back to safety and allowing space for the rest of their party. Atalia and Prince Drake were next, rolling deftly through the threshold. Accompanying them was a small, orange cat who Noble knew had to be Sir Perity.

The Scarab King's eyebrows raised in disbelief as he observed the next figure to pass through the portal – *King Matharzan-Ariebe?* Glancing toward Aarus, he noticed that the Sage showed no untoward reaction. Noble realized that Aarus had anticipated the Were-Griffin's presence. Anger and concern coursed through the King.

Noble watched as Atalia turned to re-enter the portal. Something was wrong! His suspicions were confirmed when Drake grasped her arm, refusing to let it go. Noble saw the Sage lift his hands in the air while speaking words that the King could not hear. As the translucent face of the portal cleared, Noble stared in disbelief at the frenzy in the home inhabited only a short while ago by Princess Hana and the Starchild.

∽

Sarah somersaulted through the portal, instinctively protecting her head and face. She took several more running steps forward before slowing her pace, fear continuing to cloud her mind and drive her body. She was barely aware of Dineah's presence on her shoulder or of Tazor and his brothers hovering nearby. Turning to look for her mom, Sarah stopped short as the rich smell of flora and woods filled her nostrils. But there was something else. *What was she sensing? What was this place? Why did it feel so familiar?* Looking upward, she stared in wonder at the largest, most majestic trees she had ever seen in her life. Their canopies of leaves spread across the sky in hues of vibrant greens. Facing them was a small, weathered man with stringy grey hair.

She could feel the life-force of the giant trees reach out to her, and she found herself stretching her hand out in return, all thoughts of the Gyrangers gone from her awareness. No matter where she looked, Sarah saw spirals of pulsating energy that rippled off of each plant, tree and blade of grass that made up the Ancient Forest. The fear that had gripped her mind and overridden her ability to think dissipated. At that moment Sarah's life altered as she witnessed the ancientness of the Forest and the power and magic that permeated it. Even though Sarah had never before been to this place, she knew that she had finally come home.

Abruptly her euphoria was shattered by a flash of silver that streaked through the air. Turning instantly, she watched a sword pierce the chest of a Gyranger that was under attack by Tazor – *a Gyranger that was standing over top of her mom with its own raised blade.* The Gyranger vanished into thin air.

Sarah stared, numb, as Tazor flew back to her, growling loudly. His eyes darted around frantically, continuing to search for danger. Grasping the gargoyle and hugging him tightly, she ran toward Hana.

"Mom!" she cried, trying to hold back her tears.

"I am okay, Sarah. Quickly, now! We must move away from the portal. There are still others coming through."

Sarah knew that her mom was not okay. She watched as guards helped the struggling Hana to stand, and then abruptly pulled them both away from the portal mouth. A moment later, she felt the sureness of Hana's uninjured arm wrap itself tightly around her waist.

Sarah watched her Aunt Atalia and Uncle Drake deftly somersault through the threshold into the Ancient Forest, followed by Sir Perity and Grif. Sarah knew that something was wrong when Atalia turned to re-enter the portal, but was stopped by the Prince. Looking about, Sarah realized that Silverspear was not in the Forest. A moment later, the haziness of the portal mouth cleared. Sarah's face paled as she witnessed the torturing of the Equine King. Screaming his name, she turned away, hiding in Hana's embrace.

～

Atalia knew it was time to leave. The Gyranger's were unrelenting, and there was no need to stay any longer. As she watched the remaining Legion members and Winged Warriors make their departure, she caught the eye of both the Were-Griffin and Silverspear, motioning her head toward the portal. Drake grabbed her hand and pulled her through the threshold. She landed on the other side, somersaulting neatly out of the way to ensure she would not impede those coming behind her.

Atalia then remained vigilant as Sir Perity and Matharzan emerged. She continued to watch for their final party, Silverspear. When he did not appear immediately, she knew that he was in danger. Shouting her thoughts at Drake, she turned to go back, but he caught her arm, refusing to let her go.

Suddenly the haziness of the portal cleared. Atalia's heart sank as she witnessed the persecution of King Silverspear. Eight Gyrangers were firing laser-thin bolts of light from their fingertips. *Lethal bolts of light!* It could only be the King's magic that was keeping him alive. It would not be long before the horse collapsed and the Gyrangers impaled him with their deadly pinchers. Behind her, Atalia heard Sarah scream his name.

$\sim$

Aarus was in awe of the courage and presence of the Equine King, even as the Gyrangers sought to destroy him. Suddenly Dineah was on his shoulder feverishly whispering in his ear. Silverspear's proximity to the portal had allowed her the insight that was urgently needed at that moment. He listened to the words of the tiny Firefly who had barely withstood the singing of the war song. She was now proposing an idea that could only succeed if she fully embraced her role as the Song Bearer. Aarus quickly nodded his assent, turning to face the giant Guardians.

Without hesitation, Dineah flew up, hovering in front of the same trees that only moments earlier had been restrained by Aarus. Raising her hands, she cried, "GUARDIANS, YOU CANNOT LEAVE THE FOREST, *BUT YOUR ROOTS* CAN CROSS THROUGH THE PORTAL TO AID KING SILVERSPEAR. AS THE SONG BEARER, I COMMAND YOU, GUARDIANS – FIGHT! FIGHT AND SAVE THE KING OF THE EQUINES!"

The Guardians responded immediately to Dineah's words, their earlier pent-up rage exploding into action. Dineah and

Aarus held their positions as tree roots shot by; their tips honed into razor-sharp spears that surged through the portal, impaling the Gyrangers and freeing the horse from their deadly assault. Hastily wrapping themselves around Silverspear, the roots pulled the gravely injured animal back through the portal which winked closed instantly.

CHAPTER 13

Redemption

And so it came to be that the Starchild entered the Ancient Forest along with her guardians, including the gargoyle known as Tazor, who would forever be remembered for saving the life of Princess Hana. When the Princess had thanked him for his heroic act, Tazor had grinned from ear to ear before erupting into hiccups and having to stick his head into his armpit.

Aarus sat in his tiny hut, looking back on the events of that day and the unlikely allies that the Starchild had gathered – three witches, three gargoyles, two Kings, one shapeshifter guardian created in *Atarashara*, one human who had somehow withstood the torture of the Gyrangers, and the Song Bearer, Dineah. Shaking his head in wonder, he allowed himself a brief smile. Just as quickly it disappeared. He still did not understand *Atarashara's* actions and knew without a doubt that there were more troubling times to come. Why were the Gyrangers so aggressively seeking Sarah? How had they even known about her existence?

His thoughts returned to the moment when the portal had

closed. Knowing that the Ancient Forest would resist the presence of the Were-Griffin, Aarus had quickly approached the Starchild and her guardians. He had spoken the ancient words of welcome, guaranteeing all of them, but especially Matharzan, safe passage while in the Forest.

He recalled the strain and fatigue in their faces – Princess Hana protectively holding Sarah around the waist with her uninjured arm; Tazor and Dineah sitting upright upon Sarah's shoulders, while Eblie and Sheblie fiercely perched upon the Were-Griffin's shoulders. Both the gargoyles and Were-Griffin had continued to have their guard up, their eyes frequently scanning for threats of danger. Aarus had understood why Matharzan was reticent to be here. There was history. He hoped he hadn't asked too much of the Were-Griffin to be involved in this fight.

The injured witch, Bohn, had been standing, thanks to the healers of the Ancient Forest as well as the physical support of her sister witches. Elder Mendalese had urgently addressed Silverspear's injuries, treating the wounds that would have been fatal were it not for the Elder's adept skills and immediate attention. Mrs. Gibson had stood quietly near the Equine King and lent her support by wrapping her arms around his muscular neck which had hung near the ground between his forefeet. Sir Perity had stood guard in front of Sarah, his head slowly moving from side to side as his internal senses picked up what his hollowed-out eye sockets could not see.

When Aarus had completed the formal words of welcome, he had looked to Princess Hana whose left arm had hung limply at her side. Knowing that she was in considerable pain, he had moved to stand in front of her, bowing his head in respect. He had known this child since she was born.

Princess Hana, he had said gently. *I am not a healer, but perhaps*

I can help alleviate some of the pain until the healers can see you.

He remembered how Hana had looked down at him, trying to maintain her composure and hold back the tears that had surfaced at his words. He was more than aware of how much she loved him; the feeling was mutual. He recalled her brief smile and then her response.

I have not seen you for thirteen years, and you still look as weathered and worn as you did back then. I am aware of the gift you are offering. I would be grateful, Elder Aarus.

As Hana had awkwardly knelt, Aarus had grasped her head between his hands. Pressing his thumbs flat on her forehead he had whispered words that had sent a shudder throughout her body. Upon lifting her head, the Princess's eyes had been brighter, her face less drawn. Pulling her forward, Aarus had placed his arms around her, speaking quietly near her ear.

Welcome home, child. The Guardians and I have missed you. Take heart, Princess, for you and the Starchild are safe here.

It was then that Princess Hana had lost her composure and begun to cry. Aarus knew that the magnitude of the recent events, coupled with knowing that Sarah was finally safe, had come crashing down on her. She had still been crying when her father had enveloped her in his arms, holding her close to his chest for a long time.

Drawing his attention back to the moment, Aarus felt troubled. A niggling sensation at the back of his mind alerted him that he was missing something important. He did not have the luxury of exploring the thought deeper as Sarah, Dineah, Matharzan, and Tazor would be arriving shortly for the Starchild's lesson.

Hana, the First, and the Council had agreed that Sarah would meet with Aarus for daily studies, allowing the Sage to foster a close relationship with her. Aarus's sixth sense continued to alert him that the Starchild was crucial to the success of the Song Bearer and the Ancient Forest in the forthcoming battle. He still did not know why or how this would play out, but in the time that they had together, it was imperative for Sarah to learn as much about her lineage and the Ancient Forest as possible.

Tazor also attended these meetings, for he now attached himself to Sarah's every move. Dineah and Sarah were likewise inseparable, except for when Dineah's duties as the Song Bearer drew her away. Matharzan was present at these meetings as the Forest's appointed guardian, and although they did not enter the hut, Eblie, Sheblie, and Sir Perity stood guard with the Fireflies outside the front entrance. Even though the relationship between the cat and the gargoyles had initially been tentative, Aarus knew that an alliance had developed. It was common to see Eblie, Sheblie, and Sir Perity wandering about the Ancient Forest, the brothers speaking at great length, while Sir Perity purred softly or nodded his head in response.

Aarus was also aware that Elder Mendalese and his healers had been meeting with the witches, and that a mutual sharing of knowledge was taking place, particularly concerning the healing of Mrs. Gibson. Of the three witches, Bohn was the most versed in the healing crafts. She was particularly interested in the techniques used in the Ancient Forest, some of which were similar to those used by the witches of Brendondale.

Aarus smiled as he observed that the quiet and gentle Mendalese seemed to have an extra spring in his step these days. He was enjoying spending time with the beautiful Bohn, whose black hair framed a face of porcelain skin and emerald green eyes. More than once he had caught the Elder staring raptly into those eyes before clearing his throat and quickly glancing around to see if anyone had noticed. Bohn did not appear to be bothered by the attention. Rather, she seemed to enjoy the impact that her presence was having on the Elder.

Wisteria was not aware of the attraction, for her practical, no-nonsense nature was not as in tune with others' emotions. Mrs. Gibson, on the other hand, was less tolerant of the Elder's behaviour. During her time of healing, it appeared that a residual protectiveness of the witches had developed. She now saw herself as a den mother to them, even though they were considerably older than her. On more than one occasion, Aarus had watched her find excuses to place herself between the Elder and Bohn, nudging Mendalese sharply in the ribs with her bony elbows.

It was always tender Sabrae, the one who best understood the nature of emotions, that would diffuse the awkwardness of these moments. Gently wrapping her arm around Mrs. Gibson, she would suggest that they set off to walk the many paths of the Ancient Forest and engage in its peaceful beauty. Once, Aarus had even seen her wink at the gentle Elder as she drew Mrs. Gibson away. Mendalese had smiled tentatively, his face turning red. Aarus liked Sabrae's kind and loving nature, as did Elder Borus, who often joined the two women for their walks. Aarus was not surprised, for he knew that Borus had found a twin spirit in Sabrae.

Aarus continued to reflect on all that had happened in the short period since the Starchild and her allies had arrived at the Ancient Forest. Each of them had settled into the rhythm that was the way of life in the Forest. Even the Council meeting at which Hana and Atalia had been called to disclose their actions, felt longer ago than it had been.

Again Aarus's mind drifted, recalling the events of that evening. Although the Council had considered having Hana and Atalia meet privately with the King, the gravity of the situation had required a full trial. In fact, it had been Atalia who insisted that they follow etiquette. She was adamant that the Royal Family not be granted favouritism.

The Council had gathered together in a semi-circle in the Sacred Grove of the Ancient Forest – Prince Drake and Matharzan situated at a right angle to them; Sir Perity, Sarah, and Dineah to the left. Aarus remembered how quiet and solemn young Sarah had been while Atalia and Hana had faced the Council and shared the events that had drastically changed their lives thirteen years earlier.

Aarus could still recall the tension and uncertainty at the beginning of the meeting, from both the Council and the Princess sisters. The allegations, particularly against Atalia, had been staggering. Not only had her actions justified an immediate stripping of her title and an exile from the Forest, but it had meant that her father, as King, would enforce the punishment. Princess Hana's sentence would be no less severe given that she had not disclosed her sister's actions to the Council.

The meeting had begun with Elder Aczartar spelling out the charges. Atalia had then been ordered to disclose the events that had occurred thirteen years earlier. Aarus's heart had swelled with pride as Atalia had risen to stand in front of the Council, her head held high. Only he, Noble, and undoubtedly Hana, had known the toll that her disclosure was taking, for Atalia's hands had been clasped tightly behind her back, and the muscles in her jaw had clenched and unclenched. As Atalia had spoken, her words had been direct and filled with truth, with no attempts to sway the listeners or gain favour. She had disclosed how *Atarashara* had called her to it that fateful evening, pulling her forward as if in a trance. As Aarus had listened to Atalia, his earlier suspicions had been correct. *'The field of unlimited possibilities'* had interjected! But, why?

So spellbound was Atalia that she had entered the portal without honouring the traditional protocols, knowing that she was breaking the sacred customs of the Forest and the trust of her people. She had also known at that moment that such actions could mean forfeiting her life, for entering *Atarashara* required sacred rituals to ensure one's safety – but she had not cared!

Elder Tenor had gasped in shock at Atalia's words. As the keeper of the Forest's chronicles, he had worked closely with her on many occasions. He, better than anyone, knew that her actions had compromised her character. Atalia was relentless in demanding appropriate custom and etiquette.

Atalia had gone on to share the visions that she had seen in *Atarashara*, struggling to keep her poise as she finally disclosed after thirteen years, the tragedy that would befall the Forest and those that she loved. Even with tears coursing down her cheeks, her dignity and stature had remained intact. Taking a deep breath, she had told the Council of a time when the inhabitants of the Forest would lose everything dear to them – their songs, their stories, and mostly, their relationship with the Ancient Forest, which would be forgotten. They would have no recollection of who they were, or who their ancestors were before them. Without the stories to feed and sustain the Guardians, the loss would directly impact the delicate balance that the Forest played as the gateway to, and guardian of, the Karrian Galaxy. The people of the Forest would struggle even to want to stay alive. They would need something to will them to live, for their very existence would be at risk.

Elder Tenor had stared with his mouth open, tears also streaming down his cheeks. Aarus knew that Atalia's words had been a personal blow to the tiny librarian whose life purpose was safeguarding the stories and history of the Ancient Forest.

Then Atalia had disclosed in words that lacked boasting or false pride, what she had done after seeing the visions. Taking an extraordinary risk, she had drawn upon the magic of *Atarashara*. Framing her intention and amplifying it with heartfelt emotion, she had released it to *'the field of unlimited possibilities'*, hoping to change the course of the future, or at the very least, to help the Ancient Forest face the future she had witnessed.

Sarah Starbright, she had said, *so named by Atarashara, was the result.*

Atalia had paused as every being present in the Sacred Grove had turned to look at the young girl sitting quietly to their left; the Song Bearer perched on her shoulder.

Through this intervention, she had continued, *Atarashara created Sarah to help the Ancient Forest and its inhabitants in their darkest hour.*

Aarus recalled the silence that had filled the Sacred Grove that eve. There had been no response to what Atalia had revealed. Any need to find fault in her actions had disappeared, for her full admission had presented a new set of alarming concerns for the Council.

Atalia had known that there was still more the Council needed to hear. Taking a deep breath, she had told them how *Atarashara* had appointed Princess Hana as Sarah's custodian and then created Sir Perity as her protector. Many of the Council had been surprised by the admission of Sir Perity's true identity, glancing at the small, sightless animal. Knowing that it was imperative that the Council understood what Sir Perity was, she had turned her head toward him and nodded curtly. It had gone unnoticed by no one that even though blind, Sir Perity had responded by moving away from Sarah to stand in front of the Council.

No one had spoken as they had witnessed the tiny animal bear his head down and press his weight forward into his front legs. The air had begun to shimmer. Within moments *Atarashara's* mighty guardian had been present. Throwing his head back, Sir Perity had roared a challenge to the Council, letting them see the deadly fangs that could rip his foes apart. He had then slowly paced up and down in front of the Elders, muscles rippling under his orange fur, and eyes pulsating with the magic of *Atarashara*. Walking toward the Were-Griffin, Sir Perity had stopped in front of him.

Standing and placing himself alongside the cat, the Were-Griffin had spoken.

I have fought with Sir Perity twice now, though the first time we met, we almost destroyed each other. That would have been unfortunate.

A growl of consensus had sounded from Sir Perity's throat as he had bunted his monstrous head affectionately against the Were-Griffin's leg, causing the King to be pushed sideways.

Regaining his balance, Matharzan had looked directly at each of the Council members before continuing.

Doubt not the ability of Atarashara's guardian or his adeptness at protecting the Starchild. You would be fools if you thought anything less. He will play a crucial role in the unknown danger we are facing. And hear me when I say this. If you are willing to accept me once again as an ally, thus re-granting unlimited entrance to the Ancient Forest, I will fight with the guardian of Atarashara to protect the Starchild, the Ancient Forest, and all its inhabitants.

Once again the Council had sat in stunned silence. Finally, Elder Aczartar had responded.

You have not fought with us for many a year, Matharzan, though I understand that you were asked to seek out the Starchild and lend your services in protecting her. I will admit that I was concerned when I found out what Aarus had set in motion.

Concern had crossed his face as he had glanced at Aarus, and muttering had been heard from several of the other Elders. Raising his hand, Aczartar had signalled silence while simultaneously dipping his head in respect toward the Sage.

But given what we have heard and seen thus far tonight, as always, Aarus's instincts have proven right, and I am glad you are willing to align yourself with us ... though tenuously. We thought to never hear those words from you again. I would be remiss if I didn't acknowledge the damage you inflicted upon the Guardians many years ago, and that those events remain etched in the collective memory of the trees. Can we be assured that time has allowed wounds to heal and that your actions will not occur again? I am sorry for the bluntness of my questioning and acknowledge the delicate nature of the past, but also know that the Guardians will destroy you without pause if they sense a threat from you. You owe them, Matharzan, and will need to make redress.

The Were-Griffin had said nothing for a moment, lost in his thoughts. The pain in his eyes had not gone unnoticed by those present. Looking at Elder Aczartar, he had quietly responded.

I was not of sound mind at that time. I am not proud of what I did and acknowledge that I do owe the Guardians redress. You have my word that I will make amends. I am committed to realigning my relationship with the Forest and all within it.

Turning his head, he had looked at Sarah Starbright.

At that moment Aarus had understood how Sarah Starbright, the Starchild of *Atarashara*, had given new purpose and meaning to his old friend. Perhaps she would play a role in releasing long-standing pains and sorrows. Aarus, more than anyone, had understood what had caused Matharzan to act out, harming those who had been considered allies.

Transforming back into his original form, Sir Perity had returned to Sarah, where he had promptly sat down and begun licking his paws to clean behind his ears.

Elder Borus had started to chuckle and not unkindly said, *Ye won't eat the little animals of the Forest, will ye? Ye scared us half silly with that mighty roar of yours.*

Sir Perity had purred as the Elder had talked, his head eagerly turned toward Borus's voice. Walking over to the gnome, he had allowed Borus to rub his chin.

Leaning close to his ear, the Elder had continued to speak.

Thank you, guardian of Atarashara, we are sorely in debt to your presence and protection of the wee lass here.

The Elder had looked at Sarah, smiling as he had spoken.

Aarus had watched her smile in return, remembering that Borus and Felix had met Sarah one day long ago on her return from school.

Princess Hana had then stood to speak, continuing from where the First had left off. She had explained how Atalia had arrived under duress at her home, carrying a bundle of cloth that had held the Starchild. Upon seeing Sarah, Hana had known without question that she was to protect her at all costs. Like Atalia, Hana had spoken succinctly and without apology. To avoid revealing Sarah's true identity, they had left the Forest to keep her secret safe until it was time for her return. Hana had then quickly reviewed the events that had occurred in the forty-eight hours before their arrival to the Forest, including the Gyrangers' attacks, Sarah's newly-pledged guardians, and Sarah's healing of the Song Bearer.

At that point, Dineah had flown above Sarah's head, ensuring that the Council could see her fully restored health, visible through her brightly pulsating glow light. The leaves of the Guardians had rustled in approval.

Lastly, Hana had admitted that she was at a loss as to how or why the Gyrangers knew of Sarah's existence and what their interest in her was. Looking to Elder Tenor for his expertise, she had asked if he would search the chronicles for insight. Nodding his head up and down, he had agreed.

Silence had filled the Sacred Grove as the sisters had ended their narration. Retiring to their seats, they had sat, continuing to face the Council. Aarus had noticed the similarities in their behaviour; how they both sat with their hands clasped in their laps, heads proudly held high, willing to face whatever decision was made by the Council, *and both refusing to look at their father.* He knew each sister well enough that the latter observation was for very different reasons. For Hana, looking into her father's eyes was a reminder of his enduring love for her, no matter the circumstances. She would not have wanted to break down and lose face in front of the Council. For Atalia, facing her father meant witnessing her self-judgment reflected back in his eyes. The simple truth was that Atalia would never forgive herself for her actions thirteen years earlier. Because of that, she could not believe that anyone else could either.

At this point, Sarah had stood and gone to stand behind her mother and aunt, placing her hand on each of their shoulders. Aarus had watched Hana's face light up at Sarah's touch. Atalia's stoic face had not changed, but she had patted Sarah's hand with her own.

During this time, the Council had erected a wall of silence, discussing the outcomes of the testimonies they had heard. As the Council members had looked at each other, no one had felt the need to point out the obvious – had Atalia not entered *Atarashara* that fateful night, the Elders and the Ancient Forest would have never known of the inevitable events coming their way. Not only had *Atarashara* initiated contact with Atalia, but it had shown her the future of their people and then created the Starchild in response to her intention. Given the complex and troubling circumstances, they could not exile or punish Atalia or Hana for their actions. Once again, Atalia's exemplary decision-making under duress had been demonstrated. Few others would have thought to have used *'the field of unlimited possibilities'* to their advantage under such stressful circumstances.

There had been some discussion that Atalia and Hana's decision to withhold Sarah's identity had placed all of them at great risk, as was evident by the narrow escape from the Gyranger attack on Fairy Lane. But it had also allowed Sarah's secret to be kept hidden for thirteen years. In the end, the Council felt it inappropriate even to berate Atalia and Hana for the confidence they had diligently maintained, and left it to the King to address it privately with his Princess daughters. When a vote had been called to absolve the sisters of wrongdoing, all of the Elders had voted in agreement. Upon lifting the wall of silence, Elder Aczartar had announced the Council's verdict, clearing Hana and Atalia of all charges.

Aarus had watched Hana take Atalia's hand and envelope it in her own. Atalia had not seemed to notice, her focus on the ground in front of her. When Atalia had finally looked up, for the first time, she had sought out eye contact with the King. Aarus had not missed the look of surprise on her face upon realizing that her father had stepped away from the Council and was standing a short distance away, waiting to be acknowledged. Quickly glancing at the King, Aarus had been stopped short by what he had seen in Noble's face – raw fear, and the terror of losing both of his daughters. The moment had seared Aarus's heart for it had brought back too many memories. He had also known that Atalia's burden of guilt would not have prepared her for the pain she was witnessing in her father.

Aarus had watched Noble, who knew his older daughter so well. He had reached out his hands toward her, palms facing upward, and smiled; his face filled with fierce love and pride. Atalia had stared at him, and then, ever so slowly returned his smile. For the first time in many years, Aarus knew that something had been rekindled between father and daughter. Atalia had turned and shared a private look with Hana before squeezing her sister's hand and taking the few steps it took to reach her father. Placing her hand on his shoulder, she had leaned forward and kissed his cheek. Taking her hand in response, the King had cupped it gently between his own. Aarus had known that this was the most either of them could give; that it was more than they had given in years.

As Atalia had departed, Hana had stood, moving into her father's arms for the second time in days. Without prompting, Sarah had jumped forward, throwing her arms around both of them, for she was also profoundly moved by what she had witnessed. Her previously solemn appearance had hidden her anxiety and uncertainty. In true teenage fashion, she had begun to talk non-stop, releasing the tension she had been holding inside. No one had pointed out that her behaviour lacked protocol. No one had dared to, as they had watched Noble's joy at listening to his granddaughter's youthful prattle.

Sighing, Aarus brought his attention back to the moment. The cloth doorway of his hut was pulled aside as Sarah made her entrance. Dineah flew past her, performing a perfect figure eight before pausing in mid-air to bow her head in respect to the Forest's Sage. Aarus nodded in approval. Dineah had not only returned to her full state of health, but had matured into her role as Song Bearer. It had not gone unnoticed by the Guardians or the Council that her exceptional thinking during the battle had saved both the Starchild and King Silverspear. Aarus knew that the Guardians had done well in their choice of Song Bearer. He also knew how highly revered Dineah was as she moved through the Forest these days. Her relationship with Sarah was steadily growing stronger, and for that he was also pleased.

Aarus inwardly smiled as he observed Matharzan bend his body to fit into the hut, his giant wings causing the loose fabric to poke outward. He had also watched the developing bond between the Were-Griffin and the Starchild. Aarus knew that Matharzan's passionate commitment to Sarah's safety had become an act of redemption; an opportunity to make amends for a tragic past. Aarus fervently hoped that the outcomes would be very different this time for his long-time friend, for Matharzan would not recover from another such loss. For that matter neither would Aarus. Lighting some sage to clear the energy in the hut and motioning the Fireflies to close the flap that was the door, he began Sarah's lessons for the day.

CHAPTER 14

_____

A New Life Begins

Sarah sat nestled within the roots of a majestic Guardian, surrounded by Fairies, some of whom were perched on her arms and shoulders, while others dangled from her hair. She could feel their excitement as she slowly turned the pages of her journal, showing them the sketches within. She couldn't help but smile at how animated they became each time one of them was recognized. Collective "oohs" and "aahs" were followed by shrieks of joy from the Fairy whose likeness appeared in the now renowned journals of the Starchild. The ecstatic being then flew in circles around Sarah's head to receive congratulations and high-fives from all of the other Fairies ... and Tazor of course. Sarah wondered how long it would take her to get through all of the journals given how long it took to look at only one page. She still couldn't believe that these beings were real and not just birthed from dreams or her imagination. And how had she drawn these pictures while utterly unaware of her true origins? That was the hardest part to wrap her head around.

She had noticed a change in the behaviour of the Fireflies

and Dragonflies after she had started meeting with the Fairies. The Winged Warriors remarkable airborne dives and rolls had been amazing to watch ... until Sarah had realized that they were shyly peeking into her journals to see if they were present. Their actions had so moved Sarah that she had made a special announcement, asking for models for her drawings.

If the creatures of the Forest could be so kind as to help her out please...

Sarah recalled the first morning after she had made the request. Stepping into the clearing where she often sat to draw, she had found the area brimming with hopeful candidates. She was unsure of how to handle the awkwardness of the moment, until the ever astute Dineah had suggested through their mind link, that Tazor take charge. Sarah had raised her eyebrows at the idea, wondering if Dineah had drunk too much nectar! Although at first skeptical, Sarah had watched as the little gargoyle had taken over and in his unique way ensured the inclusion of everyone.

Flying into the centre of the clearing, Tazor had hovered in the air staring straight ahead ... and saying nothing.

Tazor, you need to say something, she had whispered.

The gargoyle had responded by bursting into wild laughter, struggling to get himself under control. Then, ever so slowly, Tazor had begun to talk in his low, gravelly voice.

Good morning ... very nice creatures of Ancient Forest! You happy this beauty morning?

Tazor had bounced up and down in the air, snickering while he spoke. When no one had responded, he had looked nervously at Sarah, mouthing his next words.

Sarah, I think they no hear me. But no worry, I try again!

Turning back to face the crowd, he had started again, speaking loudly and slowly and enunciating each syllable.

Gooodd ... morr–ningg ... verr–rry ... deafff ... creaa–turess ... of Ann–cient Forr–restt. I ... Sarr–ahh's friendd ... and guarr–diann. If you ... friendd of Sarr–ahh's, ... you friendd of meee. I ... loveeee ... frienddss, so ... lets alllll be ... frienddss ... too–ge–therr. How bout BIG CHEER WITH TAZOR!

As multiple voices had erupted in unison, Tazor's face had lit up. Adding excited yips of joy to the chaos, he had begun somersaulting in the air.

Sarah had glared at Dineah who had pointedly refused to return her look.

You want Sarah to draw you, line up and SHOUT OUT you name. More loud! More better!

Another cheer had erupted from everyone in the clearing. Sarah had watched in stunned silence as Dragonflies, Fireflies and creatures that she had never seen before, had laughed and nudged each other while lining up in front of Tazor. The gargoyle had continued to hover in the air, patting his plump tummy as he smiled and snorted, his eyes splayed in opposite directions. Quickly grabbing her journal, she had written down each name as it was shouted out.

Looking about her, Sarah couldn't help but feel like she had lived in the Ancient Forest all of her life. The vibrancy of it filled her, confirming the sense that she had finally found a home; a place where she fit in and belonged. In the evenings before going to bed, Sarah would snuggle with her mom, sharing all that she had learned that day. As always, Hana would listen, and then often share her own stories of growing up in the Forest with her siblings Drake and Atalia, as well as her life as a Princess of the Royal Family. Sarah was enjoying learning about the parts of her mom's life that Hana had been unable to share while Sarah's Starchild identity had been hidden.

Feeling a tickling sensation near her ear, Sarah smiled and

brushed away the vine that was moving down her shoulder toward her drawing tools. She had lost so many of her sketching pencils since coming to the Forest! Sarah now understood how the magic that pulsated through her veins drew the inhabitants of the Forest to her. Sarah was no longer oblivious to its presence or to her true nature.

On that note, Sarah thought, *it is time to take a walk.*

Announcing this out loud, she slowly began to close the journal, careful not to crush the Fairies that had been standing on its pages, and giving them time to relocate to ... well, it seemed her fingers and the top of her hands. As anticipated, the response was audible sighs and moans of disappointment.

"Come on everyone," she said. "You know we will meet again in a couple of days."

"How about tomorrow, Sarah?" asked a Fairy child who hovered at Sarah's eye line, a hopeful look on her face.

Sarah suppressed a grin. She had anticipated this. It was the same every time.

"No, Polli, you know how this works. One morning is spent looking for your pictures in my journals; the next time we meet, I sketch new models."

"Ah, come on Sarah. How about this afternoon?"

"No, Polli, you know that after lunch I have my lessons."

"Ah, geez Sarah."

Sarah tried not to laugh as "yeah, geez Sarah," was repeated from above, behind and beside her. She enjoyed the playful camaraderie of the Fairies and how much they loved to tease. As each Fairy took their leave, she noticed how they took a moment to touch her, gently stroking her hair, or patting her arm.

Putting her journals into her packsack, she waited as Tazor and Dineah settled on her shoulders. Scooping Sir Perity into her arms, she began to walk, knowing that Eblie and Sheblie were nearby, always aware of her whereabouts. Grif did not join her for these morning sessions, trusting in the gargoyles' and Sir Perity's abilities to keep her safe.

Sarah knew that the Ancient Forest liked to play tricks on Eblie and Sheblie, sometimes moving foliage to hide her from their view. Tazor delighted in these moments, but inevitably his frenzied laughter would reveal their location. Today appeared to be no different.

Sarah caught her breath as a tree suddenly shifted into Eblie's path. Barely avoiding a collision, Eblie dodged it, turning just as swiftly to fly back and face the tree. Sarah tensed, wondering if the ordinarily tolerant gargoyle was angry ... until he wiggled his stubby paws from behind his ears and stuck out his tongue. Sarah started to laugh, as did the tree whose leaves quivered in response.

Continuing to walk, she watched as paths materialized in front of her. She looked up in appreciation at the Guardians whose treetops towered high about her. She knew that they were creating pathways and shifting their roots so that she did not stumble as she moved among them. She felt humbled by their presence. Sarah sensed that the Guardians' respect for her was as much because of her friendship with the Song Bearer as it was because she was the Starchild. Dineah had told her that the giant trees would never forget that Sarah had saved her life.

As if reading her mind, the foliage opened to the one place in the Forest that Sarah visited every day, for it drew her – every day. As she looked at the portal entrance, her mind began to slow. *Atarashara* was her home, her birthright, the place where she felt an unending sense of peace.

Sarah had not known the sensation of really knowing herself until the first time she had stood at *Atarashara's* doorway.

She could still recall the pure, life-affirming magic that had awakened inside her, moving and coursing through every part of her body. Only then, had the Starchild fully comprehended why she was a beacon to any who could feel its presence, for the magic had poured from her and into her, filling her lungs with every breath, swirling around her every limb, pulsing outward with each beat of her heart. She had felt the life rhythms of the Ancient Forest match her own, and then she had felt her awareness extend even further, synchronising with the stars, the planets, the galaxy. For the second time in her young life, she had experienced the intelligence known as *Atarashara* move within her – but this time, she had welcomed it. Sarah had shared this with no one, not even Dineah, for she could not put into words the experience of coming home to herself.

Sarah knew that she travelled somewhere when she met with *'the field of unlimited possibilities'*. Even though her body remained rooted in the Forest, her consciousness went elsewhere. She had little recollection of where she went, or what occurred while she was there. But each time she returned, Sarah felt refreshed ... renewed ... more solidified, as if *Atarashara's* magic was more entrenched within her.

Kneeling in the grass, she put Sir Perity down and then allowed herself to relish in the pulsing energy that radiated from the portal. Barely conscious of Dineah or Tazor on her shoulders, or of Sir Perity's purring, she closed her eyes and allowed her awareness to drift and connect.

Welcome, Starchild ...

Sarah felt the whisper gently brush her mind. She responded in kind.

Good morning, Atarashara.

Nothing more was said as Sarah felt the now familiar and

loving sense of her birthplace envelope her mind as if in a cocoon, and hold her. And then she remembered no more.

Upon opening her eyes a short while later, Sarah had no sense of how much time had passed. Slowly standing and rocking back and forth on her heels, she struggled to focus her attention on the Forest floor. Returning was always the hardest part. Oddly, it was Tazor who somehow understood.

"Why you eyes shine like stars, Sarah? Where you go? You come back always, okay? Promise, Sarah, promise?"

Lifting the little gargoyle from her shoulder, she hugged him. "I promise, Tazor."

Welcome back Sarah, said Dineah through their mind link. *I can feel that your visit with Atarashara has made you very happy. Want to have some more fun before your lessons of the day begin?*

Sarah began to giggle. Dineah and Tazor were very good at making sure that between her visits to *Atarashara* and the many lessons that made up her day, she had fun. Turning to her beloved orange cat, she asked the same question.

"What do you think, Perry? Should we play?"

"*Pprruuuuuuttttt!*" was his enthusiastic response.

Dineah spoke out loud. "We haven't made music with the Guardians for a while now. I think it is overdue!"

Tazor let out a whoop of joy.

Sarah smiled at the little gargoyle who had shown a surprising aptitude for rhythm, especially when adding syncopated yips, chirps, growls, trills, and howls to the music … while simultaneously tumbling through the air, of course. She fondly realized that this was yet another regular part of her new life – music making within the Ancient Forest.

Sarah loved the natural harmony of the Forest and how the leaves of the Guardians whispered in song as the wind moved through them, while their roots rumbled in rich baritone counterpoint. Coupled with this was Dineah's silvery voice, the songbirds of the Forest, the drone of the wings of the Dragonflies, the pulsing rhythm of the Fireflies' glow lights, the Fairies' ethereal sounds, and Tazor's unique contributions. To all of this, she added her voice and accompaniment on the keyboard.

As she turned to depart, Sarah noticed that a pathway had already been created, guiding them forward. Laughing aloud, Sarah scooped Sir Perity into her arms and began to walk, her protectors and closest friends accompanying her.

∾

Hana watched Sarah and her unusual but endearing entourage, who had just finished their lunch and were preparing to leave for the first lesson of the day. Matharzan stood patiently outside, waiting for the clamour to settle so that he could accompany Sarah to her studies with Wisteria. Eblie and Sheblie sat on the end of the table, having cleaned the plates of mushrooms and root vegetables that had become the diet of the gargoyles since arriving at the Ancient Forest. Hana doubted that this was their typical diet, but they were not allowed to eat the creatures of the Forest.

Tazor hovered over the table, looking for more table scraps. She had noticed that Tazor ate more than his brothers, and so always made sure that he had an extra helping on his plate. Not that it made a difference. He still flew around the table at the end of each meal and licked off every platter – which explained why his tummy was getting rounder. Hana listened to the gargoyle's snorts, growls, and tweets as he flew, and smiled to herself. At first, she had wondered about his behaviour, until Sarah had explained that he was practising his singing.

Hana was enjoying the liveliness of their life since returning to the Ancient Forest – mainly because of the uncharacteristic blend of personalities that filled the walls of her home each day. She selfishly had to admit that she was also appreciating having time with her family again, especially her sister. Hana had gladly fulfilled her agreement with Atalia to keep Sarah safe, but returning to the Forest was allowing the Princess companionship and the opportunity to resurrect her life and responsibilities as a member of the Royal Family. She loved teaching Sarah about the life of royalty, and was relishing the support of others in growing the Starchild to her full potential.

After careful consideration with Aarus, Matharzan, Atalia, the witches, and the Council, Hana had agreed upon a daily regime of studies for Sarah. Lessons typically began with Aarus, followed by visits to Elder Tenor in the Forest's library, where Sarah studied the origins and history of the Ancient Forest and the timeless role it played in overseeing and protecting the Karrian Galaxy. Allotted time with the other Elders allowed Sarah to understand the unique skill set that each of them added to the daily functioning of the Forest.

Gathering each evening in the Sacred Grove for storytelling was Hana's favourite time with Sarah, for it initiated the Starchild into the vibrant and pulsating community that was the Ancient Forest. It was at this time that Elder Ravensong and Elder Tenor narrated the stories that had been passed down since the inception of the Ancient Forest. Hana knew that as the Starchild, it was crucial that Sarah understood what only members of the Forest knew – that the practise of storytelling was central to the Forest's survival, for the energy in the words of the stories fed the Guardians in their timeless cycle of longevity.

Hana ensured that Sarah also spent frequent time with the

witches, whose primary goal was to teach her to control and direct her magic. They had rightfully argued that Sarah could augment her skills and defences by learning spells commonly used by witches. As a result, part of Sarah's daily regimen included lessons with Wisteria, Bohn, and Sabrae, who collectively or individually instructed her in methods specific to their particular strengths.

Today Sarah was meeting with Wisteria, who was adept at manipulating energy and moving objects using her mind. It was she who had formatted the shield, facilitating the deathtrap for Gyrangers teleporting onto the earth plane. It was also she who had effortlessly opened and maintained the vital mind link with all of the covens, creating time for Sarah and Hana to retreat to the Ancient Forest. And it was Wisteria whose profound relationship with crystals allowed her to wield them like a master sword fighter would wield a sword.

Hana knew that Wisteria's matter-of-fact, no-nonsense personality was difficult for Sarah, for she pushed the Starchild to her limits. Hana was okay with this. Because the witches had witnessed Sarah resurrect Dineah from the edge of death, they were more than aware that *Atarashara's* power pulsed through the Starchild's veins and that Sarah could intuitively draw upon the most potent well of magic that existed. They also knew that there was a short period for Sarah to learn to control her power. Hana recalled only too vividly how Sarah had been unable to manage her fear and access her magic when under attack by the Gyrangers at Fairy Lane.

To offset the fullness of the afternoons, Hana set time aside each evening after storytelling for just the two of them. It was then that she would gather Sarah in her arms and listen to her talk about her day. Listening to Sarah's experiences allowed Hana to see the Forest with fresh eyes. It also reminded her of the demanding regime and expectations that they had thrust upon her daughter. The latter made Hana's heart heavy. Sarah had gone through so much in such a short period, and would continue to – it was the nature of her existence. Even so, it was a lot for a thirteen-year-old girl to assimilate, even a child born of *Atarashara*.

"Mom, we're ready."

Hana looked at the girl she had raised since a baby. Sandy-blond hair tumbled around shoulders that as usual held a backpack and two passengers – Dineah and Tazor. Eblie, Sheblie, and Sir Perity had gone outside to wait with Matharzan. Already, she could sense changes in Sarah – depth and solidness that had not been evident when they lived in Brendondale. At times, Sarah's beautiful, blue eyes shone with the sparkling starlight of *Atarashara*.

Sarah is not the only one changing, Hana thought to herself, aware that her role as Sarah's primary guardian was shifting. A sense of loss filled her, immediately followed by a feeling of unease. Quickly curbing it so no emotion showed on her face, she responded to Sarah with a smile and a nod of her head. It was often this way – an endless, nagging fear that nestled at the back of her mind; residue from the events that had forced their departure to the Ancient Forest. Why did the Gyrangers want her baby girl? Gathering Sarah into her arms, Hana hugged her tightly.

"Enjoy your lesson with Wisteria."

Hana smiled as Sarah rolled her eyes.

"She's bossy, Mom."

"Well, yes, she's a strong personality."

"You mean she's bossy!"

Struggling not to laugh, Hana hugged her again.

"What are you learning today?"

"We're still practising moving stuff from one place to another, but I think it is going to be harder today."

"You can do it, Sarah. I know you can."

Hana's heart leapt at the smile that lit up Sarah's face.

Giving Hana a tight hug around the waist, Sarah opened the door and ran out to join the others, Tazor and Dineah holding tightly onto her shoulders.

~

"Sarah, you're not focusing," accused Wisteria who stood with her arms crossed and toes tapping, a frown on her face.

Wisteria shot a quick glance at Matharzan who was sitting on a boulder near the edge of the woods, silently watching the interplay between teacher and student. Dineah was settled quietly on the Were-Griffin's shoulder, and Tazor – well, Tazor was absent after being banned from the lesson. As heartbroken as the little gargoyle had been at not being able to control his outbursts, Wisteria could not tolerate distractions. Today's teachings were a culmination of several weeks of training.

Focusing again on the Starchild, Wisteria had to admit that the girl's movements were creative. Unfortunately, they had nothing to do with the lesson. It was clear that Sarah had decided to take a break from Wisteria's demanding pace, for she was completely ignoring her teacher while floating horizontally in the air. Wisteria knew that she had let Sarah's behaviour go on for too long.

"Sarah, I said I wanted to see you raise that rock above the tree and then lower it back to the ground, not for you to elevate yourself!"

Sarah continued to ignore Wisteria. Tucking her knees into

her chest, she splayed her arms upward and kicked outward, gracefully twirling slowly through the air.

Wisteria's temper rose.

"You show disrespect by ignoring your teacher, Sarah Starbright," flatly stated the Were-Griffin. "You are the Starchild, born of *Atarashara*, and daughter to the Princess of the Scarab King. Some insolence is tolerable, but you go too far."

Wisteria's jaw dropped at Matharzan's tone of voice. She had never before witnessed him admonish his charge, and was glad that she was not the one receiving the reprimand.

Sarah's reaction was instant. In a split second, she was on the ground standing in front of the guardian who had challenged her; indignant at the way he had spoken to her.

"I have *not* gone too far, Grif, I was just … ah … taking a break."

Turning quickly to look at Wisteria, she spoke with sincerity in her voice, her face red.

"I'm sorry that I wasn't listening. That was wrong. I was caught up in the moment."

Still angry, she turned back to the Were-Griffin.

"Grif, I don't appreciate you talking to me like that! You should apologize."

Sarah's colour rose as she spoke to the Were-Griffin who levelled a blank stare back at her. She did not back down.

Wisteria's eyebrows raised on her forehead.

The kid has guts, she thought to herself. *I have to give her that.*

"You are acting like a child, Sarah, and as much as I grant you minor indulgences, I will not condone disrespectful behaviour toward those who are giving their time and skills to mentor you. The Lady Wisteria has asked you to perform a task. We await your response."

Sarah stared at the Were-Griffin in shock as she unconsciously clenched and unclenched her fists while rising up and down on the balls of her feet. Her chin began to tremble as she fought back tears at being chastised. Sarah knew that Matharzan was right, but she was not ready to admit it out loud. At that moment she was far more disappointed that she had caused the Were-Griffin to speak to her in such a manner. They stared at each other for several more moments before Sarah backed down, trying to salvage some grace.

Turning and facing Wisteria, she asked, "Is there any boulder in particular that you would like me to move, Wisteria?"

"One of the largest you can find, dear. I want to see if you understand how to manipulate the concept of size and weight."

Focusing on Wisteria's request, Sarah felt the anger leave her body. Scanning the forest, the Starchild paused for a brief moment, noting where the Were-Griffin and Dineah sat. She then turned to Wisteria, a mischievous look on her face.

"I found the perfect one, Wisteria."

Wisteria could tell that Sarah was up to something. The witch's eyes at first narrowed and then grew wider as she watched the boulder occupied by the Were-Griffin and the Song Bearer slowly ascend.

"Sarah," said Matharzan, "what are you doing?"

"Just doing what my teacher asked me to." Sarah giggled, her face filled with delight.

Wisteria cringed inwardly.

"Sarah, put me down," said Matharzan.

"What's that, Grif? I can't hear you. In fact, where are you? I can't seem to find you!"

Sarah made an exaggerated motion of putting her hand over the top of her brow, grinning as she pretended to look around for the Were-Griffin. The rock continued to rise and finally stopped, hovering in the sky, for all the Forest's inhabitants to see.

From his position in the air, Matharzan could see that the Council had convened for a meeting in the Sacred Grove. His sharp eyesight allowed him to identify the various Elders, including those who were now standing and pointing up at him. Looking even closer, he could see that Aarus had a smile on his face and that Elder Borus was holding his belly as he laughed. Sighing, Matharzan realized that the Starchild had gotten the better of him. He was becoming the spectacle of the Forest.

"Teenagers," he muttered to himself. He felt Dineah's tiny hand patting his broad shoulder in understanding.

"Song Bearer, I am a King, and yet I have been bested by a teenager."

"That you have," said Dineah, sympathy in her voice, though her eyes sparkled with amusement.

Against his will, Matharzan found himself grinning. Although he hadn't liked admonishing Sarah today, he had been pleased that she had shown backbone and challenged him back. Knowing that it was time to get control of the situation, he lifted his giant wings and launched himself and Dineah silently off the rock. Slowly descending to the ground, he landed behind the Starchild who was now openly laughing and wiping tears from her eyes. He noticed that Wisteria was having difficulty keeping a straight face.

"Sarah," said Wisteria, trying to regain her composure.

"What ... Wiste ... ria ..." asked Sarah, while straining to get a breath of air.

"Look behind you, dear," said the witch.

Quickly turning around, Sarah yelped in surprise at the Were-Griffin who stood a short distance away.

"Grif!" yelled Sarah, shock and frustration crossing her face as she realized that she had been out-smarted. Having lost her concentration, she forgot the focus of her lesson.

"*Sarah!*" screamed Wisteria, "*the rock!*"

Looking up, Sarah saw the boulder barrelling toward the head of the Were-Griffin. Instantly, she lifted her hand, stretching it outward as her lips moved silently. The rock abruptly halted only feet above her guardian's head. Fear radiated through Sarah as she registered how badly her prank could have gone.

"Grif," she cried, "what were you thinking! I almost hurt you! I could have killed you."

For the second time that afternoon, tears welled up in her eyes.

"I would not have let that happen, Sarah," said Wisteria in a gentle voice. "I am sorry to have put you in this position, but it gave me an opportunity to see how well you have grasped your lessons."

As she spoke, Wisteria flicked her wrist, allowing the rock to gently settle on the ground.

Turning from Matharzan to Wisteria, Sarah stared, slack-jawed. She returned her gaze to the Were-Griffin who did not say a word, but raised one eyebrow.

"They both got me!" she muttered under her breath, unaware that Matharzan could hear what she was saying.

Silence filled the space as no one else spoke. Sarah knew that she needed to make amends.

"Grif," she said her voice tentative.

"Mm-hm."

"Sorry ... ya know ... for how I acted."

"Mm-hm," said the Were-Griffin as the characteristic grin tugged at the corner of his mouth.

"Apology accepted, Sarah."

Pleased with how well Sarah had handled herself, Wisteria spoke, diffusing the awkwardness of the moment.

"Well done, Sarah. That was an excellent example of self-control, in fact, the best I have seen so far in your lessons. You are improving, dear."

Smiling broadly, Wisteria nodded her head once, signalling the end of their session for the day.

Happiness filled Sarah upon hearing the praise. Impulsively she turned and hugged a surprised Wisteria, before stretching out her arm so that Dineah could relocate from the Were-Griffin's shoulder. As Matharzan turned to walk away, Sarah reached up and placed her hand in the crook of his elbow. They walked for a few moments in comfortable silence before Sarah began to talk.

"I got you real good, hey Grif?"

Matharzan snorted in amusement. He had anticipated this.

"Rather, Sarah, I think our manoeuvres far exceeded yours."

"Yeah, but Grif, the whole Forest saw you like, floating on a rock, in the air, all by yourself! Well not *all* by yourself, but they didn't know that Dineah was with you."

Sarah started to giggle again as she pictured it in her mind.

The Were-Griffin cringed as the memory replayed itself in his head. He paused a long time before sighing deeply.

"Mm-hm," was all he said.

CHAPTER 15

Betrayal Lurks

The Gyranger Queen was upset at being interrupted. Turning her head sharply to reprimand the intruder, she stilled her tongue upon realizing it was Straeger, her Principal Advisor.

"Where is the Starchild, Straeger?" she snapped, unable to fully contain her anger.

"You know where she is Graziel, or perhaps it is wiser if I call you, Your Majesty. I can see you're in one of your moods and will find any excuse to berate me."

As she glared balefully at him, he continued, unrattled by her behaviour.

"As I said, you know perfectly well where she is and that we have no way of penetrating the Ancient Forest and abducting her. There is one piece of information that I have learned though, which may bring a smile to your face. King Matharzan-Ariebe has emerged from wherever he has been hiding all these years to join forces with the Ancient Forest, and guard the child. It appears that they have agreed upon some form of alliance. Hard to believe after all this time, isn't it?"

A sinister smile spread across the Queen's face. She was indeed pleased with the news.

"Matharzan ... after all this time. Long I have regretted not getting my hands on the King of the Were-Griffins. What changes I could have made to our race. You see, Straeger, I find Matharzan intriguing, someone that I would like to own and control."

"I am sure, Your Majesty, that if he gazed upon your unsurpassed beauty, he would find himself compelled to know you better ... and likely do whatever you wanted him to."

Both the Queen and her advisor laughed, knowing full well that Graziel's ability at mind control was the strongest of her race. This skill, coupled with the toxic vapours that could release from the roof of her mouth, rendered her adversaries powerless, forcing them to obey her will.

Speaking quietly, Straeger continued.

"But we have done much better than Matharzan, my Queen. Perhaps our acquisition in the adjacent room could weaken his agreement with the Ancient Forest and induce him to trade for the Starchild."

"It is not just about the Starchild anymore, Straeger. Now that the Ancient Forest's role in this has been made clearer, I understand the full potential of the prophecy. Acquiring control of the Starchild is just the beginning. I also want control of the Ancient Forest. *I want the Gyranger race to rule the Karrian Galaxy.*"

Excitement coursed through her as she fully grasped what she had just said. Looking at Straeger, she saw the same eagerness mirrored in his own eyes. It was at times like this that she revelled in his company, for they were so alike. When aligned, they were unstoppable and terrifying. But she was wise enough to know that the one thing they both ultimately wanted was the one thing that drove them apart – absolute, incontestable power. There could only be one leader with that kind of control. She would always have to be cautious of Straeger.

"A brilliant idea, Straeger, but we both know that the Were-Griffin would not accept an invitation to my court. On second thought, maybe he would if he knew you were here," she said cruelly. "Perhaps we should offer you as a sacrifice? But no, Straeger, your loss would be too great to me."

"I am touched by your consideration, my Queen, and pleased that you do not wish to dispose of me."

"For now," she said quickly.

She couldn't help herself. It was not in her nature to be pleasant.

"Even if Matharzan knew you were here, he would not trade the Starchild – he is too loyal. There is another way that I believe we may be able to infiltrate the Ancient Forest. Let me think further about it, Straeger."

"You cannot enter the Ancient Forest, Your Majesty. In trying, you will expire."

"No, but I can enter an area that the Forest no longer protects. Some call it the Forest's blackthorn."

"The Shadow Forest," said Straeger in a subdued voice. "You are correct Graziel, you can enter it, but I must insist on myself and the guards accompanying you. You still put yourself at great risk being that close to the Ancient Forest."

The Queen was surprised at Straeger's shift to her first name and the sincerity within his suggestion. She was even more startled at her response, for she was pleased with the concern in his voice. What was happening to her? Since when did she feel anything toward Straeger except contempt and a need to stay one step ahead of him? She was reminded of the visions she had been having and of their increasing regularity. Her inability to understand what was happening to her fueled a sense of loss of control that quickly flared into anger. Turning to Straeger, she directed her frustration at him, speaking harshly.

"Do you think your Queen incapable of protecting herself, Straeger? Do you not recall who lives in that place of death and decay and what her relationship is to the woman we have captive in the adjoining room? This mission requires a female presence, not a group of males to remind that fool how she was cast aside for another!"

Straeger's only response was the clicking of his pinchers. Graziel knew he was angry at her rebuke. She also knew that his advice had been sound. She watched him school his features carefully, his next question void of emotion.

"What are your plans, Your Majesty?"

"Oh don't pout, Straeger, it doesn't become you," she sighed. "You are right – I need an entourage to accompany me ... *not* because of how close we will be to the Ancient Forest, but because of what lurks in the cesspool that the Shadow Forest has become. I have heard strange things about that place – things that could be used to our advantage."

Lost in her thoughts, she was unaware of how intently Straeger studied her.

Breaking the silence, he said, "Thank you, Your Majesty. As your Principal Advisor, I will make arrangements for us to travel with a guard of five Gyrangers. If I deem it too dangerous to travel to the Shadow Forest, might I suggest that the person you seek come here, or meet in an agreed-upon place? I could initiate communication and set up a point of contact."

"No – we go there. She will not leave her hole. Plus, I have heard she is not ... well. I am not certain if she is in the right state of mind to even agree to what I have planned."

"Do you wish to run your plan by me, Your Majesty?"

169

Turning so that they had direct eye contact, she responded, deliberately reminding him who was in charge.

"No, Straeger, I'll enjoy keeping you guessing. You may leave now."

After Straeger had departed, the Queen opened the door to the adjacent room and quietly entered. Moving to its centre, she took up a stance beside the tall glass cylinder that reached to the ceiling. She waved her hand briefly, clearing the milky liquid that obscured her view from the delicate woman who floated within. Her auburn hair splayed around a face of refined features.

Graziel was astounded to feel fear, an emotion that until recently had been foreign to her. Recalling the images that had been surfacing of late, she focused her attention inward to locate the anger that steadily simmered within her. Instinct told her that this woman had something to do with the visions and feelings she was experiencing. Quietly, she dialogued with the comatose woman.

"Can you hear me, Ourelia? I think you can. What are you doing to me, Ourelia? What game are you playing? Do you know who I am? *Do you know what I can do to you?*" Graziel's last words came out in a fearsome whisper.

Ourelia showed no signs of hearing the Queen's words. Graziel did not care. She could not say with certainty that the woman had been trying to influence her but it no longer mattered, for the Queen had worked herself into a cold fury.

"I thought I would share some of my plans with you, Ourelia, so that you know what I do to anyone who tries to cross me. Poor Ourelia – what a sad story you are – raised by one of the most powerful figures of the Ancient Forest, bride-to-be to a King that no longer believes you exist, a sister who has … oh yes, I believe that you don't like to talk about your sister or the shell that she has become. Not quite how you saw life unfolding is it?" she said coldly.

Leaning close to the glass, the Queen continued to speak, ruthless in her delivery.

"That ridiculous excuse of a Were-Griffin is going to lead me to the one thing that will give me absolute power – the Starchild. But first we will entice your sister to join us, and then we will use her as bait. After all these years I think she will relish the opportunity to seek revenge on the man she loved, but who chose you instead. What a tangled love story the three of you weave. One by one I will destroy each person that is close to you, Ourelia. I will particularly relish killing your father, the old fool."

Graziel's next words dripped with malice. "See what happens when you annoy me!"

Preparing to leave, she paused, delivering one last blow.

"Do you think Matharzan still loves you? He may, but he won't after he spends time with me! By the time I have finished with his mind, he will have no memory of you in his life."

Tapping the glass sharply with her fingernails, she turned, striding from the room. Engrossed in her thoughts, she did not register the shift in the other woman's awareness.

Ourelia's eyes opened wide at the same time that her hand reached toward the glass. As the door closed, she threw her head back, her mouth open in a silent howl of anguish and pain.

∾

Sarah and Matharzan walked through the Forest, having completed the Starchild's lessons with Aarus. Dineah and Tazor were leading the way, playfully trying to out-fly each other, while Sir Perity, Eblie, and Sheblie flanked Sarah and the massive Were-Griffin. Upon seeing the Starchild safely home, Matharzan took his leave and retraced his steps to Aarus's hut.

As the Were-Griffin drew near, he heard Aarus call out, inviting him in, while dismissing the Fireflies who were standing guard. Matharzan smiled briefly, knowing that Aarus had sensed his return even before he had arrived. Settling himself on the earth floor of the hut, he assumed the same position as Aarus – legs crossed underneath him and hands resting lightly on his knees. Without preamble, he began to speak.

"I know you too well, Seeker. What troubles you Aarus?"

Aarus remained silent for a long time before answering.

"I felt her presence."

The Were-Griffin recoiled in shock.

"What are you saying," he demanded, speaking more harshly than he had ever spoken to the gentle Sage.

"The day of the battle, when I travelled out of body … just before I detected the Gyranger Queen, I felt Ourelia's presence."

"But that is impossible!" said the Were-Griffin, struggling to calm his breathing and gain control of himself. "How could you have? For so many years we have believed she was dead! What are you saying, Aarus? Explain yourself! You know how difficult it is for me even to have her name spoken out loud."

"And no less difficult for me, Matharzan?" asked Aarus sharply, his heart filled with grief. Quickly regretting his tone, he closed his eyes and drew a deep breath.

"I am sorry, that was not necessary. I know this is hard, old friend – please believe me when I say that I do not take this lightly. It has been troubling me deeply."

Aarus sighed before continuing.

"I am unable to explain it; I can only tell you that I felt her presence."

"How can she be alive, Aarus?" whispered the Were-Griffin, his face tense with the strain of what the Sage had shared.

Aarus stared at the King of the Were-Griffins for a long time before responding. Finally, he spoke.

"I have travelled out of body since, back to the same place in time. In each instance, I sense Ourelia for a brief moment before I detect the Gyranger Queen. She is alive somehow, somewhere, but I do not know how or what form she holds. Was she trying to make contact with me? Is her spirit dislocated from her body? So many questions, Matharzan. All of which leave me with a sense of hope ... and foreboding. Why now? Why is she showing herself to us now? Is her presence connected to the danger we are facing? Is it related to the surfacing of the Gyrangers? You, more than anyone, knows that Straeger's presence preceded the battle that she died in."

"We all believed her to be dead, Aarus. You and I both saw her gruesome death. And I still do not believe that her body disappeared because of the blast. I know deep within me that she was teleported away by that worm, Straeger. I still search for him to this day. Even though I have tried to come to terms with the loss of Ourelia, I *will* have my revenge on that creature."

"Even our attempts to lure him out of hiding by discrediting you were not successful. I am sorry for that, Matharzan – it only created a further division between you and the Ancient Forest."

For a long time, the Were-Griffin did not reply, lost in his memories.

"Sadly, Straeger has gone underground, but mark my words, Aarus, when he reappears, he will not live long." The Were-Griffin shook his head in frustration. "I am sorry, Aarus. I know that you do not want to hear my ramblings and unresolved feelings. She was and still is your daughter ... forgive me."

"And she was the love of your life, Matharzan," said Aarus gently. "Betrothed to you in what was to be a marriage of genuine love that would unite our worlds. I am not offended by your words."

Pausing, he cleared his throat before quietly continuing.

"I feel old and tired today, Matharzan. This situation is taking more out of me than I thought possible. Anytime I think of Ourelia, my mind wanders to Aniese, who was also the light of my life. I will not speak more of her now, Matharzan, for I know that saying her name grieves you too. Please believe me that my intention is not to dredge up old wounds."

"I am sorry about Aniese, Aarus," was the Were-Griffin's response, sorrow in his voice.

The Sage did not reply. *Pain,* he thought – *there is so much pain in this story.*

"I will think further on this and let you know what insights come to me, Matharzan. In the meantime, I ask that you give an old Sage his rest and privacy. I will not make for good company tonight."

Matharzan sensed that Aarus was holding something back, but he did not push the Sage further. Bowing his head in respect, he reached out and touched Aarus's shoulder before taking his leave.

Aarus hardly registered Matharzan's gesture. His mind kept going back to the presence he had felt on the day of the battle. He could not tell Matharzan that he had also sensed an aura of darkness within Ourelia's presence. Where was his daughter and what had happened to her?

Aarus's heart beat fast in his chest as an uncharacteristic wave of rage swept through him. Now that the possibility existed, he wanted nothing less than to know for certain that his daughter was alive. Aarus still could not say why he believed that Ourelia's sudden reappearance was significant, but he felt that there was a connection between her emergence and the return of the Gyrangers.

Looking up, he realized that he hadn't bidden the Were-Griffin an appropriate farewell. He knew that Matharzan would be concerned. Aarus wished that he could share his thoughts with the King of the Were-Griffins, but knew it would only reopen old wounds that would distract Matharzan from his current obligation – Sarah Starbright. Aarus decided to keep his thoughts to himself … at least for now.

CHAPTER 16

Duties of a Song Bearer

Dineah had not slept well through the night. Dreams had plagued her sleep, filling her with unease and tension that had coursed through her tiny body. Against her will she nodded off again, only to be caught up in the same whirlwind of terrifying images.

Flying beside Sarah who is running down an endless sterile corridor ... shift ... pausing outside a door in the corridor – something through that doorway is calling to her ... shift ... she and Sarah are now on the other side of that door, in a room that contains a large glass cylinder filled with swirling, cloudy liquid ... shift ... standing with Sarah beside the glass container. It reaches all the way to the ceiling; the movement within it is calming and hypnotic. Drowsiness overtakes ... shift ... being awoken by a tapping sound coming from inside the cylinder. A form is taking shape within the milky liquid – a hand – now the body of a woman wrapped in white linens that loosely cover her ... shift ... masses of Gyrangers in the hallway, the clicking of their pinchers betraying their excitement, for they know that the Starchild is in the room ... shift ... yelling at Sarah, trying to rouse the Starchild who has become spellbound by the swirling motions in the cylinder ... shift ... the tapping sound is louder, more insistent ... shift ... the door to the room is opening – the Gyrangers are entering ... shift ... a hand is urgently striking the inside of the cylinder ... shift ... the woman's face is against the glass. Her eyes snap open as she silently screams, "SAVE ME SONG BEARER."

Dineah awoke with a start, gasping for air as a sense of dread filled her. She focused on her breathing, trying to calm the beating of her heart. Something about the woman's eyes had been familiar. Dineah knew that this was another form of the foretelling; that her capacity at foreseeing had strengthened since being chosen as the Song Bearer. Elder Aarus had warned her that this would happen, especially as the danger to the Forest drew nearer.

She needed to tell Aarus about the dream, for it gave her a terrible sense of foreboding. She knew that he was in a meeting with the Council until noon, but she had to see him as soon as possible. The dream was important.

Feeling the presence of her old friend, the wind, she saw a flower petal lightly waft through the air and land beside her. Still shaken from the dream, Dineah tenuously smiled as she drew the petal gently to herself to wipe away the light sheen of sweat that covered her body. Looking around, she was surprised to see that she was not alone. To her right hovered the butterfly Mari, strategically placed to protect Dineah from the light of the rising sun. On her other side was the Fairy child Polli, squealing and jumping excitedly now that Dineah was awake. Dineah presumed that the bowl of fresh nectar that the child was holding, well actually spilling, was for her. Flying quickly to Polli, she took the nectar, but not before placing a kiss of gratitude on the child's cheek.

Movement above her head made her look up, causing her

heart to leap into her throat. Sitting on a vine quietly above her was none other than Bronte, the second in command to the Winged Warriors. Dineah heard the wind begin to chuckle. She had shared her feelings about Bronte with the wind. She knew she wasn't the only one in the Forest who was impressed with him … the way the light reflected off his skin, his dazzling aerial skills, his remarkable stature. Sighing, she knew she wasn't acting as a Song Bearer should, but it still set her heart aflutter that he was here guarding her. As if sensing her gaze, he turned to look at her with his enormous eyes, shifting his body and causing the light to refract colours of iridescent greens and blues. Realizing that she was opening staring, Dineah sought to regain her composure. Flimsily waving her fingers, she smiled – far too brightly! Grinning, he bowed his head in response before resuming his guard. Dineah cringed inwardly, mortified, as the thought passed through her mind, *I have just acted like a teenage Firefly!*

Seeking a place to hide her crimson cheeks she plunged her entire head into the bowl of nectar. Almost instantly, she felt a jolting vibration throughout her body. Needing air, she quickly pulled out of the liquid and looked for the source of disruption, nectar dripping down her head and face. Lying on his stomach beside her was Tazor, drumming his nails on the earth. Taking a big breath, he leaned close to her, whispering in a rumbling voice that caused the flowers around Dineah to vibrate.

"What is wrong, Song Bearer? Why you play hide and seek in your food? You upset? Is something … ohhh!"

Tazor's eyes had moved about as he spoke. When he spotted Bronte, he began to grin, his voice getting increasingly louder.

"I knows why you swim in your breakfast. You *like* him!"

Tazor's right eye continued to point toward Bronte as his left eye began to float merrily in the opposite direction.

Chapter 16

"You can tell me – I no tell anyone, I promise. I know what it is like because I have big heart for Sarah. I tell no one though, only me and I know ... well and now you."

And half the Forest, thought Dineah as she looked up at Tazor. She didn't know how to tell him that although his attempt at discreetness was charming, his whisper was loud enough for everyone to hear – which meant that Bronte was listening to their entire conversation. Dineah motioned Tazor to silence with her finger. Glancing upward, she noticed that Bronte had discreetly turned his back to her, but not before taking a moment to look over his shoulder and smile. Warmth filled her. Well, he hadn't mocked her; in fact, he had seemed to like it.

In the short time since becoming the Song Bearer, Dineah had felt a change within herself. She knew that the inhabitants of the Ancient Forest no longer looked at her the same way. Before, she was Dineah Firefly, Oracle of the Forest. Now, as the Song Bearer, she carried even more responsibility for the future of the Ancient Forest. And thanks to Sarah's magic she was healthy and active again. It was during the healing that the mind link they now shared had developed. Dineah liked that she and Sarah could communicate telepathically. They had told no one about their secret, not even Elder Aarus or Princess Hana. Both she and Sarah had agreed that it was best to keep it unknown, although they couldn't explain why.

Drawing her attention back to the moment, she noticed that more creatures had gathered, hoping to have a moment to speak with her. Her days were like this now. Frequently they wanted to check in on her and know that as the Song Bearer, she was safe and well. Sometimes they would ask her questions about the future, needing reassurance. Often, she couldn't answer their questions because she just didn't know – not that it seemed to matter. They merely needed to be in her presence where they

179

could voice their fears and uncertainties. In allowing for this, she knew that they left feeling calmer and more assured.

Looking up at Tazor, she began to smile. What an unlikely friend she had found in the gargoyle. Since motioning him to silence, he hadn't said a word. She knew that he wouldn't until she told him to.

"What are you doing here this fine morning, Tazor?"

"Waiting to see you," he replied, still grinning, his eyes splaying wildly. "Sarah still sleeping so I check on you, 'cause you my friend, Song Bearer, and that what friends do."

Flying upward quickly, Dineah landed on the bridge of Tazor's nose, hugging him.

"Stay with me, Tazor, while I meet with those who have gathered to see me."

"Okay, Song Bearer. Afterwards, we fly to Sarah's house and shake water droplets on her head when she leave her home?"

Giggling loudly, Dineah clapped her hand over her mouth, realizing that once again she wasn't acting as a Song Bearer should. Tazor had a way of bringing that out in her. Nodding her head eagerly up and down, she grinned broadly before flying back to drink the nectar that was her breakfast.

～

Sarah could tell that Dineah was troubled.

"He asked me the strangest question, Sarah. He wanted to know if the woman in the dream was his daughter, Ourelia. She's been dead for years! Why would Aarus ask me that?"

Sarah lay on the ground, idly twirling a twig between her fingers and trying to absorb what Dineah was telling her.

"I didn't know that Aarus had a daughter. He never talks about her."

"He had two, well actually still has one. It's a terrible story, Sarah ..."

"Two daughters! He still has ... WHAT?"

Sarah quickly sat up to watch Dineah who was zipping back and forth as she spoke, her glow light creating a horizontal afterglow. The Firefly was clearly agitated!

"He still has one daughter, Sarah. Her name is Aniese. She does not live with us. She lives ... elsewhere."

Folding her arms, Sarah gave Dineah an exasperated look.

"I'm not trying to hide anything, Sarah. It's just that no one ever talks about the place."

"What place?" asked Sarah, frustration creeping into her voice.

"The Shadow Forest."

Sarah felt a chill move through her. "And Aniese?" she asked quietly.

Dineah responded just as softly. "No one talks about her, either."

Sarah could feel sorrow through the mind link she shared with Dineah.

"Oh Dineah, what happened? Why does this make you so sad?"

Landing on the twig that Sarah had been playing with, Dineah settled herself, placing her chin in her hands.

"Ourelia and Matharzan were promised in marriage."

"WHOA! STOP! Grif was going to marry Aarus's daughter?"

"Yes, Sarah. Everyone said that they truly loved each other. All the beings of the Ancient Forest were excited, as were the people of Matharzan's planet. I was a much younger Firefly, Sarah, but I still remember the day that changed everything in the Ancient Forest ... in all of us. So much loss."

Dineah paused, her face stricken.

"Friends, family members, whole sections of the Forest." Her next words were barely audible. "It left a hole in our hearts."

"What happened?" whispered Sarah, tears shining in her eyes.

"There was a surprise attack that no one anticipated, a terrible battle that ended in an explosion that damaged the Forest horribly, and killed Ourelia. At least that is what some say – there are so many different stories. Some believe that Ourelia was dead even before the blast and that when Matharzan found her, he went insane, blaming the Gyranger Ambassador who was present that day. When the Ambassador tried to flee through a portal, Matharzan attempted to stop it from closing. It exploded. The worse part, Sarah, is that no one ever found Ourelia's body. In trying to seek revenge, did Matharzan destroy it? That is what some say. Others believe that the body disappeared before the explosion. No one knows to this day."

"Regardless, do you understand, Sarah? That is why Matharzan had to make amends with the Guardians to be able to stay in the Forest as your protector. It is programmed into their very existence to protect, yet they lost fellow Guardians as a result of that day, as well as segments of the Forest and many beings that they loved and were responsible for keeping safe. They associate that loss with Matharzan. As the Oracle of the Forest, I have always felt a sense of disquiet over what happened. Something isn't right – it's as if a piece of the story is missing. I believe that a time will come when we will know the truth of what took place. Until that happens, Matharzan continues to carry a heavy burden. I don't think that the Elders believe him wholly responsible either; if so, they would never have allowed his return."

Pausing for a short while, she slowly began to speak again.

Chapter 16

"In a very short timeframe, the damaged portions of the Forest became very sick, as did anyone inhabiting them. The healers were able to restore some parts of the Forest, but the destruction was so vast that they couldn't save everyone. The radiation from the explosion caused transmutations in the Forest creatures, and the trees and foliage withered and turned black. Darkness descended over these areas. It slowly began to spread and touch everyone. In order to contain the sickness, the affected areas were separated from the Ancient Forest, becoming the Shadow Forest. Aniese was one of the people who lived through the blast, but it altered her. Everyone believed that she was going to have a full recovery, but one day we were told that she had left to live in the Shadow Forest. Aarus did not come out of his hut for several days. He aged, Sarah. He aged overnight. Only a year earlier his wife had died. She was the highest sought healer in the Karrian Galaxy and had been working with others to stop a plague that had spread on a planet outside of the galaxy. She caught the sickness while there and came back to the Ancient Forest, only to die a short while later. Aarus lost the three people that he loved most within one year, Sarah."

Sarah didn't try to stop the tears that were now coursing down her face.

"Did you lose family, Dineah?" she asked gently.

"No, but a good friend, and Fireflies and Fairies that I was close to ... even some of the Guardians. It was a sad time in our history."

"So Aarus thinks that Ourelia is in danger and needs your help?"

"I guess so, Sarah, but that makes no sense. The woman in the dream seemed familiar, but I didn't recognize her."

"I don't know what to say, except that we'll figure it out somehow, Dineah."

Dineah didn't respond, only nodding her head up and down, her mind still caught in the tragic past.

CHAPTER 17

Taking Advantage

Aniese sat where she had fallen. Standing, she tried to regain her balance but slipped again, sliding in the green slime that covered the path and oozed between her fingers. Lifting her hand, she watched the slime drop to the ground, causing her to laugh wildly out loud and relish in the intoxication that clouded her mind and kept the ghosts at bay. She looked upward and saw the flickers of light hovering around her; horrible aberrations of former Fireflies. They followed her everywhere, protective of her – loyalty still a part of their nature. Their minds weren't well, like hers, but they would not forget who she was. She shook her head, not wanting to continue down that train of thought.

Once again she was drawn to their lights. Reaching her hand toward them, they quickly moved away. Her muddled brain knew better, but she couldn't remember why? It would all come back when she awoke clear-headed in the morning – unbidden memories of the explosion that had transformed their glow lights into long strands of lethal, coarse hair that shone fluorescent in the dark. Strands of hair that looked safe enough, but a mere touch caused excruciating pain and momentary paralysis.

Settling into a sitting position, she crossed her legs, vaguely aware of the dense liquid seeping through her leggings and burrowing into her skin. She did not care. This place was her domain; a world she had retreated to many years ago to survive the betrayal and torment that had marked her life. She had no one here ... well, that was not entirely true. There were the Forest creatures of course; the ones that had survived through metamorphosis.

Shuddering, Aniese closed her mind, refusing it access to the images of her current dwelling place in its former state of beauty. The Guardians had refused to stay here after the change. Those who were unable to return to the Ancient Forest had chosen to leave their physical form, shifting back into pure energy. *Such a loss,* she thought, tears moving down her cheeks.

They had named this place the Shadow Forest. She shook her head, trying to shake away the thoughts that threatened to break through her barriers. *So many memories – so much pain!* Reaching behind her, Aniese grasped a bowl containing the fermented nectar that could help her forget. Tipping it up, she realized it was empty. Angrily she slammed it down beside her.

The memories were starting to slip through, and she had no way to push them away. She screamed in frustration, tears coursing down her face as she began to sob, her body shuddering with each intake of breath. No matter how hard she tried, she could never rid herself of the memories ... and the pain ... there was so much hurt and pain.

Searching again, she found another bowl. Lifting the container to her lips, she gulped down the sweet liquid. A moment later, the drink took its effect. As her eyes rolled backward into her head, she collapsed to the ground, unconscious. Fluorescent lights circled her protectively.

Aniese awoke to voices – a female voice, a male voice, and then a clicking noise. She sat up quickly, instantly recognizing the sound of the Gyrangers' pinchers. Floating in front of her were six hideous beings surrounded by a protective orb.

Smart, on their part, she thought.

Aniese knew that they were protecting themselves from the Forest. Already she could see that the vegetation had stretched apart, weakening the soil's ability to hold weight. Had they been standing on the ground, it would have caved in, swallowing the trespassers as if they had never existed.

Why would the Shadow Forest seek to destroy them? Simple – because they were here, where no one was welcome. She did not dwell on what the Shadow Forest was capable of doing for it unsettled even her. She could see that the Fireflies had formed a circle around her, like a halo. Laughter bubbled up at the thought of a halo around her head. She did not carry that kind of energy anymore. She had changed too much; become too dark. Standing, she wobbled on her feet. She was surprised that her words did not slur.

"Fools! What are you doing here? Do you not know where you are and how quickly the Forest will destroy you? Not that I would object – your slow, painful deaths would be my pleasure."

The only response was light, tinkling laughter. Aniese watched as a figure emerged from behind the group of Gyrangers – a petite woman of breathtaking beauty. Aniese immediately knew who it was. She struggled to control her knees which had started to shake.

"Oh we know exactly where we are, my sister," purred the Gyranger Queen.

"I am not your sister, you vile creature. How *dare* you set foot in the Ancient Forest – *you are not welcome!*"

"Hmm," said Graziel, "last time I checked this was no longer part of the Ancient Forest. Word has it that this place has been disowned, hence the name, SHADOW FOREST!"

Screaming the last two words, the Queen threw herself forward, the orb flexing with her movement but remaining intact. Floating in the air, she stood nose to nose with Aniese, her next words filled with cruelty.

"You are a pathetic fool. Daughter of the greatest Sage alive, you could have used the death of your older sister to your advantage and become one of the most powerful women in the Forest. Instead, you wallow here in your pitiful legacy of thwarted love. How can you stand yourself? You sicken me!"

Graziel's tone dripped with malice. Everything about this woman shouted weakness and Graziel had no tolerance for anything that threatened her need for supremacy. She sought to gain control of her contempt. She was going to use this woman and then throw the rest of her away. She chose her next words carefully.

"I know of your pain, Aniese. I know that you sit in this hell-hole, rotting. I know who created all of this … who hurt you."

Graziel paused, turning in a circle to study what was formally part of the majestic Ancient Forest. Everywhere she looked was devastation. How had Matharzan wrought this much damage? And all because of a woman? Graziel shook her head. She still did not understand why the Ancient Forest had aligned itself with him again – not when she witnessed firsthand the devastation he had created.

There were different stories, most of which had come from Straeger, which didn't assure her of their truth. She was only too aware of his unnatural obsession with Aarus's eldest daughter.

Straeger claimed that Matharzan had blamed the Forest for Ourelia's death and in his rage and grief had cursed the Forest, creating an explosion that had threatened its very role as a guardian to the Karrian Galaxy. To protect itself, the Ancient Forest had banished the Were-Griffin and then cut itself off from the damaged portions that in time had become known as the Shadow Forest. Indeed the name was apt, for everywhere she looked was charred evidence of what had existed. Now, green slime covered the vegetation, and a grey mist rose from bubbling abscesses that reeked of decay. Everything here was lethal ... including the Fireflies, she noticed. Thanks to Straeger's inquiries she was also aware of the dangerous and hideously malformed creatures that hid within the equally perilous vegetation that could strike without warning.

Turning back to face Aniese, she said, "I can help you seek revenge on King Matharzan-Ariebe, Aniese. I know where he is. Would you like to see him dead?"

Aniese's head was swimming, her intoxicated mind struggling to comprehend what was happening. Why was the Queen of the Gyrangers in the Shadow Forest? Why had Aniese not been notified? Inside, Aniese already knew the answer. The Forest would have tried to inform her, but she had been unconscious, unable to heed its warning and direct an appropriate response. She was still the closest thing to royalty that existed in this shadowland, and the inhabitants of the Shadow Forest continued to follow her leadership. Thoughts continued to mull through her mind until she was brought up sharp by the Gyranger Queen's question. Before she could stop herself, words flew from her mouth.

"Yes, I want him dead. I want to see him rot and pay for everything he has done to me."

So strong was her response that spittle flew from her lips.

Struggling to stand and hold herself steady, she pointed her finger at the Gyranger Queen.

"Your reputation precedes you, Graziel, and it is not complimentary. What are you scheming at this time? Why are you here and what do you want? *Speak!*"

Command rang in Aniese's voice. Briefly, it reminded her of the strength she had once had ... before the fall, and the sickness that had enveloped her mind. She knew she was not well. There was a hole in her, a sense of emptiness. For many years she had lived in the Shadow Forest, feeding the void with nectar, and drowning in hatred and a promise of revenge at the two people who had destroyed her life. When she would awake from her drunken stupors she would remember that one was already gone; dead long ago. She would try to shut away from the pain, but it never worked. In time, she began to target her feelings at the one who still lived – Matharzan-Ariebe, King of the Were-Griffins – the only man she had ever loved.

She had never known love until the moment she had set eyes on him. Her mind drifted back to that day – the announcement of his arrival; the anticipation it had created in the Ancient Forest. She and Ourelia had stood beside their father, directly to the left of the Scarab King, his Princess daughters and Prince Drake. It was a significant moment, a great honour, for the King of the Were-Griffins had elected to attend personally, rather than send an Ambassador. Aniese had watched Matharzan stride into the Sacred Grove and had felt her breath catch in her throat. Was it possible to know love at first sight?

Evidently, it was, because when the Were-Griffin's eyes conducted a quick sweep of the welcoming party, they bypassed everyone including Aniese, until they landed on Ourelia. At that moment, Matharzan's composure had faltered. As the King of the Were-Griffins looked at Ourelia, Aniese witnessed the same expression of longing that she knew to be in her own eyes. Ourelia! Her sister! The one person she loved more than anyone in the Forest.

Closing her eyes, the image of Matharzan continued to fill her mind, along with the litany of questions that she had asked herself a thousand times.

Why had he fallen in love with Ourelia, her only sister? And why, why had Ourelia responded, knowing now Aniese felt? Or had Ourelia known?

Aniese couldn't remember anymore, her mind too clouded now by darkness and hatred. The only time she and Ourelia had ever fought was because of the Were-Griffin. That was the same day that Ourelia had died and that Matharzan had inadvertently in his grief, destroyed a portion of the Ancient Forest, changing Aniese's life forever. Did she want him dead? More than anything! But how could Graziel possibly know where Matharzan was?

Thinking of him brought up memories of Ourelia who had died so many years ago. Aniese's throat constricted. She wasn't sure if it was from anger or grief; she couldn't tell anymore. And now this foul insect was taunting her by claiming she knew of Matharzan's whereabouts. The Gyranger Queen had not responded to her demand. Aniese spit at Graziel, the saliva striking the orb and sliding downward.

"Here, here," said the Queen in a whisper, unmistakable rage filling her face. "Let's not forget who you are dealing with."

Any sense of reason shattered into giddy delight at witnessing the Queen's anger. Aniese allowed her ignited emotions to course uncontrolled. If Graziel didn't disclose her intentions quickly, Aniese was going to order a full attack on the Gyrangers.

Graziel did not seem to be aware of the escalating situation, but someone else was.

"My Queen, I suggest that you answer Lady Aniese's question and that we depart … quickly."

Looking beyond Graziel, Aniese saw who had spoken.

"YOU BRING THIS SNAKE, STRAEGER, TO MY FOREST! LEAVE NOW GRAZIEL OR I WILL HAVE THE FOREST KILL YOU ALL!"

The Queen moved in front of Aniese, obscuring her view of Straeger. Graziel was tired of dealing with this woman.

"I will deliver Matharzan into your hands, but there is one thing I want in return. Are you willing to negotiate? If you try to kill us now, you will never know what my offer was, *and* you will have lost an opportunity for vengeance. Get control of yourself, Aniese! Make a decision! I have lost my patience."

Aniese's mind clouded with rage. She knew how badly Straeger had desired Ourelia. He had met Aarus's eldest daughter on one of his visits to the Ancient Forest as Ambassador of the Gyrangers. From that moment on he had persistently sought to gain her affections. Ourelia was bothered by Straeger's actions. She had not liked him and had mistakenly confided this to Matharzan, sparking tension between the Gyranger and Were-Griffin that had escalated until the two men could not bear to be in each other's company.

No one could have predicted that Ourelia would die in the surprise attack that fell upon the Ancient Forest so many years ago. Matharzan had claimed that Straeger had facilitated the assault and ultimately, Ourelia's death. Seeing Ourelia's mangled body lying on the ground, and steeped in the midst of battle lust, he had set to take his revenge. Uncertain if his claims were valid, the Elders had sought to intervene, driving the Were-Griffin into more of a rage. Moving to follow the terrified Straeger who was fleeing through a self-created portal, the Were-Griffin had tried to stop its closure, setting off an explosion that had created unbelievable damage to the Forest and its inhabitants. Once the aftermath had cleared, both the attacking force and Ourelia's body had disappeared.

The Ancient Forest had immediately prepared to launch an attack on the Gyrangers. Upon hearing of the Forest's intentions, the Queen of the Gyrangers had initiated an emergency meeting with the Elders. Risking her safety under volatile circumstances, she had personally attended the Sacred Grove, claiming that she had released Straeger from his role as Ambassador several months earlier due to increasingly peculiar behaviour. She had not been aware that he had continued to attend the Ancient Forest as the representative of the Gyrangers, nor did she know where he was presently residing. She was allowed to leave that day unharmed, but relations between the Ancient Forest and the Gyrangers were never the same after.

Some believed that Ourelia's body had ceased to exist because of the detonation. Others, like Matharzan, thought that Straeger had abducted Ourelia's body. Aniese no longer knew what she believed. What was clear was that the Gyranger Queen had realigned herself with Straeger, which meant that the already fragile alliance with the Ancient Forest was now utterly broken. As she moved around the Queen to look again at Straeger, Aniese realized that she hated him as much as she hated Matharzan. Without looking at Graziel, she said in a quiet voice.

"What is it you want in return for the Were-Griffin? What act of betrayal are you working at this time?"

Graziel tried to hide her reaction to Aniese's words, but a sharp jerk of her head betrayed her. Looking at Aniese, she saw clarity within the woman's eyes and felt a moment of unease.

"Matharzan is protecting a young girl that I want. They are both currently residing in the Ancient Forest. Find out his plans. I want to know when the Were-Griffin next leaves the Ancient

Forest, for him and the girl are inseparable. We will work with you to reroute his destination, ensuring that he ends up in the Shadow Forest. Once Matharzan realizes where he is, he will immediately try to leave. You will have to distract him long enough for my forces to move in and take the child. After that, he is yours to do whatever you want with him."

Looking once again at the dark and dismal setting, she added, "I am sure this rotting stench hole has little secrets that can cause him adequate amounts of pain."

"How do you expect *me* to get any information from the Ancient Forest, Graziel?"

"That is not my problem, Aniese. Just do it and report to me."

"No. I am not interested in your schemes, Graziel. Be gone from this place and leave me in peace."

Turning, Aniese made to walk away.

Pulling a small, round device from her robe, Graziel rotated the top half of it. Instantly, a light pulsed from the object and the air shimmered, revealing an image of a narrow glass cylinder filled with a clouded liquid.

Straeger's gaze whipped toward the image at the same time that he drew in a sharp breath. As Graziel glanced at him, he barely concealed his agitation in time.

Aniese had already begun walking but stopped, noticing that the sounds of the Forest had stopped. Slowly she turned to look back. Her stomach lurched as she saw the image that was floating in the air between her and Graziel. She already knew who was inside the cylinder. Shock followed by a torrent of nauseating fury moved through her.

"That is right, Aniese. We have Ourelia ... always have, in fact," sighed Graziel glibly.

"You have no right to have anyone from the Ancient Forest as a captive," snarled Aniese.

"What difference does it make, Aniese? You hate her anyway. We have done you a favour by keeping her out of everyone's hair all these years."

"Give her to me," said Aniese, her voice flat.

"Give us the child, and I will deliver Matharzan to you, as well as your sister. That is my final deal; I have no more time to negotiate. And don't try to betray us – no one will believe anything you have to say."

Suddenly Graziel lunged toward Aniese, the orb moving with her. Quickly reaching through the translucent sphere, Graziel grabbed Aniese's forearm, using her razor-sharp fingernail to carve a half-shaped moon into the other woman's skin. Aniese pulled back, crying out in pain and then watching in shock as the surface began to bubble up.

"What have you done?" she cried, unable to retaliate at the Queen who had already retreated within the orb.

Aniese watched as the skin healed, leaving only the moon-shaped mark that now protruded upward from her arm. Rubbing her finger on it, she noticed that the skin felt cold and hard. She could also feel a painful pulse coming from beneath the mark.

"When you need to make contact with me, push down on the *satae* that I have placed on your arm. It will open a link to me that will allow us to talk to each other."

"What is this?" snarled Aniese.

There was something very unnatural about what now lay under her skin. A sense of coldness had begun to spread outward from the mark.

Graziel did not respond. Turning, she looked at Straeger, who bowed his head in response before reopening the portal for their exit. Quickly stepping through, the Gyrangers and their Queen were lost to view.

"Tell me more about my sister!" Aniese screamed at the

closing gateway. Falling to her knees, she placed her hand over the now throbbing half-moon, her matted hair falling to cover her face.

≈

Ourelia knew that Straeger had entered the room. She continued to float freely, her arms splayed to the side, feigning unconsciousness. Barely opening her eyes, she saw him standing quietly in the doorway, a look on his face unlike any she had ever seen before. She could vaguely hear his murmuring.

"I will *not* let her discard you, *not when we are so close!*"

Solemnly approaching the glass cylinder, he placed his hand on it and spoke in a quiet voice.

"I know that you can hear me, Ourelia. I have known for a while now, but I have kept your secret from Graziel. I hope this proves that you can trust me."

He paused as if struggling inside himself.

"Ourelia, it is now time to share something that I have wanted to tell you for years. You would not have understood before, nor would you have heard me out. Now, I know you will. The time is soon, Ourelia. After all these years, you are finally ready to take your place among the Gyrangers … by my side. I have always loved you, Ourelia. You know that. I was never able to hide my intentions from you. I knew that you didn't feel the same way, but circumstances did not allow you to develop true feelings for me. You were too busy, too distracted by Matharzan. That is why I took such drastic measures so many years ago to have you brought here. You needed to separate yourself from the illusions that were controlling your life."

"I knew you would be angry at the time, which is why I had to wait these many years before I could tell you. But time has passed, and you – well you have changed. Ourelia, your genetic make-up is now both Gyranger and your former self. You will now think and act as part of the collective mind of the Gyranger race. You may not be aware of it yet, but once released from this liquid cocoon, you will know of what I speak.

Straeger's next words came out as a whisper.

"Together, you and I will be unstoppable, Ourelia."

Ourelia could feel the passion in his voice. Her stomach churned at the Ambassador's twisted demonstration of love.

"There is something I need to tell you, Ourelia. There cannot be any secrets between us any longer. It was I, Ourelia, who orchestrated the attack on the Ancient Forest that day. It was also I who rendered you unconscious before I took your body through a portal, leaving a hologram of you that appeared dead. Upon my return to the Ancient Forest, Matharzan sought me out and blamed me as I knew he would. Feigning fear for my safety, I created a portal and prepared to leave. What I did not expect was for him to foolishly try and stop the closure of it as I was departing. It did not kill him Ourelia, but it did cause destruction both in the Forest and to people dear to you. I will not take the blame for all of it, Ourelia. It was Matharzan's rash behaviour that created tremendous damage, in ways I had not thought possible."

Straeger's voice had risen as he spoke, hatred seeping through his words.

"For years the Ancient Forest exiled him as a result of his reckless actions. Some even thought that he had caused your death! I did not dispel the rumours, Lady. In fact, I fostered them by adding more. I know you may not want to hear this, but everything I did, I did for you, Ourelia, and for us."

Dropping to one knee, Straeger pressed the tip of his head against the glass encasement.

"Believe me, Lady. I always knew that I could offer you more. That is why I removed you from your birthplace, and the man you foolishly thought that you would marry. And soon, after all these years, you will see how I have proven my love for you."

Standing, he began to move toward the rear of the glass cylinder, continuing to speak.

"Ourelia, it is time to release you from the liquid enclosure you have been immersed in for so long. You may feel discomfort as your lungs adjust to breathing air, but do not panic, your body will naturally adapt. You have changed, Ourelia. You have abilities that you did not have before."

Reaching to the back of the glass, Straeger pushed a button which began to flash, causing liquid to discharge from the cylinder into a drain in the floor.

"It will not be long, Ourelia, before you fully integrate as a hybrid into our formidable race. I look forward to hearing your voice, and to looking into your eyes again."

Caressing the glass tenderly, he bent his head in a deep bow before turning to leave the room.

Ourelia noticed for the first time that the door did not lock upon his departure. She could already feel a pressure change in the cylinder, forcing her attention away from the distressing conversation she had just heard. Carefully shielding her churning emotions, she continued to focus on the two things that had kept her alive all these years – escape and revenge.

CHAPTER 18

Next Steps

Aarus sat in his hut reflecting on his lessons with Sarah. He was pleased. For weeks now she had met with him daily to learn about the inner functioning of the Ancient Forest, as well as its role as a safeguard to the Karrian Galaxy. He had used the hidden realms as a teaching arena, after instructing the Starchild to project her consciousness out of her body. It had been an easy and efficient way to draw her awareness back in time, and show the Starchild events which would otherwise have entailed hours of teaching.

Aarus found Sarah to be a quick learner, soaking in her studies tirelessly. He knew that her ability to integrate the vast amounts of information was directly related to her birthright as a child of *Atarashara*.

She continued to regularly meet with each Elder to understand their unique role in maintaining the equilibrium of the Forest. She had even spent several days with Elder Effley who was responsible for screening and processing new candidates seeking permanent resident status in the Karrian

Galaxy. Wisteria had not agreed to this until she has placed a concealing spell on Sarah that had not only changed her appearance, but had veiled her magic so that it did not draw unwanted attention.

Sarah continued to have individual lessons with Sabrae, Wisteria, and Bohn, who all agreed that she learned at a remarkable rate, but still said there would never be enough time to teach her all that they knew. And every evening she went with Dineah, Sir Perity, and the gargoyles to the Sacred Grove to hear the Orators of the Forest – Elders Ravensong and Tenor - tell their stories. Aarus knew that Sarah particularly enjoyed Elder Tenor's style of oration. Aarus understood why, for Tenor was a remarkable storyteller. It was the only time that the Elder lost his ordinarily meek stature.

Aarus was aware that Sarah set aside time each day to visit *Atarashara*, where she would quietly commune with her birthplace. During these times, Sir Perity, Eblie, and Sheblie protectively hovered around her, readying themselves for any possible danger or threats. Not that there were any, for the Guardians continually watched over both the Song Bearer and the Starchild.

Aarus was surprised to see that Sarah did not ask for solitude during these visits. Rather, Dineah would sit quietly on one shoulder, and Tazor would sit … well as quiet as was possible for Tazor, on the other shoulder. Aarus sensed that *Atarashara* was patient with the tiny gargoyle whose hyena-like outbursts had on more than one occasion, caused Forest creatures to run and burrow in their dens.

Aarus knew that Princess Hana still believed that Tazor was essential in what was transpiring, despite the gargoyle's struggle to keep his mind intact. Hana argued that Tazor had already demonstrated loyalty and quick thinking when he had saved her life at the time of the cross-over to the Ancient Forest. Tazor's response had been instinctual and ferocious. Hana also maintained that although Tazor's behaviour was unpredictable, and particularly unsettling when directed at his enemies, she never feared for Sarah's safety.

Bringing his attention back to the present, Aarus thought further on the relationship between Sarah and *Atarashara*. Aarus never asked Sarah for details about her meetings with *'the field of unlimited possibilities'*. He was too respectful of their bond. Intuition told him that there would come a day soon when *Atarashara* would once again act outside of its normal protocols and seek contact. As each day passed, he felt a heaviness settling in the Forest as if something were pressing upon it. He knew that others felt it, for he was aware of the many Forest dwellers who took counsel with Dineah, wanting reassurance that all would be well. He also knew that the heaviness was not only linked to the danger foretold in Dineah's song. It was now common knowledge between the Forest creatures that the Gyrangers had tried to abduct the Starchild. The Forest and its inhabitants had come to love Sarah in the short time that she had lived among them. They did not want to see her harmed and were very protective of her.

He had observed the Elders bending as they walked as if weighed down, and realized that he was likely doing the same thing. He had also noticed that the Guardians were more tense and formidable than he had ever seen them. Something was coming – of that, he was sure. A sense of foreboding was everywhere.

There is still something that doesn't add up, thought Aarus. *Are the Gyrangers capable of the destruction that was foretold by Atalia's visions in Atarashara thirteen years earlier? Are the Gyrangers the threat to the Ancient Forest, or is there something else that is not yet in my awareness?*

Aarus knew that the day of action was drawing near. He just did not know how or when it would manifest. As if in response to his thoughts he felt the stirrings of a message move through his mind. A moment later, a voice began to speak. He recognized it instantly.

Elder Aarus, we seek your attention, whispered *Atarashara*, its silky voice caressing his mind.

"What is it, Honourable *Atarashara*?" replied Aarus, his head bent in reverence.

You have done well with the Starchild's teachings, Elder. But she still requires more knowledge – there is another that must teach her. Have her attend to the planet Oorse and meet with Monserat. Take heed, for time is short.

Aarus's mind began to clear as *Atarashara* took its leave. '*The field of unlimited possibilities*' had very seldom initiated direct contact with him in the past. Once again Aarus was struck by the irregularity of this. Why was *Atarashara* abandoning the etiquette it had lived by since its creation?

Putting it from his mind, Aarus concentrated on *Atarashara's* request. He knew well of Monserat, the High Priestess of the mysteries of the Great Mother. In particular, he was aware of her close relationship with *Atarashara*, for it was she who taught initiates the protocols and rituals that were necessary to interact with the consciousness that existed within the sacred portal. Aarus respected Monserat profoundly and considered her a steadfast friend and ally. He was intrigued by *Atarashara's* request but did not have the luxury of reflecting upon it at the present moment. He began making preparations immediately, asking the Firefly guards to contact Matharzan who arrived within minutes. Once the Were-Griffin had settled himself on the floor of the hut, Aarus wasted no time in getting to the point.

"Sarah's next level of teaching will occur on the planet Oorse, with Monserat. Gather your party, Matharzan, and escort her there. I will contact Monserat tonight and apprise her of our need." Pausing he added, "The direction came directly from *Atarashara*, Matharzan."

The Were-Griffin looked at Aarus sharply, his eyebrows rising.

"Be prepared to leave within forty-eight hours, old friend. Who will accompany you?"

"The same group that escorted Sarah from Brendondale to the Ancient Forest. I will contact Silverspear and have him join us. What will you tell Monserat, Aarus? How will you explain Sarah's magic?"

"I will disclose Sarah's true identity to Monserat. There is no sense hiding anything from her, for she will sense the child's magic immediately and will have questions. She is the High Priestess who oversees the training of initiates entering *Atarashara*. It is not a coincidence that Sarah is being sent to study under her. I would also suggest that members of the Legion escort you, including the First."

"So be it," said Matharzan.

"I will prepare the portal that will give you direct access to Oorse from the Ancient Forest. I will also ensure that upon your arrival, Monserat's guards will be available for additional security. I will leave it to you to inform your party and have them prepared."

Suddenly Aarus paused, sensing an invisible presence in the hut. Continuing to give the Were-Griffin instructions, he did not disclose its existence or the feelings that it evoked in him. Calling the meeting to an end, he bid Matharzan goodbye. As Matharzan exited the hut, so did the presence. Instructing the Fireflies to guard his entrance and allow no further visitors,

Aarus closed his eyes, reaching out and offering an opportunity for his daughter to return and present herself. She did not respond. Sadness filled him. In all the years that Aniese had exiled herself to the Shadow Forest, this was the first time she had travelled out of body back to the Ancient Forest. Aarus was not concerned about what she had heard, for it would have meant nothing to her. What saddened him was that she would have seen Matharzan in the hut. Aarus knew that Matharzan's return to the Ancient Forest would have felt like a betrayal to her.

Aarus recalled that fateful day so many years ago. He had never fully understood what had happened to Ourelia. One moment she had stood among the Guardians, gallantly fighting in the battle that had caught them unawares. The next moment she was laying on the ground, her neck twisted, her arms and legs grotesquely distorted as if caught in a whirlwind that had torn her bones from their very sockets. Aniese was the first to find her, followed by himself and Matharzan. He would always remember the look on Aniese's face – her vacant expression. He knew that a piece of her very soul had left at that moment, brutally torn away. He also knew that she and Ourelia had fought earlier – over what he wasn't sure, but he guessed that it had something to do with Matharzan. He knew that both of his daughters had loved the King. He also was painfully aware that they had seldom fought in their lives. It had saddened him deeply when he found out it was their last communication before Ourelia's death. The breaking point for Aniese had not only been Ourelia's death but Matharzan's open display of grief upon finding her dead. It had been more than Aniese could bear.

Matharzan was certain that Straeger had been behind the attack and Ourelia's subsequent death, for he knew that the

Ambassador of the Gyrangers had tried relentlessly to win Ourelia's affections. The King of the Were-Griffins had gone mad after seeing Ourelia's body, turning his wrath on the Gyranger who had been a guest of the Ancient Forest that day. Straeger had tried to retreat, fearful of the enraged Were-Griffin. In his grief, Matharzan had mistakenly attempted to take control of Straeger's exit portal. In trying to halt its closure, he had caused it to implode, leaking harmful emissions of radiation that had damaged anything close to the gateway.

Aniese was among many who were affected, burned beyond recognition. In time, Elder Mendalese was able to mend her burns, but she discontinued treatment before her mind could fully heal. She was never the same, withdrawing into herself and becoming more and more argumentative. Without the badly needed healing, she became a shell of her former self. Aarus knew that like Matharzan, something had died within Aniese that day. Aarus was not surprised the morning he had found out that Aniese had left the Forest. He was devastated to learn that she had retreated to the Shadow Forest, a toxic place filled with the contaminated overflow of the explosion. For years he had sought communication with her, and for years she had declined. He had never tried to visit her – there was too much risk for him in the Shadow Forest.

Not for the first time, he shook his head and wondered how a moment in time could change one's life forever? He had lost two daughters that day, and his dear, sweet Kerri one year earlier. They had been the light of his life, what had given him meaning each day that he awoke. His next breath came out as a shudder as he tried to contain his distressing thoughts. Would his heart ever stop aching?

Closing his eyes, he focused his mind and sent out the message, initiating contact with his longtime friend, Monserat.

CHAPTER 19

The Death of a Friend

Elder Tenor huddled under his dark robe, careful not to reveal his face. As nondescript as he was, he was still an Elder of the Ancient Forest, a position which came with responsibilities and protocols. Keeping his identity hidden was important, which was why he did not want his travel to the planet Marsa and more specifically the city of Starai, to be public knowledge. He was here to negotiate information off of the black market.

Elder Aarus never begrudged Tenor's ingenious attempts to acquire the information he was seeking, but he always expected discreetness. One positive aspect of Tenor's quiet demeanour was that very few were aware of the extraordinary network of informants he had created over the years. Even fewer were aware of his adeptness at covert activities. Small in stature, with mousy, unruly, brown hair, and eyes that appeared twice their size due to the thickness of his lenses, he did not stand out in a crowd, going unnoticed as he discreetly listened to conversations and gathered information.

These days Elder Tenor was deeply troubled and plagued with

restlessness. Since hearing of the visions Atalia had witnessed in *Atarashara*, there was a niggling feeling at the back of his mind. If asked what it meant, he would that said that time was running out. As the librarian of the Ancient Forest, he felt solely responsible for keeping the stories and histories of the Forest safe. Any threat to their security deeply disturbed him. As a result, he was determined to find a way to eliminate the danger foretold by Atalia. So far he had been unsuccessful.

In addition, he had been asked by Princess Hana to discover how the Gyrangers knew of Sarah's existence and more importantly why they wanted to capture her. He had taken to this task like a Firefly seeking out nectar. For weeks he had discreetly canvassed his informants, seeking information that would shed any light on why the Gyrangers were willing to risk a battle with the Ancient Forest over a thirteen-year-old girl. This search had been more successful. Today he was to find out, having been promised that an answer had been found – for an extraordinary price of course. Not surprising given how dangerous obtaining the information had been.

Tenor had consulted Aarus who hadn't argued with the price. Seeking information on the Gyrangers was a risky venture and one that put the seeker in peril. Gyrangers had no qualms disposing of anyone asking questions about them.

Moving away from the street and looking through the dark shadows that lined the alley where the meeting was to take place, Tenor saw a tall figure clad in a dark green robe. Tenuously approaching the creature, the Elder began to speak, the high pitch of his voice betraying his nervousness.

"Greetings to you, Faramir. Long has it been since we met. Do you have the information that I sought?"

The dark figure's only response was a nod of its head before drawing its cloak aside to reveal a cylinder that it pulled from its belt and handed to Tenor. Tenor glanced down at the hand that had only four fingers, each edged with talons. That was the only piece of the creature's physical identity that he had ever seen. Not hesitating, he pulled a bag of gold from his pocket and handed it over.

"Beware, Elder," hissed Faramir. "You must return immediately to the Ancient Forest. The Gyrangers have been tracking me since I obtained it and they are not far away. I will distract them so you can seek safety, but you must move quickly."

Tenor's heart began to beat wildly as he quickly nodded his head up and down. He was a gatherer of knowledge, not a fighter. He knew that Faramir was going far beyond duty in protecting him and would speak to Aarus about further compensation.

Bowing once to the tall creature he turned to move back toward the main street, his pace hurried. As he drew near the entrance of the alley, he heard the familiar sound of a portal opening. Looking back, he saw Faramir square off with two Gyrangers that had just emerged from the portal. One looked Tenor's way and started forward, but Faramir blocked it.

Tenor felt sick. He did not want to leave the creature who had risked so much to help the Ancient Forest, but knew that he could add no physical support if he stayed. Assisting in the only way possible, Tenor fingered the tiny pebble in his pocket that opened a mind link to Aarus, and sent a message – *two Gyrangers! Danger! HELP!* He then began to run, more than aware that he was in peril. Not worrying about being discreet, he wove in and out of crowds, thankful that his small stature concealed him.

Tenor had travelled for many of the city's long blocks before pausing. Out of breath, he approached a vendor's wagon, quickly climbing onto the wheel to look above the heads of the crowd for the Gyranger. He saw it almost immediately, paling when he realized how close the creature was *and* that it had also seen him. Not only did the Gyranger begin to move faster, but a path began to clear as others recognized that the deadly monster was on a hunt.

Fear coursed through Tenor, for he should have been able to lose the creature. Was it possible that the cylinder that Faramir had passed to him was a beacon, marking his presence? Tenor knew that he could not possibly win a fight against a Gyranger. Never fearing death before, he wondered if he had gambled too far today. Turning right, he ran down an alley, hoping to find a backdoor exit. He was unaware of the dark shadowed figure that noiselessly entered the lane immediately after him.

Too late Tenor realized that the alley came to a dead end. Spinning, he began running back to the street. Abruptly he was stopped as arms roughly lifted him off the ground slamming him backward, a hand covering his mouth. He froze, unable to move or speak. He knew he was about to die.

"Do not say a word," said Atalia softly, her breathing sure and steady.

Continuing to hold him tightly against her, she moved further into a recessed doorway that he had not noticed in his panicked state. It did not completely hide their presence, but it made it possible to overlook it. Struggling to calm his breath, Tenor continued to hang limply; his mind grappling with the fact that he wasn't going to die. He tried to stand, but his legs betrayed him, unable to hold him up.

A second later the Gyranger came into view, gliding silently across the doorway. A feeling of terror shot through Tenor, and he began to shake. When the Gyranger stopped, he knew that once again his presence had been detected. As the creature slowly turned its head toward the darkened recess, Tenor felt

Atalia release her hold on him and shift her body, quietly loosening her sword from its scabbard. He bent his still shaking legs, ready to throw himself to the side so as not to impede the First's movements.

The Gyranger turned its body to face the recess where they hid, lifting up both of its blackened hands. The clicking of its pinchers betrayed the creature's excitement. It knew its prey was cornered and was ready to move in for the kill.

Atalia did not hesitate, releasing the dark cloak she wore around her neck and drawing her sword as she stepped out of the darkness to meet the Gyranger.

It hissed upon seeing her. It had not anticipated encountering the First. Stepping back hastily it also withdrew a sword, its pinchers continuing to click off rapid staccato pulses.

Tenor watched the Gyranger rear up in front of Atalia, and his heart wept. He did not doubt the First's ability to fight, but she looked far too small in comparison to the six-foot monster. Looking past her into the creature's eyes, Tenor was stopped short by the evil that shone from them. He could not bear to watch. Burying his head in his knees, he held the cylinder tightly as he closed his eyes and huddled in the darkness.

The sound of metal clashed as they moved away from the doorway. Tenor knew that the Gyranger would seek to fight earnestly, hoping to wear the First down. He also knew that he needed to do more than hide in the darkness, but his fear imprisoned him, making it hard to think clearly. He knew he needed to try harder, but he simply was not brave. Standing on still shaky legs, he forced himself to open his eyes and take a step forward, but not before he heard a strangled sound, followed by abrupt silence. Knowing that one of the two fighters was injured, he slowly peered into the alley. Atalia lay on the ground, her head raised toward the Gyranger who was slowly lifting its sword in the air, enjoying the moment as it prepared to strike.

Tenor's fear fled as he registered what was about to happen. Running toward the Gyranger, he screamed, rage filling his mind. As he neared the creature, his right leg buckled in pain, and for the second time, arms pulled him back and held him tightly. Tenor stared in astonishment as the Gyranger shot up into the air. The creature's limbs splayed outward as a green glow spread around its form before bursting from its abdomen. A moment later, the severed spirit of the Gyranger stepped outside of its body before floating upward and disappearing. Its body hit the ground, disintegrating into ashes.

Standing behind the mound of ashes was Prince Drake, the Emerald Sword glowing brightly in his hands. His eyes quickly scanned the darkened alley, affirming that Atalia and Tenor were alone. Moving forward, the Prince reached down and pulled Tenor to his feet, bending to dust off the Elder's cloak.

Tenor's mouth opened, but nothing came out. He continued to hold onto the Prince's hand, not even turning when he heard movement behind him. A moment later, Atalia spoke.

"Thank you for trying to save me, Tenor, but I had to stop you as there was no need. I was feigning injury to distract the Gyranger. You are brave, Elder."

Still, in shock, Tenor's next words were barely a whisper.

"I ... am not ... so brave."

Atalia continued to stare at him but did not respond. Turning to her brother, she said, "It took you long enough."

"You were handling it beautifully," answered Drake, a smile lighting up his sombre face as the battle fierceness began to leave his eyes. "And we both know you would have managed it without me."

"Yes, I would have," she said, "but I am glad you were here.

What *did* take you so long?"

"I had to dispose of the other Gyranger. I am sorry, Elder Tenor, but your friend did not make it. In trying to protect you … his life was lost."

"He wasn't my friend; he was an infor …"

Tenor stopped speaking, dismayed at the words that he had been about to say. Faramir had given his life for the tiny Elder. Tenor began to shake. He knew that his face betrayed his churning emotions for Atalia stepped forward and put her arm around his shoulder.

Her uncharacteristic display of empathy surprised him, causing the cylinder to drop from his hand. The lid released as it hit the ground. Out slid a thin piece of white paper, scratches of hastily written words on it. Adjusting his glasses on his nose, Tenor bent over to read the writing on the paper. The sharp intake of breath and the swearing behind him told him that Atalia had done the same thing. Standing to look at her, he was unaware that his eyes were as round as saucers, enlarged even more by the thickness of his lenses.

"*First*," he cried, "*we must get back to the Ancient Forest, immediately!*"

"Tenor, open a mind link to Aarus," she responded sharply. "Tell him that Sarah mustn't leave the Forest. Drake, the portal, NOW!"

As she finished speaking the portal shimmered into life. Grabbing Tenor's hand, Drake pulled him through the gateway, Atalia close behind.

CHAPTER 20

The Worst Kind of Betrayal

Sarah sat across from Aarus on the dirt floor of his hut; her backpack pushed to the side. She was alone with the Sage, for Dineah and Tazor were still preparing to leave for the planet Oorse. Sir Perity was sitting outside with Eblie, and Sheblie, and the Firefly guards. She could hear the gargoyles talking animatedly, and smiled to herself. She wondered if their entire race was as chatty as the three brothers who had pledged allegiance to her safety and well-being, and who she had come to cherish.

Sarah was selfishly enjoying having Aarus's company to herself. As much as she loved all of her mentors, it was the Sage's powerful but gentle and compassionate nature that felt the most comfortable to her. Sarah knew how the beings of the Forest respected him, and that many were in awe, perhaps even fearful of him. She was not afraid of Aarus at all. Instead, Sarah felt profoundly safe with him. She also knew that her mom, who had known the Sage all her life, loved and trusted him.

On more than one occasion, when Sarah had been with the

Fairies, either sketching or pouring through her journals, she had observed them become silent as they watched Aarus move through the Forest. It was at that time that she had learned of the now legendary story of Aarus's courage and wisdom on the day that she had crossed to the Ancient Forest. The Fairies had spoken in a whisper, reverence in their voices as they recited how the tiny Sage had stood up to the Guardians, refusing them exit from the Ancient Forest to go to the aid of the Song Bearer. They said that he had used his willpower to stop the giant sentinels from crossing through the portal to their deaths. The Guardians had lashed out, furious at being opposed, but never once harming the Elder. Then, despite the chaos and frenzy, he had shown the foresight to utter the necessary ancient words of welcome that had ensured King Matharzan-Ariebe's safety within the Ancient Forest.

As Sarah watched the aged Elder who sat across from her, his eyes closed, palms upon his knees, she was acutely aware of the rare gifts he had granted her in their time of study together. In particular, her new ability to project her consciousness out of body. She knew this was not customary. Only Seekers, those destined to roam the other realms and seek knowledge for the higher good of all, learned this skill. She did not understand why Aarus had gifted her with this teaching. She still recalled his response when she had asked him.

It is not always necessary to know things at each moment, child – you will understand when the time is right.

Aarus's proximity reminded Sarah of what Dineah had disclosed about his family. A feeling of sadness engulfed her.

"Aarus," she said quietly.

"Starchild."

"I ... "

Pausing, she suddenly felt uncomfortable. Not knowing

what to say or how to say it, she blurted out her next words.

"I'm sorry about what happened to your family."

For a long time, Aarus did not reply, his breathing steady.

But Sarah had felt a shift in his presence when she had spoken. As he slowly opened his eyes, she found herself drawn to the brilliance of the cloudy blue eye that was the gateway to the world of spirit. Her sensitivity as the Starchild of *Atarashara* enabled her to look deeply into it and witness the complex layers of sorrow that her words had evoked. She regretted having spoken. Not sure what to say next, she awkwardly continued, her words tumbling out.

"I ... I don't know what I would do if my mom died. I can't imagine what it was like for you. What ... what happened? I mean, I know some of it because Dineah told me, but what happened to your wife?"

Aarus continued to stare at her without saying a word. Although she was asking about the most painful period of his life, he was struck by the sincerity and innocence in her voice. Sighing deeply, he spoke.

"I should not be surprised that this is happening. Nothing should surprise me with one born in *Atarashara*. I would not normally share my thoughts on this matter with anyone, and yet the fact that we are alone, and that you have been moved to ask me these questions tells me not to take it lightly. And oddly, child, you are somehow linked to it, given your origins. I now understand why Matharzan says you challenge him to his core."

"Grif says I challenge him to his core! That's not true!" squealed Sarah, indignant at Aarus's comment.

Aarus began to chuckle.

"Yes, his comment is completely unfair given how quiet and orderly you always are."

"I'm quiet! Well ... not always, and ... he said I challenge him to his core?"

Sarah's face reddened with embarrassment, but she found it hard to stay angry as Aarus continued to laugh. Trying to suppress a smile, she attempted to look sternly at the Elder.

"Calm now, child; you are the best thing to have happened to the Were-Griffin in a long time ... but don't tell him I said that."

"But ..."

"Enough. Let me answer your question, for the time draws near for you to leave. I will be brief as it is not easy for me to speak of this. My wife, Kerri, was a renowned healer, equalled only by Elder Aczartar himself. On more than one occasion, her compassionate nature drew her healing skills outside of the Karrian Galaxy, particularly when it affected large masses. It was this very occasion that summoned her to a planet called Hearse. A rare plague had begun to spread, leaving its victims with unusual physical deformities and mental deterioration, followed by a slow, painful death. Kerri felt that there was something unnatural about the plague, and questioned its origins. Her attempts to find out more about it resulted in a barring of information by the leaders of Hearse, and the abrupt termination of her services."

"She returned home shortly after that, but the Forest's alarms erupted upon her arrival. She was infected and a carrier, making her presence dangerous to all within the Forest. Elder Aczartar was devastated at having to place her in quarantine. Her ability to speak declined almost immediately, but not before she made an unusual request. She asked to enter the sacred gateway and die in *Atarashara*, claiming that in doing so, the sanctuary of the portal ensured no one else could be infected. This type of request was unheard of, but when Monserat, the High Priestess of Oorse, made the request, *Atarashara* sanctioned it. I have always felt there was more to this incident than meets the eye, but even as the Forest's Sage, have never been able to discern what happened once Kerri entered the portal to die. That was the last day my daughters and I ever saw her."

Silence filled the hut as Aarus finished speaking. Sarah wanted to respond but didn't know what to say given the gravity of what Aarus had just shared. The interruption of a Firefly guard announcing Princess Hana's arrival drew the moment to an end. Impulsively jumping up, Sarah threw her arms around Aarus, hugging him tightly for a moment before reseating herself.

"I am sorry for all the awful things that have happened to your family, Aarus. I will not forget what you have told me about Kerri. And … I'm sorry to have made you sad."

Closing his eyes, Aarus nodded his head in acknowledgement of Sarah's words.

"Be at peace, Starchild. Now go, as it is time for you to travel to the planet Oorse and begin your next level of studies. I will be in daily communication with Monserat to check on your development and to determine when you will be returning to the Ancient Forest."

Bowing her head in respect, Sarah gathered her backpack and left the hut to join Hana. She was not aware that Aarus continued to stare at the cloth flap that she had exited through for a very long time, lost in thought.

~

Matharzan stood in front of the shimmering portal, ready to escort Sarah to Oorse. He surveyed the accompanying entourage, struck by the unlikely blend of allies who had once again, without question, agreed to ensure her safety. Sir Perity sat in Sarah's arms, purring as she rubbed his chin. Dineah and Tazor held their usual positions on her shoulders, not unlike Eblie and Sheblie who were on Matharzan's shoulders. There had been some question as to whether the Song Bearer should leave the Ancient Forest, but given that Oorse was the Forest's close ally, arrangements had been by Aarus and Monserat to ensure that the giant sentinels could retain an active connection to her from afar.

At times Matharzan found himself shaking his head, wondering when his stern, unfeeling shell of a character had started to change? He attributed it to being with the Starchild, and because he was back in the Ancient Forest. Although the Forest held the most painful memories of his life, being here again had finally allowed his heart to open and heal. One could not stay shut down amidst the vibrant life and energy that permeated the hub of the Karrian Galaxy.

Becoming Sarah's guardian had also reawakened a sense of purpose for the Were-Griffin. Her innocent, yet defiant youthfulness challenged him. In fact, at times she pushed him to his limits! He hadn't realized how much he had longed for this until now. In return he demanded a lot from her, challenging her back, making her responsible for her actions, her beliefs, and her magic. Sometimes they would disagree, and he would push her even further, but in the process, Sarah was finding whole pieces of herself that had lain dormant on Fairy Lane. She was a child of *Atarashara* – filled with gifts and knowledge and possibilities that she had not yet even begun to tap. Matharzan understood this. He also knew that he was a good mentor. He knew when it was time to allow Sarah space for introspection; using her drawing and music to integrate the changes and the new life that had been thrust upon her.

His commitment to always be brutally honest with her had forged a profound trust between them.

Continuing to take stock of the travel party he noticed that Bohn, Sabrae, and Wisteria had fanned themselves around Sarah, all but invisible in their black robes with hoods drawn. Silverspear and Hana were next in line, facing each other as they engaged in a telepathic dialogue. Matharzan knew that Hana's unexpected presence was because of Atalia's absence. Both the First and Drake had been drawn abruptly away without explanation by Aarus. Matharzan briefly wondered if he should be worried. Just as quickly he pushed the thought from his mind, knowing that Aarus would inform him of anything that could impact the safety of the Starchild. Lastly, four Legion members made up the rear of the guard. Atalia had handpicked these men, herself. They stood without moving, but Matharzan knew them to be constantly vigilant. He remembered these men from years before; they were the best.

Matharzan had met briefly with Aarus, who was staying alert to the outcome of Elder Tenor's meeting, the contents of which the Were-Griffin would learn upon his arrival to Oorse. Given the high level of security both in the Ancient Forest and awaiting them on Oorse, there was no fear that the resulting information could compromise their mission. Matharzan hoped that Tenor's expedition would illuminate the Gyranger's unhealthy interest in the Starchild.

Clearing his throat, Matharzan prepared to speak but was interrupted when static and sounds of murmuring came from behind him. Turning, he watched in surprise as the light of the portal dimmed and jagged streaks of energy shot across it. Removing Eblie and Sheblie from his shoulders, he stepped closer, turning his ear toward the flickering gateway.

Odd, he thought, *I'm sure that I heard voices coming from inside here.*

Moving even closer he continued to listen, but there was nothing further. Interference with the portal was impossible given that Aarus was its creator. Only the initiator or someone of the same blood could alter an existing gateway. He knew this only too well given the results of tampering with Straeger's portal years earlier. He did not allow his mind to wander any further down that painful track.

He continued to watch the portal closely for several more minutes. When nothing further happened, he decided that it was one more of the anomalies that were occurring in the Forest these days – things that were unexplained. Aarus assured him that this was not uncommon following the foreshadowing of the war song.

Returning his attention to the group of beings escorting Sarah, he watched as conversation ceased and everyone gave him their full attention. He also noticed concern on Princess Hana's face. He knew that she would need more assurance once they had landed safely in Oorse. He understood her constant worry. Clearing his throat again, he addressed the group.

"We will enter the portal and cross to Oorse in the same order that you are currently standing. Monserat's guards will be waiting for us upon our arrival. I want this to occur quickly and efficiently. Although we should not anticipate any danger, we must keep our guard up. Protecting Sarah is of the utmost importance. Sarah – step in line behind me, with Sir Perity, Eblie, and Sheblie at your rear."

Sarah stepped away from the witches and moved closer to Matharzan as she placed Sir Perity on the ground. Sir Perity immediately took up position behind her, Eblie and Sheblie hovering in the air directly above him. Dineah and Tazor remained on her shoulders.

"I stay on Sarah's shoulder. I protect her with my life," Tazor announced solemnly in his gravelly voice.

Eblie and Sheblie nodded their heads vigorously in agreement. The gargoyles and Sir Perity were Sarah's first line of defence.

Looking toward the rear of the guard, Matharzan made eye contact with Silverspear and Princess Hana before nodding at the four guards who each acknowledged him with a response. Turning, he jumped through the portal, anticipating the lush fields of Oorse, a planet he has visited on more than one occasion. Emerging on the other side, he fell to his knees, noxious fumes stinging his eyes and burning his lungs, forcing him to cover his mouth. Struggling to rise and warn the others he stumbled and fell again, unable to see through the tears pouring from his eyes. Moving back toward the portal, he blindly began to scramble on all fours but was stopped by the sound of growling. *Tazor!*

"Tazor – where is the Starchild?" he gasped, struggling to speak because of the fumes.

"I protect her and the Song Bearer, King Matharzan," said the gargoyle in a deadly calm voice that set Matharzan's nerves on edge. "They here with me. I okay with the fumes – they no bother me. I guard until you can see again."

Matharzan knew that something was very wrong. Anger surged through him as he struggled to gain control of his senses. As he listened to Sarah coughing, he blindly moved toward her, wiping at his eyes until he was able to focus. To his dismay he saw that they were in a clearing, surrounded by what appeared to be a haze. He realized that this was the cause of the toxic fumes. Matharzan watched as it began to clear away, slowly revealing Sarah's form. She sat huddled on the ground with her head tucked into her chest, still coughing sporadically. Dineah stood quietly on her shoulder, her face grey and her glow light dimmed. Looking about, he found Tazor several feet away, rigid as a statue and poised to attack.

Dismay filled him as he realized that no other guardians had made their way through the portal. For the first time, he also registered that the gateway had disappeared. Fear slowly wormed its way into his stomach. Looking around again, he noticed that as the smog had cleared, pinpoints of light had created a circle around the four of them. The lights reminded him of Fireflies ... grossly deformed Fireflies with long strands that trailed behind them, radiating a fluorescent glow. *Where in the Great Mother's name were they?*

"Matharzan, it has been many years," said a voice that he knew instantly. Emerging from the darkness was a single, ghost-like figure. He watched her gently caress the last strands of haze before pushing them away. He no longer had any doubt where he was, or who was controlling the toxic mist.

"Aniese, *what have you done!*" he rasped, his throat raw and painful.

"What have I done? It's time for retribution," she said, cackling as she moved forward, her body becoming clearer in the light produced by the Fireflies.

Like the Fireflies, something about her was ... off.

"Retribution for what?" snarled Matharzan.

Anger rang through Aniese's voice.

"For what? You destroyed my life! You took everything that was important away from me! You shattered my relationship with my sister!" Breathing hard, she turned away.

Matharzan could hear Aniese continuing to speak, but to whom he didn't know. He watched as she wrapped her arms around her body as if protecting herself, and then turned back to him, her face slack.

"Do you remember, Matharzan?" she asked, her voice vulnerable and childlike.

When he didn't reply, she lunged toward him, yelling the next words into his face.

"DO YOU, MATHARZAN? DO YOU REMEMBER?"

Aniese began to wail, rocking her body back and forth, trying to control the battle waging within her. She had waited so long for this moment – to have him in front of her, to tear him apart, to make him hurt for all of the pain that she felt. But being near him again had brought back the other feelings, the ones that had initially drawn her to him.

"King of Were-Griffins!" whispered Tazor urgently. "Something broken. Don't let her go bye-bye. Bring her back! Keep her here, Matharzan!"

Matharzan didn't understand what Tazor was saying, but he tried to gain Aniese's attention nonetheless.

"You know that I did not kill Ourelia. You know that, Aniese! Something else did, and then the body was gone. *Aniese! What have you done here today?*"

Aniese abruptly stopped rocking, the tone of the Were-Griffin's voice cutting through the chaos that had threatened to consume her mind. As her eyes focused on Matharzan, her mind cleared, a brief respite of clarity.

"Aniese, I don't know what you have done, but you have to return me to the Forest, immediately. I know how difficult this has been for you. We can talk more about this, and I will do whatever is in my power to make it up to you, but right now I *must* get this girl back to your father. He created the portal, so you have the power to reopen it. Please! Open the ..."

Matharzan paused.

"It was you that I heard, wasn't it? It was your voice that I heard through the portal? You somehow altered it."

"Yes, me … and others," said Aniese in a clear, flat voice that unnerved the King. "You know, for years I thought I would feel better when this moment happened, but I don't. Why couldn't you love me, Matharzan? Why did you choose my sister? You nev …"

Aniese stopped talking as the Were-Griffin finished her train of thought.

"… ver loved you," said Matharzan in a quiet voice. "No Aniese, I never did. I truly wish I could say what you want to hear, but it would be a lie."

"And you could never lie," said Aniese.

Her knees folded and she dropped awkwardly to the ground as if the Were-Griffin's admission had drained all of her energy.

"You will never love me. Finally, after all these years I have heard it from your mouth."

As quickly as she had collapsed, Aniese rose to stand, erect and proud.

Matharzan's breath caught. Ourelia used to stand the same way.

In an eerily calm voice, Aniese said, "What have I done here today? I could say that I have sold my soul, but my soul left a long time ago … because of you. I have made a deal with the Gyrangers, Matharzan. They want this child, and in return, I get you … whom I wanted to see dead …"

As she spoke, she stroked her forearm. Matharzan could see a raised mark on her skin, shaped like a half moon. Aniese began to cry.

"You know, Matharzan, all that you would have had to say was that you loved me. It would have changed everything that is about to happen. Why couldn't you say it, just this once?"

As Matharzan looked into Aniese's eyes, he could tell that there was no madness. At that moment she was utterly lucid ... and vulnerable. Sadness swept over him as he was forced to recall the tragic story that was theirs.

"I am sorry, Aniese. I truly am."

"I believe you," she said sadly, "and for that, I love you even more."

Touching her forearm again, he watched her fingers stop at the mark and press it.

"Goodbye, Matharzan. I no longer have any desire to kill you, nor do I want to be reminded of what I can never have. I know you will fight to the death to protect this child and if you somehow bypass that, the Shadow Forest will quickly rectify it. I will not protect you from it again."

Turning away from him, she watched as portal upon portal opened into the Shadow Forest. Her next words, softly spoken, were filled with sorrow.

"Matharzan," she paused. "It is well known that my mind never fully recovered from the blast and that it is ... frail. At this moment, I am clear in my thinking. I want you to know that my next words come from a place of truth. Tell my father that I love him ... and that I am truly sorry for the pain my actions will cause him. I also want you to know that I will continue to hate you as much as I love you. The two emotions are so strongly entwined within me that after all the years of feeding them both, I can no longer separate one from the other. What I will do though, is demonstrate my love for you, one last time."

Closing her eyes and focusing her mind, she spoke words quietly.

Matharzan did not understand what Aniese was doing, his mind too intent on the influx of Gyrangers filling the Shadow Forest.

"Tazor," he commanded, "protect Sarah at all costs!"

Glancing behind him he saw Sarah standing quietly, her eyes fearful but resolute, Dineah standing tall on her shoulder.

"Dineah – hide," whispered Matharzan so that Aniese could not hear. "Hide in Sarah's hair. No one must know who you are or that you are here. Sarah – be prepared to fight! You have been taught by the best. Do not allow yourself to be injured. If we have to surrender to protect your life, we will!"

Matharzan watched as a small figure stepped out of the nearest portal. The Queen of the Gyrangers.

Great Mother, he thought. *Could this get any worse!*

"I have delivered my side of the bargain, Queen; you best not forget what you have agreed to," said Aniese, laughing manically and stumbling to the side.

Matharzan started. Quickly glancing at her, he could tell that the Aniese of only a moment ago was gone, taken over by the darkness that she had valiantly keep at bay. Spittle flew from her mouth.

"I will follow through on that promise, but not until the Starchild is securely in my hands. You have done well, Aniese."

"Do not compliment me, Queen," she spat, her frenzied laughter stopping as quickly as it had started. "You are vile! Your words mean nothing to me. Mark my words, Graziel, I *will* hold you true to your promise."

Turning, Aniese stumbled again as she left the clearing and followed a path into the Forest while babbling to herself.

Tears welled up in Tazor's eyes as he watched Aniese depart. He alone knew that she was pretending her madness. It was as if the arrival of the Gyrangers had strengthened her determination, allowing her to hold herself together for just a little while longer. He recognized only too well the chaos that reigned in Aarus's youngest daughter's mind. Because he continued to watch her depart, he was the only one who witnessed Aniese's last conscious expression of love. As she neared the Forest's edge, she paused quietly, making small motions with her fingers before disappearing into the dark, stale foliage. The Gyranger Queens next words abruptly brought the gargoyle's attention back to the clearing.

"Hand her over, Matharzan. You cannot protect her against my forces. Let us do this peacefully."

Flexing his wings, Matharzan took a fighting stance, unwilling to stand down.

"There is nothing peaceful about this, Graziel. You have taken advantage of Aniese's vulnerability and used it to turn her against the Ancient Forest. I didn't think you could stoop any lower. Was this your idea, Graziel, or the worm, Straeger's?"

"Why Matharzan, you're assuming that Straeger is once again in my company," purred the Gyranger Queen.

"And you are correct, Matharzan," said Straeger, as he moved out of the darkness from behind her, a smile splitting his grotesque features.

Hatred boiled through Matharzan's veins.

"I will not hand her over, Graziel, to you or that coward behind you."

The Were-Griffin did not even turn as he heard yet another portal opening behind him, knowing that Gyrangers were continuing to teleport into the Shadow Forest. He did not care, his mind consumed with seeking revenge on the creature that had killed Ourelia and was now planning to harm the Starchild. So absorbed was he in his hatred that it took a moment to register the sound he had just heard. As a rage-filled snarl exploded throughout the Shadow Forest, the orange blur of *Atarashara's* guardian landed to his right, slamming into Gyrangers and ripping them apart with his deadly fangs and claws. Quickly looking over his shoulder, Matharzan saw the First and the Legion pouring through, accompanied by Prince Drake and masses of Fireflies, Dragonflies and their Fairy riders. His mind briefly registered Eblie and Sheblie swiftly moving through the ranks, their heads scanning back and forth.

Great Mother, he thought, *the portal to the Ancient Forest has reopened.*

Turning back, he could no longer see the Gyranger Queen. Desperately looking around, he tried to locate Straeger, and then Sarah, barely stopping the pinchers of a Gyranger from attaching onto his neck. Sweeping it aside only resulted in two more taking its place, joined by a third Gyranger to his right. As he turned to square off with all of them, he saw white hooves move through the air, striking the Gyranger on his right. Matharzan watched Silverspear rear up a second time. He could feel the fury emanating from the King of the Equines. The white of the horse's eyes showed as he bared his teeth, and lunged at the other two Gyrangers.

Matharzan immediately began to search for Sarah again. He briefly felt a sense of relief upon seeing her, but then frantically screamed to warn her as he watched the Gyranger Queen slowly approach the girl from behind. Despair filled the Were-Griffin as he witnessed Graziel grasp Sarah's shoulder and turn her. As the Gyranger Queen blew into the Starchild's face, Sarah gasped and clutched her throat before collapsing.

Pushing wildly, Matharzan tried to make his way to Sarah, but he could not break through the frenzy. He watched as Tazor, who was ferociously using his claws and teeth to fight off a Gyranger, was forced apart from Sarah. The Were-Griffin then saw Straeger strike Tazor from behind, causing the tiny guardian to drop to the ground and disappear.

Roaring in frustration the Were-Griffin tried to use the

razor-sharp tips of his wings to sweep an opening around him, but to no avail. Helpless, he watched Straeger lift the unconscious body of the Starchild, while Gyrangers created a circle around him and the Gyranger Queen, clearing a path to the nearest portal. As they leapt through, the portal winked shut.

Matharzan became crazed. *He had failed!* Time slowed down as he met attack after attack. At one point both Atalia and Drake with the Emerald Sword covered his back, in the next moment Sir Perity fought beside him. As exhaustion threatened to overtake him, he finally noticed an open circle of space around him and realized that the fighting had stopped. His eyes moved quickly around the clearing, seeking out Tazor. Where was the gargoyle? Had he withstood the force of Straeger's blow? He saw others also searching – Hana running with Eblie and Sheblie through the debris, calling Sarah's name. Sir Perity standing in one spot as his head moved back and forth, his inner senses scanning for Sarah's presence. Matharzan's heart ached to watch it all.

"She is no longer here," he cried out. "She was taken by Straeger and the Queen. I am sorry. I have failed you all!"

Sir Perity let out a deafening roar, his head raised in the air. Matharzan knew that the giant cat's heart was breaking, as was Hana's. She stood utterly still, not saying a word, and covering her face with her hands. Prince Drake moved quickly to her side, but it was Atalia who grabbed her by the shoulders and began speaking urgently to her, shaking her roughly. Turning away from her sister, Atalia ran to where Matharzan was standing.

"Quickly, Matharzan, we have to get back to the Forest. I'll explain once we're there. Gather everyone up and move them through the portal. NOW! We have no time to waste."

Matharzan tried to force himself to move but knew he was in as much shock as everyone else.

Atalia grabbed his shoulder.

"It is not your fault, Matharzan. I'll explain once we are back in the Ancient Forest. We now know why the Gyrangers have abducted Sarah. We have no time to waste."

"I will gather the others, Atalia, but first, we have to search for Tazor. He is either dead or injured. I cannot leave him in this place. Take Hana with you, and leave me with the others. We will be along as quickly as we can."

Atalia closed her eyes for a moment, pain and frustration written on her face. Sighing, she nodded her head curtly and turned to go.

"First," said the Were-Griffin. "There is one more thing you need to know. The last I saw of the Song Bearer, she was hiding in the Starchild's hair. I think that the Gyrangers have both the Starchild and the Song Bearer."

Atalia's face paled.

"Great Mother," she gasped, "the Forest!"

Raising her voice Atalia shouted sharp commands to the gathered forces to return to the Ancient Forest. She then ran toward Hana and Drake. A moment later, the three siblings sprinted to the portal, leaping through at a dead run.

Looking grim, the Were-Griffin made his way to the three witches who were huddled together; their eyes closed as they held onto the amulets that contained Sarah's blood. He knew they were trying to sense her presence.

"Where is she?" he asked.

"We don't know where she is. We believe that she is alive but unresponsive," said Wisteria.

"She is. I saw the Gyranger Queen render her unconscious."

A shocked silence followed his words. Finally, Bohn spoke.

"That explains what we are sensing. We are careful not to probe too deeply as we don't want to risk revealing our presence. Sarah feels distanced from us by some form of barrier, but it is not penetrating the protective shield of our magic."

"Witches, we must return to the Ancient Forest as soon as possible," said Matharzan. "Atalia has information on why the Gyrangers want Sarah, but first, I need your skills to locate Tazor who was injured in the battle and is lying somewhere on the Forest floor. I do not know if he is alive or not – I have to admit, I fear the worst from what I witnessed."

"Oh," gasped Sabrae, her hand moving to cover her mouth. Concern filled her gentle brown eyes.

The witches began searching immediately, using their sensing skills to try and detect Tazor's presence under the mounds of Gyrangers that littered the Forest floor.

Matharzan pulled Eblie and Sheblie aside, gently explaining what had happened to Tazor. Both gargoyles began to sob, devastated that their brother may be dead. With encouragement from Matharzan, they moved methodically through the air, shrilly calling out, knowing that Tazor would respond to the sound.

Everyone worked together to try and locate the tiny gargoyle – Silverspear using his hooves to paw down to the Forest floor, the witches casting sensing spells, and Sir Perity swatting the bodies of Gyrangers aside effortlessly. Try as they might, not one of was able to locate or feel Tazor. Filled with sadness at the outcome, the Were-Griffin drew the search to an end, advising that there was an urgent need to return to the Ancient Forest.

Both gargoyles wept as they sat on his broad shoulders, their shoulders shaking, and tears streaming down their faces. Bohn and Sabrae gently lifted them from Matharzan's shoulders, holding them close while they passed through the portal. Sir

Perity's tail continued to switch in agitation as he repeatedly moved his massive head back and forth. Growling, he leapt through the threshold, the hair on his back and tail raised.

Once everyone had exited the Shadow Forest, Matharzan waited a moment longer before leaving. He stood motionless, layers of grief washing over him.

"Are you there, Aniese," he cried out.

No answer.

"I know that it is you who reopened the portal, Lady."

Still, there was no answer.

Turning to face the gateway, he stepped through to the Ancient Forest.

CHAPTER 21

The Crossroads

Dineah slowly crawled out from the nape of Sarah's neck, careful to stay hidden from view. Looking around, she gaped at the room of pristine white walls that shone with unnatural light and emitted a sterile odour, both alien and offensive to her senses that were so attuned to the earthy vegetation of the Ancient Forest. Sarah continued to lay unconscious on a flat, metal table that Dineah knew was cold to the touch. She had stood on it for only a moment before climbing back onto the warmth of Sarah's skin. Instinct told her not to speak out loud, and so Dineah continued to try and awaken Sarah through the mind link that they shared. She could feel Sarah's consciousness slowly return as she emerged from a dormant state. Dineah knew that the Gyranger Queen had used a toxic vapour to render Sarah immobile.

Dineah was troubled, not only because they were captive, but because by now the Ancient Forest would have sensed her absence. She knew this because it felt like her connection to the Guardians had been severed; she could not feel them at all.

Dineah, like everyone in the Forest, knew that the Song Bearer's presence was critical to the well-being of the Guardians. She had no idea what the full impact of her disappearance would be, but her sixth sense warned that the results would be catastrophic.

Sarah Starbright! Awaken Starchild; it is me, Dineah. Wake up, Sarah! Wake UP!

Sarah groaned and lifted her hand to her forehead.

Dineah knew that Sarah's head was pounding for she could feel the pressure through their mind link. She continued to bombard the Starchild with thoughts, knowing that she could not let Sarah slip back into a slumber.

Sarah Starbright, you are the child of Atarashara, manifested through Atalia, the First, and daughter of the Scarab King. Awaken Starchild. Release yourself from the grip of unnatural sleep. It is urgent that you awaken! You are in danger!

Sarah sat up abruptly, panic flooding through her. Breathing hard, she was unaware that she had almost dislodged Dineah.

Calm, Sarah, calm down. I am with you, but hidden. Do not speak aloud. This place feels ... different, as if the walls have ears. We cannot let them know that I am here.

Sarah listened to Dineah's voice, letting the steady flow of words settle inside her while she sought to get her bearings. The grogginess still had a tight grip on her, making her thoughts break apart and scatter. Sarah was thankful for Dineah's reassuring presence for it allowed her mind to focus.

Sarah tried to recall what had happened. Her last memories were of fighting in battle, surrounded by Gyrangers who she had desperately tried to keep at bay with blasting spells taught by Wisteria. She had succeeded at clearing a space around her. It was then that she had felt a firm hand on her shoulder. Thinking it was Matharzan, Sarah had turned ... only to look into the eyes of the beautiful woman who had arrived with the Gyrangers. Time had slowed down, and the sounds of battle had diminished as Sarah had been drawn in by those eyes, unable to think or act. And then she had felt both fear and dread as she watched the woman lift her hand to her mouth, blowing a gentle breath of air that smelled of decay and ...

You collapsed at that point, Sarah. That woman is the Queen of the Gyrangers. She appears human, but she is a shapeshifter. Don't be fooled. She carries the most lethal traits of the Gyrangers – she uses her eyes to hypnotize and paralyze her prey and then renders them unconscious with a harmful vapour that she releases from the glands in the roof of her mouth. Aarus warned me of this a short while ago.

Where are we Dineah? I feel so ... cut off, as if there is a wall between Atarashara and me. I can't sense any of the guardians, Dineah, not one of them!

Sarah's words only elevated Dineah's sensation of disconnect from the Ancient Forest. She quickly pushed the thoughts from her mind, not wanting Sarah to sense her fear.

Can you feel the protective shield of the witches?

Sarah answered slowly.

Yes, I can. I can feel it, but it is more ... I don't know ... subdued.

That is likely why you are already conscious. I think that without it the Queen's toxic gas would have impacted you far worse than it has. Focus your attention on the shield and try to sense Wisteria's presence. She is the strongest of the three.

Sarah was quiet for a long time. Finally, she let out a deep sigh, her shoulders falling forward.

I feel blocked, Dineah. It is like a wall I cannot penetrate. I will try to sing Silverspear's name, but I am certain ...

Don't, Sarah, said Dineah hurriedly. *Something here must be physically blocking you, and I have a feeling that the Queen controls it. Do not sing or speak Silverspear's name. It is best that the Gyrangers stay unaware of how you communicate with your guardians. The less they know the better.*

I am terrified, Dineah – for me, for you, and the others. What became of Matharzan and Tazor? Tears welled up in Sarah's eyes as she turned to look at the Song Bearer. *Do you think that they are alive, Dineah?*

Dineah could feel panic building in the Starchild. The Song Bearer breaths shortened and her heart pounded, as she struggled to distance herself from Sarah's emotions as they flooded the mind link. The Starchild's thoughts too closely echoed her own. Dineah vaguely recalled the portal to the Ancient Forest reopening but had seen little else from where she had hidden in Sarah's hair.

Listen to me, Sarah. We must figure out what the Gyrangers want with you and then we will find a way to escape. You are a child of Atarashara, and I am the Song Bearer. We are not without resources. Do not panic, Sarah! Stay strong and connected with me. Once we escape, we will find out what has happened to our friends.

But I can't even feel Atarashara, Dineah.

Once again Dineah guarded her emotions, for she knew that she could easily slip into the same hopelessness as what the Starchild was feeling. Fighting to stay calm she settled on Sarah's shoulder, sending waves of reassurance through their mind link. She barely hid her presence in time, as a door opened, and the Queen of the Gyrangers entered the room.

Don't look her in the eyes, Sarah.

Sarah quickly looked down, focusing on the floor in front of her.

"Well, child, you are resilient. I didn't expect you to be awake."

When Sarah refused to answer, Graziel continued to speak, her words direct and firm.

"Sarah, I needed to restrain you to gain control and bring you here. I knew that you would never accept an audience with me unless I distanced you away from Matharzan and the other influences of the Ancient Forest."

"Did you hurt my friends?" asked Sarah, her chin trembling.

"Casualties occur in battle, child. If you are going to feign naivety, there is nothing I can do about that. I do not know if your friends were harmed or not, but I can tell you that many of those who accompanied me, died! I do not like when the numbers of my race expire, Sarah, so don't expect sympathy from me. It was supposed to be a quick manoeuvre with few if any causalities. We were there to remove you and depart, not battle our ally, the Ancient Forest."

"You are not an ally of the Forest! You lie!" spat Sarah, angered by the Queen's disregard for Matharzan and Tazor. "You have attacked my family, my friends, and the Ancient Forest. Do not pretend to be a friend! You are mean and selfish, and … and … awful! I hate you, and I hate your race."

The Queen stood quietly, her lips pursed and arms folded across her chest. The only sign of agitation was her fingers drumming on her arm. No one spoke to her this way, or if they did, they did not live long. Fool girl! Finally, Graziel spoke, having come to a decision.

"I am not going to coddle you, Sarah, nor am I going to ask forgiveness for whom and what I am. You are right. I am ruthless, and it would serve you well to remember that. I don't allow emotions to influence my decision making and I don't expect you to either. I do whatever needs to be done to ensure the longevity and survival of the race that I rule." Leaning her face closer to Sarah, her voice intensified. "That is why my race is the strongest alive, and soon to be stronger, girl."

When Sarah refused to respond to the Queen, a look of

frustration passed across Graziel's face. Taking a step back, she continued to speak.

"I have always had good relations with the Ancient Forest. Some years ago they were strained when the Gyranger Ambassador at the time caused a rift between our two races. He had been released from his role and was not acting as my representative when he allowed *his emotions* to rule, causing an incident that severely damaged my relationship with the Ancient Forest. I was able to stop a war between us after convincing the Council that Ambassador Straeger had acted on his own accord.

"Do you think I'm stupid?" sputtered Sarah incredulously. "Straeger was with you in the Shadow Forest. He is back in your servi ..."

"Yes, he is back in my service. Years later I allowed him to rejoin me, but not in his former role. Straeger is well monitored now, trust me on that, child."

Graziel's eyes lit up with a sinister look that made Sarah's throat constrict. This small, beautiful woman scared her.

"You must wonder why I have taken such lengths to bring you here, Sarah. Hear me out, child, for I am going to offer you something that I offer no one. *Power, Sarah! Power more magnificent than you could ever imagine!*"

Moving to sit on the table beside Sarah, she took the girl's hand and continued to speak, her voice melodious and compelling. When Sarah tried to look away, the Queen lifted the girl's chin, forcing the Starchild to stare into her eyes.

Sarah, shouted Dineah through their mind link. *Break eye contact! Now!*

Sarah could hear Dineah's voice in the back of her head, but she could not pull her attention away. Suddenly the Gyranger Queen snapped her fingers, causing Sarah to jolt upright, unsure of what had just happened. She could hear Dineah shouting frantically through their mind link. Looking at the Queen, Sarah knew that once again, her thoughts had been overridden by this woman. Fear coursed through the Starchild as she realized how quickly it could happen.

Graziel spoke as if reading her thoughts.

"I could control your will, Sarah, but I would rather that you listen to what I have to say and agree to align yourself with me freely. I think it is clear that I can rule your mind if I choose. Believe me when I say it is not my desire to do so. I want to create an alliance with you, rather than forcing you to do my bidding."

Sarah nodded her head up and down slowly, without saying a word.

"Listen carefully, girl, for this is important. Thirteen years ago I dreamt of you, Sarah, in a dream that was a foretelling. Known as the Gyranger prophecy, it resides in the collective mind of the Gyranger race. In the dream I saw the birthing of a magical girl child – a Starchild, not born of humans, but raised by nobility in a human world. In her thirteenth year, the Starchild would align with the Gyranger race, taking her rightful place and raising the Gyranger race to a level unheard of in their history. So powerful was the dream that I took steps immediately to find you. After thirteen years of searching, I have finally brought you here where your rightful place is – beside me. You are the Starchild, Sarah. Together we will see the Gyranger race rise to greatness as we control the Karrian Galaxy. You were born to rule beside me; otherwise, you would have never been part of my race's prophecy. Welcome, Sarah – welcome to your fate. Accept it! Join me! It is your time to fulfil your destiny!"

With the Starchild so close, the Queen's urge to dominate

was so strong that it took all of her willpower to not plunge her pinchers into the side of the girl's neck and drink in her magic. She was unaware of the tiny whispers of toxic vapours leaking from the roof of her mouth as she spoke.

Dineah was acutely aware of the vapours for not only could she see them, but she could also feel a shift in Sarah's awareness. It was as if the girl's senses were being battered and shut down.

Mistakenly taking the girl's silence as consent, the Queen continued to speak.

"It was a Gyranger called Banzen, posing as one of your teachers, who was the first to locate you. She died in the process of bringing you to my awareness and was a great loss to my race. Sarah, I will not bring harm to the Ancient Forest and those you hold dear unless they resist me. It will be up to you to ensure that the Ancient Forest surrenders and relinquishes its control as the port of entry to the Karrian Galaxy."

Grasping the girl tightly by both arms, she looked Sarah in the eye.

"With you by my side, I will control the galaxy. Do you understand, girl? Can you see our future, Sarah? I have lived my life for this moment. Are you willing to be part of the strongest race alive and rule beside me?"

So stunned was Sarah by the Queen's disclosure and by the toxic vapours that were hammering at her senses, that she struggled to make sense of what she had heard. Was she part of a prophecy? If birthed in *Atarashara*, how could she be created to assist a race as evil and destructive as the Gyrangers? Was she as capable of evil as the Gyrangers were? Had her mother known of this? Had Aarus or her Aunt Atalia? Nothing that Sarah had experienced in her short life had prepared her for what the Queen had just said. Worse yet, she felt the truth within the Queen's words and a surge of excitement over having that much power. What did that make her? What wickedness was she capable of that she felt drawn to this evil creature's offer? It would mean turning her back on the Ancient Forest and all those who were dear to her ... but ... yes ... they would understand. She knew that her mother would forgive her; that Aarus would allow her to make her own choice. Suddenly a voice broke through her thoughts.

No, Sarah! Don't listen to her! The poisonous vapours are distorting your thinking! What she says is not true! The Gyrangers will destroy everyone and everything within the Forest.

As Dineah's words flooded Sarah's mind, so did images of the Shadow Forest and its destruction, and of Matharzan and Aniese's story of pain and betrayal. At that moment she understood how the Queen had found the weakness in the Forest's defences, and manipulated it. Holding tightly to the link that she shared with Dineah, she allowed anger to blossom within her, slowly replacing the former apathy and disorientation that had filled her mind. Anger: for Aniese's brokenness, at how Aarus would be heartbroken that his daughter had let down the Ancient Forest, that her mother would be panic-stricken at her absence and that after finally finding her family, she had almost betrayed them. She may be part of the Gyranger prophecy, but she still could make a choice. Looking fearlessly into the eyes of the Gyranger Queen, Sarah felt the strength of *Atarashara* move within her. She was unaware that stars shone in her eyes as her next words rang out.

"All you do is use people and hurt them. I am not going to be like you. I WILL NOT BETRAY THE PEOPLE I LOVE! I will never follow you, Queen of the Gyrangers, for I am the Starchild. I don't care what your prophecies say; you *will not* control me."

Graziel's head recoiled abruptly. Fearing that she had lost her opportunity, her patience dissolved, replaced by fury and an instinctual need to dominate her prey.

"You *will* obey me, Sarah!" she snarled.

Moving quickly, she sprung forward, shapeshifting into her Gyranger form and plunging her pinchers into the side of Sarah's neck, releasing poison into the girl's bloodstream. A second later the Queen was projected across the room, hitting her head on the wall with a large crack before sliding to the floor. Dazed by the blow, she struggled to get her bearings. Fearing another attack, Graziel continued to cower against the wall, shifting back into her smaller human form. Relief filled her as she watched Sarah collapse into unconsciousness. The poison had taken effect. Rising slowly, Graziel edged along the wall toward the door.

Dineah had witnessed the exchange between Sarah and Graziel. She saw the moment when the Gyranger Queen had snapped; when she had stopped trying to negotiate and instinct had moved her to override by force. In that split second, Dineah had barely hidden in time. Dineah knew that the deadly bite would make the Starchild a mindless pawn to the Gyranger Queen unless Dineah could maintain a connection with Sarah. And so, the tiny Firefly began to chant, repeating the same words over and over through their shared mind link.

You are Sarah Starbright; you are my friend. You saved me when no one else could. You are a child of Atarashara, manifested through Atalia, the First, Principal Commander of the Legions and a member of the Royal family. You are Sarah Starbright; you are my friend. You saved me …

As the Gyranger neared the door, she stopped, tenderly touching the back of her head where it had struck the wall. Hatred seeped from her as she spoke, her face twisted into a sneer.

"Yes, I will control you, Sarah. I will force you to help me gain control of the Ancient Forest. You should be very afraid, for I am going to manipulate you and hurt those that you love, all while you rule beside me. I will make you love power, until you are willing to sacrifice anything for it. You shouldn't have angered me, stupid child. I tried to offer all of this to you freely, but you had to be difficult. Now that the poison is in your system you will have no choice but to do what I tell you. It would have been nice to have had a little backbone in you, Starchild, but it is too late for that. You are one of us now, Sarah, just like the other fool down the hall."

Opening the door, she shook her head in disgust. "Two now, from the Ancient Forest ... such weakness!" Turning, she left the room, the door still ajar.

Dineah's chant stopped in mid-stream. Two from the Ancient Forest? Who else was here? Matharzan? Hope burst within her ... and just as quickly left, for in the precious seconds that she had stopped chanting the words that were Sarah's lifeline, the link had severed. She could no longer sense the Starchild's mind. The poison was moving faster than Dineah had thought possible.

Flying upward to view Sarah from above, Dineah was terrified by what she saw. Now only had Sarah stopped breathing, and her complexion turned grey, but her body was convulsing, forcing her back to arch unnaturally. Dineah put her hands to her mouth, stifling the scream that wanted release from her tiny body. Was Sarah's body going to accept the poison, or was she going to die? Dineah knew that if Matharzan was here, she needed to find him. Flying to the doorway, she looked up and down the hall, unsure of which direction to go. Seeing a door open down the corridor, she watched the Gyranger named Straeger step into the hallway. As he turned and walked away, she flew to the room he had just left, entering it before the door closed.

As a result, she didn't see the bright flash of light that came from Sarah's room or the faint auric shield that pulsated once before dissipating into nothingness. She felt it though – through the mind link that was now re-established with the Starchild. Relief flooded through Dineah as she spun around to leave the room and return to Sarah … only to watch as the door clicked shut. Turning to look for other exits her eyes never got past the giant glass cylinder located in the centre of the room. Dineah's breath caught in her throat as she recognized this place from her dream.

"You're from the Ancient Forest," said a voice that seemed to come from the other side of the glass cylinder.

Dineah's heart pounded fiercely in her chest. What was this place? She was trapped. She needed to get back to Sarah!

The voice continued, softly, yet groggy.

"I have only been out of cylinder for a week. I am still so weak and tired. Are you my saviour, Firefly? I would have hoped for something a little more … substantial. I wish you could have come earlier. I have waited so long. I tried to withstand their … alterations, you know, but I was not successful. I am not quite the person I used to be. Perhaps you remember me. WAIT!" the voice cried out. "You're more than a Firefly! I can feel it in you. *You're the Song Bearer!* What, in the Great Mother's name, are you doing here?"

Dineah pressed herself against the wall, too scared to reply.

CHAPTER 22

All Alone

Hana sat beside Atalia in the Sacred Grove, the Council flanking each side of the Princess sisters. She knew that this seating arrangement was not the usual protocol for the Elders. It was a demonstration of their grave concern for her. Hana tried to feel grateful, but couldn't. She couldn't seem to register anything beyond numbness. Her logical mind said that she was still in shock, as was Sir Perity, who was sitting on the ground in front of her. Hana knew that he felt as lost and empty as she did. She barely heard what the Council was discussing; her mind continually going back to the events of that day.

She had seen Matharzan turn questioningly to the portal – had even seen the unusual patterns of static herself. Why had she not questioned it further, especially when Atalia and Drake had been urgently called away by Aarus? Why had she been so confident that Sarah would be safe in the Ancient Forest after the Gyrangers' unrelenting attempts to abduct her?

Hana's mind continued to drift as the images began to replay yet again. Matharzan, jumping through the portal, followed by Sarah, Dineah, and Tazor. The portal closing shut! The sound of Aarus's urgent voice as it boomed through the Forest, commanding them to halt the crossing. Sir Perity, bellowing and leaping at the air where the portal had been, so distraught that he shapeshifted into his warrior form before falling back to the ground. Atalia running toward them, her eyes frantically scanning for Sarah as they moved down the procession of guardians. The look on Atalia's face! Great Mother, that image would be burned into Hana's mind for the rest of her years. *Never* had Atalia look so vulnerable, *and never* had Hana felt such fear through their mind link.

Hana vaguely recalled her legs collapsing beneath her. She didn't know where her father had come from – but suddenly he had been there, his strong arms holding her, encouraging her, stroking her hair. Elder Mendalese had been there too, his hands placed on her chest which had ached and felt like it was about to burst. It had been so hard to breathe. Why? Because the child she had raised from a baby was in danger, and they could do nothing to help her.

She had watched Aarus arrive, out of breath but calm and composed. She had drawn strength from his presence, trusting in his ability to deal with the terrifying circumstances that they faced. Standing where the portal had been, he had raised his hands in the air, working to re-establish the gateway that should never have closed without his consent. Time moved far too slowly. She had registered the look of surprise on his face when the gateway had suddenly reappeared and opened on its own volition, at which point Sir Perity had exploded through, followed by Atalia, Drake, and their armies. Hana had gone too, fearful of what she would find on the other side of the portal.

That was when she had found out that Sarah was gone, and

realized that all the years of protecting the girl had accounted for nothing. The thought re-elevated Hana's anxiety, causing her breath to shorten and her chest to tighten. Immediately, Elder Mendalese's healing hand touched her shoulder, filling her with warmth and allowing the band around her heart to relax. She looked up at him and nodded in appreciation, patting his hand with her own. She knew that he was keeping a close watch on her. She also knew that Atalia was watching her from the other side, worry coursing through their mind link.

She had listened to Elder Tenor's report. Sarah was a fundamental piece of the Gyranger prophecy. She would be turned against the Ancient Forest so that the Gyrangers could gain control of the Karrian Galaxy. She knew that Sarah would never agree to such a thing, which made Hana feel even sicker. Something would be done to Sarah to change her, to taint her, to destroy her mind and gain control of it. Hana bit back a sob. She saw Atalia again turn to look at her. What did Atalia expect? She was as close to a mother that Sarah had ever had! *Her child was helplessly alone and in danger!*

She had listened to Matharzan tell the Council that Straeger was back in the company of the Gyranger Queen. She did not doubt that he had aided in the abduction; the whole situation stank of him. She had watched the Were-Griffin struggle with his next words – that Aniese's vulnerable state had been used to betray her people and aid the Gyrangers in the abduction of the Starchild. Atalia had spoken at this point, confirming that the Gyrangers had known of the plans for Sarah to travel to Oorse today. No one spoke out loud, but everyone's thoughts had come to the same conclusion. The only person who could have given that information to the Gyrangers as well as altered the portal to Oorse, was Aniese. Hana's heart ached, watching the noble little Sage grapple with the unfaithfulness of his only surviving daughter, and the implications of her behaviour for the Ancient Forest. She knew that his heart was breaking as much as her own.

And then, when she thought that it could not get worse, it was revealed that Tazor was believed to be dead and that Dineah was gone, likely abducted by the Gyrangers at the same time as Sarah. Hana had thought that the Guardians would lash out at this news, but they stood tall and stoic. Aarus must have already spoken with them. Dineah's absence was the most tragic news of all, for without the Song Bearer, the Forest was virtually defenceless. Uncertainty filled Hana as she wondered if the images witnessed by Atalia in *Atarashara* so many years ago, were coming to fruition. She could sense a web of fear and uncertainty coursing through the Forest.

Knowing that the Council would be meeting for many hours yet, she looked at Elder Mendalese, motioning that she wanted to leave. Hana needed time alone to collect herself and act like the Princess that she was. Touching Sir Perity's head, she was not surprised when he turned to leave with her. As Hana stood and prepared to go, Elder Borus shifted his chair to face her, grasping both of her hands with his own. Even in her dark state of mind, she felt bolstered by the smile of peace and reassurance that filled his face. Hana's heart filled with gratitude.

Borus pulled the Princess close to him, whispering in her ear.

"Believe, Princess Hana – believe that we will get her back. Don't let fear fill ye heart. Sarah is a resourceful lassie."

Felix dipped himself low to the side of the Elder's head, gently stroking her hand. Then lifting its tip so that it was eye level with Hana, the hat spoke in a voice that was not its own.

"Hold a place of hope, Princess – Sarah Starbright is born of magic – let miracles happen. You have protected her well for years. Do not doubt the ability of a child born in Atarashara."

Chapter 22

Hana stopped short in her ruminating, realizing who was speaking to her. So stunned was she by *Atarashara's* direct contact that she said nothing, staring blankly at the hat.

"What is it, Princess Hana?" asked Borus, concern filling his eyes.

Looking down at Borus, she slowly released his hands, but not before squeezing them tightly and smiling to show her appreciation. She was unaware of his discerning gaze as he watched her move on, followed by Sir Perity. She hardly noticed the many beings who gently touched her, offering comfort and support.

And so it happened that Princess Hana was not present a short time later when the witch guardians of the Starchild gasped in unison, bringing the Council meeting to an abrupt halt. Many turned in time to witness Wisteria, Bohn, and Sabrae grab the amulets around their necks followed by a sharp command by Bohn to link. As the witches joined hands, a pulsating glow of light grew around them. Their faces tightened in concentration, while Bohn murmured words of magic under her breath.

"What is it, Aarus?" demanded Matharzan, who had risen, his vast wings unfolding into a fighting stance.

"The Starchild is under attack," answered Aarus who had also risen to his feet, his face tense with concentration.

"What can we do?" demanded Matharzan.

"Nothing, King of the Were-Griffins," said Aarus. "We cannot join this battle. It is up to our witch sisters."

Matharzan continued to stand, rigid as a statue.

"Hold," whispered Bohn, through clenched teeth. "I have done all I can do. Hold tight; do not let it take her, sisters! Men … da … lese …" She could barely speak his name.

Aarus watched, helpless, as the light surrounding the witches began to dim. He knew by the pained expressions on their faces that they were struggling … badly. He turned to look for Mendalese who steadily strode to Bohn, placing his hand over her own. Lifting his head and tapping into the energy of the Sacred Grove, the Elder directed his strength into the floundering glow of power held by the witches. In short order, other healers arrived to link with him, each adding their strength.

Suddenly the light exploded outward, illuminating the entire Sacred Grove for a brief second before plunging it into near darkness. Aarus wiped at his eyes, desperate to clear the spots that filled his vision. He heard the cries of pain before he saw them. Standing, he tried to make his way toward Mendalese and the other healers who were lying on the ground, struggling to rise and regain their eyesight. It was then that he saw the witches, injured and on the ground, burn marks covering their faces and chests where the amulets had been. Aarus could also see that the charms were gone. Amplifying his voice to fill the Forest, he released a command.

"ANCIENT FIRE CARRIERS, WE HAVE INJURED IN THE SACRED GROVE! ATTEND, NOW!"

In moments the air was filled with the whirling sound of Firefly wings, their glow lights ablaze. Without hesitation they descended upon Wisteria, Bohn, and Sabrae, covering the witches' bodies. A shrill cry rang out at the same time that multiple glow lights began to pulse simultaneously, growing brighter until they filled the space with unbelievable heat. Aarus was forced to step back, though unlike the others, he refused to cover his eyes. On and on the light pulsed. As it diminished and stopped, the Fireflies moved aside, creating space for Aarus, who bowed his head in gratitude. He could see that the witches' skin had healed, though their clothes were beyond repair.

Bohn was the first to recover and look to her sisters, shock and fatigue evident in her eyes.

"The connection with Sarah is broken," she said, her voice flat. "I cannot feel her at all. Her blood could not remain in the amulets that were under our protection."

Murmurs and questions filled the Sacred Grove.

"Elder Aarus," she continued, "the Starchild was attacked by what could only have been a Gyranger. Toxicity was spreading through her bloodstream at an alarming rate, so fast in fact, that she was dying. The protection of our magic could not tolerate that level of toxicity – in her body, or in our amulets, which is why the amulets exploded."

"Does she live, daughter?" he asked.

"I can't be certain, though I would believe so given the severity of the explosion and the disappearance of the amulets."

Looking at Wisteria, she sought confirmation.

Wisteria nodded in agreement. "I agree with my sister. As the blood broke free of the amulets, the toxicity would also have released from Sarah's body. Whether we stopped the spread of it completely, I cannot say, but we may have prevented it from consuming her entirely. Sadly, I have to admit that we have done as much as we can from where we sit. Sarah is truly on her own now."

Out of the corner of his eye, Aarus saw Atalia close her eyes and lower her chin to her chest. Matharzan reached down and gathered her hand in his.

"Elder Borus," said Aarus. "Take the news to Princess Hana and Sir Perity."

Aarus watched as Mendalese joined Borus before the two Elders left the Sacred Grove together.

CHAPTER 23

The Downfall of Innocence

Tazor awoke with a terrible pain in his head. Touching the back of his head with his paw, he winced and began to growl. It hurt so much! He could hear someone whispering, but did not recognize who it was.

"He is awake," said a female voice.

"Get ready then, we must be ready to restrain him, Lewna," murmured a deeper voice.

"What if we can't, Kaiten?" asked Lewna, who continued to speak in hushed tones. There was no response to the question.

Who they talk about, thought Tazor? He decided to ask; maybe he could help out.

"Why we whispering?" asked Tazor softly, his rumbling voice sparking a squeak of surprise from somewhere above him. "Who we need to control?"

No one responded.

Suddenly he realized they were talking about him! Forgetting to whisper he cried out, "Hey! Why you want to control me? I a nice gargoyle – I be your friend. You no need to control me!"

Tazor's outburst had made him dizzy and his head even sorer. Opening his eyes, he saw many pretty lights shining above him in the air. In fact, there were many blurry lights that seemed to multiply the longer he stared at them. What fun this was! Reaching out his paw, he tried to touch one. Something screeched and moved back, causing many of the lights to shift with it.

"Did you see that, Lewna? He tried to get me. Be ready – he's going to attack!"

"Have peace, Kaiten. I don't think he was trying to harm you. I think he is … confused."

Tazor did feel confused. A sense of urgency was permeating his mind. Was he supposed to be doing something? Anxiety began to build in his chest. The bubbles of laughter that he struggled so hard to contain started to move upwards from his tummy, demanding release. A grin spread across his face at the same time that an uncontrollable spurt of laughter escaped from his throat. Trying to regain control of himself, he focused on the voices and where they were hiding.

"I hear you, but I not *seeee* you," he said playfully. "You playing hide and seek with me? I *love* to play hide and seek. I a good hider. You can't find me unless bubblies start to come out, then it super duper easy to find me."

"Silence!" shouted Kaiten, whose attempt to take charge vanished when his voice cracked.

"Oh, so *fun-nay!*" Tazor shouted back, snorting as his laughter escalated out of control.

Looking up again, Tazor noticed that the number of lights decreased each time he blinked his eyes. Delighted with his discovery, he began blinking rapidly, moving his head first up and down and then back and forth from left to right.

"What is he doing?" asked Kaiten, his voice distressed.

"Maybe the blow to his head made him – you know, cuckoo?"

"Cuckoo? What is cuckoo? You mean crazy? On no," said Tazor cheerfully. "I already cuckoo. Hey, there only two lights now. Before, so many more. So pretty," he sighed, disappointed that the other lights had left.

As Tazor's vision continued to clear, he was able to make out two tiny, winged bodies that hovered in the air. Each of them had long strands of hair that hung downward, radiating a fluorescent glow. They reminded him of someone he knew. Why did they look so familiar?

"Dineah!" he blurted out. "You like my friend, Dineah! Where is she? *Where my Sarah?*" he snarled, a growl rising in his chest.

The sense of urgency returned to Tazor as memories began to fill his mind. He recalled the portal closing and trapping them in the Shadow Forest, followed by the argument between the Lady Aniese and Matharzan. He also remembered the battle between the Ancient Forest and the Gyrangers where he had tried to protect Sarah and Dineah. It was after he had felt a sharp pain at the back of his head that he remembered nothing more. Why was he here alone? Where were his brothers?

"You know Dineah?" squeaked Lewna, struggling to control her nervousness.

Tazor squinted at the light on his right and realized that this was the source of one of the voices.

"Then it was her, wasn't it?" Lewna continued, growing more confident. "It was Dineah on that girl's shoulder, right?"

"Where my Sarah?" Tazor snarled again. He was trying so hard to be polite, but no one was answering his questions.

"If you mean the girl that Dineah was with, they were both taken by the Gyranger Queen," answered Kaiten.

Tazor was stunned into silence, uncertain that he had heard correctly. How could they have gotten past Matharzan? How could Sarah have been captured? *He had broken his promise to Sarah – he had not protected her.* Guilt and then terror swept through him, for suddenly they were there – the voices in his head that Tazor had been able to keep at bay since pledging his loyalty to Sarah. Frantically he looked around him. Where were Eblie and Sheblie? They were the only ones who understood the deep well of darkness that haunted their brother's mind. He needed them to help keep the voices away. Tazor began to whimper, pressing his paws against his ears. The darkness slowly descended upon him, delighted by the gargoyle's vulnerability.

Oh, poor, foolish gargoyle, you have failed. Poor, poor Tazor. You try so hard, but you never quite make it, do you? We understand, gargoyle. How could someone like Tazor Gargoyle protect someone as important as the Starchild? So foolish to have made such a promise! Silly little gargoyle. Such a disappointment! You can never return to the Ancient Forest, Tazor. You have let them down. You have no home gargoyle, no place where you fit in. Silly, hopeless, little Tazor Gargoyle. You couldn't help but fail, could you ... because you always do. Come to us, Tazor. Come and join the darkness. Your brothers are gone. You were always meant to be. We have waited a long time. Join us, Tazor.

Tazor clasped his paws to his ears even harder, trying to drown out the words that filled his mind. Angered by his resistance, the voices became more cruel and insistent.

Hopeless, pitiful, little gargoyle! Matharzan and Aarus will be so disappointed in you! Princess Hana will wail in grief! You will have no place to go! You are doomed! Do not stay away from us any longer, Tazor. Come, live with us. Turn your back on your brothers and the Starchild. COME, LIVE IN THE DARKNESS ... FOREVER!

Hopelessness swept through Tazor as the voices screamed in his head, laying all of his fears and doubts bare. What about his brothers? What had become of them? Were they dead? Overcome by despair, he felt himself slipping into the darkness, unaware of the heart-wrenching howl coming from his throat.

"What have we done, Kaiten?" cried Lewna. "We have driven him to madness!"

"We didn't mean to," wailed Kaiten, his previous attempts at bravado, gone.

"I just wanted to know if the Firefly I had seen was Dineah," cried Lewna. "What do we do now, Kaiten? How do we stop him? His sounds will alert the others. They will know that we removed him from the battle and shielded him so he could not be detected. You know we will be punished."

Kaiten struggled inside. When Lewna had told him that she thought her childhood friend was in the Shadow Forest, he had agreed to help her determine if it were true. Not because he cared about her friend, but because he had a crush on her. Now things had spiralled out of control, and the strange little gargoyle appeared to have lost his mind. Unsure of what to do next, Kaiten made a decision. Sweeping down toward Tazor, he struck the gargoyle's arm with the tip of his fluorescent tail. Tazor's howling stopped immediately. For a moment, silence permeated the Forest … only to be replaced by another sound.

"OWWWWW," yelled the gargoyle, his attention pulled away from the darkness. He could feel paralysis moving up his arm and into his neck. Relief flooded through him, for the voices in his head had vanished.

"Oh thank you, thank you shiny light for pulling me from the blackness," Tazor sobbed, tears coursing from his eyes. "I no want to go away. I no want to go with the voices. I no … OWWWWWWWW. That hurts so much! Why you do that shiny light? Why you hurt me so bad? OWWWWWWWWWWW!"

Kaiten looked helplessly at Lewna, realizing that the gargoyle's cries were as loud as before.

"Help him, Lewna! You know you can!"

When Lewna had lived in the Ancient Forest, she, like her friend Dineah, had displayed unique talents. From an early age, Dineah was singled out for her ability to foretell. Lewna, in turn, had been identified as a healer. Even after the blast had changed her physiology, she had been able to heal others, albeit not as effectively as before. She had been discreet with this knowledge, aware that not all within the Shadow Forest were open to her abilities. In addition to Kaiten, only Commander Baire and the Lady Aniese knew.

Pushing her fear aside, Lewna floated down toward Tazor's injured arm, landing lightly on it. The gargoyle howled even louder. She knew that even a touch as light as hers would make the pain more excruciating. Closing her eyes and focusing inward, she altered the colour at the end of her tail hairs, allowing a purplish hue to pulse into the strange little creature's arm. There was immediate silence. Opening her eyes, she found herself looking into two round, tear-filled, hopelessly-crossed, brown eyes. She wondered which one to focus her attention on?

"What is your name, friend of Dineah?" she asked, attempting to sound stern but failing miserably. It was not in her nature to be cruel.

"Tazor ... Gargoyle," sniffed the overwhelmed creature.

"Hello, Tazor Gargoyle. I too am a friend of Dineah's ... well, at least I was long ago."

"Lewna," whispered Kaiten urgently. There is a light approaching. Someone must have heard Tazor's screams. What will we do?"

Looking at Tazor's eyes which were floating loosely in their sockets, Lewna came to a decision. She could not say why, but she felt a need to protect the endearing yet strange little gargoyle known as Tazor.

"Tazor, we will play a game together."

"A game?" whimpered Tazor. "I ... like games. Please no more hurting. I no like hurting."

"No more hurting, Tazor. We will play a game of pretending. You will pretend that I have captured you and that you are scared of me. I will pretend to be mean, but I won't be. I promise. Okay?"

"Okay," said Tazor, brightening up. "I like games," he said again in his raspy voice.

As the light drew nearer, Lewna flew above Tazor and raised her voice, nodding encouragingly at him as she spoke.

"Do not move, gargoyle, or I will be forced to harm you."

Tazor grinned in response. This game was going to be fun.

"O ... KAY!" he shouted enthusiastically.

Lewna cringed and motioned him to be more subdued.

Tazor immediately stopped grinning and responded again but in a deep, bass voice. He was going to do his best!

"No, please, evil shiny light, no hurt me."

Tazor couldn't help himself. He began to giggle.

Kaiten placed his head in his hands. They were doomed!

As the light grew and filled their location, both Lewna and Kaiten turned to give their full attention to the Firefly that now hovered in front of them. Relief flooded through Lewna when she saw who it was.

"Commander Baire," said Kaiten. "We found this creature unconscious in the Forest. Upon awakening, we subdued him with pain. We were preparing to take him to the Lady Aniese. Please excuse us as we have the situation under control and are on our way."

"Well done, Fireflies," said Commander Baire, who looked discerningly at Kaiten. "I was on my way to see the Lady myself. I assume it is alright if I assist you with the escort?"

Kaiten and Lewna exchanged a look of apprehension.

The Commander moved to take a closer look at Tazor. Lewna moved at the same time, obstructing his view. When the Commander shifted in the opposite direction, she did too. Putting his hands on her shoulders, he held in her one place as he peered over her shoulder. Staring up at him from the ground was the oddest little creature that Baire had ever seen. When it started to grin and wave its hand back and forth in greeting, he turned his gaze back to Lewna, his hands still on her shoulders.

"I can see that you've really subdued him, Lewna. Did you invite him for nectar while you were at it?"

"Nectar! My friend, Dineah, loves nectar," said Tazor conversationally. "She has it every meal. I can no catch her when she's on that nectar … stuff …"

Tazor's words faded out as he realized he had forgotten to play the game.

Lewna hung her head, closing her eyes and sighing.

Kaiten spoke next, desperate to clarify the situation.

"Commander, there was a Firefly on the shoulder of the girl who was taken by the Gyranger Queen. This gargoyle, Tazor, has told us it was Dineah Firefly, Oracle of the Ancient Forest. We thought it was important that the Lady Aniese know."

Commander Baire's eyes widened.

"The Oracle is being held captive by the Gyrangers!" he exclaimed.

"She is also a friend of mine … from before …" Lewna said quietly, not finishing her sentence. "That is why when Tazor Gargoyle was struck unconscious, we shielded and hid him for questioning. I wanted to be certain before we brought this news forward. Commander, we must let the Lady know."

Commander Baire was quiet.

"You are right," he finally said. "I am not certain if the Lady is open to visitations. She has been … indisposed … since the battle. We will try nonetheless. Can that … uh … creature … fly?"

"I a gargoyle, Sir Commander," said Tazor proudly. "I CAN FLY!"

Tazor rose up into the air, turning quickly from one direction to the other while growling and baring his teeth, demonstrating his agility and ferociousness.

"I out-fly Fireflies, oh Commander of Lewna and Kaiten," he said excitedly. "I show you? Have we a race? So much fun!"

The three Fireflies stared at Tazor, as uncontrolled hyena-like laughter erupted from his pudgy little tummy.

"Great Mother!" was all the Commander could say as he stared in shock. Was this creature really from the Ancient Forest? Taking the lead, Baire motioned for Tazor to follow him, Lewna and Kaiten following in the rear.

Although the Commander had not allowed it to show, Lewna's news had deeply unnerved him. He did not fully understand what had occurred before the battle, but since then, the Lady Aniese had been more withdrawn and difficult. Baire was uncertain if she would even care that the Oracle of the Ancient Forest was missing. Looking behind him, he noticed that the gargoyle was in a full-fledged conversation with itself – all the while snorting with laughter. He wondered if the blow to the head had harmed the creature. He did note that the gargoyle was true to his word – he certainly had no problem keeping up with the Fireflies.

It was not long before they arrived at the home of the Lady Aniese. The Commander was the first to see her as she stood outside her hut, swaying slightly on her feet. She appeared to be talking to someone.

"I will return her to you, immediately. I told you my word was good. You shouldn't have doubted me, Aniese."

Why is that voice familiar? thought Baire.

Stopping in mid-flight, he motioned to those behind him to stop. Unfortunately, Tazor was looking elsewhere. Missing the cue, he flew straight past the Commander, stopping abruptly beside the Lady Aniese.

"Oop ... sie," rumbled Tazor in his gruff voice.

Aniese slowly turned toward the gargoyle, her reflexes sluggish from intoxication. Surprise showed in her face.

It was only then that the Commander recognized the voice he had heard. Alarms went off in his head as he realized that they had interrupted a meeting with the Queen of the Gyrangers.

"Who is that ugly little creature?" barked the Gyranger Queen.

Tazor bared his teeth and growled. *He knew this woman! She had taken his friends.*

Immediately, the three Fireflies surrounded him, their lethal fluorescent points levelled at his head and chest.

Tazor did not move, only too aware of the pain that the points could inflict. Struggling to control the rage that coursed through him, his next words came out as a snarl.

"Where my Sarah and my Dineah? What you done with them?"

With a signal from Commander Baire, the Fireflies moved as one, forcing Tazor to back away from the Lady Aniese and the Gyranger Queen. Thinking quickly, the Commander began to speak.

"We found the gargoyle unconscious. He is confused and does not make sense when he speaks. I had thought it best to bring him to you, Lady Aniese, but I see that you have more important matters at this moment. I will deal with this intruder myself. Forgive me for interrupting you."

Turning his back to the Lady Aniese and the Gyranger

Queen, he looked Tazor directly in the eye, and made subtle hand motions, signalling him to turn around – *quickly!*

"Who is Dineah?" asked the Gyranger Queen sharply.

"Yes, who is Dineah, Commander," repeated Aniese.

A look of frustration crossed Commander Baire's face. They had been so close to getting away! Before he could respond, Tazor cut him off.

"You not know who Dineah is?" asked Tazor, surprise in his voice. "Why, she the Song Bearer. Everyone know that!"

Frowning, he shook his head in disbelief.

Sharp intakes of breath filled the air. Commander Baire watched the Lady Aniese's head snap toward the gargoyle, her eyes widening, as understanding and fear flashed through them. She turned her gaze to Baire. She had never looked so uncertain.

Let this go, please let this go, he chanted inwardly while subtly shifting his head back and forth. He barely stopped himself from sighing aloud with relief when he saw that the Lady, even in her inebriated state, had understood the slight movement of his head.

"This creature is deranged," she snarled, her words slurred. "You have interrupted me, Commander, and we will talk of this later. For now, remove your party. I am in the middle of an important matter."

"Wait!"

Graziel's voice cracked like a whip. Narrowing her eyes, the Gyranger Queen moved menacingly toward Tazor, licking her lips as she advanced, her hands flexing open and shut.

"Is what you say true, gargoyle? Was the Song Bearer with the Starchild?" cooed the Gyranger Queen, her voice hypnotic.

Tazor began to growl as his defences alerted him to danger ... except he found himself relaxing as he listened to the Gyranger

Queen speak. She was so ... pretty ... so patient. Leaning forward, he hovered in the air, placing his head on his paws and gazing wistfully at her.

"Yes," he answered blissfully. "Dineah play hide and seek in Sarah's hair."

Why couldn't he stop smiling?

Laughing loudly, the Gyranger Queen leaned toward Tazor, her next words filled with malice.

"Thank you, you little fool! You have just delivered the Ancient Forest into my hands."

Tazor felt the Queen abruptly release the mind control she had used on him. Devastated by what he had disclosed, he let out a piercing wail and dropped his head between his paws. *He had failed again!*

Graziel's face flushed with excitement.

"The Song Bearer! Think about it, Aniese. If the Song Bearer is missing, then the Ancient Forest is vulnerable. Here is our opportunity! Fight with me, Aniese! Bring the Shadow Forest to fight against the Ancient Forest – I know you have wanted this for years! The time is upon us – the prophecy is coming to fruition! Help me in this matter, and I promise you power and glory! As the second daughter of the most powerful Elder, your rightful place is to rule the Ancient Forest with the Gyrangers as your ally and protectors. Do not worry about your father, Aniese, for when all is said and done that fool will no longer even remember his name. Aniese, you will finally be where you belong instead of in this cesspool of a Shadow Forest."

Aniese's nectar-fogged brain struggled to comprehend what she was hearing. A chance to get back at the Ancient Forest. Did she want that? As she asked the question, a feeling of excitement began to grow, closely followed by doubt.

"I ... I don't ... I am not interested in ruling the Ancient

Forest, Graziel. Just give me my sister back so that I can be done with her and find peace."

"But think of how many others you could destroy, Aniese! They didn't do anything to help you after the explosion. Look at you, at how pathetic you have become, reduced to ruling in this place of slime and decay. Where were they then? This war is your opportunity for revenge! You could rid yourself of them all!"

But they did try to help you, argued a voice in Aniese's head. *You were the one who chose to leave.*

As Graziel continued to talk, any thoughts of reason were replaced by a fire that began to build in Aniese, fed by the hatred and anger that she had kept at bay since her meeting with Matharzan. It compelled her … calling to her … enticing her.

Yes, she thought, as the feeling continued to grow. *I will seek revenge and make them pay for what they had done.*

That is what she had wanted to do with Matharzan, so why had she let him go? She realized now that she had made a mistake. A delicious feeling began to spread through her. Not only would she destroy her sister, she would kill everyone in the Ancient Forest!

"I will fight, Graziel. Now send me my sister."

"Not yet, Aniese. Not until we have conquered the Ancient Forest. Your sister will be the first of many rewards … and acquisitions." Shrewdness oozed from Graziel. "I will deliver her to the Forest where all can see that she is alive. You will destroy her then – in front of them all."

Graziel giggled like a small child as she continued to muse.

"The Song Bearer! It all makes sense, Aniese. Haven't you noticed that the Shadow Forest looks different than it did yesterday? No, likely you haven't. I can tell you that the decay and foulness are even more pronounced, which means that the Ancient Forest is also changing. We must strike now – you, me, and our armies side by side. Gather your forces and be prepared to fight within the next twelve hours, Aniese! I will have an entourage sent here to accompany you to the Ancient Forest, ensuring that your portal opens adjacent to my own. Remember – it is important that you enter the Ancient Forest directly beside me."

The Commander watched the Lady Aniese stare blankly ahead. He knew that the intake of nectar coupled with the manipulation of her emotions had overwhelmed her and shut down her ability to reason. The Commander struggled to keep his breathing calm. Everything had spiralled hopelessly out of control.

Turning glazed eyes toward the Commander, Aniese said in a vacant voice, "Prepare the Shadow Forest to fight."

"You can no fight the Ancient Forest," cried Tazor. "It your home!"

"Get him out of here," said Aniese, "and get me more nectar … and lots of it. I don't want to be clear-headed again until after the battle."

Graziel's face shone with ecstasy. Opening a portal she left the Shadow Forest.

CHAPTER 24

Deception

Straeger entered the Gyranger Queen's quarters. He knew he was late, having checked yet again on Ourelia whose transition from the cylinder to an air-breathing environment was noticeably slower than it should have been. He guarded his features, ensuring that Graziel did not sense the emotions that ignited whenever he was close to Ourelia. Since abducting her from the Ancient Forest, he had been careful to downplay his feelings, wanting the Queen to believe that Ourelia's sole purpose was to better the lineage of the Gyranger race. He could not let the Queen know of his true intentions or that his feelings for the woman had never changed. Graziel would not tolerate it ... again. She saw emotion as a weakness.

He was uncertain of her mood for she had been distant since capturing the Starchild. He had found out that she had travelled off-site earlier today, her whereabouts unknown. That level of secrecy was unusual for her and bode poorly for him. Upon entering the room, he knew his instincts were correct. The gaze that she directed at him was lethal.

"You're late!" she snapped. "Do I need a new advisor, Straeger? Are you too enthralled by your pet that you do not have time for your Queen?"

Dropping quickly to one knee, Straeger bent his head in subservience.

"Do you think that possible, Graziel?" he asked softly. "I am sorry. Please accept my apology and do not question my allegiance."

He knew that using her first name would throw her off. At one time that would have never happened but it appeared that the genetic sharing with Ourelia had softened the Queen's armour and made her more vulnerable. His gamble paid off, for her temper dissipated as quickly as it had flared.

"Oh stand up, Straeger, and quit grovelling."

Glancing at her, he noticed her face flush with colour. A searching look filled her eyes. Satisfaction filled him. He was enjoying toying with her emotions and slowly weakening her defences. Before he could speak further, she began to talk excitedly.

"The Ancient Forest is ours, Straeger. Soon the Gyrangers will control the Karrian Galaxy."

Straeger stared at her, speechless.

"Why Straeger," said Graziel laughingly, "I don't believe I have ever seen you at a loss for words. It becomes you."

"I see that you are as pleasant as always, Your Majesty."

Straeger smiled to put some warmth in his words, but inside he was unsettled. What had she done, and why had she not discussed it with him? Masking his fear, he continued to speak, ensuring that his voice mirrored her excitement.

"That is a bold statement you make. Please, tell me more, you have my full attention!"

Gliding gracefully toward the advisor, Graziel began to circle him, speaking as she walked.

"It would appear, Principal Advisor, that when we abducted

the Starchild, we may have also inadvertently acquired the Forest's Song Bearer. I did not see the Song Bearer when I was with the Starchild, but it doesn't matter anyway; she is missing from the Ancient Forest. The Forest is vulnerable. I am declaring war on it shortly, and the Shadow Forest has agreed to align with the Gyrangers in the fight. Be ready Straeger, for our time has come."

Straeger felt a sense of excitement burst through him as he contemplated the Queen's words. He was delighted that she had included him in her last sentence; this would serve his plans very well. To hide his eagerness, he bowed his head in feigned respect.

"You have done well, Your Majesty. Once again you demonstrate your ability to lead our race toward greatness. How can I assist you in achieving your legacy?"

"You will lead the attacks with the Lady Aniese, from the Shadow Forest. You will be responsible for ensuring that the arrival of the Shadow Forest's army coincides with our own."

Straeger nodded his head in assent.

"I will prepare."

"Do so, and leave me for now. I have more planning to do."

Bowing his head again, Straeger turned to depart. He was stopped short by her next words.

"Oh and Straeger ..."

His stomach clenched at the tone of her voice.

"Prepare Aarus's daughter for departure to the Ancient Forest. I want the inhabitants of the Forest to see that after all these years, Ourelia is very much alive."

A sinister smile lit up her face.

"And then we'll have Aniese kill her," she drawled, the smile stretching even further. "Anyway, we have made a promise to Aniese. We no longer need Ourelia now that we have the Starchild."

Straeger kept his head turned away so that the Queen could not see the panic on his face. He had been wondering if this moment would come, stupidly convincing himself that the Queen would not follow through on the promise she had made to the Lady Aniese.

"We have gone to such lengths to change Ourelia for our purposes, Your Majesty. Would it not be better to keep her here and exploit her new resources now that she is out of the chrysalis state? I know that the Lady Aniese will initially be angry, but she is so ... unwell, that I doubt that she will even recall our agreement. Graziel, you saw her on the battlefield! Truly, we owe her nothing!"

"No, I want Ourelia gone. I gave my word, and I want to maintain a relationship with the Shadow Forest, particularly because of how weak Aniese is. I am sure there will be other ways that we can manipulate her. She foolishly believes that I will relinquish power of the Ancient Forest to her after we overtake it. She may become its figurehead, but she certainly will not be controlling anything. Anyway, I am tired of that wench in the next room. Prepare her for transport to the Ancient Forest."

Straeger regretted his earlier actions to make the Queen feel vulnerable. He guessed that the emotions he had aroused were playing into her current decision. The advisor knew that Graziel had felt increasingly threatened by Ourelia, though he wasn't sure why. Knowing Aarus's first daughter as he did, Straeger guessed that Ourelia was making the Queen's life difficult in any way possible.

He must not panic! He needed to stay calm. Taking a deep breath, he turned back toward Graziel, looking her full in the eyes as he spoke his next words.

"You are correct, Your Majesty. Now that we have the

Starchild, the Lady Ourelia no longer offers us the advantage that she once did. And the commitment to the Lady Aniese does need to be fulfilled. I will see to the preparation of Ourelia, myself."

Straeger bowed again before walking away. As he opened the door to leave, he looked back one last time.

"Can I make a suggestion, Your Majesty? Might I propose that the Lady Ourelia attend with me to the Shadow Forest? I think it would be … impactful, if both the Lady Aniese and the Lady Ourelia were seen entering the Ancient Forest at the same time. Let us play upon the confusion and shock it will create. This arrangement will also allow me proximity to both sisters. If Aniese gets cold feet, then with a little mind control I can ensure that she strikes and ends Ourelia's life in front of all present. I especially want her father and Matharzan to witness this event. At that point, I would suggest a full-out attack and annihilation of the inhabitants of the Ancient Forest."

Pausing briefly, he continued.

"One more thing, my Queen. If it is not too much to ask, I would like permission to focus solely on the destruction of my long-time foe, King Matharzan-Ariebe. It would be my absolute pleasure."

Trying not to hold his breath, he waited, allowing a smile to cross his face that did not reach his eyes. Graziel raised her head and stared at him with a calculating look. He did not look away. Soon he was rewarded with a similar smile that spanned the Queen's face.

"Why Straeger, you are as evil as I," she purred.

Bowing one last time in deference, he departed through the door, murmuring to himself.

"You have no idea, Graziel."

~

Dineah was worried. Although she could feel Sarah's presence through their mind link, there was no response from the Starchild. She was equally concerned about Ourelia, who lay stretched out on a metal table, draped in white sheets that fell to the floor. Ourelia was asleep, her breathing laboured.

Dineah now understood her dream – this room, the glass cylinder, the face inside it. Although she barely recognized the woman that she had known as a young Firefly, she was not surprised once Ourelia had identified herself. Aarus had been correct, as had been her foretelling – Ourelia had never died.

Ourelia was not well. Dineah had repeatedly tried to explain why the Gyrangers were holding her and the Starchild captive, but Ourelia had fallen asleep … again, unable to concentrate long enough to listen. Dineah stared down at the woman who was part of the tragic love triangle that had brought such devastation to the Ancient Forest. She did not remember much about the eldest daughter of Aarus, for Dineah had been but a child when the tragedy had occurred. She did vaguely recall how Ourelia had been small and fine-boned. Dineah thought that her mother, Kerri, had come from a Fairy lineage.

Ourelia had told Dineah that after being removed from the cylinder of fluid, her lungs had not adjusted back to an air environment. Dineah had listened without comment, for it seemed that Ourelia had needed to talk. Dineah wondered how long it had been since Ourelia had spoken with anyone? How could the Gyrangers have done this? Ourelia's status as the daughter of Aarus was equivalent to one of the Royal Family. Not only had the Gyrangers held a member of the Ancient Forest against her will, but they had spent years conducting tests and forcibly taking genetic coding that was specific to the lineage of the Forest's only Sage. Ourelia had not elaborated, but Dineah knew that the procedures had altered the woman.

She watched Ourelia's face ripple and shift as she slept, transforming from human to … she didn't know what? Dineah felt nauseous, barely able to consider what Ourelia had endured. As the skin on Ourelia's face and neck continued to writhe, Dineah leaned closer. Suddenly she gasped, scrambling to fly back as fast as she could. For a brief moment, a Gyranger lay atop the metal bed, its eyes open and staring coldly at her. A second later it transformed back to Ourelia, the same eyes continuing to bore into the Firefly.

"What did you see, Song Bearer, that scared you so? What have they done to me?" she whispered, her raspy voice causing shivers to move up and down Dineah's spine. Before Dineah could answer, Ourelia spoke again.

"Hush, someone draws near. Hide yourself, little one."

"I must go to the Starchild, Lady. I have to make sure that she is alright. Then we will return, together. I promise."

Ourelia's face twisted in confusion, as if not understanding what Dineah was saying.

"The Starchild, Lady. We are here together. I promise, Lady – we will come for you. You will not be left alone."

"I have been alone from the Ancient Forest too long, Song Bearer. I know not of whom you speak."

On impulse, Dineah flew down and kissed Ourelia's cheek. At that moment the door to the room opened. Dineah zipped to the shadow of the glass cylinder to conceal her presence, knowing that she had to make it to the door before it closed. As footsteps approached, Dineah hurriedly flew around the opposite side of the glass cylinder. Frustration filled her as she heard the door click shut. Even though it meant risking discovery, she knew that she must cross the open room and take cover near the door. Slowly rising, she hovered in the air, careful that her glow light remained unlit.

"Ourelia, my love, you are awake," murmured Straeger as he glided around the cylinder toward her bed. He stood looking down at her, wringing his hands together, his pinchers clicking excitedly.

Dineah heard a terrible hissing sound and realized that the Gyranger was laughing.

"I have done it, Ourelia. I have sealed our fate. Finally, after all these years, I have created the moment that will allow us to manifest the life that we have always deserved. You will be central to it, Ourelia. Do not be worried, for you are ready. Soon, you and I will direct the future of the Gyranger race."

Dineah continued to hover in mid-air, confused by what she was hearing.

"I have great plans for you, Ourelia, with me at your side of course. I will tell you later, for I must leave to prepare for battle. Think of me while I fight, and upon my return, be prepared to live the life you were born to."

Ourelia knew that Straeger wanted to reach out and touch her, but she kept her face turned away, fearful that the loathing she felt for him would be evident if she turned to look at him.

"Who do you fight, Straeger?" was all she had the energy to ask, hoping to stall him and help the Song Bearer depart undetected. He did not respond, having already turned to leave. As she felt sleep overtake her, Ourelia wondered if the Song Bearer had been able to escape.

The brief moments of conversation between Straeger and Ourelia had allowed Dineah time to fly to the doorframe. Flattening her tiny body against the wall, she heard Straeger's final words before he turned and walked directly toward her. Her heart pounded, making it hard to breathe. Thankfully, he was so consumed by his thoughts that he did not raise his head to peer above the doorway. Once he had opened the door, Dineah waited a brief moment before zipping out. As his long strides took him to the left, she flew in the opposite direction, praying to the Great Mother that he would not turn around and see her.

Upon arriving at Sarah's room, she found the girl lying on the metal table. Her complexion had returned to its natural state. Try as she might, she could not awaken Sarah from the deep sleep that consumed her. Sitting near her ear, Dineah repeated Sarah's name while also sending assurance and hope through their mind link. It was several hours later when Sarah's eyelids fluttered and then opened.

Do not speak out loud, Sarah. I am on your right shoulder. How do you feel?

What happened, Dineah? asked the Starchild groggily.

The Queen of the Gyrangers bit you, but something repelled her, throwing her across the room. I think it was the protection spell of the witches. It was awful, Sarah! Your body went into convulsions, and you turned a terrible colour. Honestly, I thought you were going to die! I left the room to try and find help, but while I was away something changed. I could feel it through the mind link. Somehow, you were okay again. I mean, I think that you're okay? Are you? Do you remember anything?

Sort of, I think. I remember being bitten and then this terrible pain filling my body. I couldn't bear it Dineah, but then a bright light seemed to come out of nowhere. It filled the room and exploded. That is all I recall before waking up. I feel awful, Dineah – like there are bruises all over my body. How can I be this sore? I think I am going to be sick.

Sarah clutched her stomach.

It is the poison that entered your bloodstream, Sarah. It will take a while before it entirely leaves your body. Can you still feel the protective shield of the witches?

Silence filled the bond as Sarah focused her attention.

Chapter 24

No, it is gone, she said, worry and fatigue in her voice.

Dineah did not give her time to ponder. She needed to get Sarah out of the room and to a place of safety.

We must leave this room immediately, Sarah. The Gyrangers are going to war. I overheard it when I was next door. Sarah, I fear that it is against the Ancient Forest. We must try to do something.

But how can we?

I don't know, but follow me. We are going to hide in the room down the hall. Quickly, Sarah! I don't know if the Gyrangers plan to use you in this war, but they are going to have to find you first.

Sarah struggled to rise, barely getting her feet under her. Lurching forward, she followed Dineah, clutching her stomach as she ran. Upon reaching the doorway, Sarah grasped the doorframe, her breath coming in gasps. Hastily checking that the hallway was empty, she stumbled to the right. Dineah flew to the first door on the left, hovering in one spot while Sarah caught up.

Quickly, Sarah, open the door! We can't let anyone know where we are!

Once they were inside the room, Sarah let the door close quietly behind them. Leaning against it, she slid to the floor, nausea and fatigue enveloping her. As her eyes adjusted to the lighting, she made out a strange glass cylinder situated in the centre of the room. An awful feeling began to form in the pit of her stomach.

What is this place, Dineah? It feels ... horrible. What has happened here?

There was a long pause before the Song Bearer replied.

Come, Sarah. It is time for me to introduce you to Ourelia, eldest daughter of Aarus.

Sarah did not respond. She didn't need to. Dineah could feel her shock through the bond that they shared.

CHAPTER 25

I Believe in You

T azor barely remembered flying with Kaiten and Lewna to the hut where he now sat, alone and utterly defeated. He felt broken inside, with no idea of how to fix himself. He had tried to summon the bubbles of laughter, but even they could not face him. He had messed up so badly! Many people were going to hurt because of Tazor. Covering his eyes with his paws, he began to sob.

Tazor knew that he needed to fight the hopelessness that was slowly overwhelming him, but the reality of what he had unintentionally set in motion had torn him apart, leaving him more vulnerable and defenceless than he had ever been in his life. The voices in his mind knew this. They were slithering back into his head, soft and soothing as they coaxed him, encouraging him to follow them and slip away. He knew that surrendering to them would mean never coming back. He would never see his brothers again, or Sarah Starbright, Dineah, or any of the new friends he had made in the Ancient Forest. But staying meant he would live knowing that he was responsible for the ruin of the Ancient Forest and of those he had grown to love. That thought, he could not bear. Because he knew of no way to undo the mess he had made, Tazor Gargoyle came to a decision.

Shuddering, he took a deep breath, relaxing the last thin barrier that kept the voices of madness at bay. Immediately, they intensified, luring him forward and welcoming him home while the darkness simultaneously enveloped his mind. Tazor felt as if he were slipping into an abyss where blackness and numbness tumbled over him, making it hard to breathe or to think. Never had he gone this deep before. He was vaguely aware of his thoughts fragmenting like pieces of a puzzle pulling apart. As they detached and floated away, he felt himself gradually diminish, becoming smaller … and smaller …

Tazor, whispered a voice that flitted across his mind. *Tazor Gargoyle, trusted guardian of the Starchild.*

Tazor brushed a paw across his forehead. Something was annoying him, interrupting the numbness. Pushing the voice away, Tazor felt the blackness begin to envelop him again, like the closing of a heavy curtain.

Tazor, come back. Tazor, the voice called again.

Why wouldn't it leave him alone? Was one of those Fireflies circling his head? Hunching his shoulders down, he tried to ignore it.

Tazor, Sarah needs you, the voice whispered.

Tazor growled. Sarah? Sarah who? Oh *that* Sarah. She didn't need him. All he had done was mess things up.

"Leave me alone," he whimpered.

Tazor Gargoyle, whispered the voice, while continuing to caress his mind and push back the darkness. *Brave and loyal gargoyle, Atarashara calls you. Why do you give up, little one?*

"Because I no protect Sarah and the Ancient Forest! I *fail!*"

Tazor began to sob again.

Come Tazor, come out of the darkness, faithful guardian. You have not failed. You still have more to do.

"But I have! I fail! Many soon die because of Tazor."

Tears rolled down Tazor's pudgy cheeks. The numbness was retreating, replaced by a pain in his chest. He didn't want the numbness to go away. Why did his chest hurt?

Feel the ache in your heart, Tazor. Feel it and hold onto it. Release the darkness. You cannot leave, gargoyle – it is not your time. You made a pledge to protect the Starchild, and you must keep your word. Are you forsaking your pledge, Tazor? Are you going back on your promise to Atarashara, and abandoning the Starchild? That is not like you, loyal gargoyle.

Tazor watched a pinpoint of light slowly grow in the darkness. As it continued to build, he felt a sense of warmth and hope envelope him. Relishing in the feeling, it took him a moment to grasp who was speaking with him. Clarity burst through the gargoyle, like the sun burning off the early morning mists – followed by white-hot anger. Abandon the Starchild? How dare *Atarashara* say that he would not keep his word!

"I no break my promise to Sarah! What you mean, *Atarashara*! I keep my word! I ferocious! I let no one hurt my Sarah! Why you talk like that! Why you say those things? I a loyal gargoyle! I …"

Pausing to catch his breath, he felt *Atarashara's* presence still encompassing his mind and realized that the voices and darkness had utterly vanished. They were gone. Relief flooded through him. As Tazor took a deep breath; he understood what *Atarashara* had done.

"Thank you, friend, *Atarashara*," he said quietly. "You help me. Tazor almost break his promise, but you help me to remember. Now, Tazor no break his promise. You a good friend."

Tazor Gargoyle, time is limited. We ask one more thing of you. Will you help Atarashara yet again?

278

Tazor closed his eyes and focused his attention, his brow furrowing.

"I listen, *Atarashara*! See?" He pointed at his furrowed brow with his paw.

Lady Aniese, whispered *Atarashara. Guard the Lady Aniese. Keep her safe.*

With that *Atarashara* was gone and Tazor was alone once again in the hut. No longer was he filled with pain and self-loathing, for *'the field of unlimited possibilities'* had come to him, Tazor Gargoyle, and given him a purpose. *Atarashara* believed in him, just like his brothers did! He was not going to let *Atarashara* down!

Slipping back the cloth that covered the doorway, he flew out of the hut, surprised to see that it was nightfall and that there were no guards present. *Odd,* he thought to himself as he began to make his way to the Lady Aniese. The Forest was surprisingly quiet. *Too quiet,* an inner voice told him – *something wasn't right.* And then he remembered. The Shadow Forest was preparing for battle.

∾

He found the Lady Aniese sitting on the Forest floor, her body slumped forward, matted hair covering her face as she mumbled softly to herself. Empty bowls surrounded her. As he moved closer toward her, he could make out her words.

"Kill them all ... destroy the ... Ancient Forest ..."

"Why you want to destroy the Forest?" asked Tazor softly.

Aniese jerked up violently, her hair flying away from her face. Moving her hand frantically behind her, she failed to find the weapon she sought. Grabbing one of the empty bowls she leapt up, arm raised and ready to strike. Her eyes, swollen from crying, had purple hues under them.

"Why you want to destroy the Forest?" he asked again, his large eyes filled with innocence.

"LEAVE ME ALONE!" yelled Aniese, her words slurred, as she moved to hurl the bowl at him. Slipping, she lost her balance and fell to her knees, the container falling harmlessly to the ground. Folding her arms around herself, she slowly lowered the rest of her body to the ground and began to moan.

"Your heart so sad, Lady Aniese. So many big tears. You no want to destroy your home. Please, no join fight with evil Gyranger Queen."

"Stupid gargoyle, what do you know? And what are you doing here? Where are my guards? GET THIS CREATURE AWAY FROM ME!" she yelled.

There was no response.

"WHERE ARE MY GUARDS?" she cried again.

The silence ensued.

"Why is no one here?" she asked in a childlike voice. "Why am I alone … Great Mother, what have I done? What have I agreed to? *What have I done?*" Aniese began to cry; mumbling incoherently.

Tazor watched the battle that raged within her, witnessing a torment that only he could recognize. He knew that *Atarashara* had helped him and now he needed to do the same for the Lady Aniese.

If asked, Tazor Gargoyle would have said that there was nothing special about him. That he was just a gargoyle who in his words, had bouts of uncontrolled bubblies that caused havoc and got him into loads of trouble. What he was not aware of, was that he exuded a naive and childlike nature that allowed him to view life most simply. This character, as well as his fierce loyalty, drew others to him. Tazor could not see evil in another unless they tried to hurt someone he loved. As much as he could have disliked the Lady Aniese for betraying the Ancient Forest, he had witnessed her act of love for Matharzan when she had reopened the portal to the Ancient Forest. Something in her despair touched him, for he understood it. And so in true Tazor fashion, he spoke from the heart, his gravelly voice carrying into the silent night.

"Hold on, Lady Aniese! Hold on and keep the fight! Do no give in to bad voices! You have good in you, too! I know – I saw it. Sometimes I do things I no can control, but my brothers, Eblie and Sheblie – they still believe in me. It okay as long as someone believe in you. Even when people laugh at me, it okay because my brothers love me …"

Tazor stopped talking, for Aniese had ceased her mumbling and turned to look at him. Actually, she seemed to be glaring at him. Very good! He had her attention. Their conversation was going so well!

"Look at yourself," she said scornfully. "Can you blame them?"

Tazor tilted his head, questioningly. Unaware that he had been insulted, he continued to speak.

"My brothers, they always believe in me. And Sarah, she too believe in me. And Princess Hana, too. Oh and Dineah, she my friend. She believe in me too."

"You are a joke gargoyle," snarled Aniese. "Look at the mess you made this afternoon in front of the Gyranger Queen. Now I have aligned with the Gyranger race to kill my people. How has it come to this?" she asked, her voice trembling.

"You can no kill your people, Lady Aniese! Why you talk so bad? You must tell the Ancient Forest what is to happen!" cried Tazor.

"And who should I tell, you simple-brained, flying dog! MY FATHER?" she screamed.

Tazor's brow furrowed as he looked around. *There no dogs here,* he thought to himself.

"Yes, you must tell Elder Aarus because he fix things when they bad. Elder Aarus help when I made Wisteria mad and her hair stood on end and sparkled! I catched the sparkles with my paws, and she got so more angry."

Tazor's shoulders shook with laughter. Looking up at Aniese, he was stopped short by the look on her face.

"You are pathetic," she said in a voice filled with contempt. "Leave here now, gargoyle, and do not come back, or I swear by the Great Mother that I will see you dead."

Aniese rose unsteadily, staggering as she turned to walk away.

Tazor was stung by her words. For the first time, he realized that their talk wasn't going well – at all. The Lady Aniese had just told him to leave. But he couldn't, for Tazor had made a promise to *Atarashara.*

Perhaps I talks quieter, he thought to himself.

"I think Elder Aarus like to see you," whispered Tazor.

"REALLY!" screamed Aniese, turning around so abruptly that Tazor scrambled backward.

"Even if I betrayed him, betrayed what he has spent his entire life protecting? What if I broke contact with him for years, ignoring my obligation as his apprentice and surrounding myself in the foulest existence alive? What if I loved the man that my sister was betrothed to marry? Do you think he would like to see me, gargoyle, especially when he finds out *I am going to kill his other daughter and my only sister!*"

Manic laughter followed Aniese's last words. Grasping her head in her hands, she tried to force the chaos away. She knew that if she gave in to it, there would be no memory of her actions from here on in. She *wanted* to recall, to remember every treacherous act she was about to commit, for then she could add it to the rest of the wreckage that was her life. Continuing to cradle her head in her hands, she dropped to her knees. Her laughter diminished, turning to sobs that wracked her body. The presence of the Shadow Forest wrapped around her in silence, a quiet witness.

Padding up to her, Tazor settled by her side. As the sobs subsided, he began to speak.

"I know what it like to have the darkness," he whispered. "I know how hard it is to stop the voices from taking you away."

Aniese continued to hang her head down, hair covering her face.

"It want to take me all the time, but I no let it, Lady."

"How do you keep it at bay?" asked Aniese, just as quietly.

"I made a promise, and I no can break it, because that's not what you do when you make a promise. That keep the bad voices away. Sometimes I get excited and laugh too much, but I loyal." Pausing, he added, "You can count on me, Lady."

"Well, I am not loyal gargoyle and …"

Interrupting her, he said awkwardly, "Lady … my name is Tazor, Tazor Gargoyle, but you can call me just Tazor. I be your friend if you want, Lady. I a good and loyal friend, I promise. But, please call me by my name cause that what friends do."

Aniese stared at him again, a bewildered look on her face.

"You are a strange one, Tazor Gargoyle. Wise for a … strange little gargoyle."

Tazor shrugged. "I not wise, but my friend, *Atarashara*, help me, and now I help you."

Aniese's head jerked backward in shock. She struggled to absorb what the gargoyle had just said.

"*Atarashara*? Here?"

"It came to visit me in the hut when my mind was going far

away. It stopped my mind from floating off ... forever," he said quietly.

Aniese turned her head away.

Tazor barely heard the next words that she spoke.

"*Atarashara* has never talked to me, not even after my mother died within its walls, or the day of the explosion; the day that was believed to be my sister's death. Even when the healers worked to heal my mind, *Atarashara* never sought me out. *Atarashara* does not intercede in the life of those within the Forest."

Turning back to face him, she demanded, "What are you saying gargoyle? How is it that *Atarashara* would talk to *you*?"

"*Atarashara* ask me to protect you."

As Aniese stared at Tazor, a look of hope and then yearning crossed her features.

"It is too late, Tazor Gargoyle. There is no longer any hope for me. Too much has been set in motion."

A long silence followed Aniese's words.

Finally, Tazor spoke in his gravelly voice, his large eyes crossed and brimming with truth.

"Sometimes, when we can no believe in ourselves, someone has to believe for us. I will believe in you, Lady Aniese, until you can once again."

Planting his feet firmly on the ground, Tazor stuck his jaw forward, further testimony to his commitment.

Aniese stared at him, her face vulnerable and raw. She turned away, unable to hold his gaze, needing something to wash away the painful feelings and memories that their conversation was igniting. Almost immediately, she saw the bowls of fermented nectar that had gone unnoticed earlier. Aniese stood and moved toward them, staring blankly before slowly lowering herself to her knees. Turning to look at Tazor once again, she watched him for several long moments. Shrugging her shoulders, she turned and began to drink each bowl until they were empty. Laying down, she curled up into a fetal position, letting the liquid consume her.

Tazor watched as Aniese slipped into unconsciousness. Padding over to her, he used his claw to gently gather the hair that covered her face, placing it behind her ear. He then stood guard, keeping his promise to *Atarashara*.

It wasn't long before he sensed movement in the space where the Lady Aniese lay, motionless. Vines began to untwine and make their way down the trucks of the trees, while roots surfaced from underground and slowly inched forward. Soon, Tazor and Aniese were surrounded by the foliage of the Shadow Forest which had crowded in around them. Tazor began to hear whispers in the air. As he sat quietly, he sensed an underlying tension that he hadn't noticed earlier.

"We will fight against the Ancient Forest and take back what is ours ..."

"Fools, you know we will be destroyed in the process. The Gyranger Queen cannot be trusted ..."

"The Lady Aniese has ordered us to prepare for battle. We must follow her orders ..."

"No, we mustn't. The Lady Aniese is also untrustworthy! Look at her! She is no longer fit to command. We should not fight in this battle ..."

"But we must!"

"No, we should not fight against the Ancient Forest..."

The whispers continued to argue and talk over each other until one voice cried out.

"SHE IS NOT ABLE TO COMMAND. HER TIME AS OUR LEADER IS OVER! THE LADY ANIESE MUST BE DESTROYED!"

An unnatural silence descended upon the Forest and the whispers stopped ... for a moment.

Tazor caught his breath for he knew something had just changed, and not for the better. The hair on his back rose as the voices resumed, more frantic and ferocious than before.

"Yes! Yes! The Shadow Forest must destroy her ... we must take control ... it is time for the Shadow Forest to have its revenge!"

Tazor watched as the roots that had gathered around them inched closer to where Aniese lay. A growl formed in his chest. The next words he heard made his mouth pull back in a snarl.

"She must die ..."

"Yes, yes, she must die ... we will swallow her up ... we are so hungry ... she will be so delicious ..."

"Yes! Then we must destroy everything! The Song Bearer is gone. The Ancient Forest is going to die anyway, as are we. Let us end in battle, fighting those that left us alone so many years ago. The Ancient Forest has turned its back on us, just like the Lady Aniese ..."

The voices went on, frantic and crazed, increasing in loudness as they argued among themselves again.

Tazor could feel the sickness of the Forest and the fury that was escalating out of control. Snarling, he rose into the air, hovering protectively over Aniese. Suddenly a root lashed out and wrapped itself around her foot, another one bursting up and reaching for her hand. Tazor attacked instantly, his teeth severing first one and then the other. The shrieks of pain from the demented roots sent shivers up his spine.

"I protect the Lady Aniese!" he cried. "I MADE A PROMISE!"

Instantly, Tazor found himself buffeted by a whirlwind of debris and twigs that obscured his vision and made him cough. Just as suddenly the wind receded, and the voices stilled. The vines and roots slowly withdrew, slithering menacingly away. As the foliage opened up, Tazor witnessed the glow of hundreds of deformed Fireflies, their fluorescent tails aglow and ready for battle. Tazor recognized Commander Baire, flanked by Lewna and Kaiten.

Raising his voice, the Commander spoke firmly and clearly.

"We will fight as a unified front. The Lady Aniese has commanded that the Shadow Forest join the Gyranger race in the battle against the Ancient Forest. If that is her command, then it will be done. Settle for the night, and prepare yourself for battle."

The frenzy of a moment ago was gone.

Flying close to Tazor and speaking quietly, Commander Baire added, "It seems you have changed your fate, Tazor Gargoyle. You have just saved the life of the Lady Aniese. I no longer have the time or guards available to consider you a prisoner. Nor do I consider you a threat. Watch your back for you have made enemies. I cannot guarantee your protection here, for the Shadow Forest becomes more unpredictable each day. From here on in, you will assist in protecting the Lady Aniese."

"I know," said Tazor, surprised by the Commander's words. "*Atarashara* already tell me."

Commander Baire looked sharply at Tazor before being drawn away by one of the Fireflies. Upon returning, he asked, "*Atarashara* told you to guard the Lady?"

Tazor nodded his head up and down.

Commander Baire said nothing, only staring at Tazor for a long time. Finally, he spoke.

"Who are you, gargoyle?"

"Tazor," the little gargoyle innocently responded. "Don't you remember? I Tazor, Tazor Gargoyle."

CHAPTER 26

The Forest Is Dying

Aarus walked back to his hut in silence, flanked by two Firefly guards. He was appreciative of the reprieve, knowing that it would not last for long. He had work to do. Following the explosion of the amulets and the healing of the witches, had come the distressing realization that not only was the Starchild without the support of her guardians or the Ancient Forest, but any possible link to the Song Bearer via Sarah was gone. The Elders had disbanded the Council meeting and met in private throughout the night, deciding that Aarus, as the Forest's Sage, would journey to the spirit world for wisdom and insight at how to deal with their current situation. Aarus knew that the Elders were struggling with everything that had happened. Without the Song Bearer, the Forest was utterly vulnerable. He had watched Elder Tenor depart from the Sacred Grove early, looking unusually pale as he begged leave due to illness.

Aarus knew that everyone, including himself, was filled with shock and grief. He did not have the luxury at the moment to think further about Aniese's actions, but his heart ached nonetheless, fed by renewed feelings of sorrow and a newer emotion of betrayal. As he continued to walk, he couldn't help but notice the fatigue that permeated his body. When had he started to feel this old and frail? He hadn't thought about his age for years. Why now? Was it because of the Forest's exposed state? Was he worried about their survival? Without warning, other thoughts began to seep through, doubts that typically did not penetrate the resilient defences of the Sage's mind. The Ancient Forest was strong, impenetrable, and filled with layers of protective systems and resources that had always allowed it to guard the Karrian Galaxy effectively. How had it become so severely compromised? How had the protective shields been breached, and both the Starchild and the Song Bearer abducted? How could events of so many years ago come back to play themselves out now – events inextricably linked to his two daughters?

He had lost his wife, Kerri, the love of his life, and then both Ourelia and Aniese, through a series of events that had shattered the world as he had known it. Now Aniese had been used to compromise the security of the Ancient Forest. He knew that the Gyranger Queen could be persuasive, but it did not leave his second daughter void of responsibility. At some level, she had agreed to sacrifice her home, her friends, and everything that had been her life … including him. That was more than he could wrap his mind around. And his heart … well, he needed more time than what the present moment allowed for his heart to even begin to comprehend what had happened.

To redirect his troubled thoughts, Aarus focused on the Fireflies who moved with him. He was grateful that they honoured his need for silence, and drew strength from their unwavering loyalty and presence. It was best that they did not know how uncertain he felt. *Uncertain* … the word barely described the dilemma they faced. He knew that the Ancient Forest walked a road it had never been on before; that its circumstances were dire. The absence of the Song Bearer left them exposed, though no one was quite clear how that would play out. Changes were occurring though, for Dineah's brief absenteeism had already impacted the Guardians. They were aging in front of his eyes, their trunks bending forward as if unable to hold themselves as erect and proud as before. Never before had he witnessed such confirmation of the Song Bearer's connection to their life source.

Alarm moved through Aarus as he watched wilted leaves pour down upon the path that he walked, their colours having changed from former green, to yellows, oranges, and browns. Slowing his walk, he bent to pick one up. His Sage's instinct told him that the trees were rapidly dying. He would have never believed it could happen this quickly. Straightening again, he began to hurry. Aarus now understood that time was short. As the Forest's Sage, not only did he need to journey and determine what the future showed, but it was imperative that he speak with *Atarashara*. He had to understand why *'the field of unlimited possibilities'* had created a magical child that was foretold to save the Ancient Forest, but also destroy it, if the Gyranger prophecy were true.

Turning to instruct his Firefly entourage, he was interrupted by a horrifying scream. Immediately, his movements were impeded by Fireflies and Dragonflies with Fairy riders that had appeared from nowhere, creating a protective circle around him. A roar filled the early morning air, followed by the nearby trees being rent apart as a giant orange head and body pushed through, massive white fangs slashing at branches that obstructed his movement. Landing in front of Aarus, Sir Perity continued to growl, his enormous head swinging back and forth in search of danger, the hair on his back and tail, raised. Pounding feet marked the arrival of Atalia and Matharzan, Atalia's sword unsheathed and in her hand. Aarus's astute mind understood immediately.

"First, why do you fear for my safety?" he asked, his voice quiet, but filled with authority.

"Because any attack on the Forest will begin by targeting you," said Atalia, just as levelly in return.

He could see the concern in her eyes ... and strength, so much strength.

"Even before the King?" he asked wryly.

"You underestimate yourself, Aarus. You are core to the existence of the Forest ... but you already know that," she said quietly.

Aarus fell silent, deep in thought. He knew her words to be true. Even so, he disliked that they were worried about him.

"Yes, I do know that, Lady Atalia. And you are right. Removing me would be a strong tactical move. Forgive my insolence. You forget though, that I am not without resources. Now ..."

"I apologize for interrupting, but as the First, I am assigning additional protection to you at this time. Do not dispute me, Aarus. You know that what I speak is true."

"Ah, my dear Atalia, you are the most brilliant Commander I have ever met. But we are in dark times, and the Guardians are ... not themselves."

A gasp escaped from one of the Fairy riders, shocked at Aarus's admittance.

Aarus continued to speak.

"Without their full support, our remaining resources are stretched far too thin. We don't have the luxury of assigning a guard to me ..."

Aarus's words were interrupted by a rumbling sound. Turning to its source, he watched Sir Perity seat himself so that his eyes were level with the Sage's. As *Atarashara's* guardian continued to purr, he gently butted his head into Aarus's stomach.

Placing his hands on the giant cat's head, Aarus felt a lump form in his throat and his eyes moisten. He understood the gift that Sir Perity was offering. It took him a moment to be able to speak.

"I am deeply honoured, guardian of *Atarashara*, and although I think your presence could be used better elsewhere, I accept," he said softly.

Slowly removing his hands from Sir Perity's head, he cleared his throat before continuing.

"Now let us move forward and find out what ..."

Aarus was interrupted by the sound of running footsteps. As one of the Legion guardsmen approached, Aarus had a sinking feeling in his stomach. He knew this man to be a seasoned fighter, yet his face was ashen.

"Elder Aarus, Sir. You must come, quickly. It is Elder Tenor. He ..."

Aarus moved forward quickly, not even allowing the guard to finish his words. He was barely aware of the entourage that ran to accompany him. As he approached Elder Tenor's hut, he noticed Elder Borus standing outside, holding Mrs. Gibson, who was distraught and weeping.

Moving to pull back the cloth doorway, Aarus did not miss Sir Perity blocking his way so that Atalia could enter the hut first. Nor did it escape him that the First paused unusually long before turning back to him, her face void of emotion as she nodded at Sir Perity. As Aarus's newly assigned guardian made space for him, he entered the hut, walking to where

Elder Tenor lay. Nothing could have prepared him for what he saw.

Elder Tenor had aged exponentially since leaving the meeting of the Elders. His skin was translucent and stretched tightly over the bones of his face, and his breathing was raspy. Crater-like holes existed where his eyes should have been.

Mendalese's quiet voice could be heard soothing the Elder, as he spoke in hushed tones, his hand resting on Tenor's shoulder. He quickly rose when he saw Aarus, gesturing for an apprentice to take his place. Pulling the Sage aside, he continued to speak quietly.

"The Fireflies were able to convince his spirit to stay, and I have slowed the aging process, but it is not good, Aarus. Elder Tenor's life-force is rapidly deteriorating, and he is dying. *He is aging by the second.*"

Aarus's brilliant mind instantly understood. Turning to Mendalese's other apprentices, he cried, "Elder Ravensong – go to him and have him brought here, immediately. Our Orators are under attack!"

"I don't understand, Aarus," said Matharzan. "What is happening?"

"The Forest is dying, Matharzan. The trees are losing their vitality because the Song Bearer is gone. I should have realized that the Song Bearer's absence would also impact the Orators of the Ancient Forest."

Matharzan did not respond.

"Don't you see, Matharzan? That is why we have gathered every night in the Sacred Grove since the beginning of time and listened to the storytellers. Their words feed into the energy that sustains the Ancient Forest and most importantly the Guardians. Like the Song Bearer, their stories are the heartbeat of the Forest. Now the storytellers are dying. They were the only ones who could have slowed the lifeforce that is leaving the Ancient Forest. Matharzan – it is imperative that we get the Song Bearer back and ..."

Aarus paused as a pulsating alarm began to ring through the Forest. Turning quickly to the Firefly guards, he watched as their glow lights turned a blood red, pulsing in time to the alarm. He was not surprised by the sound. His instincts had been trying to warn him of this. Without the Song Bearer, the Forest was defenceless. As fury coursed through him, he quickly reined it in, containing it until the proper time to unleash it ... *and unleash it he would!*

"Aarus!" shouted Matharzan. "What is happening?"

Turning to look at Matharzan, Aarus placed his hand on the Were-Griffin's forearm.

"We are under attack, old friend. It can only be the Gyrangers. Prepare yourself, King of the Were-Griffins, for we are truly fighting for our existence. I cannot say with certainty that the outcome will be in our favour. Sir Perity, protect both Matharzan and me. They will seek to destroy him as readily as myself. Fireflies! My staff! Bring it to me. We go to war!"

Amplifying his voice to project throughout the Forest, Aarus cried out.

"THE ANCIENT FOREST IS UNDER ATTACK. PREPARE FOR WAR!"

He knew that his next words were crucial.

"RISE, GUARDIANS, AND MOVE! A BATTLE IS UPON US! YOUR TIME IS NOW! FIGHT, SENTINELS! PROTECT THE GALAXY YOU HAVE BEEN BORN TO DEFEND!"

Inwardly, he wondered if the Guardians would be able to. Great Mother, he hoped that his words had rallied what energy they had left.

Turning to Matharzan, he continued in a quieter voice.

"I could not have asked for a better ally, Matharzan. I wish you had become my son-in-marriage."

Staring down at the small Sage, the Were-Griffin felt calmness spread through his body. How he loved this man! He responded, his voice rough with emotion.

"We are not dead yet, Aarus. Stand with me, Elder. Let us give them a fight they will never forget."

Sir Perity lifted his head, releasing a thunderous roar of agreement.

CHAPTER 27

A Sudden Change of Events

Straeger stood at the portal mouth, ready to cross into the Shadow Forest. He knew that the Queen had started the assault on the Ancient Forest, and that very shortly he would join her, accompanied by the Lady Aniese and the Shadow Forest. The Lady Ourelia had not accompanied him for he had made a small change in their plans – he just hadn't told the Gyranger Queen. The heightened decay of the Forest assaulted Straeger's senses as he emerged from the portal. He was stunned by the deterioration that had occurred since the battle less than thirty-six hours earlier. It was as if the Shadow Forest were dissolving into itself. Graziel had been right. The Forests' were dying due to the absence of the Song Bearer.

He had dismissed the Gyranger bodyguards who were to accompany him, for it was imperative that no one witness what he was about to do. Abominations that were former Fireflies settled in front of him, acting as an honour guard. It was not long before they stepped into the clearing where Aniese stood. He watched her sway slightly from side to side. Perfect – she was inebriated! Surprisingly, he found a gargoyle settled on her left shoulder. The creature seemed oddly familiar to him.

"Look who she sent!" Aniese chortled. "Didn't she want you on the front lines, Straeger? Was she worried about you creating another incident that she would have to fix?"

Rocking dangerously to one side, Aniese righted herself before falling over, forcing Tazor to hover in the air until she had regained her balance.

Behind her, Straeger could see the forces of the Shadow Forest gathered.

So many demented, wounded, lethal creatures, he thought, giddily. *My lifetime of planning is so close!*

"The Queen is ready for your army to join the Gyranger race, Lady Aniese. Let us go."

Turning, he began to walk away, but then paused.

The turning point – this was the turning point.

"Oh, and there is one more thing you should know, Lady Aniese?"

"What is that, traitor?" slurred Aniese.

"The Gyranger Queen has no intention of returning your sister to you. She plans to keep her for further experimentation." Pausing, he added, "In truth, she never had any intention of giving her to you."

Continuing to move forward, he revelled in the shriek that filled the air. A thin smile passed his lips.

"WHAT DO YOU MEAN THAT SHE IS NOT TURNING HER OVER TO ME? SHE PROMISED ME! SHE PROMISED THAT SHE WOULD GIVE HER TO ME, TODAY! SHE PROMISED!"

Turning back to face Aniese, Straeger put his head down, pretending to focus on his hands. He wanted to ensure that his next words were perfect.

"I know, Lady. It is terrible. Acquiring Ourelia was your moment to seek revenge and find peace once and for all. I do not know what has changed the Queen's mind, but in doing so, she has taken that possibility away. I argued with her. I told her that it was imperative that she follow through with her commitment, but she would not see reason."

Spittle flew from Aniese's mouth as she lurched forward, her eyes filled with rage.

Commander Baire tried to interject and speak, but she waved him away.

"Take me to her, Straeger! Commander Baire – the portal will stay open. Hold the army back until you have a direct command from me to move forward. The Shadow Forest will not fight if the Gyranger witch refuses to uphold her end of the bargain."

Moving closer, Straeger fell into step beside her. He noticed that the annoying little gargoyle had left her shoulder but continued to hover several feet behind. As Aniese concentrated on opening a portal into the Ancient Forest, Straeger moved closer to her. Compelling her to look into his eyes, he spoke quietly, overriding her mind and taking control of it.

"It is not right, what the Gyranger Queen has done to you, Lady Aniese. She has lied to do. You will not stand for this! You want revenge! You know what you need to do."

Turning his body to block the gargoyle's view, he slipped a knife from underneath his cloak and passed it to Aniese. Stepping back, he nervously watched as her eyes glazed over. She shook her head, fighting the mind control. How could she be so frail and yet so strong?

"The portal, Lady Aniese, you must open the portal."

A moment later, the portal opened into the Sacred Grove of the Ancient Forest. Aniese began to scream, even before fully crossing through the gateway. She ran straight toward the Gyranger Queen, Straeger close behind.

~

Aarus stood with Matharzan, Atalia, and Noble in the Sacred Grove, surrounded by the Forest's armies and the Guardians that had tumbled lifelessly to the ground. The trees were dying in front of his eyes. As a result, the Forest's defence systems had been unable to stop the opening of multiple portals into its depths. He could see thousands of Gyrangers waiting for the command to pass through. The Gyranger Queen stood at a safe distance from him, beautiful and regal as ever. Perhaps he should have destroyed her that day when they were both travelling away from their bodies. It seemed so long ago. There was no time to think about that now. He was stung at the arrogance within her words.

"Do not take all day, Aarus. I would prefer not to destroy the Forest that I plan to inhabit. We have the Starchild and the Song Bearer. Surrender the Forest to us, and we will take control of it with minimal causalities."

"You forget who you speak with, Graziel," said Aarus, his voicing ringing throughout the Sacred Grove. "Even in our weakened state, we have the power to override your army. Do you truly think that you can step upon the sacred soil of the Ancient Forest and overtake us? This Forest is our home. We hold the greater power here!"

"But the Gyrangers are not alone, Aarus. *The Shadow Forest fights with us!* Your daughter has betrayed you ... *once again!*"

Hissing and clicking of pinchers could be heard through the portal openings as the Gyrangers responded to the Queen's words.

A wave of shock moved through Aarus's body. He heard Matharzan's sharp intake of breath and felt the Were-Griffin's hand on his shoulder. The Sage couldn't believe what he was hearing. How could he have been so foolish that he had not considered this possibility? Aniese had already betrayed them once. If the Shadow Forest turned against them, then the Ancient Forest was indeed lost. Time seemed to slow as he turned to first look at Noble, and then at the First, whose face looked carved as if from stone. He knew her extraordinary mind was trying to figure a way out of this.

Vaguely he felt the air shimmer as yet another portal opened. He watched as a gaunt figure leapt through the air toward the Gyranger Queen, thrusting its arm forward and screaming words that he could not decipher. The being stepped back seconds before the Queen fell to the ground, a knife impaled in her chest. It was only then that Aarus recognized who had attacked the Queen of the Gyrangers. Great Mother! It was his daughter, Aniese! He also knew who had entered the Forest behind her. Straeger!

Aarus knew that Aniese's strike had landed true, for the leaderless Gyrangers immediately went berserk, surging through the portals into the Ancient Forest. The Gyranger Queen was dead, and her army was out of control. He watched as Straeger did nothing to bring them under control.

Rough hands grabbed Aarus, pulling him to safety as the armies of the Ancient Forest moved forward to meet the onslaught of crazed, insect-like creatures. Wrenching himself free, he ran to the portal belonging to the Shadow Forest, striking at Gyrangers with his staff as he went. Quickly murmuring words into the shimmering threshold, he closed it, ensuring that the Shadow Forest could not join the fight. As members of the Legion circled him in protection, he sensed the opening of another portal. Turning, he was baffled to see Straeger depart from the battlefield.

He gave it no further thought as swarms of Gyrangers pressed upon them, pulling his guards away and leaving him exposed and vulnerable. Two Gyrangers slid menacingly toward the Sage, their pinchers snapping as they stretched their arms out, fingers reaching for him. Raising his staff, Aarus began to swirl it, almost striking the whirling blur of teeth and claws that distracted the beasts until the guards could dispose of them. Aarus shook his head to clear his vision. Who was that creature darting through the air, waving frantically at him … and smiling? *Tazor Gargoyle?*

"Elder Aarus, I protect you. I protect you, Elder Aarus, just like I protect the Lady Aniese. *I made a promisssseee,*" yelled the little gargoyle, continuing to smile as he flew backward, smacking squarely into Martharzan's shoulder.

"Sorrreeeeey!" he yelled, yips of glee filling the air when he saw the Were-Griffin.

Matharzan's eyes opened wide as he turned to see Tazor Gargoyle bouncing up and down in the air.

"I back, Matharzan, I back!" he yipped.

The Were-Griffin frowned as he returned his attention to the two Gyrangers that had paired against him.

"I made a promise to *Atarashara!*" Tazor continued to yell, barely missed being struck by a guard's sword. The gargoyle's sounds then turned to hyena-like laughter as he returned to taunting Gyrangers that had drawn close to the Sage, piercing the tops of their heads with his razor-sharp claws. Cries of joy radiated from Eblie and Sheblie who had heard their brother's yelps and were speeding toward him.

"I over here, brothers," shouted Tazor, "I back, I back Eblie and Sheblie!"

Aarus continued to gape at the gargoyle. Was Tazor having … *fun?* Having lost his concentration, he barely swung his staff in time to stop a Gyranger from impaling its pinchers into his neck. Aarus watched as both Atalia and Matharzan moved toward him, desperately trying to create a pathway to remove the Sage from the battle area. Aarus knew that it was useless – they could not fend off the massive numbers of Gyrangers in their feverish state. He continued to fight knowing that without the Guardians as allies, he was inevitably going to die in battle.

It was then that he heard the growl that brought a smile to his face. Hope blossomed through the Sage as he watched Gyrangers scrambling to clear the way. As *Atarashara's* guardian broke through, sweeping his massive orange head back and forth and piercing Gyrangers with his fangs, Aarus grabbed a tuff of hair at the base of the great cat's neck, swinging onto his back. Out of the corner of his eye, he saw Tazor hovering in the air and clapping his hands, his laughter cackling through the air.

Sir Perity instantly turned his head toward the sound, roaring his joy as they made eye contact. Bunching his haunches, the cat sprang through the air, clearing the heads of the Gyrangers, and removing the Forest's Sage from the heart of the battleground.

CHAPTER 28

Returning Home

Sarah stood beside Ourelia, who lay on a metal table covered in a white cloth. She could feel the woman's life-force rapidly declining. Sarah knew it wouldn't be long before the eldest daughter of Aarus died.

"Ourelia, wake up – we have returned," said Dineah, standing at the base of her ear.

As Ourelia awoke, Sarah found herself staring into eyes that she recognized.

"Your eyes are just like Aarus's," was all she could say. Sadness engulfed her.

Ourelia's surprise was evident in her face.

"You are filled with magic, child! Who are you?" she asked in a raspy voice.

Sarah's throat constricted. She cleared it before speaking.

"I am Sarah Starbright; born of *Atarashara*, and raised by Princess Hana on the planet they call Earth."

Ourelia continued to stare. Suddenly, her eyes lit up with awareness.

"Born of *Atarashara!* I have heard of you. You are the girl child sought by the Gyrangers. But why has *Atarashara* intervened?" Ourelia turned her head away as tears filled her eyes.

"There is so much I no longer understand."

Lost for words, Sarah did not respond. She watched Ourelia fall back to sleep.

"What do we do, Dineah?" Through their mind link, she continued to speak.

She is dying, Dineah. I can feel it.

Can you do anything, Sarah? SARAH! WHAT IS WRONG?

Sarah felt the barrier restraining her snap so violently that she stumbled backward. At the same moment, Ourelia screamed, clutching her hand to her chest. Her cries continued until finally turning to muted whimpers. She curled in upon herself, gasping for breath.

"What is it, Ourelia, what has happened?" cried Dineah, distraught at watching the woman's pain.

"The Queen is dead! He comes to me. I feel him … approaching," she whispered, her face stricken. "Don't let him …" Ourelia's eyes glazed and her breathing stopped.

"Do something, Sarah," cried Dineah. "If the Queen is dead then you can access *Atarashara* and your magic. Save her, Sarah, as you did me! You can do it, Sarah! You *must* do it!"

For the second time in her young life, Sarah was being asked to save the life of someone who was dying in front of her – except that this time she knew what to do. Calmness permeated her as she opened up to the magic of *Atarashara* and allowed it to move through her. Sarah was awestruck by the pureness of the tone and energy that emerged from her throat. Stretching her arms outward, she felt wave upon wave of vibrations leave her hands to enter the Lady Ourelia.

At that moment Ourelia's life was laid bare as Sarah witnessed the kaleidoscope of images and memories that arose from the woman's heart. Ourelia's love of Matharzan, tainted by the horrible argument with Aniese the last day they spoke. The betrayal of Straeger whom she had disliked, but trusted. The years of torture and pain while her body was forced to change. The increasingly shared bond with the crazed Gyranger Queen. And the anger, the suppressed anger that had slowly eaten away at Ourelia over time, while she had tried so hard to resist what she had finally become.

All of this Sarah saw, right up to the instant that Ourelia felt the blade enter the Gyranger Queen's heart. At that moment, through Ourelia's eyes, Sarah knew who had killed the Queen. She also heard the fateful words spoken.

You promised Ourelia would be mine to kill! Where is she? Where is my sister?

Sarah knew that this, more than anything else, had been the final blow for Ourelia. Knowing that her sister wanted her dead had broken her heart.

Sarah felt *Atarashara* continuing to flow through her, allowing the darkness that had permeated Ourelia's heart centre to shift … to become lighter … to release. Time ceased to exist, and then … slowly … ever so slowly … the heart began to beat … once … twice … and then it continued. Sarah watched as the spiral of life-force that was circulating through Ourelia's body restored organs that had not healed after emerging from the chrysalis state of the glass cylinder. Ourelia slowly opened her eyes, and for a moment the stars of *Atarashara* were present.

The sound receded from Sarah's throat and finally came to a stop. She lowered her arms to her sides.

Ourelia gazed tranquilly at Sarah.

"Thank you, Starchild of *Atarashara*," she murmured.

Struggling to push herself up, Ourelia stepped down from

the table, testing her legs to ensure that they would hold her weight.

"Lady," said Dineah. "You must rest."

"There is no time to rest, Song Bearer."

Sweat began to bead on Ourelia's forehead. Turning her head toward the door, she spoke.

"There is fighting everywhere. The Queen is dead, and the Gyrangers have gone mad. Straeger is coming for me, and he is not alone. He has rallied Gyrangers to follow him. They are leaderless and will look for any form of authority, no matter how vile," she spat. "Is the door locked?"

"No," answered Dineah, as she turned toward Sarah who had left Ourelia's side to stand near the door.

Sarah, what are you doing? she asked through their mind link.

Sarah stood with her eyes closed, her hands directed at the steel base that held up the glass cylinder. Using one arm to guide the glass upward, she focused the other one at the bottom structure. Sweat slid down the sides of Sarah's head as she shifted the massive base toward the door. Footsteps approached in the hallway, as well as the unmistakable sound of pinchers.

"Hurry, Sarah," cried Dineah, "they are here!"

"I ... can't ... go ... faster ..."

"Release the cylinder, Sarah," commanded Ourelia. "Put all of your strength into the base. Dineah, quickly ... come with me and take cover!"

Grabbing the sheet from the bed, Ourelia moved to the farthest wall, crouching as she threw the sheet over Dineah and herself.

The cylinder crashed to the ground, glass shattering around the room. The base thumped firmly against the door at the same time that the doorknob turned from outside the room.

The door did not budge.

"Ourelia," cried Straeger. "What has happened? Are you hurt, my love? Open the door, Ourelia."

"Well done, Sarah," whispered Ourelia who rose slowly, using the wall to support herself. "But now we are trapped in this room. What now, Starchild?"

A mischievous grin appeared on Sarah's face. Looking at Dineah, Sarah sent a thought through their mind link. Dineah began to giggle, clasping her hands to her mouth.

"Interesting," murmured Ourelia, as her head turned back and forth between the Starchild and the Song Bearer.

Throwing back their heads in unison, they sang his name aloud. The tone rang through the room, creating sparkles like sunlight on a snowy winter's day. He was there immediately, his silvery coat ablaze. Head held high and forelegs raised, he was ready to strike.

Ourelia's knees gave way as she realized who stood in front of her. She slid against the wall to the floor, all dignity lost.

The pounding at the door continued. The hallway was now teeming with Gyrangers. The door began to push open ever so slowly, moving the steel base aside.

Sarah ran to Silverspear, wrapping her arms around his neck.

"Thank you for coming, Silverspear. I have missed you so much. Please, you must take us to the Ancient Forest, immediately."

Looking up, she noticed that he was staring at Ourelia. Shifting his violet eyes to gaze at her, she heard his gentle voice in her mind.

Of course, Starchild! Long have I waited to hear you call my name! I knew that you would do it, Sarah, that you would find a way to contact me. I never stopped believing in you, for you are the Starchild, born of pure magic. I will gladly return you to the Ancient Forest, but first, there is an acknowledgement that I must make.

Walking to Ourelia, Silverspear bowed his head in respect before speaking to her telepathically.

Lady Ourelia – long has it been since our paths crossed. It is indeed my privilege to see you again. Would you allow an old horse to bear you to safety?

Ourelia sat entranced as she listened to the soothing voice of the Equine King. Smiling for the first time in what she knew to be a long time, she responded.

"You are hardly an old horse, Your Majesty. And yes, it would be my honour."

As Silverspear bent his forelegs and gracefully folded the front half of his body to the floor, Sarah helped Ourelia mount the winged horse. Scrambling up behind Ourelia, Sarah made sure that Dineah was firmly attached to her shoulder. The door opened further, the leg of a Gyranger protruding into the room.

In her head, Ourelia heard Straeger's shriek of frustration, followed by a collective howl of Gyrangers. Clasping her ears to muffle the noise, she almost lost her balance on Silverspear's back. A moment later, a silky voice filled her mind, accompanied by the smell of fresh rainwater and roses.

Listen to my voice, child, and allow it to push the noise away.

Expanding his thoughts to include Sarah and Dineah, he continued.

Hold on tight, Starchild, Song Bearer, and daughter of Aarus, for we return to the Ancient Forest.

∼

She circled lazily through the mist, not wanting to awaken from the peaceful slumber that embraced her. She wondered where Sir Perity was. He usually kept her company, curling up near her feet.

Sarah Starbright, Starchild of Atarashara, whispered a voice.

Was the voice speaking to her? It was so ... dreamlike. She must be having a dream. Sarah did not open her eyes as she continued to slowly twirl, savouring the feeling of tranquillity that filled her.

Sarah, whispered another voice, like silk rippling across her mind. *Awaken!*

Should she know that voice? Why was it so familiar? The smell of rose blossoms permeated her bedroom. Who had brought flowers into the room? All she wanted to do was sleep and surrender to the peacefulness that ...

"Uh, Sarah ... Sarah ... SARAH!" yelled Dineah.

Sarah's eyes jolted open, snapping her awareness back into her body. Hovering in front of her was Dineah, hands on her hips and glow light bright with agitation.

"You may want to get back down here, Sarah," said Dineah, her voice strained.

It was only then that Sarah realized that she had been floating in the air. Bringing her body down to land on a surface of soft, yet firm clouds, she turned to her travelling companions and cringed, wondering how long they had been trying to awaken her. Her face turned red with embarrassment.

"Sorry about that, I was caught up in ... where are we?"

"I was hoping you could tell us that, Sarah," said Ourelia. Silverspear had targeted us to return to the Ancient Forest. It appears that we have arrived somewhere else. Can you identify this place?"

Sarah took a deep breath to quiet her heart which was still rapidly beating from being jolted awake. Stilling her mind, she let her senses expand. Instantly, she recalled the feelings that had permeated her dream. This place was … divine! Images began to flit through her mind – a child wrapped in a blanket, celestial bodies of golden stars, moons, and planets rotating around her head. Princess Hana, cradling the child who was crying, having fallen and bumped her head after her first unsteady steps. Sir Perity, patiently sitting and purring while the child pulled at his ears … and his whiskers … and his tail. The child giggling as hundreds of butterflies filled the backyard, all longing for her to touch them with her magic. The child as she lay on the ground with Princess Hana on a summer night, watching stars fall through the sky as they put on a light show just for her and her mother. A smile spread across Sarah's face as she understood where she was.

Welcome home, Starchild, whispered the voice of *Atarashara* in her mind.

"Thank you," she murmured aloud in response.

Turning to face the others, Sarah was unaware that her face was glowing, or that her eyes were alight with stars.

"We are inside the portal of *Atarashara,*" she said.

She heard Dineah gasp and watched Silverspear bow his majestic head in reverence. Only Ourelia did not seem surprised, or overly pleased.

"Why are we here, *Atarashara?*" asked Sarah.

"Yes, *why!*" demanded Ourelia abruptly.

Sarah turned to stare at Ourelia, shocked at her tone of voice. She noticed that Ourelia's face was pale and drawn, and that sweat rolled down the sides of her face.

Have peace, Lady Ourelia, whispered the voice of *Atarashara* through the minds of everyone present. *Your body will align quickly enough – it has undergone many changes and is adjusting to its return to the Ancient Forest.*

"But why are we here!" she demanded again, no less harshly.

When there was no response, Dineah interjected, desperation in her voice.

"*Atarashara* – it is crucial that you return me to the Ancient Forest, immediately. I am the Song Bearer. I am worried about the Forest and what my absence has done …"

Suddenly a portion of the clouds cleared, revealing the Sacred Grove. Dineah gasped in horror. Guardians that had stood for a millennium had toppled, others had been set afire. Gyrangers fought anyone that crossed their path, including their own kind. Matharzan was injured, his right wing torn and hanging loosely by his side. Sir Perity was surrounded by four Gyrangers, two of whom were about to attack him from behind if not for the typically gentle Sabrae setting them on fire, her face filled with fury. Wisteria was blowing up segments of earth and hurtling large rocks that were wiping out multitudes of Gyrangers. Mrs. Gibson stood guard in front of Elder Tenor's hut holding a large stick, her face fearful but resolute. The Scarab King bellowed as he charged a group of Gyrangers, lethal in his display of swordsmanship; the First and Prince Drake with the Emerald Sword joining him a moment later. Lady Aniese sat near a felled Guardian, holding her head in her hands while Tazor, Eblie, and Sheblie fought to keep Gyrangers away from her.

"Sarah!" screamed Dineah. "Do something! I have to get back to the Forest."

Sarah stood helpless, stunned by *Atarashara's* apathy.

"*Atarashara*, why did you bring us here?" she cried. "Why did you not return us to the Ancient Forest? The Gyrangers are destroying it. If the Forest is wiped out, so are you! Please, return us and help me to put an end to this. You've created me for this moment. *Tell me what I must do!* "

The Gyrangers are crazed without a leader, whispered *Atarashara*.

You can achieve nothing, Sarah Starbright, until they are under control.

"Then I will lead them!" Again she cried, "Show me what I must do."

"Sarah, you cannot lead them," said Dineah dismally. You have to be of their blood to be part of their collective mind. They would not follow you anyway."

Floating down to rest on the clouds, she put her head in her hands, overwhelmed with despair.

There is nothing you can do, Starchild. This moment belongs to someone else.

"It is not Sarah you are addressing, is it, *Atarashara?*" declared Ourelia, her voice raw with pain and fury. "You knew all along, didn't you? Do you truly understand what they did to me? What it cost me? What it cost my father? My sister? My betrothed? Why, *Atarashara? You* created the Starchild, so let *her* resolve this situation and let me return to my home and the people I love!"

Lady Ourelia, whispered *Atarashara. Have you become so embittered that you refuse to see what your heart knows to be true? Your father is the greatest Sage alive. Look deeper within, sweet child, for like your father, you have the sight.*

Ourelia stood motionless, speechless at what *Atarashara* had just called her. A memory bubbled up from her unconscious. She was a small child, and something had scared her. She had run toward her mother who had smiled and gathered her into her arms. She recalled the words that Kerri had spoken. *Why do you cry, sweet child? There is nothing to fear. You are always safe in my arms.*

Sweet child. She was not sweet or innocent any longer. Ourelia did not want to look within, for she was terrified of what she would see. For so many years she had merely tried to survive; now the bonds had been released. A disturbing thought had been niggling at the back of her mind since arriving at 'the *field of unlimited possibilities*'. It was too encompassing even to consider. Reluctantly she drew her attention inward, allowing the light that had been closed for so many years to open in her mind's eye.

She immediately returned to another battlefront – one that she recognized instantly. Lying in front of a portal was herself, or what she now knew to have been an illusion of herself. This was the battle scene where Straeger had betrayed and kidnapped her from the Ancient Forest. As time and images flipped forward, she watched the many years of genetic restructuring that her body had undergone. She saw Atalia manifest the Starchild in *Atarashara*, and relived the Gyranger Queen's prophecy dream that had launched the thirteen-year-long search to find Sarah Starbright. She witnessed the birthing of the Song Bearer and felt the war song reverberate through her blood, setting it on fire. She came to understand the connection between the Starchild and the Song Bearer as she watched Sarah save Dineah's life, and realized how Sarah's capture by the Gyrangers had ultimately saved her own life. And then she saw an image of herself and what she had become as a result of *Atarashara's* healing through the Starchild. An aura of light surrounded her, containing a darkness that permeated her body. She was both dark and light. At that moment she understood how the synchronicity of everything had brought them to the present moment. Taking a risk, she looked further in time. She saw darkness, an emptiness … that shouldn't have been there. How could there be total darkness? And suddenly she understood. She wondered if her father knew. Opening her eyes, she was once again in *Atarashara*.

"I understand, *Atarashara*," she said quietly. "Is there any hope?"

There is always hope, Lady Ourelia. Remember where you are.

Closing her eyes she focused her willpower, setting a heartfelt intention for her people and the Ancient Forest, and praying to the Great Mother that it would be enough. A long moment later her eyes reopened.

"I have done all I can for now. Let it be enough."

Turning to look at Silverspear she commanded, "Everyone! Mount King Silverspear. It is time to return to the Ancient Forest!"

CHAPTER 29

The Battle in the Sacred Grove

Aarus had been fighting the two Gyrangers for what seemed an eternity. Although Sir Perity had tried to shelter him from the heart of the battle, the number of Gyrangers had been too vast. Having arrived initially at the Sacred Grove, the insect-like creatures were now steadily progressing through the Ancient Forest.

Stepping back, Aarus stumbled over the exposed root of a Guardian, its body drooped and defenceless.

The Gyrangers hissed in rapture for they knew that he was trapped.

Aarus watched them lunge toward him, their pinchers dripping with the toxic poison that would take his life. Raising his staff to fight, he was thrown off his feet as the ground beneath him erupted. Jumping to the side barely in time, he stared in wonder as tree roots sprang forward, spearing the Gyrangers and throwing them high in the air.

It was then that he heard the war song. Tears filled his eyes as he felt the power of the Song Bearer's voice move through his veins. He knew that the Guardians would be sensing it too. Looking upward, he witnessed the transformation of tree trunks that had fallen in on themselves and lay dormant, miraculously resurrected to their former glory. Many of the giant sentinels already stood tall and strong, their fresh green leaves creating a canopy that filled the sky. *The Song Bearer had returned!* The ground continued to explode as more Guardians broke from their static positions, moving forward into the heart of the battle. Protecting the Ancient Forest was their highest purpose. They were ready for combat!

"Fight, brothers, fight!", shouted the ecstatic Sage, cackling while he waved his staff in the air and jumped from one foot to the other. He watched in awe as enormous tree branches swept down, their massive strokes wiping out multitudes of Gyrangers. Aarus could feel the rage of the Guardians, knowing how they had been forced to passively witness the destruction of the Forest while helpless to do anything. He knew they would destroy every Gyranger present.

Father! The fighting must stop! The Guardians cannot destroy the Gyrangers!

Aarus shook his head, stunned by the words he had just heard in his mind. Could it be? Was it possible? *Where was she?*

He frantically looked around, his vision bombarded by the chaos and fighting. Frustration filled Aarus as he frantically tried to locate the source of the voice. A moment later, his thoughts were interrupted by another sound that filled the air *… one that was very different from that of the war song.* Aarus felt the magic of it, immediately.

≈

Chapter 29

Ourelia sat upon Silverspear's back with Sarah and Dineah, watching the frenzy and destruction that was claiming her birth home. Urgency gripped her. She knew it had been instinctual for Dineah as the Song Bearer, to launch the war song to restore the Guardians into their power, but now they were rapidly destroying the Gyrangers. It needed to stop. Ourelia telepathically sent a message to her father. When he did not respond, she frantically considered other options. It was then that a thought came to her. Turning slowly to stare at the Starchild, she wondered if her instincts were correct. Was it possible? Taking a deep breath, she spoke sharply.

"Sarah Starbright, child of *Atarashara*, you may not understand what I am about to say, but I saw a vision while in *'the field of unlimited possibilities'*, and I speak the truth. The fighting between the Ancient Forest and the Gyrangers must stop. Help me, child! You are born of magic! You must use your magic to bring this war to an end, *now!* Go into your heart, Sarah, and focus! Focus on the battle coming to an end! You can do this, for you *are 'the field of unlimited possibilities'!*"

Ourelia knew it was unfair to put such responsibility on the young girl's shoulders. She wasn't even certain if Sarah understood how to manifest her magic, but she knew firsthand of Sarah's profound capabilities. Although still a child, Sarah's presence and powers were well beyond her years. This could only be because of Sarah's birthright as a child of *Atarashara*. At that moment, Ourelia was banking on that birthright to manifest a miracle. Holding her breath, she watched as the Starchild slowly registered what Ourelia was asking from her. As Sarah closed her eyes and took a deep breath, she raised both her arms and head toward the sky. Nothing could have prepared Ourelia for the pureness of tone and energy that emerged from the Starchild's throat.

~

The magic of the sound called to Aarus, filling him with a sense of peace like nothing he had experienced in his long life. He was not aware that his staff had dropped from his hand until he saw it lying on the ground. Grabbing it quickly, he honed his Sage's sight to locate the source of spiralling energy that was permeating the Forest. It was only then that he realized that the battle had stopped, for everyone, foe and ally were silent … listening … mesmerized.

Continuing to push his way forward, the Legion fell back to create space. As the final guards cleared away, Aarus stepped into the middle of the battlefield. It was then that he saw Silverspear, his head held high and his nostrils flared. On his back sat Sarah Starbright, her face turned to the sky as she continued to bring peace and order through the magic that flowed from her voice. The Song Bearer hovered nearby, her glow light ablaze with fire.

Aarus's breath caught in his throat as he saw who else sat upon King Silverspear. Although he had recognized the voice in his head, a part of him had still refused to believe. Now he knew it to be sure. A surge of joy spread outward from his heart, filling his whole being as words passed through his mind.

She is alive. My daughter is alive!

He had been right – she had not died! Moving forward, he stretched his arms toward her, blinking his eyes rapidly to clear away the tears that threatened to break free. He watched as Ourelia slowly dismounted from Silverspear's back and turned to face him. As he looked into her eyes, his Sage's sight exploded in alarm.

Uncertainty and then dread filled Aarus as he registered the changes in Ourelia. At that moment, his instincts told him that once again his life was about to change forever, and although he did not understand the plan of the Great Mother, he surrendered to it. Quietly, he stepped back and lowered his arms … and then swept them upward again as he amplified his voice, crying out words in only a language that the Guardians would understand. In doing so, he set a spell of protection for his precious daughter who was not the same woman that she had once been, and whom the Guardians would seek to destroy when they truly understood. And then he spoke the formal words of welcome to the Ancient Forest.

"Welcome, Ourelia, eldest daughter of myself, Elder, Sage, and Seeker of the Ancient Forest. You are welcome and safe here in the Ancient Forest."

"Welcome home, my beloved girl," he added quietly, for her ears only.

Aarus saw a look of understanding pass over Ourelia's face. His sweet, intelligent child understood what he had just done. His joy instantly disappeared as he sensed once again that something of great consequence was about to happen. As Ourelia began to speak, Aarus knew his intuition was correct.

"There is something I must do, Father. Trust me, please."

~

Ourelia felt wave after wave of sound move over her body, filling her with a sense of tranquillity that she had not known since living in the Ancient Forest. She watched as the Guardians ceased their crazed pursuit to destroy the Gyrangers, drawing themselves proud and erect, their leaves lightly fluttering in response to the vibrations of the Starchild's song. She saw both the Gyrangers and the inhabitants of the Ancient Forest still, and then stand quietly, their attention focused on the source of the sound instead of at each other. And then she saw her father, her dear, aged father, using the support of his staff as he made his way toward her through the mangled state of destruction that filled the Sacred Grove. Stopping, he slowly raised his arms toward her. Dismounting from Silverspear's back, Ourelia turned to face him.

Fear consumed her as she watched him step back and lower his arms. *He knew!* His Sage's instincts had alerted him to what she had become, and he could not accept it. Her father was rejecting her! But no – for he raised his hands again, amplifying his voice as he cried out the sacred words that ensured her safety, safeguarding her from her own home and people. It was only then that he spoke the formal words of welcome to the Ancient Forest.

"Welcome, Ourelia, eldest daughter of myself, Elder, Sage, and Seeker of the Ancient Forest. You are welcome and safe here in the Ancient Forest."

Her heart felt like weeping. She fully understood her father's actions and the risk he was taking in protecting her. The Guardians would have sought to destroy her, and likely still would when they found out. Her father knew what she was … and yet he loved her nonetheless. His next words confirmed it.

"Welcome home, my beloved girl."

For a second, time stopped as Ourelia committed the moment to memory, savouring her father's unconditional love despite the darkness within her. It filled her with hope, giving her the courage to speak her next words.

"There is something I must do, Father. Trust me, please!"

Wasting no more time Ourelia amplified her voice as Aarus had taught her so many years ago, and raised her hand in the air as she spoke.

"Hear me, Gyrangers. Your Queen is dead. Rally to me!

Rally! I am the new Queen of the Gyrangers!"

Ourelia vaguely heard Matharzan's tortured cry, for the chaos of the collective Gyranger mind overwhelmed her, making it hard to stay focused. Even so, she did not miss the approach of the man she had once promised her life to as he beat his way to the front of the ranks, pushing both Gyrangers and Legion guards aside in his haste.

Ourelia began to panic. She had so little time, for she could sense the uncertainty coursing through the insect-like creatures. Although their shared mind confirmed that Ourelia was one of them, on a physical level they recognized her as one of the Ancient Forest. Ourelia knew that if she did not immediately gain control, the Gyrangers would relaunch into battle frenzy. Closing her eyes, she forced Matharzan from her thoughts, focusing solely on the Gyrangers' collective mind.

"NO, it can't be! What are you doing, Ourelia! Are you mad?"

Her focus was abruptly jolted away as Matharzan moved to stand in front of her. She watched her father step beside him and touch his arm. Her heart ached as she looked at the Were-Griffin, the man that she had loved more than life itself. Seeing his pain and confusion was more than she could bear, but she could not explain. She was out of time.

"I am sorry, Matharzan. I am so sorry," she whispered.

Closing her eyes again, she surrendered. Allowing herself to embrace what she had rejected for so long, she shapeshifted into a Gyranger. Ourelia heard a scream of utter anguish. Opening her eyes for a brief second, she saw that Matharzan had fallen to his knees, and was covering his face with his hands.

Maintaining her Gyranger form, she amplified her voice a second time.

"The battle is over. I repeat – as of now, the battle with the Ancient Forest ceases. There will be no more fighting. The

Ancient Forest is now, and forever will be, our ally. It is time to withdraw our forces. As your Queen, I command you to move to the portals and prepare to return home."

Ourelia held her breath, aware of the complex stillness that permeated the Sacred Grove. Time seemed to stretch out, but then, ever so slowly, the Gyrangers began to stir, reassembling themselves as they moved toward the portals that had allowed their entry to the Ancient Forest. As she shapeshifted back into human form, she turned to Matharzan, desperate to speak with him. Once again her focus was abruptly interrupted.

"You've become one of them, you piece of filth!"

Ourelia's face paled as she watched the gaunt and haggard shell of her younger sister stride toward her in clothes covered in decay.

"Ourelia," cried another voice. "My Queen! Why are you here! How did you get here?" Straeger approached swiftly, confusion marring his features. "What is going on? Why have you stopped the battle?"

Aniese stopped short of Ourelia and Straeger, rage filling her face. Shaking her fist in the air, she screamed at Ourelia.

"You sided with them? All this time you have been working together with them?"

Sun reflected off the metal of the knife that Aniese held.

"Aniese, no," Ourelia said, her voice strained. "That is not what happened!"

"Allow me to finish her, my Queen," snapped Straeger. "While I had you encased in the cocoon state we used this pathetic creature's vulnerable state to gain access to the Ancient Forest. Through mind control, I directed her to kill Graziel, ensuring your place as the rightful Queen of our race. She is a pitiful excuse of a being and one that we no longer need. I know it is distressing for you to see what she has become. Give me but the command, my Queen."

Ourelia and Aniese continued to stare at each other, Ourelia's face pale and drawn; Aniese's sickness evident through the gleam in her eyes.

"Aniese, *please*, I didn't know about any of this! You've got to believe me! *I … am … your … sister*," Ourelia whispered, desperation in her voice. She saw something flicker in Aniese's eyes.

Aniese lurched forward swinging her arm upward at the same time that her fingers opened, releasing the knife that flew through the air. Leaping forward, Ourelia grasped it, turning swiftly to drive the blade forcefully into Straeger's heart.

"*You will never harm my sister or me again, Straeger!*" cried Ourelia. "You are dead to me. I have *never* loved you, and *never* will!"

Turning the blade and wrenching it sideways, Ourelia was unprepared for the strength of Straeger's blow that struck her, causing her to fall heavily to the ground.

Pain exploded inside Straeger, making it difficult to breathe. Slowly removing the knife from his chest and dropping it to the ground, he looked at the blood pouring from his chest and knew that he was gravely injured. Grief and betrayal filled him as he realized that all of his dreams had been for naught. After all the years he had committed to Ourelia, to creating their life together, she had never come to love him. At that moment Straeger needed to strike back at her, to hurt her in the same way she had just done to him.

Pretending to stumble, he stretched his hands toward Ourelia, shooting bolts of laser-thin light from his fingertips. He was unprepared for the staff that struck him from behind, knocking him off balance. Straeger became crazed as he recognized the thwarted opportunity for revenge. Turning to face Aarus, he lunged at the Sage, intent on impaling his poisonous pinchers into the tiny man's neck.

Straeger gasped as he was struck in the back by a blinding force that shot him upward, forcing him to hang, suspended in the air. Looking down, he saw a glow of emerald green light growing around his body. A moment later, it burst outward from his chest. He barely registered the roar of *Atarashara's* guardian or the sound of ancient Scarab words that shattered the life-line connecting his soul and body.

Straeger collapsed to the ground, dead, his body instantly disintegrating into ashes. Behind the now fallen Gyranger stood Prince Drake, wielder of the Emerald Sword. Flanking him were King Matharzan-Ariebe and Sir Perity.

CHAPTER 30

A Time to Heal

Sarah's awareness had slowly returned as the spirals of magic that had flowed through her voice had softened and come to an end. Looking about, she had seen that the battle had stopped, which meant that she had succeeded in what Ourelia had asked of her. How, she had not known? Somehow, she had once again accessed the magic of *Atarashara* in a time of urgent need. Sarah should have been pleased with this, but instead had only felt confused and disoriented. It was then that she had been drawn from Silverspear's back and enveloped in her mother's arms, at which point she had no longer cared about the battle in the Sacred Grove. She had only wanted to be with Hana, and safely back in the Ancient Forest. Hana had summoned guards to assist in removing them from the carnage that filled the Sacred Grove.

Sarah was cherishing the feeling of being safe with her mom inside their home. She now knew what had transpired after she and Hana had left the battleground, and of the newly formed alliance between the Gyrangers and the Ancient Forest. She was not overly surprised that Ourelia had stepped forward as Queen of the Gyrangers, not after what she had witnessed while in *Atarashara*.

"What happened next, Sarah?"

Sarah started, realizing that she had stopped talking mid-sentence. She was trying to tell Hana what had happened after her capture by the Gyrangers but was finding it difficult to remember. There were holes in her story; spaces of time that Sarah could not recall.

Worry filled Hana as she saw the distant look in her daughter's eyes. She could see how confused and vulnerable Sarah was, *which was why she needed to know everything that had happened to her at the hands of the Gyranger Queen.* When Sarah did not reply, Hana prompted her again.

"After you called Silverspear, what happened?"

"He came, Mom. Silverspear came when Dineah and I sang his name. He was so glad to see me and ... he already knew who the Lady Ourelia was." Sarah paused as this clarity came to her.

"Go on, Sarah."

Sarah sighed, struggling to keep her train of thought.

"He took us away just as the Gyrangers were entering the room."

"They were inside the room?"

"No, they were just opening the door as we left."

"That's when you arrived at the Sacred Grove?"

"No, we arrived at *Atarashara*, first."

"You what!" exclaimed Hana.

"We were inside of *Atarashara*. It was then that we saw the battle in the Sacred Grove. It was horrible, Mom," said Sarah, her voice a whisper. "I tried to tell *Atarashara* to send me to the Forest to end the fighting, but it said that the Gyrangers were out of control and that they needed to have a new leader. That was when Dineah said that the leader had to be one of their blood. There was nothing I could do," she said in a distant voice.

"And then?" gently prompted Hana.

"Then Ourelia got really mad, and I didn't understand what was happening. She seemed to think that *Atarashara* was telling her to lead the Gyrangers. She asked *Atarashara* if there was any hope, and then she closed her eyes for a long time. After that, she said that she had done all she could, and told us to mount Silverspear. The next thing I knew, we were at the Sacred Grove where Ourelia asked me to stop the battle."

Hana did not respond, for Sarah's words had set off a new set of alarms. What had Ourelia witnessed while in 'the field of unlimited possibilities' that had moved her to manifest the portal's magic? Something told the ever astute Hana that it went beyond the battle that had occurred in the Sacred Grove. She knew that Ourelia had proclaimed herself as the Queen of the Gyrangers and that the Forest and the Gyrangers were now allies, but after hearing Sarah's story, Hana knew that she needed to talk with Aarus.

Hana's heart ached at the pain and turmoil she could see in Sarah. She had just gotten her baby girl back, and yet she needed to let her go again for Sarah to heal fully.

"Sarah, you need to return to *Atarashara* and rest in the magic of your birth home. That is where you will heal from everything you have undergone."

Sarah sat up in protest. She did not want to leave her mom so soon after being reunited. Turning toward Hana, she was stopped short by the look on her face. It was only then that Sarah understood how painful her absence had been for

Hana. She also knew deep inside, that her mom was right. For some reason, she needed to return to her birthplace.

"Okay, Mom," she said quietly, fiercely hugging Hana, who in turn, drew Sarah into her arms.

~

Sarah watched Mrs. Gibson depart. She had insisted on having a moment with the Starchild before Sarah entered *Atarashara*. It had been this way with many of the inhabitants of the Ancient Forest. They had either lined up in front of the portal or flown about her, in the case of the Fairies, needing to see with their own eyes that she was safe and unharmed. Sarah had tried to be patient with them, but she was exhausted by her emotions and the toxins that still lingered in her body from the Gyranger Queen's attack. More than anything, she disliked having to be parted from her mom, again.

Thankfully, Sir Perity had stayed by her side, noisily purring while rubbing against her leg. Sarah had watched Sabrae, Bohn, and Wisteria check-in, but from afar. Even though they had smiled and waved, she had seen the worry on their faces. She had motioned them toward her, but they had declined, not wanting to step in front of those patiently waiting in line.

Sarah felt a stab of worry as she briefly glimpsed Grif. She wondered how he was coping with Ourelia's drastic transformation. Ourelia – the woman who had been the love of his life. Sarah's head still spun at everything that had happened, both past and present, and how it had caused such tremendous pain and suffering to so many people.

Sarah knew it was time to enter *Atarashara*. Hugging Hana tightly one more time, she then turned to her usually stern Aunt Atalia. She was surprised to see tears in the First's eyes as she gave Sarah a back-breaking hug. As Sarah moved toward the portal entrance, Sir Perity walked alongside her. Grateful for the companionship of her longtime friend, Sarah gathered the small cat in her arms. It was then that she was interrupted by the arrival of a very agitated Tazor and his brothers, Eblie and Sheblie.

"Where you go, Sarah Starbright? You scare me so, Sarah! Why you leave? I suppose to protect you. Do no scare me so, Sarah! Why you go without Tazor?"

The pain in Tazor's voice pulled at Sarah's already overwhelmed heart.

"By the way – you notice? I back Sarah! I sorry Gyrangers get you. So vera vera, sorry, but someone hit me on my head and poof ... no more Tazor! But then Tazor make new friends and protect Lady Aniese because *Atarashara* tell Tazor to... well, kind of new friends, because some of them want to eat Tazor, especially after Tazor bite them ... but now ..." Tazor shrugged his shoulders in explanation as a smile spread across his face. "... it all okay!" Just as quickly the smile was replaced with earnestness.

"I miss you, Sarah! I protect you because I made a promise. Okay? Where you go, Sarah?"

For the first time, Tazor stopped and looked around him.

"Why everyone have leaky eyes?"

No one said a word after Tazor's passionate oration. Sarah saw that her Aunt Atalia's mouth was hanging open in astonishment. Suddenly feeling giddy, she barely stopped herself from laughing out loud. Sarah guessed that it was *Atarashara* appointing Tazor as guardian to the Lady Aniese that had put Atalia at a loss for words. It wasn't often that she saw her aunt speechless.

"I am going inside *Atarashara*, Tazor. I don't know exactly why, but I need some time to be alone, and it has to be in here."

Sarah motioned toward the threshold. She was surprised by Tazor's solemn response.

"Tazor come too, Sarah. Tazor come with you to *Atarashara*. *Atarashara*, Tazor's friend. Tazor no let Sarah alone again. Tazor made a promise. Tazor be *really* quiet! See!"

Tazor clamped his mouth shut while flying to hover between Sarah and the entrance to the portal.

Sarah watched as the gargoyle's face turned red, and realized that he was holding his breath.

"Tazor, you have to breathe!"

Gasping for air, he continued to speak. "Please, Sarah, tell Tazor, yes."

Be at peace, Tazor Gargoyle, whispered a voice in the mind of everyone present. *You may accompany the Starchild and her guardian safely through the portal. Atarashara is proud of you, brave and ferocious gargoyle. You have served Atarashara well. Be welcome, little one. You will be Sarah's messenger while she resides within these walls. Can you do that, Tazor Gargoyle? Will you help out yet again?*

This time a look of shock appeared on both Hana and Atalia's faces, followed by Tazor's yipping sounds of joy.

"You are a lucky one, gargoyle. Entering the portal without the proper preparation is unwise. I know of this only too well," said Atalia in a quiet voice.

"You must go now, Sarah," said Hana. "It is time."

Turning to face Tazor, she continued.

"Thank you, Tazor. Your presence is a blessing. I am glad that you will be Sarah's messenger while she is away."

With Tazor settled on Sarah's shoulder, and Sir Perity in her arms, the Starchild faced the portal entrance. Turning one last time to her look at her aunt and mom, she waved briefly and then disappeared into the shining light of the portal mouth.

CHAPTER 31

Reunited after so Long

Ourelia sat with Aarus in his hut. She had visited the Ancient Forest often in the past weeks, though she knew that her primary home was now with the Gyrangers. She had been unusually quiet on this visit and appreciated how her father had not pressed her, giving her space to say things in her own time. He sat quietly in meditation. She couldn't help but notice that he looked as worn and weathered as she had always remembered him. A smile crossed her lips.

"What do you smile at, Ourelia?"

A thought flashed through her mind.

How does he do that? His eyes are closed!

I am looking at your timeless face, Father."

"How nice of my daughter to humour me," he said, his eyebrows rising in speculation. "Is that a polite way of saying I look *old*?"

Laughing, she allowed herself to relish in the feeling of being with him. Slowly her smile faded, and her face became serious.

Opening his eyes, he looked at her.

"What is it, Ourelia? What is the burden that you carry?"

"The danger foretold by the Song Bearer's song is still upon us, Father. I saw it while in *Atarashara*. It will take our combined forces to fight it, likely far more than even that, which is why the Gyrangers needed to align with the Ancient Forest."

"What of Atalia's visions and the birth of the Starchild – were they not true?"

"No, they are correct. But, there is something more, a ..." Ourelia paused.

"Darkness," said Aarus. "I know, Ourelia. I too have seen this, though I did not have the same clarity as you at the time. What do you think it is?"

"I don't know yet, Father, but I believe that the threat foretold by Atalia's visions and the Song Bearer's song, still looms. We are not safe yet."

Nodding his head slowly up and down, Aarus closed his eyes again.

"This battle is like none we have ever faced, Ourelia. There are too many discrepancies, including the fact that in the history of the Ancient Forest, *Atarashara* has never taken an active role like it has done this time, starting with the creation of the Starchild thirteen years ago. In my recent journeying, I have seen how '*the field of unlimited possibilities*' directed the gargoyle, Tazor, to guard your sister's life. I do not understand what *Atarashara* is doing, and I am both intrigued and troubled by it."

"Yes, my sister," was all that Ourelia said, a sadness infusing her face.

"Go talk to her, Ourelia. Allow the past to be released."

He watched as a tear rolled down his eldest daughter's face. Knowing there was nothing more that could be said, Aarus quieted his mind and drew his attention inward.

"Shall we journey on this road together, Daughter?"

Smiling, she closed her eyes, drawing her breath in synch with her father's.

"I would be honoured," she said.

~

Aniese watched Elder Mendalese leave the infirmary, having completed the final healing that had restored her mind to full wellness. Having endured madness for so long, she had not believed the day would come when she would be whole again. What patience the Elder had shown! Aniese had not been a willing patient at the beginning, her thoughts riddled with hatred and paranoia. The radiation incurred from the blast many years ago had created an illness in her mind that had eventually become a way of life.

Moving to stand at the window, she stared at the activity taking place outside. Every inhabitant that lived in the Ancient Forest was involved in clearing debris away and restoring the Forest to its former state. She watched as Elder Tenor passed by, waving at her as a huge smile split his face. Aniese was glad that the little librarian had survived. She couldn't imagine living in the Forest without Elder Tenor and Elder Ravensong orating stories each night in the Sacred Grove. How she had missed those stories! She noticed that Mrs. Gibson was spending a lot of time with the tiny Elder; another blessing that had come from all of this.

Aniese saw the Song Bearer and Lewna, laughing as they flew together, Tazor Gargoyle trailing behind. He too was smiling and talking aloud … to himself. Upon spotting Aniese, he began to coast sideways, waving with both hands, and letting out yips of joy. Laughing softly, she waved back. What a wonder that one was. She had heard that he had developed an immense crush on Lewna.

She was pleased to see that the Shadow Forest had responded well to the healing that was occurring. Not only was it working to reclaim its place in the Ancient Forest, but families were reunited that had not been together for years. She couldn't have been happier, and yet something still troubled her. As if on cue, she heard soft footsteps entering the hut.

"Hello, sister," said Ourelia, softly. "May I enter?"

Turning to look at Ourelia, Aniese nodded her head. They had hardly spoken since the day of the battle several weeks ago. She wondered why Ourelia had come. Motioning toward two pillows, they both sat down.

"Were you really going to kill me, Aniese?" asked Ourelia softly.

Ah, she had wondered when this conversation would come up. Trust her sister to cut right to the chase.

"Is that what you believe, Ourelia?" Aniese asked sadly.

She heard more footsteps, entwined with an occasional thud of a staff. It looked like this was going to be a family discussion. Aarus entered the room quietly, stopping when he saw his daughters sitting across from each other. She waved him in and continued to speak. Her father needed to hear this as well.

"Deep down inside I never wanted to kill you, Ourelia. There were times ... in my madness that I would have done it though. I was not myself. I cannot take back what happened, or what you heard me say. I am sorry though ... sorry that you heard me say those words ... sorry that you will have the memories for the rest of your life."

"I too am sorry for so many things, Aniese. I truly did not understand the impact that my love for Matharzan had on you."

"How is he handling your ... you know ... new role?" asked Aniese.

Ourelia laughed softly, though sadness infused her face.

"He still wants to be with me, believe it or not."

"And?" asked Aniese.

Looking directly into Aniese's eyes, she answered.

"It is not to be so, sister. I have another relationship that I need to make right first. It is the one between you and me. I am not the same woman that I was those many years ago when betrothed to Matharzan. I need time to understand who I am now. And I need you to know that I will never again agree to a union that tears apart my relationship with my only sister."

Aniese looked away, tears welling up in her eyes.

"Anyway," continued Ourelia, "my ability to shapeshift from Gyranger to human form will likely scare most suitors away."

This time it was Aniese who began to laugh. Turning to look at her father, Aiese saw contentment on his face as he watched his two daughters whom he loved more than life itself. But she could tell that something troubled him.

"What is it, Father?"

"Why, Aniese? Why did you not bring the Shadow Forest to fight us? You could have reopened the portal and brought their forces through."

Looking at both her father and sister, Aniese stood and strode to the window. It didn't take long before she saw the little gargoyle who was trying to impress a particular Firefly with fancy tumbles in the air. Both Dineah and Lewna were laughing uproariously, egging him on. His hyena-like yips rang through the Forest. It took a long time for her to respond.

"Sometimes, when we can't believe in ourselves, someone has to hold that belief for us until we can," she said quietly.

Her throat constricted as she heard the next words in her mind, spoken in a low, gravelly voice.

I will believe in you, Lady Aniese, until you can once again.

Turning, she sighed.

"Sit down, Father. Let me tell you and Ourelia the story of a strange little gargoyle who played a significant role in saving the Ancient Forest from its shadow side."

Gathering pillows for Aarus, she continued.

"By the way, his name is Tazor, Tazor Gargoyle, but you can call him just Tazor. He has two brothers named Eblie and Sheblie, who love him and believe in him ... no matter what he does. He is loyal and ferocious ... and can be *incredibly annoying!*"

It was dusk by the time Aarus and his two daughters emerged from the healing hut to attend to the Sacred Grove for storytelling.

CHAPTER 32

Your Destiny Awaits You

Sarah sat inside the pristine iridescent walls of *Atarashara* with her eyes closed, revelling in the sense of peace and calm that filled her. Slowly opening her eyes, she instantly witnessed the pureness and serenity that embodied her birthplace. Sarah could feel the magic of *Atarashara* expand and release with her every breath. More than ever, Sarah understood how she was a part of this place. Every molecule of her being was made up of the consciousness that existed within this sacred site.

Sarah knew that she had been deeply affected by her contact with the Gyranger Queen and in learning that she was central to the Gyranger prophecy. Knowing that she had nearly aligned herself with the Gyranger race still haunted her. What would she have done had Dineah not been there – a voice of reason, a light that had shone through the darkness and stopped her from walking a sinister road? Sarah was still trying to make sense of it all. Thankfully, the sanctuary of *Atarashara* was allowing her solitude; a time to be with her thoughts and to let her physical body release the last of the toxic poison that had been forced upon her by the Gyranger Queen.

Turning her head, she looked for Tazor and found him curled up a short distance away. He had slept continually since entering *Atarashara*. It appeared that Sarah was not the only one healing. She had no idea what had happened to the gargoyle in the Shadow Forest, but he seemed changed, as if more intact.

Sarah knew that she too had changed. The releasing of poison from her body had heightened her already enhanced senses. Sarah could not *see* the change in Tazor, she could *feel* it. Even from within the walls of *Atarashara*, she could sense the vibrancy and anticipation of the Ancient Forest as its inhabitants pulled together in reparation and healing. A pang of loneliness filled her. Sarah knew that she still needed time alone, but she was missing her friends and family. Moving instinctively, Sarah waved her hand briefly and gasped in surprise as *Atarashara's* walls shimmered and transformed, revealing Dineah flying through the Forest with her friend, Lewna.

"How did I do that?"

Quickly flicking her hand again, the scene of the Forest was gone, *Atarashara's* walls once again in place.

"The Sacred Grove," she said, unsure of how she knew what to say. A view of the Sacred Grove immediately appeared. Sarah realized that she had not moved her hand.

"How am I able to do this?" she exclaimed loudly.

"Sarah okay?" murmured Tazor sleepily.

"It's okay, Tazor, go back to sleep," mumbled Sarah, her focus on the scene in front of her.

Sarah stared in amazement at the changes in the Sacred Grove since the battle. Much of the debris had been cleared away, and many of the Guardians had returned to their former state of health, their vibrant green canopies once again filling the sky. Elders Mendalese and Borus, and his talking hat Felix, were tenderly treating the giant sentinels who had suffered from the fires. Other healers, including Wisteria, Bohn, and Sabrae, worked within make-shift tents, housed with creatures receiving healing from the radiation of the blast so many years ago.

Sarah knew that the inhabitants of the Shadow Forest were reuniting with their families after years of being apart. Tears filled her eyes as she thought of Hana.

"I miss my mom," she whispered.

Instantly, the scene shifted to Aarus's tent. Seated within it was Princess Hana who was speaking earnestly with Elder Aarus, Atalia at her side. Sarah could hear their conversation.

"How can that be, Aarus?" said Hana incredulously. "I thought that the battle was ..."

Sarah watched as Aarus raised his hand, motioning Hana to silence. Moving his head slowly back and forth as if searching, he suddenly turned, looking directly at Sarah, his opaque blue eye flashing.

He sees me, howled Sarah in her mind.

Aarus slowly raised one eyebrow.

Waving her hand frantically to clear the scene, Sarah jumped to her feet, gasping for air. She barely heard her mother's next words as the scene faded away.

"What is it, Aarus?"

Sarah's heart pounded in her chest. What was going on? The moment she thought of something, it happened, and now she had just eavesdropped on a private conversation between her mom and Aarus! Sarah felt sick at the thought of her next meeting with the Elder. Covering her face with her hands, she desperately wished she could disappear. Instantly, she felt a change in her body. Slowly moving her hands away from her face, her mind flooded with fear. The floor of *Atarashara* was visible through her hands. They were transparent.

"Tazor!" she screamed.

Instantly, he was awake and airborne; his mouth pulled back in a snarl as he flew through the air searching for her.

"What wrong, Sarah! What wrong? Where are you? I come, Sarah?"

"I'm right here, Tazor!"

"Where, Sarah! I no see you! Sarah, where are you?" cried Tazor, frantically flying in circles.

"Tazor, it's okay. I ... somehow ... made myself invisible," she said, her voice trembling.

Tazor stopped in mid-air, turning his head toward Sarah's voice.

"You play hide and seek, Sarah?" he asked, his body quivering with excitement.

"Well, sort of. I don't know how ... I made myself disappear, Tazor."

"Sarah, I *love* hide and seek! Tazor play too! Okay, Sarah, *you start!*"

"Tazor! I can't play right now. I have to figure out how to become visible again."

"How you become invisible, Sarah?"

"I don't know, Tazor. It just seems that ... well, everything I think about or long for ... it ... happens."

"Well then, think Sarah back to visible, silly Sarah," said Tazor, loudly snorting as he shook his head back and forth in amusement.

"Oh, uh, good idea, Tazor," said Sarah sheepishly.

Closing her eyes, she wished with all of her heart to be visible again.

"There you are, Sarah," said Tazor, softly. "You done it! How you do that, Sarah?"

"I don't know, Tazor, but, it seems like it is more than just thinking about it."

Pausing, she thought for a moment.

"I also have to feel it, here," she said, pointing at her heart.

"So try again, Sarah! What do you heart want, Sarah?"

"Well," she said hesitantly, before blurting out her next words.

"I want to be a warrior princess, just like my Aunt Atalia!"

Instantly she was garbed in the magnificent iridescent colours of the Scarab armour, her right hand raised, holding a sword in the air.

Tazor tumbled backward in the air, yipping in joy.

"What else, Sarah?" he cried. "What else you want?"

"I want to have wings, like you and Dineah, and the Fairies," giggled Sarah, impishly.

Immediately, the armour vanished. Sarah closed her eyes, feeling a surge of joy and excitement move through her as she imagined the extensions on her back.

"You do it, Sarah! You have wings," screamed Tazor in excitement.

Opening her eyes, Sarah found herself hovering several feet in the air. Slowly propelling herself forward, she flew toward Tazor, halting awkwardly in front of him, her face flushed with excitement.

You are growing in your understanding of the magic of 'the field of unlimited possibilities', Starchild, whispered the voice of *Atarashara.*

"I, WHAT?" shouted Sarah, surprised at the voice in her head. Glancing toward the floor, she panicked at its distance. Immediately, her wings disappeared, and she dropped ungracefully to the floor.

Inside the portal, your magic is heightened, causing whatever you focus on to manifest immediately. Hence the name, 'the field of unlimited possibilities'. You are already capable of doing what initiates train for years to accomplish. Hello, Tazor Gargoyle.

"Hello, friend *Atarashara*," said Tazor, cheerfully, delighted to hear its voice in his head.

"But, wait!" cried Sarah, struggling to contain the churning emotions that had ignited. "I don't understand. I may be able to control my magic now, but what about when I needed it! I couldn't use it to protect myself when the Gyrangers attacked our home on Fairy Lane because I was too scared. I couldn't access my magic when captured by the Gyranger Queen, and I almost gave in to the Gyranger prophecy. I would have hurt the people I love!"

Sarah's lip trembled as she tried to hold back tears.

But you instinctively accessed your magic to save Dineah's and Ourelia's lives, and to bring the battle between the Ancient Forest and Gyrangers to an end. You have not failed, Sarah. Your birthright as the Starchild has guided you all along, even gathering the right people to you to ensure that you succeeded. Observe, Starchild.

Instantly the walls of *Atarashara* were alight with images: Wisteria, Bohn, and Sabrae in the Sacred Grove, holding tightly to the amulets that carried Sarah's blood, desperate to stop her body from being consumed by the Gyranger Queen's toxic venom. On an adjacent wall, Sarah watched the deadly spasms of her body end at the same moment that the amulets exploded, releasing the poison. Suddenly, a new set of images appeared: the abduction of Sarah in the Shadow Forest, Dineah hiding in her hair. On the neighbouring wall was the sterile room where Sarah's willpower was being overpowered by the Gyranger Queen, only to be saved by Dineah's presence through their shared mind link. The images changed yet again: King Silverspear, standing tall upon a hilltop, the wind blowing his mane and tail while his head slowly moved back and forth … waiting. Suddenly, he reared on his hindquarters, letting out a fierce neigh. Sarah knew what he had heard, for at that moment she heard it too – the sound of her and Dineah, *singing his name.* He disappeared, reappearing a moment later on the adjacent wall, in the room where Sarah, Dineah, and Ourelia were trapped.

Think about it, Starchild – the witches protective magic from afar, Dineah Firefly as your voice of reason, King Silverspear, a guardian with the ability to transport you through time and space, removing you from the clutches of the Gyrangers. Do you understand, Sarah? Do you see the synchronicity, the magic within all that happened? You were never alone, and your light would not have allowed you to turn to the darkness. You are born of the magic of Atarashara. You … are … the … Starchild!"

"But why, *Atarashara?* Why was I part of the Gyranger prophecy? Why did so many people that I care about, have to hurt?"

You were foretold in the Gyranger prophecy to ensure that the Gyranger race and the Ancient Forest aligned at this moment in time, and to prepare the Karrian Galaxy for the battle that has been forewarned by the Song Bearer's war song.

"What do you mean, *Atarashara?*" cried Sarah angrily. "The battle has happened, and the Ancient Forest was not defeated. Anyway, I don't want to be part of any prophecy, or fighting, or … " Sarah lowered her head, trying to hide her tears. "I just want to stay in the Ancient Forest with my mom and my friends," she said in a whisper.

Suddenly an image appeared on the wall in front of Sarah. Her throat constricted as she watched a swirling mass of blackness swoop back and forth, billowing out and then folding in upon itself. A piercing, high-pitched sound accompanied the movement, forcing Sarah to place her hands over her ears. The dark mass filled her with dread, for she could feel its chaos and destruction. For a moment, it rippled upwards through the air like an enormous serpent before turning and plunging downward toward her, its darkness filling her vision. Wrenching her head sideways, she found herself gasping for air.

Just as suddenly it was gone, replaced by an image of a small-framed woman with delicate features and short, curly hair. Although of human size, the woman reminded Sarah of a Fairy. The woman's gaze fell upon Sarah.

"A plague that was never truly a plague. The time is soon, Starchild," she said, and then she too was gone.

Sarah stared at what was now the pristine wall of *Atarashara*, not understanding what she had witnessed. Her attention was abruptly brought back to the moment.

It is time for you to return to the Ancient Forest, Starchild. You may not feel ready, but you are. There is healing yet to take place in the Forest, and your abilities will expedite it significantly.

"I still don't know what I am supposed to do?" cried Sarah.

You will know when the time is right. Your destiny awaits you, Starchild, but first, you must learn to control your magic – the magic of 'the field of unlimited possibilities'. You will soon travel to the planet Oorse and study under the High Priestess Monserat, where you will come to understand who you fully are. You are strong, Starchild. The survival of the Ancient Forest hangs on a thread, but you were born for this, Sarah. Your time will come, not so long from now. Now go, Starchild, and return to the Forest.

With that, the presence of *Atarashara* left Sarah's mind and was gone.

AUTHOR BIOGRAPHY

 M. Louise Cadrin lives near Vancouver, British Columbia, Canada. Through the power of music, and her many years as a music therapist in palliative care, she has seen the strength of the human spirit, and witnessed the complex, heart-warming layers of the human story. These experiences, coupled with her belief in Fairies and her sensitivities to the mysteries found in nature, have profoundly impacted her creativity and ability to weave a fantastical tale.

Louise spends as much time as possible exploring and taking sanctuary within nature.

www.mlouisecadrin.com
www.thestarchildofatarashara.com
author@mlouisecadrin.com

CPSIA information can be obtained
at www.ICGtesting.com
Printed in the USA
LVHW031531061218
599502LV00019B/781/P

9 781999 499808